HISTORICAL

Your romantic escape to the past.

Regency Christmas Weddings
Christine Merrill, Liz Tyner & Elizabeth Beacon

Their Convenient Christmas Betrothal
Amanda McCabe

MILLS & BOON

A MISTLETOE KISS FOR THE GOVERNESS
© 2024 by Christine Merrill
Philippine Copyright 2024
Australian Copyright 2024
New Zealand Copyright 2024

First Published 2024
First Australian Paperback Edition 2024
ISBN 978 1 038 93535 9

THE EARL'S YULETIDE PROPOSAL
© 2024 by Elizabeth Tyner
Philippine Copyright 2024
Australian Copyright 2024
New Zealand Copyright 2024

First Published 2024
First Australian Paperback Edition 2024
ISBN 978 1 038 93535 9

LORD GRANGE'S SNOWY REUNION
© 2024 by Elizabeth Beacon
Philippine Copyright 2024
Australian Copyright 2024
New Zealand Copyright 2024

First Published 2024
First Australian Paperback Edition 2024
ISBN 978 1 038 93535 9

THEIR CONVENIENT CHRISTMAS BETROTHAL
© 2024 by Ammanda McCabe
Philippine Copyright 2024
Australian Copyright 2024
New Zealand Copyright 2024

First Published 2024
First Australian Paperback Edition 2024
ISBN 978 1 038 93535 9

MIX
Paper | Supporting
responsible forestry
FSC® C001695
www.fsc.org

Published by
Harlequin Mills & Boon
An imprint of Harlequin Enterprises (Australia) Pty Limited
(ABN 47 001 180 918), a subsidiary of HarperCollins
Publishers Australia Pty Limited
(ABN 36 009 913 517)
Level 19, 201 Elizabeth Street
SYDNEY NSW 2000 AUSTRALIA

Cover art used by arrangement with Harlequin Books S.A.. All rights reserved.

Printed and bound in Australia by McPherson's Printing Group

Regency Christmas Weddings

Christine Merrill
Liz Tyner
Elizabeth Beacon

MILLS & BOON

Christine Merrill lives on a farm in Wisconsin with her husband, two sons and too many pets—all of whom would like her to get off the computer so they can check their email. She has worked by turns in theater costuming and as a librarian. Writing historical romance combines her love of good stories and fancy dress with her ability to stare out the window and make stuff up.

Liz Tyner lives with her husband on an Oklahoma acreage she imagines is similar to the one in the children's book *Where the Wild Things Are*. Her lifestyle is a blend of old and new, and is sometimes comparable to the way people lived long ago. Liz is a member of various writing groups and has been writing since childhood. For more about her, visit liztyner.com.

Elizabeth Beacon has a passion for history and storytelling and, with the English West Country on her doorstep, never lacks a glorious setting for her books. Elizabeth tried horticulture, higher education as a mature student, briefly taught English and worked in an office before finally turning her daydreams about dashing piratical heroes and their stubborn, independent heroines into her dream job: writing Regency romances for Harlequin Historical.

A Mistletoe Kiss For The Governess

Christine Merrill

MILLS & BOON

Dear Reader,

Regency Christmas was a time for eating, drinking and playing parlor games. I mention snap dragon and bullet pudding this year, as I have in past stories, but did not dwell on the rules.

To play snap dragon, merrymakers would put raisins in a bowl, cover them with brandy and set it on fire. Then they would try to pick up the raisins without getting burned. Not something I would advise you to do, especially not after drinking a few glasses of strong Regency punch.

For bullet pudding, a mound of flour was poured onto a plate, and a bullet was placed on top. Then players would try to pick it up without using their hands and would end up with a face full of flour. Since I live in a house with a curious cat, I'm not going to try this game, either.

Happy reading!

Christine Merrill

To Annie Warren. Off to a great start.

Chapter One

Major Frederick Preston stared out of the window of the hired carriage at the bustle of London, still amazed to be home. It had been five years since he'd been in England, but now that Napoleon had been exiled to Elba, he was confident that the war was over. There was no reason he should not return to see how much his daughters had grown.

'How is the leg?' This comment came from his travelling companion, a captain in the Fusiliers who was sharing the ride into the city.

Frederick flexed his knee, trying not to grimace at the injury that was still not healed, though it had been over six months since he'd taken a ball at Toulouse. 'Fine, thank you.'

In truth, it was beastly. When he had been on the ship from Calais there had been space to walk around and keep the joint limber. But on the ride from Dover, it had grown stiffer and more painful by the mile.

'It will be better once you are home with your family,' the Captain said, ignoring his lie. 'The last time I was in London, I enjoyed dinner and a delightful evening of cards with your daughters. It is most kind of you to open your house to junior officers when you are not there. We are all very grateful for your generosity.'

Frederick smiled and nodded. 'I know how lonely it can be when one is between postings and without the proper time to have a decent meal. The least I can offer is dinner now and then. And in her letters my girls' governess assures me they appreciate the company.'

'Mrs Lewis?' the man said with a smile.

'You have met her then?' he asked, trying not to appear too curious.

'She is never far from the girls when we are there,' the Captain assured him.

'Lewis has been a godsend,' Frederick admitted. 'I hired her through an agency while I was in Portugal and she took everything in hand with barely a word of instruction from me.'

'You have never met her?' the man said, surprised.

Frederick shook his head. 'We correspond frequently, but I have been rather busy these last years...'

The Captain laughed at this assessment of a long and brutal war, then said, 'You will be pleasantly surprised, I am sure. Mrs Lewis is a favourite of the regiment.'

'Like a mother to you all,' he said, for didn't all governesses have a maternal air about them?

There was a strange pause, probably caused as the carriage bounced in a rut. Then the Captain gave a weak nod and said, 'You really have not met her.'

'But I am looking forward to it,' Frederick replied. 'I wish I'd had her on the front lines to teach my Lieutenants how to write reports. Her letters were succinct without missing a detail.'

'A useful skill,' the Captain agreed.

'And the old dear follows orders like a seasoned campaigner. When it comes to the care of my children, I have but to ask and she obeys.'

'The old dear,' the Captain said, smiling into the dark.

The carriage was slowing now and Frederick smiled as it proceeded the last few yards to stop in front of his town house. 'Home at last,' he said, slapping his knees with his hands to pound the blood back into his legs. 'We shall see you at dinner soon, I hope.'

'I welcome the invitation,' the other man said, reaching to open the door for him. 'Give my regards to the girls. And Mrs Lewis, of course.'

'Of course,' Frederick said. While he had missed his children and was eager to come home to them, he felt a similar excitement at the prospect of meeting the woman who had cared for them. After years of correspondence, he viewed her more as a friend than an employee. Her letters had been a source of comfort on some of his most difficult days, giving him little slices of the life he missed to raise his spirits. Even when relaying a domestic crisis, she solved the problem with maturity and wisdom and ended the letter with a happy outcome to assure him that all would be well when he returned.

And now, at last, he was coming home to enjoy the fruits of her governance. He took one last, steadying breath before grabbing his stick and heaving himself out of the carriage with a smile, then limped to the front door.

'Father is here!' Eleanor Preston stood in the little window by the door to the town house, bouncing from side to side with excitement. 'The carriage has stopped. The door is opening.'

'Let me see,' her sister Jane said, pushing her out of the way.

'Ladies,' Charlotte Lewis said with gentle admonition, 'remember your manners. You are no longer children and you do not want your father to think he is coming home to a pair of hoydens.'

The sisters immediately calmed themselves and stepped away from the window to stand side by side and straight ahead like a pair of their father's soldiers.

Charlotte smiled in approval. At sixteen and nineteen respectively, the girls were not quite of age. But they had been children when their father had last seen them and she wanted the Major to be impressed by how much they had changed. They were lovely young women now and a credit to his name.

'I was so afraid he would not be here in time for the ceremony,' Jane whispered, raising up on the balls of her feet for one last peek through the glass.

'He promised he would come,' Charlotte reminded her. 'It would take more than Napoleon to keep him away from your wedding.' He had assured her of it in his letter, but his homecoming had been delayed several times already and it was hard to believe that their waiting was finally over.

She resisted the urge to peer through the window for a first glimpse to assure herself that he was well. In truth, she was just as excited by this homecoming as the girls were, though it was not her place to be so. She was only a servant. Her happiness did not signify.

All the same, her heart leapt when the door opened and a man in a dashing red coat limped though, shaking snowflakes from his hat before setting it on a side table and turning to accept the embraces of his daughters.

She recognised him instantly, for she had seen his face often enough in the little miniature portrait that Jane kept on her bedside table. That picture had been painted years ago, when he had been younger and war had not taken a toll on him. He was still tall and broad-shouldered, but there were touches of grey in the temples of his brown hair and a small scar slicing though his right eyebrow.

She could see lines around his mouth as well, signs of the barely contained pain that his injury must be causing him. It was bad, she was sure, and she ached for him. But she offered a silent prayer of thanks that he was here and on two legs. For some time after the Battle of Toulouse, they had feared him dead. Even after he had been found and taken to hospital, two months had passed when he'd been too weak from blood loss and fever to write them. It had been months after that before he'd been strong enough to travel.

The wait for news had seemed interminable. She'd been as distraught as the girls during that long silence and rejoiced with them when it had ended. And celebrated again, when alone in her room, hugging herself and smiling at the thought that the meeting she'd longed for would finally occur.

His letters had been so much more to her than mundane correspondence from an employer to an underling. He'd filled them with stories of the places and people that he saw, hinting at the glories and terrors and boredoms of his days in a way that her late husband never had bothered with. Though he'd been away at sea for much of their marriage, his letters had been brief and irregular.

But the Major was a natural storyteller. Perhaps that was why she felt such a connection to him. And now here he was, an arm wrapped around each daughter, staring at them in amazement as they squealed in delight.

'So tall,' he said in an awed voice. 'My dear Jane, you are taller than your mother was when she passed.' He glanced to the other. 'And my little Eleanor. Not so little any more.'

'You are being silly,' Eleanor said with a laugh. 'Jane is to be married and next Season I will be out.'

'You certainly will not,' he said with a mocking smile. 'You are far too young. And you, Jane, cannot mean to leave me just as I have finally come home.'

'We already have your consent,' she reminded him. 'Jeremy saw to that before offering.'

'He is a fine young man,' her father agreed, giving her a peck on the cheek. 'But I still have you for several days and mean to make the most of them.'

The footman was bringing in the luggage and Eleanor broke free to open the nearest valise.

'Here, now,' her father said. 'What are you doing?'

'Searching for presents,' she said, showing no shame.

Charlotte cleared her throat to remind her not to be greedy and the Major glanced up, noticing her for the first time. Then he smiled and she felt the warmth to the tips of her toes. 'Christmas is not for two days, Eleanor. Your gifts will wait until then. For now, you must show your manners and introduce me to your friend.'

'Our friend?' said Eleanor with a laugh.

'You know Mrs Lewis,' Jane said.

'She has been here for ever,' Eleanor agreed.

His smile faded as he stared at her, confused. 'Lewis?' he said, furrowing his brow.

She had been longing to hear that single word for months, for he never called her Mrs Lewis in his letters. This abbreviation of her name had come to feel familiar, rather than dismissive, as if he was speaking to a comrade. It was never, 'Lewis, do this' or 'Lewis, do that' as if commanding an underling. Instead, he might write 'The most interesting thing happened the other day, Lewis...' The name felt like a touch on the shoulder, drawing her into a private conversation, away from the rest of the world.

But now it was spoken with confusion, as if he could not quite place who she might be. Had he really forgotten her, after all the letters they'd exchanged? She hid her disappointment beneath a professional smile and dropped a curtsy, eyes bowed. 'Sir.'

'Lewis,' he said in the same dazed tone, then gave a small shake of his head and said, 'Of course.'

'It is good to have you home, Sir,' she said, for what harm could there be in saying so? 'Tea has been laid in the sitting room, in anticipation of your arrival.'

'Tea,' he repeated in the same dull tone.

'And sandwiches and cakes,' she assured him. 'If you prefer something stronger, you have but to ring.'

'Of course,' he said, still staring at her as if she was a stranger.

If she were a lady, she might have flounced away at this cold greeting. But she was his servant. It was not her place to come and go as she pleased. He needed to dismiss her and she prayed it would be soon, for she could not stand another moment of this unexpected awkwardness between them. 'If there is nothing else,' she prompted, 'I will leave you alone with your family.'

At last, he seemed to remember himself and said, 'That will be all, Lewis.'

'Thank you, Sir.' She turned before he could see her expression of disappointment and hurried up the stairs to her room. What had she been expecting? He was tired after a long journey and she was only a member of the staff.

She would take this time alone to get hold of herself and banish any nonsense she'd imagined about their first meeting, how he would greet her as an old friend, or perhaps, something more. If she did not learn to hide her feelings, it might mean the end of her position here. Her affection for him would be an unwelcome embarrassment.

For now, she would stay away until summoned. The family did not need her to watch their reunion. They had much to talk of and she had no part in it.

Chapter Two

As the girls led him into the sitting room, Frederick cast a confused glance back at the woman retreating up the stairs. In his experience, governesses were old. The lady who had raised him had certainly been.

In the five years since he'd hired her, he'd had ample time to create a similar image of Lewis in his head. His Lewis, his faithful sergeant on the home front, was an elderly woman, still in mourning black for a husband she'd lost long before he'd hired her. Though she was childless, she treated his girls as her own and was as vigilant of their honour as a hawk watching over her chicks.

That image, of a bird of prey, formed much of his picture of her. Her features would be sharp and her gaze as steely as the grey in her hair. Despite her stern appearance, she was not humourless, for her letters revealed a sly wit and an ability to laugh at herself and the antics of her charges. She was tough but fair and the girls loved her like a mother.

How was he to reconcile that with the petite blonde who had been standing in the hallway just now? That woman... No. That girl had been rosy cheeked with a halo of curls that framed her perfect, heart-shaped face. Her eyes were not steely but wide and blue, full of humour and kindness.

The expression in them as she'd looked at him had been so warm and gracious that he'd felt irrationally happy just to be near her. He wanted to bask in that gaze, to bathe in it like the waters of a healing spring.

He blinked to clear such thoughts from his head. She was a servant and it would not do to be gawping at her like a moon calf, especially when he had his own two girls both eager for his fatherly attention. There would be time enough later to speak with Lewis and to decide what, if anything, needed to be done about his misunderstanding.

Several hours had passed and it was clear that his girls lacked Lewis's reticent nature. They talked without stopping for breath, as if it were possible to tell him the events of half a decade in a single afternoon. When the housekeeper came to summon them to dinner, he was ready for a peaceful meal.

But apparently they were not. Eleanor took one look at the place settings and stopped in the doorway as if refusing to enter. 'This is wrong,' she announced.

'There is no place set for Mrs Lewis,' Jane agreed, reaching for a bell pull.

'Because staff does not dine with family,' he said automatically, surprised that they did not know the fact.

'Mrs Lewis is not staff,' Eleanor said, puzzled.

'I beg to differ,' he replied, taking his place at the head of the table. 'I distinctly remember hiring her.'

'And she has been eating with us each night since you did,' Jane said.

'But I am home now,' he said shaking his napkin into his lap.

They stared at him in silent disapproval. Apparently, though they had been treating him as if he'd hung the moon for the last three hours, his sole presence now was not enough.

He sighed. 'Call her to dinner, then. It seems that I will have no peace until she joins us and I have been looking forward to a meal at home for longer than you can imagine.'

There was a brief delay as the governess was called for and the table rearranged with a place set a ways down from the family.

'Satisfied?' he asked his daughters.

'She usually sits to the right.' Eleanor pointed to the seat next to him.

Mrs Lewis cleared her throat. 'That is Jane's place, until she marries and leaves the house.'

The single quiet phrase was all it took to secure his daughters' obedience. They sat and the meal began.

It was clear that the cook meant to impress him with a lavish repast though Christmas was only a few days away. The table was crowded with more fish and game than he had seen in ages.

But his mind was not on the food. He could not seem to pull his attention from the woman sitting in silence down the table from him. 'Lewis,' he said at last. 'It seems you have been presiding at meals in my absence.'

'Necessity dictated,' she said, meeting his eyes with the same pleasant smile she'd worn to greet him in the hall. 'Your daughters are far too old to be eating in the nursery and required instruction in the manners required to eat at the adult table.'

He nodded, not convinced.

'And of course, there were frequent gentlemen guests,' she added. 'Someone had to chaperon, if we were to entertain officers every night of the week.'

'So, this change protocol was of my making?' he asked.

'Since there were no specific instructions, I did what I thought was best,' she said.

'And did not feel it necessary to tell me about it in your letters,' he added. Suddenly, her efficient communication felt suspiciously brief.

'There was not space to tell you everything,' she said, in the same reasonable tone she'd been using.

'I see.'

'She will stay with us in the sitting room after dinner as well,' Eleanor announced.

'That is not up to me,' Lewis informed her, looking down at her plate.

Now both girls were looking at him to affirm that this stranger would be tucked into the midst of the family for the evening.

Of course, she wasn't a stranger. She was Lewis and he knew her well. But when had he ever, even in the most desperately lonely moments of the last five years, wished to see Lewis wearing a low-cut dinner gown and not the practical buttoned-up uniform of a governess? The Lewis he'd known had been a trusted aide-de-camp. This woman, with her trim figure and inviting smile, was as dangerous to his nerves as a French brigade.

The girls were still staring at him, waiting, and he surrendered with a sigh. 'She will join us at table and in the sitting room after. Because, apparently, that is the way things are done here.'

Then he went back to his meal and did his best to ignore her.

The Major was displeased with her.

Charlotte smiled down into her empty plate, her expression unwavering, for she did not wish the girls to know how much this troubled her, nor would she let her employer see her wilting at his disapproval.

She'd suspected that she had overstepped her authority on more than one occasion. But she'd known nothing about being a governess when she'd taken the job. Though her father had been a gentleman, her family had been poor and her parents had raised and educated her without the help of one.

When she'd accepted the position in the Preston household, there had been no lady of the house to guide her and the Major was away in Portugal. So, she had followed her own judgement in setting rules and hoped for the best. For the most part, things had gone well. Both girls were sweet tempered and well mannered, and Jane had already found a man that the Major approved of.

She had known that things would change with his return and that one did not cross the master of the house, especially not on his first day home. She had tried not to do so. She had planned to take dinner alone in her room like a proper servant and sit the night by her own fire, not disturbing anyone with her company.

But he had summoned her and she'd had no choice but to obey. The fact that he did not seem happy to have her here was not something she could change. Perhaps, if she were quiet and stayed in the corner of the sitting room when they retired after dinner, he would forget all about her again.

But that was not to be. When she retrieved her work basket from its place by her usual chair and carried it to the back of the room, Jane said, 'Do not be silly. You cannot sew a straight seam in the dark. Come sit by the fire, as you always do.'

The Major, who had taken the large wing chair that they'd always saved for him, looked surprised. 'Lewis, are you in the habit of sitting there?' He pointed to the smaller chair, just across from him.

'I did when you were away,' she said, hoping that he and the girls would drop the subject and let her return to the corner.

'That is the seat for the lady of the house,' he said, still staring at her.

'But Mama has been gone even longer than you have,' Jane said. 'And it seemed foolish for her to sit at the back of the room alone when her job was to watch over us.'

'I see,' he said, giving Charlotte a stern look. 'Well, then, by all means, liberty hall. Take your seat.'

She gathered up her work again and went back to her usual chair, staring down into her mending basket so that she did not have to watch him watch her.

'Would you like to hear me read, Papa?' Eleanor asked, ready to distract him.

'Of course, my dear,' he said, smiling at his daughter and immediately forgetting his irritation.

She reached for the book they had been reading and Charlotte tried not to wince.

'I will catch you up on the plot,' Eleanor said. 'It is called *The Animated Skeleton* and is about the unfortunate Count Richard who is usurped by Albert and Brunchilda. They are terrible, but there is a skeleton that is thwarting all their plans. Let me begin.'

She took a deep breath and intoned, *"'I would this minute kill thee and banish thy vile soul from the earth which thou emcumberest, wert thou not reserved for greater torments.'"* She finished the line with a diabolical laugh that made the Major nearly start out of his chair.

As she read on, describing the lurid tortures in the book, the narrow escapes and improbable horrors with relish, Charlotte could feel the Major staring not at his daughter, but at her.

She stole a glance in his direction and could see him grow redder with each turn of the plot. Perhaps he thought that his daughters had read nothing but sermons and recipe books while he was gone. If so, it was proof that he did not know them very well. Especially not Eleanor, who had a touch of the macabre about her and devoured Gothic novels, the grislier the better.

When the clock struck eleven, the Major leaned forward in his chair and said, 'I think that is enough for the evening. Quite enough, thank you, Eleanor.'

She beamed at him. 'Did you enjoy it, Papa?'

'I found it most illuminating.' He shot another dark look in Charlotte's direction.

'It is my favourite story,' she said with pride. 'We have read it at least three times.'

'And now you are reading it for Christmas,' he said, with a grimace.

'Yes, I suppose we are,' Eleanor replied. 'And Mrs Lewis says, with my Christmas money, I shall be able to buy *The Mad Monk of Montenero*. It is just out and is supposed to be a cracking good story with a weeping ghost and a tiger pit.'

'We shall have to see,' he replied.

'Goodnight, Papa,' she said, giving him a kiss on the cheek.

'And to you, my dear,' he said, managing to smile again.

Jane came to wish him a similar goodnight. While she was doing so, Charlotte folded her work and got up from her chair, hoping she might go to her room unnoticed and put the night behind her.

But before she could make it to the door, she heard the Major's voice, sharp as a rifle shot in the silence of the room.

'Lewis.'

She turned back to him, schooling her face to a neutral mask. 'Sir?'

'May I see you in my study, please?'

'Of course, Sir.' She followed him out of the room and down

the hall, where he gestured her through the door and into his study, a room she'd rarely had reason to enter while he was away. Once inside, he shut the door behind them, taking the seat at the desk and indicating, with a sharp flick of his finger, that she take the chair facing him on the opposite side.

She sat, hands folded in her lap, and waited for the explosion.

It did not come, which was almost more terrifying than shouting would have been. Instead, he said in a deceptively quiet voice, 'Well, Lewis, what have you to say for yourself?'

She was unsure how to respond. There was something in his manner that made her want to confess every sin, even those he had not discovered yet. She wet her lips.

For a moment, his face went blank, as it had when he had first looked at her in the hall. Then he focused again, his gaze even sharper than it had been before. 'Don't think you can get around me by stalling. Tell me what you meant by taking the mistress's seat at table and in the sitting room. And what do you mean by permitting my daughters to read garbage?'

'I meant no disrespect,' she said cautiously. 'But when I arrived here, I was under the impression that there had been no mistress in the house for some years already.'

'My wife died when Eleanor was eight,' he affirmed.

'And the governess you had for the first three years was in the habit of locking the children in their rooms for their dinner,' she said, scowling back at him. 'When I met them, they had been left unsupervised and uneducated for the better part of three years, and lacked the skills and graces required of young ladies their age.'

'That is why she was sacked,' he said, giving no quarter.

'The dining room had been given over to entertaining your guests, who behaved as men will when they do not have the moderating influence of ladies,' she said. 'In short, they also lacked the dignity and courtesy one might expect of guests in a decent household.'

He leaned back in his chair, as if surprised that she had dared to suggest his friends were anything less than complete gentlemen.

She pressed on. 'In bringing the girls down to table myself,

I solved two problems in one. I took a seat near the top of the table, with the girls, but had the servants set your place and left the chair empty as a silent reminder that you might return at any time and see how they behaved.' She smiled at the memory. 'And the officers who came to dine were so embarrassed by the presence of the girls that they were, thenceforth, on their best behaviour.'

'And the sitting room,' he said, still trying to find fault.

'Is exceptionally draughty. We are all in the habit of sitting close to the fire in winter. But, as with the table, your chair remains empty.'

'And the Gothic rubbish...'

'They may be young ladies, but they are also a soldier's children and have a bloodthirsty streak that even I cannot curb. Eleanor can be particularly ghoulish.' She offered a half shrug. 'During the day, they read French and Latin with their lessons. But I allow them to choose the evening's readings when we are alone together.'

There was a long pause as he digested what she had told him. His expression was still grim, but she could not detect the barely contained fury that she had sensed when they entered the room. She waited nervously for his verdict.

'Very well,' he said at last. 'You have done the best you could under difficult circumstances. Until after the wedding, you may continue to take dinner with the family and join us in the sitting room after. But I would ask that you remember your place and know that these privileges are granted by me and can be taken away just as easily.'

'Of course, Sir,' she said.

'Very good.' He was staring at her again, as if there was something more he wished to say. And, as the seconds ticked by, the room seemed to get smaller and warmer. She stared back at him, thinking that the little portrait she had seen did not do justice to the blue of his eyes. She could stare into them for ever, if he would let her.

Then, with a little shake of his head, the connection was broken. 'You are dismissed, Lewis.'

'Thank you, Sir.'

* * *

Frederick watched as she rose and left him, letting out a long, slow breath and hoping it would cool his blood. It had all been so simple when he was in France. The employment agency had promised Charlotte Lewis was 'a woman of good character and widow of a naval officer'. From that, he'd formed his own opinions, filing her neatly in a slot in his mind for 'old governess'.

But now that he could see her, every interaction was complicated by her beauty. At dinner, she had been far enough away so that he could admire her in an academic sort of way, acknowledging that she was lovely while enjoying his meal. But in the sitting room, she'd been closer, sharing the fire with him as a wife might. At least there had been the presence of the girls and Eleanor's horrible story to keep his mind from dwelling on the way the firelight danced in her eyes and turned her hair to gold.

But just now, when he'd been alone with her, the door closed and the house asleep? He could barely think straight. If she'd dissolved into tears over his scolding, it might have been easier to stand. A display of emotion would have annoyed him, perhaps giving him a distaste of her.

Instead, she'd been as coolly logical as she had been in her letters. Except for that moment of hesitation when her tongue had darted along her lower lip. Had she been trying to provoke him? Because, for a moment, he'd been transfixed by that kissable mouth, unable to string two thoughts together. And then, when he'd managed to get all the answers from her that he required, he had not wanted to let her go.

There was only one reason to be locked away with a beautiful woman for any length of time and there was nothing proper about it. If she was to remain in this house, working for him, he must be sure that no more of these private interviews were needed. Though he'd thought himself battle hardened, his nerves were not strong enough for too much time with Charlotte Lewis.

Chapter Three

The next morning was Christmas Eve and, as she always was, Charlotte was the one to supervise the decorating of the house. The footman had stacked the front hall tables with an assortment of fresh greens: pine and bay and hawthorn, holly and ivy. The cook and housekeeper had filled bowls with nuts, apples and oranges, some of which were studded with cloves. The air was filled with the scent of spice and evergreen and she smiled and hummed a carol as she gathered ribbons to add colour to the garlands she was making.

Then she sent the girls from room to room, draping mantels and windowsills, and tying bows on sconces and chandeliers.

When the Major came down to breakfast, they were just finishing the sitting room and she was balancing on a ladder, hanging a kissing bough of mistletoe and velvet streamers at the centre of the doorframe.

'What the devil are you doing?' he said, startling her and making her teeter on the ladder.

He stepped forward automatically and reached out to steady it as she grabbed at the door for support.

'We are decorating for Christmas,' Eleanor said, craning her head around Charlotte to answer her father.

'We have servants for this,' he said, then looked up at Lewis before adding, 'Other servants.'

'Christmas would not be the same if we left it all to the house-keeper,' Jane said, smiling just as brightly. 'When I have a home of my own, I shall decorate it, just like this.'

'With a kissing bough in every doorway,' Eleanor said with a giggle.

'What do you know about such things?' the Major said, frowning at his younger daughter.

Charlotte bit back a smile. It was very naive of him to think that the sixteen-year-old Eleanor would not be curious about kissing, especially with all the handsome Lieutenants that had been passing through the house at supper.

Before she could say anything, Eleanor proved her point. 'It is hardly complicated,' she said. 'You kiss and then pull off a berry.' She pointed to her governess. 'Mrs Lewis is under the mistletoe right now, Papa, as are you.' She held out her hand in a gesture of revelation and smiled expectantly.

Though she knew it was wrong, it was what Charlotte had dreamed of when she'd thought of the Major coming home for Christmas. That there would be a random moment like this one where he realised why she had been so loyal to him all these years.

He was staring up at her now with the puzzled expression he'd worn yesterday, as if she were a problem that he could not manage to solve. And she remembered that one of the possible outcomes was to have her sacked at Christmas. He was her employer, nothing more than that.

She straightened the ball of mistletoe, then jumped from the ladder to be out of his reach just as he said, 'Certainly not.'

Then she gave Eleanor a warning look and said, 'It is a little early in the day for Christmas games. And, in any case, the decorations are not here for me to enjoy.'

'In Portugal and France, we had no time for such nonsense,' the Major said, equally firm.

'But you are back now. We finally have you home again. The war is over and that is reason for celebration,' Eleanor reminded him with a smile. Then she turned to Charlotte. 'And you are not usually so stuffy, Mrs Lewis.'

'I am not being stuffy,' she insisted, though having to scold the girls always made her feel older than thirty-three. 'I am speaking the truth. I shall have all the fun I need on Boxing Day. Until then, it is my job to help you ready the house for the season. That is all.'

The girls were looking at her in surprise, for that was never the way it had been. She'd always taken joy in the Christmas season and celebrated it with the girls as a friend and not a servant, playing games and singing carols with them, before sitting down to a fine dinner on Christmas Day. With their father gone, she had wanted to make the twelve days of Christmas as merry as possible.

But this year, they had a father to celebrate with and would not need her. The disappointment she felt was sharp and strong and it surprised her. To hide it, she grabbed a sprig of holly from the nearest table and said, 'And now I will go and be sure the cook has this to decorate the puddling.' Then she pushed past the Major without bothering to wait for a dismissal and headed for the kitchen, where the family would not see her should she shed a tear.

Frederick looked after her, then back to the girls, trying not to scowl. He was annoyed with himself and not them, for he must sound like a proper curmudgeon, railing against Christmas as he had. But his leg was paining him and the sight of Charlotte Lewis under the mistletoe had raised thoughts that an honourable man did not have towards a member of the staff. It did not help to have Eleanor suggesting that he act on them and claim it was the spirit of the season.

Now the girls were looking at him with trepidation, as if waiting for another scolding. They had done nothing to deserve it. It was he who was the problem and he had best acknowledge the fact.

He braced himself against the doorway to take the weight off his knee and folded his hands behind his back. 'I am sorry

I was so short with you,' he said. 'Sometimes I forget that I am home and do not need to be a mean old soldier all the time.'

The girls gave him a relieved smile and Jane said, 'You do not need to order us about, you know. Our love is sufficient reason for us to obey you.'

'If you do not like the decorations, we will take them down,' Eleanor said, though she did not sound very enthusiastic about the fact.

'Of course not,' he said hurriedly. 'The room looks lovely.' If he was honest, it reminded him of a part of his life that he'd thought dead and buried, when his wife, Anna, was still alive and the girls were small, and he'd had no notion of loss or war. Would it really be so bad to let a little bit of that hope return to comfort him now?

'We usually leave the presents here on the mantel until to-morrow,' Eleanor said, pointing to an empty space among the greens. 'In case you have forgotten,' she said, giving him a sharp look.

'I have not forgotten,' he assured her, thinking of the silk shawls he'd bought in Paris for the girls.

'I have taken care of the Boxing Day packages for the servants,' Jane said in a motherly voice. 'But you must find something for Mrs Lewis. After all, she remembered to give us gifts each year, in case yours did not arrive on time.'

'I…' He had made a special effort to remember their governess. There was a gift in his luggage, right now. But that had been for the Lewis he'd expected to find, an old woman with an old woman's problems. He'd bought her a sensible woollen cap to wear in bed that would keep her poor ears warm all night.

He imagined those gold curls smashed beneath the dowdy thing and winced. She would look and feel a hundred years old in such a cap.

'I have got her a box of lace handkerchiefs and Jane has embroidered her a pair of mitts,' Eleanor said, giving him a look to remind him that, as master of the house, he must do better than either of those.

'I will find something,' he assured them, trying not to grit his teeth as he said it. The last thing he'd wanted to do, on Christmas Eve day, was to go to Bond Street. He'd much rather have braved a battle. When at war, one was allowed to cut down anyone that got in one's way. One did not have to stand patiently behind other people as they dawdled. 'And I suppose you will need me to help prepare for the wedding,' he added, ready to receive his orders from the bride.

'I think Mrs Lewis has taken care of everything,' Jane replied. 'St George's is reserved for ten o'clock on the twenty-eighth. We have set the menu for the breakfast. My dress has come from the modiste...'

'Then you do not need me for anything,' he said.

'You must give me away, of course,' Jane said, sensing his disappointment.

'And what about the flowers?' he asked.

'I had thought, perhaps, some of the greenery from the house,' she said, gesturing at the decorations on the mantel.

He smiled and shook his head. 'I must know someone with a glasshouse in the country. You shall have roses, my dear. Nothing else will do.'

'Roses at Christmas,' she said, her eyes shining with unshed tears, and threw herself into his arms to kiss him on the cheek.

So he took his breakfast in the study and wrote letters to several of his friends, requesting that they send flowers immediately after Christmas. Then he summoned his carriage and set off for Bond Street.

His first stop was at his bank, to get a stack of shiny gold sovereigns to add to the staff Boxing Day gifts. From there, he went to a jeweller to find something special that the girls might wear to the wedding. He chose a pair of pendant crosses in amber and garnet hanging from fine gold chains and had them wrapped so he might give them at Christmas along with the silk shawls.

Now, he must find something to give to Lewis. The necklines of her gowns were cut too high for a necklace, but perhaps there were some earrings or a cameo here that might suit. Something small and impersonal, but as delicate and feminine as she was.

The proprietor sensed his hesitation and stepped forward to help. 'You are seeking a gift for a special lady, I assume?'

'Yes,' he agreed.

'Diamond bracelets are always a popular choice,' the man said, pointing to an elegant display. 'Or, perhaps, some earrings.' He withdrew a case from a drawer and opened it to reveal a pair so gawdy that they could only be worn by a courtesan.

'No,' Frederick said hurriedly. 'Not that sort of lady.'

'Your wife, perhaps?' the man said, gesturing to some necklaces that were just as expensive, but more tastefully designed.

'I have no wife,' he said, automatically.

'Not as of yet,' the man said, then opened another drawer and pulled out the tray to set it upon the counter.

Frederick stared into the velvet case that the man held, mesmerised. It was full of wedding bands. The ring that the jeweller indicated was set with emeralds and rubies arranged to look like the leaves and berries of a holly sprig. Without thinking, he reached out and touched it. Compared to the tiny circle of gold his hands were large and clumsy. But he could easily imagine this on Charlotte Lewis's slender fingers.

'Perfect for a Christmas wedding,' the jeweller coaxed.

He snatched his hand away. 'Not what I was looking for.' He had only known the woman two days, yet he had known her for years. He had trusted her with his daughters and she had been like a mother to them.

Not only that, she'd been his confidant. When he'd written to her, he'd often said more than he'd meant to about the loneliness and difficulty of his life away from home. At the time, he'd thought of her as a confessor. But perhaps it had been something more than that, all along.

And what had she thought of him?

It did not matter. She was a servant. He was her employer. If she saw him looking at wedding rings, she would think him a fool. He backed away from the case in confusion. 'I think the necklaces will be sufficient, thank you.'

The man looked disappointed at the loss of a sale, but wrapped the gifts he'd chosen. Then Frederick paid for them, dropped the packages into his pocket and went back out on to the street, sucking in a breath of city air to clear his head. Jewels were far too personal for Lewis, too likely to be misinterpreted as meaning something far more than they did.

Just down the way, there was a perfumery which would be much less intimidating. He used to get cologne for his mother, when he was a child, and she had been most happy with it. He would find something like that.

He pushed open the door and was instantly awash in scent, his senses muddled and his mind almost as confused as it had been in the jewellery shop.

'May I help you?' the girl behind the counter said with a sympathetic smile.

'Please,' he said, eyeing the plethora of delicate bottles around him with suspicion. 'I need a gift for a...friend.' That sounded innocent enough.

'A special friend,' she concluded. 'A lady.'

'A lady in every sense of the word,' he assured her, thinking of the gaudy eardrops in the last store.

'I am sure we have something to suit,' she said and turned to scan the shelves behind her. 'Is she young, this friend of yours?'

'Young,' he agreed. 'But not too young.' The agency had said she'd been a widow for some time when he'd hired her, so she might not be as young as she looked. He was only forty himself, older than her, but not by an improper amount.

He blinked, confused again by the direction of his thoughts.

'She is still beautiful, I am sure,' the woman hinted.

'Very,' he said, for there was no ignoring the fact.

'And her heart,' the woman asked, tapping her own chest. 'What is it like?'

This question was even more confusing than the fragrances clouding his mind. Did he dare to even wonder about that?

When he did not answer, she tried again. 'Does she have hopes? Dreams? What does she want?'

He had not presumed to wonder. He had always assumed that her best years were behind her and that she would look on his children as she might her own grandchildren. But now, after seeing her, what did he know?

'She is a widow,' he admitted. 'A young widow. She has

known disappointment, but it has not crushed her. Her heart is true. Her wit is sharp, but her nature is gentle. She is...' What was a word that would fit? 'She is a marvel.'

The woman smiled and nodded, then turned back to the shelf, scanning along the bottles before choosing one. Then she reached beneath the counter and withdrew a handkerchief, touching it to the mouth of the bottle. She wafted the cloth in the air to spread the scent in front of him.

He leaned into it, unable to resist.

It smelled of spring. Of new grass and tiny flowers and something else he could not name, something that drew him in and made him long for a future that was just out of reach.

'It will be different on her skin,' the girl warned. 'When heated by the blood, each perfume becomes unique to the wearer.'

A scent unique to her. He liked the sound of that. It was innocent enough, yet far more personal than a cameo might have been. For a moment, he imagined how small her life must have become, if she could fit all of it in the little room by the nursery that had been allotted to the governess. The scent he was giving her smelled of something much larger than a stuffy back bedroom. It was a whole world in a bottle.

He smiled. 'It is perfect,' he said. 'Wrap it for me and I will take it away.' He put the little package in his pocket and went back to the carriage, ready to go home to dinner.

Chapter Four

When Charlotte returned from her manufactured errand to the kitchen, the Major had left the house and the girls were eating oranges that had not been needed for the decorations. Her mouth watered for a taste, but she had best not join them. If the Major returned, he would think it another example of her taking advantage of her position and acting like a member of the family.

But Eleanor patted a place beside her on the couch. 'Come, Mrs Lewis, you know you want to sit down. It was a long morning and we were all very busy.'

She hesitated a moment longer, then settled into the seat and stole a walnut from the bowl on the table at her side. 'I suppose a few moments' rest will do no harm.'

'You are not usually so proper,' Jane said. 'It is because of Father, isn't it?'

'I would not dare to presume,' she said, immediately regretting it. She might as well have just said yes.

'I don't remember him as being so stuffy,' Eleanor said.

'That was probably because you were little when he left,' Charlotte said gently.

'No,' Jane said, considering. 'He was different, back then. It is probably his injury that has changed him. That, or...' She looked at Charlotte, then shared a smile with Eleanor.

Charlotte looked back at her, waiting for an explanation, but she only shrugged and nibbled on a bit of orange.

From the hall, they heard the front door open and the Major stomping his feet and muttering to the footman. Then, before she could move to a different seat, he was in the doorway, smiling at the three of them.

'Did you finish your errands?' Jane asked with a critical frown.

'Yes, Ma'am, I did,' he said, saluting her.

Charlotte tried to hide her surprise, for it seemed, wherever he had gone, he had found a measure of Christmas spirit on the way. To make sure he remained as happy as she was, she gathered up her nutshells and prepared to move to a different seat.

'At ease, Lewis,' he insisted, taking a chair opposite and helping himself to an orange.

'Yes, Sir,' she said automatically and sat back down.

He took out his penknife and peeled away the rind in an even spiral, then tossed it into the fire where it snapped and sizzled, filling the room with the pleasant smell of orange oil. Then he tasted a segment and made a disapproving face. 'Not bad, I suppose. But not as good as fruit straight from the tree in Spain.' For a moment, his face took on a distant, thoughtful look. 'Not all I experienced while gone was bad. I quite liked the people and the food, when we could get it.' He looked at them and smiled again. 'Perhaps, now that the war is over, we might travel there.'

Charlotte was surprised as his gaze fell on her for a moment, then hurried on to look at Jane.

'That would be nice,' she said with a misty smile. 'Jeremy is not sure where he will be posted, or whether I might come with him. But I should like to see Spain. And Paris, of course.'

'I want to go to Italy,' Eleanor announced. 'Venice seems very mysterious, like something out of a book.' Then she turned to Charlotte. 'And where would you like to go, Mrs Lewis?'

Moments like this showed how little the girl knew about the differences between Charlotte's life and her own. She gave the girl a firm smile and said, 'I go where I'm sent, Eleanor.'

The girl smiled, still oblivious. 'Then, when I go to Venice, you shall come as my chaperon.'

She hadn't the heart to tell the girl that such decisions were up to her father, who seemed to have mixed feelings about her presence in the family.

And then, as if from nowhere, an orange landed in her lap, making her jump.

'Eat up, Lewis,' the Major ordered with a smile. 'You will need strength for that trip.'

She could not help smiling back, for his good mood was as rare a treat as the fruit was.

'And what are we doing tonight?' he asked in a teasing tone. 'It is Christmas Eve, after all. What new family traditions am I unaware of?'

The girls both laughed and Jane said, 'Just a dinner for your friends. I have prepared the seating arrangements, just as Mrs Lewis taught me to. We shall have roast beef tonight, then parlour games, punch and gingerbread.'

'It sounds fine,' he said, leaning on his stick to rise. 'I will be looking forward to it, though you will not catch me playing Blind Man's Bluff with a room full of junior officers.' Then he limped from the room, leaving them alone again.

'Did you invite her?' whispered Eleanor, a worried expression on her face.

'I saw no way to avoid it,' Jane whispered back, her brow creased in a frown. 'This is her first Christmas alone and she hinted most shamefully that she wanted the seat next to Father.'

'Who are you speaking of?' Charlotte said, forgetting any plans she'd made to keep to her place and not meddle in family affairs.

'Major Baker's widow,' Jane said.

'According to Jeremy, Mrs Baker is just out of mourning and ready to return to society.'

'You are matchmaking?' she said numbly, thinking of the Major, still alone after so many years.

'Not as such,' Jane said firmly. 'There are always many officers here. If she is set on remarrying, perhaps she will find someone.'

'And what will your father think of such a plan?' she asked cautiously. It had never occurred to her that he might be seeking a wife, but the thought was troubling. A new mistress in the house might dismiss her out of hand. Then she would lose both the girls and the Major.

'I have no idea,' Jane said with a sigh. 'But it might be good to see him settled with someone. Now that Father is home, we want to keep him here.'

'If left to his own devices, he will wait until his leg is fully healed and will find a reason to go back to France or India or the Americas, and we will never see him again.' At this Eleanor looked truly worried.

'It is time for him to sell his commission and come home,' Jane agreed.

'That decision cannot be made by you,' Charlotte said, though she could not help but agree with it.

'We can at least see to it that his evenings are full of pleasant company,' Jane said with a strained smile that made Charlotte wonder if Mrs Baker was included in that group.

'And one wedding often leads to another,' Eleanor added.

'You make your sister's impending marriage sound like a contagion,' Charlotte said.

'I do not mean to,' Eleanor said. 'I should simply like Father to be as happy as Jane is with Jeremy. And you should be happy, as well,' she said, giving Charlotte a pointed look.

'What does any of this have to do with me?' she said, trying not to blush.

'We both love you and want to keep you with us,' Eleanor assured her.

'But we also want to see you as happy as you can possibly be,' Jane added. 'You are young enough yet that you could marry and have children of your own to care for. Perhaps Mrs Baker is not the only one who should be returning to society.'

'If I wanted such things, I would get them for myself,' she said firmly, then added, 'And it would not just be to any man who asked. He would have to be...'

She thought of the pang she'd felt at the idea of the Major remarrying.

'He would have to be the right man,' she concluded. 'If he was not? Then I should much rather stay just as I am, thank you very much.'

Both girls looked at her with frustration. Then Jane shrugged. 'I suppose we shall just have to try harder to find you the right man, then.'

'Well, do not try this evening,' she said, using the firm tone of a governess. 'I will have enough on my hands chaperoning you during the games without having to disappoint some young gentleman.' Then she rose to signal that it was time for all of them to go upstairs to dress for dinner.

Chapter Five

That night, the dining table was packed with his friends from the regiment, the first wave of officers who had been invited to celebrate Christmas with them. Two of the Captains had brought their wives and it surprised Frederick to see that the women were barely older than Jane. It was no surprise that her fiancé, Lieutenant Jeremy Tucker, was there as well. He would be the only member of tonight's company who would be joining the family again tomorrow at dinner.

Seated beside him was the widow of an old friend. Mark Baker had taken a ball through the heart at San Marcial. Frederick had written a letter of condolence to Phoebe himself. And now here she was in a bright blue dress, chattering away as if nothing had happened.

He knew that a soldier's wife could not be expected to grieve for ever. But neither did he feel comfortable with the way Phoebe was looking at him now, as if he was the answer to her prayers.

He hoped that the girls had not arranged this meeting as a hint that he should remarry. If he got them a stepmother, it would not be Phoebe Baker, who had annoyed him when she was married and whose personality had not improved with bereavement.

As she prattled in his ear, his gaze strayed down the table

to where Charlotte Lewis was sitting. As he had promised her, she was still allowed to dine with the family and was seated near the foot of the table to chaperon and round out the numbers so there were not too many single men. The gown she was wearing was as modest as her day dresses. Unlike the Widow Baker, whose neckline was low to the point of immodesty, Mrs Lewis's was filled with an organza chemisette that left everything to the imagination.

Perhaps it was because he could see nothing of her shoulders and breasts that he was fascinated by them. Did she ever long for the freedom to dress as other women did, in fine muslins and silks that would accent her beauty instead of the more sensible garments that she could afford as a servant?

As Frederick watched her converse with her neighbours, he remembered what the Captain in the coach from Dover had said about her being a favourite of the gentlemen who dined here. He'd thought nothing of it at the time. But then, he'd thought of her as a motherly figure. That officer must have been secretly laughing at his mistake, for there was nothing filial about the gazes of the officers on either side of her as she chatted with them. They looked smitten.

It annoyed him on several levels. If he had followed his first instincts, she would be eating in her room. But if she was here, guests should not be noticing her in that light. It was not her place to outshine her charges. Next to his daughters, she should be nearly invisible.

As if invisibility could be possible for a woman as lovely as she was. Even he had been imagining her in silks and satins just now, taking a place at the head of the table where the annoying Mrs Baker was still chattering.

Most importantly, he should not be sitting here, guessing at her feelings in response to the attention she was receiving from the Lieutenants beside her. Did she wish to marry and leave her position? Why did the idea bother him so? The dismay at the thought of her leaving was far deeper than he would have expected after such a short acquaintance. But the sight of the men flirting with her made him want to bark orders at them,

something that would force them to silence and have her fleeing in terror.

Of course, she did not frighten easily. Nor did she seem flustered by the gentlemen around her. As she turned from one to
the other, she glanced up the table at him and their eyes met.

And, as he did each time they looked at each other, he felt
a funny little tug on his soul that made him want to hold her
gaze until she gave up all her secrets to him. He had no right
to feel thus and no reason. He forced himself to look way, refilled his wine glass and deliberately turned to Phoebe Baker,
making some offhand comment that he hoped would prove
he'd been enraptured by her ramblings and not secretly thinking of someone else.

The meal went on for some time longer. After a dessert
course of sherry-soaked trifle, the women withdrew to the sitting room, leaving the gentlemen to their port. As Frederick
poured for his neighbour and passed the decanter, the officer to
his right said, 'We cannot thank you enough for opening your
home to us so soon after returning.'

'I am most happy to do so,' Frederick replied. 'I understand
that you have enjoyed the hospitality here before now.'

'Many of us have,' the Captain replied. 'Your daughters are
delightful company and Mrs Lewis is always there to keep us
on our best behaviour.'

'You do not find it unusual to have a governess as hostess,'
he said cautiously.

'We would not have it any other way,' the Captain said with
a smile. 'She is a favourite of the men and I swear some come
just so they can see her.'

'More than some,' Jeremy said, sipping his port. 'Half the
regiment has offered for her at one time or another.'

'Marriage?' Frederick said, shocked.

'She deserves nothing less,' said one of the men who'd been
sitting beside her. It was clear from the look in his eye that she
was on the way to making another conquest.

'And what has she done with these offers?' Frederick said,
uneasily.

'She has refused them all,' Jeremy replied. 'Graciously, of course, but refusals all the same.'

'She has no favourites?' he asked, trying to contain a rush of something that felt rather like jealousy.

'None that she will admit to. She insists that she is happy where she is, working for you.'

'Although she will not be so for very much longer,' one of the officers said. 'With Miss Preston marrying and Miss Eleanor growing closer to her Season...'

'Eleanor will not be marrying any time soon,' Frederick said, unable to keep the gruffness from his voice. 'And as for Lewis leaving? It might be several years yet.'

'A patient man can wait,' the smitten Lieutenant replied.

The fellow was an insolent puppy and Frederick could not fathom what had possessed him to invite the man to dinner.

As if sensing his displeasure, Jeremy changed the subject. 'But offers to her were not the only ones made. It was Mrs Lewis that put me in mind to go to France and meet with you, Sir.'

'Not orders from the Horse Guard?' Frederick said with a laugh. He'd still been on his sick bed when young Tucker had come to visit him with letters from home and a request that he be allowed to marry Jane.

Jeremy smiled. 'They are always looking for someone to deliver dispatches. I knew that we would need your permission, since Jane is not yet of age. But it was Mrs Lewis who reminded me that you were more likely to respect my request if it was put to you in person and not by letter.'

'So, you volunteered to go to France,' he said, surprised.

'With Napoleon captured, it was hardly as dangerous as it was during most of your time there,' Jeremy replied modestly. 'And it would not have been right for us to plan a wedding without knowing that you would be well enough to attend. A haveycavey elopement would not do. I honour Jane too much for that.'

'As well you should,' he said, giving the boy a sharp look to accompany his smile.

When the men joined the ladies in the sitting room, the parlour games began, with a round of 'Jacob, Where Are You?'.

Charlotte tied a handkerchief over Eleanor's eyes and Lieutenant Wilkerson was given a bell to help her find him. Then he darted around the room, hiding behind the other guests and ringing it as she stumbled about, calling for him.

While other guests stood ready to take their turn, the Major took a seat by the fire, turning his chair into the room, and announced that he did not intend to play, but would be judge, should one be needed.

Now that her job of starting the game was done, Charlotte took a seat at the back of the room, well out of the way of the activity. Though she always dined with family, she sat out of games like this, reminding the girls with a firm smile that it was never proper to tie a blindfold around the eyes of the chaperon.

As the game progressed, she could not help but watch the Major and notice a slight grimace of pain as he shifted his leg out of the way of the partiers. It made Charlotte wonder if he would be sitting on his dignity if his leg had not pained him and if his daughters had chosen less active games.

The answer presented itself when they decided it was time to play 'I Love My Love'. Then he acquiesced and dragged his chair into the circle, ready to join the fun.

'You must sit here,' Mrs Baker said, pulling him across the circle to sit opposite her. 'The light is better here, I think.'

'If there is anything I must read, I will keep that in mind,' he said, giving her a puzzled look and taking the chair she'd found for him.

'And you must play as well,' Eleanor insisted, taking Charlotte by the hand and leading her to a seat. 'There is no blindfold in this game, so you have no excuse.'

'It is Christmas, after all,' Jane reminded her.

'Christmas Eve,' she replied, but took the chair they offered and waited for her turn.

Mrs Baker began the game, screwing up her face in concentration before beginning. 'I love my love with a letter A because he is ardent. I hate him because he is ambiguous. I took him to Avon to the sign of the Antelope and fed him on apples. His name is Andrew Andrews.'

The room laughed and one of the Captains complained that

the surname was far too similar to the Christian name to count. But the room voted to let it stand without her having to pay a forfeit and the turn passed to the next player.

Charlotte watched as the game proceeded through B, C, and D and it grew closer to her turn. She had best come up with words that began with F so she was not embarrassed. Fanciful was good. Faithless could come next. Falmouth at the sign of the Fawn. She would feed him on fennel and his name would be...

She froze, only half listening to the room laugh as the man next to her stumbled through the E's. What name began with F other than Frederick? It was the only thing she could think of, looming large in her mind to block out all the other words. If she said it aloud, she would blush and everyone would know the truth. She was in love with Major Frederick Preston and doubted he even knew her first name.

Perhaps she could pretend to be ill. Or claim that she didn't have an answer. She would be made to pay a forfeit like hopping around the room on one foot, but a moment's embarrassment would be better than total shame.

'Mrs Lewis's turn,' Eleanor sang, leaving her no more time to think.

She took a deep breath and prayed for a miracle. Then she began, reciting the beginning of the script while her mind raced to find an ending. She had no more time. The moment was here. 'His name is...' She paused, searching. 'Francis Ferdinand.' She let out a gasp of air and smiled in relief.

The other players laughed and applauded, and the turn passed to the Captain at her left, with no one the wiser.

The play continued around the circle until it reached Jeremy, who had the letter J. Of course, he announced that his love was Jane, but insisted on giving her the last name Preston and losing the turn. It made his beloved blush and had the rest of the room calling for a forfeit. He hopped to his feet and surprised everyone in the room by standing on his head.

A little while later, it was the Major's turn and he was tasked with the letter P. Charlotte had wondered why Mrs Baker was so insistent that he take that seat, but now it was clear. She wanted him to say that his love was Phoebe Preston. As he prepared to speak the horrid woman leaned forward in her chair, her breasts nearly falling out of her gown, and gave the Major an encouraging smile.

He stared at the ceiling, as if totally oblivious. Then he recited, 'I love my love with the letter P because she is prim. I hate her because she is parsimonious. I took her to Paris to the sign of the Pigeon and fed her on pomegranates. Her name is Pamela Paul.'

The widow slumped back in her chair and the girls exchanged a look of relief as the rest of the room applauded.

But Charlotte released a held breath, slowly so as not to call attention to her special interest in this turn. Tonight, when she was alone, she would brood on each word he'd said. He could have chosen pickles in Portsmouth, but instead, it had been pomegranates in Paris, a scenario so romantic that it set her heart to fluttering and reminded her of their talk of travel earlier in the day.

She had never tasted a pomegranate, but she could imagine it, just as she did Paris and Florence, and all the other places she had not been. She must seem very boring to a man who had seen so much. Perhaps, some day, he would take Eleanor on a trip abroad and she could go along as a chaperon.

She allowed herself a brief glance in his direction and was surprised to see him staring back at her with the same unreadable expression he often had. She should look away, before anyone noticed. But for a moment, she did not. She willed him to see her for the woman she was and not just another servant. She couldn't parade before him in silks and jewels as the widow did. But she should not have to. After all the times they'd written to each other, he must have formed some idea as to her character.

Or perhaps not. There was something about the set of his mouth that made her think he disapproved. But she could not think of what she might have done to change his mood from this afternoon, when he had been pleasantly joking with her and tossing oranges.

He looked away and so did she.

The games continued until nearly midnight when the guests disbursed, going home to sleep away the first hours of Christmas. And, after seeing the girls off to bed, she walked through the ground floor, snuffing candles and straightening chairs in the sitting room before going to bed herself.

'Lewis, may I speak to you in the study, please.'

Charlotte started, turning to see the Major standing in the hall behind her. There was no trace of Christmas mirth in his expression. He looked quite grim, making her dread whatever was to come.

But what choice did she have? She was his to command. 'Of course, Sir,' she said, giving him her governess smile and following him down the hall, waiting as he shut the door behind them and took a seat behind his desk.

She sat as well, though a part of her wanted to stand so she might be ready to run at a moment's notice—he was quite intimidating when he was quiet like this. What had she done to displease him now?

She perched on the edge of the chair, nervous and waiting.

He stared at her for a moment, considering. Then he said, 'It has come to my attention that, in my absence, you have received offers of marriage from several officers of the regiment.'

'That is true,' she said, annoyed. Had the gentlemen been talking about her over wine and cigars? If so, they were not gentlemen at all.

'How many?' He steepled his fingers and stared over them, his scarred eyebrow raised in accusation.

She considered for a moment, counting, and then said, 'Seven.'

'Seven?' he repeated in a shocked tone.

When stated aloud, it did sound like a lot. 'Seven or eight,' she corrected. 'I do not usually count the last one because the gentleman was rather shy and could not get the words out. Before he could make his offer, I warned him that it was hopeless.'

'And why is that?' he asked. 'You are young enough to marry again.'

'Not so very young,' she replied. 'Three and thirty is quite old enough to know my mind.'

'Seven years younger than me,' he muttered, distracted. Then he focused on her again, frowning. 'As I said, you are young enough to marry and have a family of your own.'

'If I wished to,' she agreed.

'Perhaps you do not like soldiers,' he prodded.

She tried not to blush for she liked one soldier well enough, though he did not seem overly fond of her, at the moment. 'I was married to a naval lieutenant,' she said. 'I am well aware of the sacrifices one must make when wedded to a man in service of the King.'

'But the life you have chosen has sacrifices as well. Surely it cannot be easy to work for your keep,' he said. 'Are you not tempted to wed and have your own house, your own servants and the company of a husband?'

Was he asking her if she missed the marital act? If so, the answer was both yes and none of his business, though a part of her wished he would make it so. She redoubled her neutral smile and replied, 'The happiness of a marriage does not depend on personal comfort alone. And as for the company of a man, I had scant little of that in my last marriage, with a husband who was away at sea more than he was home.'

'So, you were unhappy, then,' he said.

She thought back to her marriage, unsure of how to answer. 'When we wed, I had no idea how alone I would be. My life was happy enough, I suppose. But it was not the shared happiness I expected when I accepted Hiram's offer.'

'And what made you seek employment in your widowhood?'

'I had little choice in the matter,' she said, trying not to frown. 'Hiram Lewis was as unlucky in postings as he was in everything else. His Captains were just as likely to lose their ships as to take prizes. When he died, I was left with a modest widow's pension, nothing more. I did not want to rush into another marriage, but neither did I wish to be alone and without the joy of children. Taking a position as a governess seemed a sensible choice.'

'You would do better if you married into the army,' he said, unable to hide his pride for his own branch of service. 'There are many officers coming home from the Peninsula with full pockets and a desire to sell their commission and find a woman to give them a reason to remain in England.'

'Is that your plan?' she said, then immediately regretted it. It was a question as personal as the ones he'd been asking her, but they were not equals and she had no right to enquire.

He looked surprised and she thought she saw the flicker of a smile before he grew stern again. 'We are not speaking of me, Lewis.'

'Of course not, Sir,' she replied, then added, 'If you are asking about my willingness to remain in my current position, despite what must seem ample temptation to leave it, you need not worry. I am content to stay here for as long as you wish me to.'

'That is good to know,' he said, giving her another of his enigmatic looks.

When he did not say anything more, she braced her hands on the edge of the desk and pushed out of her chair. 'If that is all...'

Without warning, he shot his hand out to grab her by the wrist.

They both froze, shocked by the sudden touch.

Could he feel the pulse racing under her skin? She might lie to him about her happiness and satisfaction here, but the erratic pounding of her blood when he touched her told too much of the truth.

He snatched his hand away just as quickly, as though the contact burned him. 'You have not been dismissed, Lewis,' he said. His voice was soft and warm now, making his words seem far more personal than they were.

'I beg your pardon, Sir,' she said softly, but did not sit.

'Merry Christmas,' he said staring into her eyes.

'And to you, Sir,' she whispered back. And for a moment, it seemed that there was a whole conversation in those few words, something she felt rather than heard.

Then it was gone again as he looked away. 'Goodnight, Lewis.'

'Goodnight, Major Preston,' she said and left him.

Chapter Six

The next morning, Frederick came down to find the girls already waiting in the sitting room, smiling expectantly at the little pile of packages on the mantel.

'Are you really so eager for your gifts?' he said with a smile. 'I have not even had my breakfast yet.'

Eleanor pointed to a little table where a large plate of crumpets was sitting next to toasting forks so they might prepare them over the fire. He could smell the chestnuts roasting on a pan by the hearth beside pots of chocolate and tea. 'We have everything we need, right here.'

'Everything except Mrs Lewis,' Jane replied.

'I will get her,' Eleanor said, rushing out of the room, down the hall and up the stairs to find her.

To disguise his feelings, Frederick went to the fire and stared into it, making a show of shaking the chestnut pan. He had no reason to feel so embarrassed at the thought of seeing Charlotte Lewis again. Nothing had occurred between them last night.

Nothing except for a touch on the wrist. He'd had no right to take that liberty. But she had been about to leave and, suddenly, he did not want to let her go. But once he had stopped her, he'd had no idea why it was that he'd wanted her to stay. She must think him mad.

* * *

When she arrived in the sitting room, she showed no sign of embarrassment or reticence. Perhaps he was reading too much into their interaction and she had not noticed the strangeness at all.

Instead, she walked to the mantel and set two packages with the rest.

'You did not have to give us anything,' Jane scolded.

'But I wanted to,' the governess said with a soft smile. 'You are both as dear to me as my own children, should I have been blessed with them. Part of the joy of Christmas is in giving to others. Allow me to do this small thing for you.'

The girls accepted with gracious hugs and unwrapped the two little packages to find a pair of earrings for each of them, gold flowers for Jane and tiny pearl drops for Eleanor.

As they tried them on and smiled into the mirror, Frederick watched as Lewis touched her own ear, which was pierced but bare. Suddenly, he was sure that she had taken these gifts from whatever remained in her own jewel case, to share with his daughters.

Were they gifts from her late husband, or perhaps something she had received from her parents on some long-ago Christmas? Either way, it spoke of her generous nature that she was so obviously happy to give them up.

It made him more confident in the gift he had chosen for her. If she was giving her own away, she was obviously not in the habit of wearing jewels, while in her current position. That did not mean he would not like to see her in them. Some day, perhaps, when she'd left this job behind and accepted one of the many offers she'd been given. But this Christmas was not the time and he was not the man.

Now the girls were distributing the gifts they'd got for him and Lewis: an enamelled watch chain from Eleanor and a pair of silver brushes from Jane, and, of course, Lewis's mitts and handkerchiefs. She was properly impressed with the handiwork and smiled as brightly as if she'd been gifted with the jewels he imagined for her.

It was his turn now. He gave the girls their presents and took the last package down from the mantel, shifting it from hand to hand as the girls oohed and ahhed over the shawls he had given them and took turns helping each other fasten the chains of the matching necklaces. He had not felt this awkward in decades, not since he was a green boy unsure of every word and action.

He took a breath and summoned his reserve, reminding himself that it was just a walk across the room and not a frontal assault on the enemy. There was nothing to fear. Charlotte Lewis was a lady, with a lady's manners. Even if she loathed it, she would be as polite as she had been when she'd received those tokens from the girls.

But suddenly he wanted more than weak approval. He wanted to see her face light up. He wanted a smile full of promise meant specially for him.

Maybe he should have got her jewellery after all.

But it was too late to change his mind now. He was standing like an idiot, leaning against the mantel as if he needed it for support.

Perhaps he did. He should not have left his stick by his chair.

Carefully, he took the few halting steps necessary to carry him across the room, then thrust the gift at her. 'Here, Lewis,' he said. 'In gratitude…' Then he limped back to his chair.

She unwrapped it carefully, setting paper and string aside as if she feared being seen as wasteful. Then she stared down at the little gold box, lifting the lid to reveal the crystal bottle inside.

Her response was everything he could have hoped for. She lifted the bottle out of its satin-lined compartment and held it to the light, watching the glass sparkle before daring to pull the stopper and inhaling deeply of the fragrance. Her polite smile turned to something much warmer, more dreamlike than awake, as if she could imagine whole worlds before even trying it.

Then, slowly, she moved to apply the scent. One hand dipped the stopper back into the bottle, taking up a single drop, the colour of fine brandy, on the tip of the glass applicator. The other hand turned palm-up so that the drop could fall on her wrist in the place he'd touched her last night.

'So lovely,' she whispered, as she closed the bottle and put it carefully back into its box. 'I have never smelled anything like it.' She rubbed her wrists together, making small circles, skin against skin, to spread the scent, stopping to smell it again before looking at him with shining eyes. 'Thank you,' she said in a whisper.

'It was nothing,' he said with a shrug and went to the fireside to skewer a crumpet with a fork. Then he turned his back to her, his smile broadening with satisfaction as he toasted his breakfast.

The morning passed quietly, with the family gathered in the sitting room, admiring their new gifts and snacking by the fire. Jeremy arrived in the afternoon and took a seat on the sofa next to Jane, reaching out to take her hand as they discussed their plans for the wedding, which was to occur two days after Boxing Day.

This meant that she would be gone from this house before Twelfth Night, visiting for dinner on the nights that they did not come to her new home in Mayfair.

'And of course you will visit us for New Year's,' Jane said to Charlotte, after she described the menu she was planning.

Charlotte smiled back at her, trying to ignore the tears which were forming at the thought. The little girl she'd helped raise, who had been so shy and unsure five years ago, was now a fine lady who would have a house and husband to think of. In no time at all, she would forget all about her old governess, as she should, and Charlotte would devote herself to Eleanor, until she grew up and moved away as well.

Each new beginning was an ending of something. But she would not think of that today. She took a deep breath and said with a bright smile, 'I will certainly come to dinner, if your father permits it. You must remember that my time is not my own.'

'You would not forbid her from coming to the house, would you, Father?' Jane said.

'Not on my account, I hope,' Eleanor added hurriedly. 'If we are invited as well, perhaps she shall have to come and chaperon me.'

Charlotte stared at her feet, embarrassed to be the topic of conversation. She particularly did not want to look at the Major to see if he was angry again that she did not know her place. The day had been almost perfect thus far and she did not want to spoil it by remembering who and what she was.

She stole a look at the perfume bottle in its elegant box. It had been the nicest present anyone had ever given her. Even better, it had come from *him*.

She heard him stir in his chair by the fire. She'd thought he was napping, but it seemed he'd had no trouble following the conversation.

'I would not presume to tell Jane who she may and may not invite to her own home,' he said with a sigh. 'And you are right, Eleanor. Lewis may accompany us, if we are dining at your sister's house, if she wishes to.' He gave her a sidelong glance. 'She is dining with us this evening, is she not?'

'And helping with the games and the carolling,' Eleanor said.

'It is almost time to go upstairs and dress for dinner,' Charlotte said, gathering up the wrapping at her feet and making a neat stack of her gifts, with the perfume in a place of honour at the top.

'And who are we to have this evening?' the Major said in a dry voice. 'Not another desperate widow, I hope.'

'Mostly bachelor officers who have no family near,' Jane said. 'And Captain Cummings and his three daughters to round out the table.'

'Very good,' he said as Charlotte left the room. 'Very good indeed.'

As she cleared the doorway and walked down the hall she could not help smiling. He thought Mrs Baker was a desperate widow, did he?

She could not help but agree. She should be more sympathetic, since some might see the same qualities in her own life. If they did, that would be unfair. As she'd told the Major, she'd had more than enough offers and was not the least bit desperate. He had seemed most interested in the fact when they'd been alone in the study.

Then, for no reason, he had grabbed her hand. And today he'd given her perfume. Once she was in her room she closed the door tight and set the tiny crystal bottle on the dressing table, staring at it in fascination. There was nothing exactly improper about it, but it was also a much more intimate gift than she'd expected to receive from the Major.

She opened it again, holding it under her nose for a minute before refreshing the scent on her wrists and adding another drop at the base of her throat. She inhaled again. It was a decadent fragrance, a combination of fruit and flower and spice that promised something she could not name.

It had been years since she'd smelled of anything more than soap. Hers was a practical, clean scent to match her sensible, no-nonsense life. But now she smelled like a lady. Better yet, she smelled like a woman.

She closed her eyes as a shiver went through her, touching a part of her soul that had been ignored for far too long. Wearing this scent, she felt capable of anything. She imagined running wild in a field of spring flowers. Better yet, she could imagine being caught, tumbling to the ground, her skirts raised, her legs spread, and the sweet feel of a lover, his lips at the places the perfume had touched, his body hard and eager. And when she looked into his eyes...

Her own eyes snapped open, blinking away the image of the Major smiling down at her as, with one thrust, he made her his.

She hurried to the wash basin and splashed water over her wrists, trying to rinse the scent away. But it clung to her body, her clothes, her mind. She could not shake the changes it was causing in her, this awkward awakening of the senses.

How was she to sit at table with him, after such a fantasy? It was some consolation that she would be seated far away from him, conversing with the lowest-ranked guests as she kept an eye on the girls. There would be distractions that would keep them from having one of those awkward moments when their eyes met.

But suppose he wished to speak to her alone, as he had last night? Her breath quickened at the thought of being alone with him, even for a brief conversation. But how could she make him see her as anything other than a servant?

She glanced at the wardrobe and the row of practical gowns hanging there. She went to it and pushed them out of the way to reach to the back wall. There, she found a remnant of her old life—a dinner gown that she had not cast off when she'd gone through mourning.

Pale blue silk, cut low, with puffed sleeves and a scalloped hem, it had never been worn. With Hiram Lewis always at sea, what reason had she had to go out? But she had seen it in a shop window and been unable to resist buying it for the moment he returned.

It was too elegant for her current life. Far too bold. But maybe with a tucker in the neckline... It was Christmas, after all. She slipped out of her day dress and pulled it from its peg, shaking the wrinkles from the skirt and stepping into it, doing up the fastenings and arranging her best lace fichu to fill the cleavage.

She stared into the mirror and smiled. There was nothing to be done with her hair, she supposed. She'd cut it short when taking this position so she might style it easily without a maid. But she had some combs and pins that she rarely bothered with.

She allowed herself that luxury tonight, along with tiny diamond studs for her ears. She added one more drop of perfume, spicy sweet, between her breasts, and declared herself ready to go down to see that the punch bowl and game tables were ready for the after-dinner festivities. She might look different tonight. She might feel like her old self. But she must remember that it was only an illusion. Nothing had changed.

Chapter Seven

When Frederick came down to dinner, the first guests were already arriving and his daughters stood in the front hall to greet them. They looked as lovely as they had on the previous evening, with the additions of their Christmas gifts, shawls looped loosely over their arms, necklaces sparkling at their throats. And Lewis's earrings were there, glinting beneath their hair.

Ah, Lewis. She was responsible for the beauty he saw here, the gracious manners and the poise. He had been away and could not claim credit for what his daughters had become. Her letters had assured him of what he would find when he returned home, yet it still surprised him, each time he looked at them.

But at least he was getting used to the sight of their governess and over the shock of his misplaced expectations. Perhaps tonight he would be able to dine down the table from her without staring.

Then she appeared in the hall, chatting with the housekeeper about the arrangements for the games. She floated past him in a cloud of blue silk and perfume and he was smitten all over again. Were those diamonds in her hair? Even if they were paste they sparkled like stars on an angel.

She looked every bit a lady tonight, as beautiful as any of the female guests. The only sign of her role as chaperon was that damned scarf, stuck in the bodice of her dress, obscuring the view of what he was sure were luscious breasts. That scrap of lace was the first thing he would get rid of when...

What was he thinking? He snapped his mind back to his duties as host, accepting the salutations of the pair of officers entering and directing them to the sitting room to wait for the call to dinner. When everyone was assembled, he took Eleanor's arm, allowing Jeremy to escort Jane and they all went to the dining room for a feast of roast turkey, currant chutney and sprouts, followed by a Christmas cake and a flaming pudding.

And, as he had last night, he watched a Lieutenant and a freshly minted Captain flirting with his daughters' governess, who smiled and laughed, sparkling as brightly as the gems in her hair.

At least tonight he didn't have to contend with Phoebe Baker. The ladies on either side of him were properly married and capable of holding a conversation without seeming desperate for male attention. And was it his imagination or was Lewis staring down the table at the two ladies with a look of appraisal? Was she comparing herself to them in some way?

She needn't have bothered. In his opinion, there was no comparison. She was the loveliest woman there. He smiled down to her, giving her an encouraging nod, and she smiled back and offered a playful toast of her wine glass before returning to her conversation with the man next to her.

If he'd had any doubt, he knew why there'd been so many offers for her hand. When she was in a mood like this, what man could resist her?

When dinner had ended and the party reformed in the sitting room, there were tables set for snapdragon and bullet pudding and a bucket to bob for apples. Lewis moved from station to station, attending to the games, replenishing the raisins in the flaming brandy and handing towels to wipe faces dusted with flour or soaking wet.

He wanted no part of it. His leg ached and he was longing for bed. Frederick stared at the chaos and the laughing young people around him, wondering when he'd got so old and staid.

Not so staid, perhaps, for he was imagining a warm bed and a welcoming woman, something he'd not had for many Christmases. It could be a cold time of year when all the guests had gone home and he was alone with his thoughts.

Then he stepped to the apple-bobbing bucket and plunged his head into the water, chasing a fruit all the way to the bottom before coming up a dripping mess. The cold water cleared the maudlin dreams from his head, leaving him sensible again.

As she had been for everyone else, Lewis was there at his side, offering him a flannel. As he took it, their fingers brushed and he felt a flash of heat, gone almost as quickly as it had come, but leaving the desire he'd been trying to quell.

He offered her a gruff thanks and took a mug of spiced wine and a place on the far side of the room where he could be alone with his thoughts.

The night ended several hours later, the guests wandering to the door in twos and threes, still laughing and chatting, wishing him a Happy Christmas as he stood at the door to see them out. Jeremy was the last to leave, appearing from the darkened dining room with Jane a step behind. They must have crept away from the crowd to share a private goodnight.

He gave the boy a sharp look before reminding himself that the wedding was only a few days away and there was a limit to how much mischief they could get into in that time. Thank God he'd had Lewis to navigate Jane safely to this point. He had nothing to fear, as long as she watched out for his girls.

Then he walked down the hall towards the sitting room and froze in shock. Eleanor was under the mistletoe with Lieutenant Hargraves. And he was kissing her on the lips.

'What the devil is going on?' He used his best command voice and it had the usual, desired effect. Hargraves jumped back, abandoning his daughter and snapping to attention.

'Where is Lewis?' he demanded. Wasn't her job to prevent situations just like this?

'Here.' When he looked into the room, she was sitting in the corner, her hands folded in her lap. She'd been in full view of what had been happening and had done nothing to stop it.

He turned back to Eleanor to chastise her, since it was clear that Lewis could not be bothered to. But the girl was unimpressed by his anger, which was usually enough to terrify even the most seasoned officer.

'How could you?' she said, fists balled and face red, her voice trembling as though she was on the verge of tears. Then, with a shriek of frustration, she turned and ran down the hall and up the stairs. A moment later they heard the slam of her bedroom door.

Then Jane appeared, looking just as frustrated with him. 'Father,' she said, in a tone that implied he had just ruined Christmas. She glanced at Lewis and it was as if they could share an entire conversation without saying a word. 'I will go after Eleanor,' she said, giving him one last disgusted look before disappearing up the stairs to help her sister.

He turned to the Lieutenant still standing stiff in the doorway. At least this fellow understood the danger of the situation for he was white with fear.

What was he to do with him? It was not as if he wanted to force a marriage between them. Eleanor was far too young and he knew far too little about the Lieutenant to want him as a son-in-law. 'If you know what is good for you, you will say nothing of this incident,' he said, letting his voice drop to a dangerous growl.

'Of course not, Sir,' the Lieutenant said, barely daring to breathe.

'Goodnight, Hargraves,' he snapped.

'Sir,' the man said, snapping a salute and running for the exit. A few moments later he heard the front door open and close as Hargraves departed.

That left him alone with Charlotte Lewis. He stared into the corner where she was still sitting, giving her the same glare that had terrified the Lieutenant. 'Explain yourself, Lewis.'

'What is there to explain?' she said in a patient voice. 'I was chaperoning Eleanor.'

'And a fine job you were making of it,' he said, not bothering to lower his voice. 'She was...' He waved his arms at the wretched kissing bough, which he should have torn down the first moment he'd seen it.

'She was receiving a kiss,' Lewis said, sounding faintly amused. 'It was not the first time that has happened and not even the first time this evening.'

'You allow it?' he said, looking up to see that there were berries missing from the sprigs of mistletoe, which meant that the damn thing had been used.

'It is far better that she receives a few chaste kisses with me sitting here to watch than that she tries to pull the wool over my eyes and get them in secret,' she said with a small smile. 'This way, she has her fun at Christmas and nothing gets out of hand.'

'Where did you get such a ridiculous notion?' he demanded, giving her the same glare that had broken the nerve of many strong men.

'From my own past and my knowledge of all girls her age,' she said, unflinching.

'You allowed men to kiss you,' he said, his anger turning to fury.

'When I was young and courting.' Her expression grew distant. 'My only regret is that it did not happen more often, for once I was married there was no time for such frivolity.' For a moment, there was a deep sadness in her bright blue eyes and he had to struggle not to be touched by it. He did not want to think of her, alone and unloved, feeling that her youth had escaped her.

Then she added, 'When Jane was sixteen, she was no different. She outgrew the fascination with mistletoe when she realised that she wanted a man who would kiss her without relying on parlour games. So will Eleanor, given a Season or two.'

'Or I can forbid her to do anything so stupid,' he snapped, remembering the problem at hand.

Lewis opened her mouth as if she was about to speak, then thought the better of it and closed it again.

'You have an opinion as to how I raise my daughter?' he said.

'Yes, I think I do,' she replied, tipping her head to the side as if considering. 'She will not respond well to such a command. It is liable to make her more rebellious, rather than less.'

'Then I will lock her in her room until she sees the light,' he said.

To this, she said nothing, simply staring at him until the anger began to fade. What he was suggesting sounded unreasonable, even to him, and he began to wonder who it was he wanted to punish, Eleanor or her chaperon. He stared at Lewis, remembering her at dinner looking radiant as she did now and chatting amiably with Hargraves herself. It left him wondering about the missing berries on the ball of mistletoe and who might have used them.

'This cavalier attitude to kissing, does it pertain to you as well?' he asked. There had to be something fuelling all the proposals she had told him about yesterday.

'Certainly not.' She laughed. 'I am far too old for such nonsense.'

'Are you now?' he said, stepping into the doorway, so he was positioned under the ball of greenery.

'Of course,' she said. But now she looked uneasily from him to the mistletoe and back again.

'That is good to know,' he said, then added, 'You are dismissed, Lewis.'

She was frozen in her chair, looking at him like a rabbit staring at a fox. They both knew that, to leave the room, she would have to push past him, as he stood beneath the kissing bough. Tradition said she owed him a kiss. If there was truly nothing dangerous about the custom, then she had no reason to hesitate.

'Dismissed,' he repeated, daring her to come to him.

'Of course, Sir,' she said and he watched her stubbornness win out over her fear. She rose slowly, straightening her skirts and lowering her eyes. Then she walked towards him.

Suddenly, the room seemed a hundred miles long and time stretched as she got closer and closer. There was ample opportunity for him to move out of the way and let her pass. It would be the gentlemanly thing to do. But he could not bring himself to move. She was almost upon him now, so close that he could feel the warmth of her body as she came close.

She paused for just a moment, then tried to ease past, her

breasts brushing against his coat. And in that moment, his reserve crumbled and he seized her, pulling her into his arms to claim the kiss he could not stop imagining.

He was kissing her.

She should struggle and refuse. She should pull away with a shocked rebuke and give him the set down he deserved. Instead, she melted into him, letting him crush her against his body and hold her so tightly that she could hardly breathe.

This was no innocent mistletoe peck on the lips. It was the sort of forceful, passionate possession that she had imagined when she'd dreamed of his homecoming. She was afraid to move, afraid to breathe, afraid to respond lest he come to his senses and stop what he was doing to her.

So she let him take what he wanted, opening her mouth to the thrust of his tongue, drinking in the decadence of it. His hands were on her body now, tracing her curves through the fabric of her gown. As he gripped her hips, she pressed her breasts to the front of his uniform jacket, rubbing herself gently against him and imagining his touch on her bare skin.

She would be his, if only he would ask. But that would be madness. He was not her equal. He was her employer and had hired her for her good sense and sterling character. She could not chaperon his daughters by day and be his lover by night. She would be little better than a courtesan to behave so.

But in this moment, she would be happy to let it all burn, to be left with nothing but the memory of his kisses and his love.

Then, just as suddenly as it had begun, it was over. He pulled away and set her back on her feet, and she had to resist the urge to groan in disappointment.

'Let that be a lesson to you,' he muttered. 'What you think of as a Christmas game can quickly get out of hand.' Then he walked down the hall to his study and slammed the door.

She leaned against the door frame, still weak with desire. Perhaps he was right. Tonight, the presence of mistletoe did feel dangerous in a way she'd never noticed before. Since he'd given no instruction to take it down, she left the kissing bough just as it was. But not before reaching up to pull off a berry and rolling it between her fingers as she smiled and walked up the stairs to console Eleanor.

Let that be a lesson.

Once in his study, Frederick reached for the brandy decanter and poured himself a stiff drink, downing it in one gulp.

What had he been trying to teach anyone by that shameless display? She must think him a monster, the sort of man who took advantage of the women who worked for him, then blamed them for tempting him into despicable behaviour. He owed her an apology, not a platitude.

The trouble was, he wasn't the least bit sorry. If she came into the room now, he would likely kiss her again to see if he could coax her into responding to him. Her mouth had been sweet, her body even more so. The feel of it against him as he'd held her had raised desires that he'd been trying to ignore all week.

It was not as if he'd been celibate during the war. But the couplings he'd allowed himself had been anonymous and brief, leaving him feeling lonelier than he had when he'd sought them.

But holding Charlotte Lewis had left him wanting a future that was full of warmth and, dare he say it, love. There was no indication that she wished to offer such to him and he had no right to take it, as he had just now.

But suppose he wanted to court her. How would he even go about doing so? Anything he might suggest would be seen as a command and he was far too used to giving those anyway. How did one suggest to a member of the staff that one wanted a different sort of relationship from the professional one they shared?

She had said that she did not want to be married to a military man again. She would have the right to refuse. And suppose she did? It would make subsequent interactions between them so awkward he might end up dismissing her, just to escape the embarrassment.

If she was happy in her position, she deserved to stay there. She had not asked for any of this. It was all down to his obsession with her. Better to get a hold of himself and remain silent than to speak and risk spoiling everything.

He waited until he was sure that he was alone on the main floor and then snuffed the candles and went to bed alone, just as he always did.

Chapter Eight

The next day was Boxing Day and Charlotte allowed herself to
sleep late for the first time in months. The other servants had
the day off to visit their families. Breakfast, lunch and dinner
would be cold and left over from the previous day's feast.

Since her parents had died before her husband, she had nowhere to be but just where she was: with the Preston family.
But there would be no guests tonight, so there was no need for
a chaperon, or for someone to arrange games and scold the
girls into their best behaviour. For twenty-four hours, her time
was her own.

She threw back the covers and went to the pot of chocolate
she'd left on the hob by the fire the night before. As she poured
herself a cup, she glanced at the blue gown hanging at the front
of the wardrobe and thought of the kiss she'd been given. She'd
had sweet dreams last night. Fantasies of dancing at balls and
being held too close, pulled into the shadows for an embrace as
sweet words were whispered into her ear. Promises of a future
of love and ease, of a family already made that she could be a
true part of and a new family that might begin.

She shook her head and sighed. It was romantic nonsense.
Though he had probably meant it as a punishment, she would

view the kiss as an extra Christmas gift. In time, it would be nothing more than a pleasant memory.

Eleanor's aborted kiss was another matter. Last night, she'd sworn she would never speak to her father again. There had been tears, of course, and Charlotte had assured her that she had spoken to the Major about it and would speak again if necessary to assure that there would be no punishment for Lieutenant Hargraves, since Eleanor had been the one to step under the kissing bough to tempt him.

She went to the wardrobe and reached past the dinner gown to find one of her usual, modest day gowns, then prepared to go downstairs to visit with the girls. But she reached the bottom of the stairs to find the Major, pacing uneasily in the front hall.

'Mrs Lewis, may I speak to you in my study, please?'

Was she a Mrs today? This was different from the usual curt summons she'd been receiving. In truth, she rather liked being called Lewis. Though it was genderless, it felt to her as if he wanted to call her by her first name, but could not bring himself to do it.

But today, she would take what she could get. 'Coming, Sir,' she said and followed him down the hall and into the room to her usual seat.

He gave her a grim look. 'I want to apologise for what happened last evening,' he said, looking as if each word pained him. 'I do not know what came over me.'

She maintained her polite smile, hoping it hid her disappointment. It was no compliment that he meant to treat the only kiss she'd had in years as an embarrassing aberration. 'That is all right,' she said automatically.

'I do not want what happened to come between us,' he said, though she did not understand how it could make them anything but closer. 'It was a mistake. My mistake, actually.'

'I understand,' she said, then turned the conversation to a topic which was a more important and less painful topic. 'And have you apologised to Eleanor?'

He stared down at the desk and muttered, 'You may have been right about that, as well.'

'I might?' she said.

'She would not speak to me at breakfast,' he said.

'Call her in here, as you do me,' she suggested. 'Speak freely to her and allow her to answer. She is worried about poor Hargraves.'

'Since I did not shoot him this morning, the matter is settled between us,' the Major said with the faintest of smiles.

'Men are simple creatures,' she replied. 'Women are more complicated. Girls even more than that.'

'I am beginning to realise the fact,' he admitted. 'And you...' He stopped again and her heart skipped a beat as she waited for his next words.

He smiled at her. 'You always seem to know what to do with them and I would do well to listen, just as I did when I was away from home and had only letters to follow the happenings here. I enjoyed our correspondence immensely.'

'As did I, Sir,' she said.

He sighed. 'That is all, Lewis.' This time, he rose and walked her to the door and out into the hall. Then she went to the library to find a book and he went off in search of his younger daughter, to try to make amends.

It had been a quiet day and, if Frederick was honest, he much preferred it to the continual business of the last few days. Cold turkey and bread with a healthy dollop of currants and a decent claret was more than satisfactory for a meal.

To his relief, the matter of Lewis had been settled first thing. She had accepted his apology and behaved as if nothing significant had happened. It was rather annoying to see how easily she had recovered from what had been an excellent kiss, profound in its depth and, he'd hoped, capable of arousing the passions of an average woman.

But then Lewis was not an average anything. She was really quite exceptional. He had discovered that as he'd been traipsing across the Peninsula with her letters for company. Getting to know her at home had not changed his opinion.

Of course, if he'd wanted emotion, he'd got more than enough of that during his talk with Eleanor. She had erupted in a shower of tears and called him the worst father in the world. But, in the end, she had blown her nose in his handkerchief and forgiven him, and he had promised not to lurk about in hallways, guarding the mistletoe and spoiling everyone's fun.

Then he had retired to the sitting room and spent most of the day napping and reading as the girls and Lewis played cards and guessing games. The sound of their voices had been a sweet accompaniment to his shallow dreams, which had been homey and pleasant. He had hardly noticed when they'd crept off to bed, leaving him in his chair by the fire.

It was half past eleven and rather embarrassing, he supposed, to be sleeping in a common room when he had a perfectly good bed waiting for him. But dozing in front of his own fire was a luxury he'd not had in many years and surely he could not be blamed for it.

But his body argued at his careless treatment of it. His knee was stiff from too much sitting and locked from lack of use. It would hurt like the devil when he tried to stand up.

He glanced at his stick, which he'd foolishly left on the other side of the room. He would need that before tackling the stairs to get to his bed.

He sighed, drumming his fingers on his knee before gritting his teeth and hoisting himself to his feet. He'd made it only a step or two before the joint failed him, sending him lurching towards the nearest table.

But before he could collide with the furniture, Lewis was there, taking the weight of his body on to herself and preventing the fall. She could not support him for long. He was far too heavy for her. But her intervention gave him enough time to grab the back of a chair and prevent a complete collapse.

'I thought you had gone to bed,' he said, trying to distract her from his embarrassing weakness.

'It is a good thing I had not,' she said, looking up at him with her blue eyes full of worry. 'I was just checking the door before getting a candle. Are you all right, Sir?'

'Better than I was in France,' he said, attempting a laugh. 'Death is not imminent. But if I neglect to stand and stretch every hour or so, I cannot be surprised when I pay the price for it.'

'Then it is good that I was here to help,' she said, her curls bobbing. He was standing close enough to her that he could plant a kiss on that blonde head, if he wanted to. It was sorely tempting. But there must be no more of that, even though he caught a whiff of the perfume he had given her like a whispered invitation.

Perhaps she realised the direction of his thoughts, for she stepped away to get his walking stick for him. 'Here you are, Major. Are you headed to bed now?'

'That was my plan,' he said, doing his best not to think of the previous day's mistake under the mistletoe. If they were to leave the room together, there was a chance that the incident could be repeated. It left him wavering between anticipation and dread.

'I will see you to your room,' she said, giving him a firm governess's smile.

'It is still Boxing Day for another few minutes,' he reminded her. 'You have no obligation.'

'And the footmen are still gone, or I would summon one of them, no matter the day. But I am here,' she said. 'I will not leave you alone.'

Her devotion stirred something in him, reminding him of all the letters they'd shared and the confidence he'd placed in her. If he trusted her with his daughters, why was it so difficult to lean on her now?

Because he wanted her to see him as something less than her feeble employer. 'I am...' He'd meant to announce he was fine. But as he stepped away from the chair he was holding to reach for the stick, the knee buckled again. He grabbed for the chair again, wincing. 'I am grateful for your help,' he said, surrendering.

'And I am happy to give it,' she said with an encouraging smile. Then she slung an arm under his shoulder and planted herself against his side like a living crutch.

There was nothing more for him to do but release the chair and let her lead him out of the room and towards the stairs. As they walked through the doorway and beneath the kissing bough, he held his breath, hoping that she would take it as a reaction to the pain of his injury and not the very real fear that he would forget himself and kiss her again.

They passed it without incident and he relaxed and let her walk with him, tight to his side as they reached the foot of the stairs.

'This is no longer necessary,' he insisted, trying to ignore the comfort he felt at the warmth of her body against his. 'I am doing much better.' He tested the leg, sure he could manage on his own.

'Maybe so,' she agreed. 'But it is better to be safe than sorry and have a tumble on the stairs.'

'I am not an invalid,' he replied.

'Of course not,' she agreed, but she did not withdraw her help.

He bit his tongue against any further objections. If she listened to them, she would leave him alone and he would lose the feeling of her breast pressed firmly into his side and her hip against his thigh. What kind of fool would refuse such delightful aid?

They were nearing his bedroom door, the moment when he should part from her. He was quite capable of putting himself to bed without a nursemaid, even with an injured leg. But he did not feel tired. He felt alive in a way he hadn't in ages.

As he opened the door, he turned his head to the side and surrendered to desire, nuzzling the hand that was resting on his shoulder, inhaling the scent dabbed on her wrist. The girl in the shop was right. With the heat of her skin, the innocent floral he had chosen for her had turned to a heady musk that he did not want to resist. He pressed his lips to the place where her blood pulsed, allowing himself a taste of her sweet skin.

She stiffened and sighed, but did not pull away. Her body, which had been straight and strong as she'd helped him, fit perfectly against him, curve to hollow. They belonged together. For tonight, at least.

He flexed his bad leg and, though the pain was still there, the strength had returned to it. He turned into her, wrapped one arm around her waist and dipped the other to her knees to scoop her up into his arms. Then he carried her the few steps to the bed.

Chapter Nine

It happened so suddenly that Charlotte did not know how to respond. One moment, they had been in the hall, then she was on the bed, looking up at him as he turned back to shut the door.

She should protest. The least she could do was sit up instead of lounging in the pillows as he approached her. But after years of being proper and strong, she was tired of it. Tomorrow, she might have to listen to the same hollow apology she'd got this morning. But just for a little while, she wanted to feel like a woman and not a guardian of someone else's innocence.

He paused a few feet from the bed, his hands on his hips, a soldier ready to do battle. With his dashing red coat and the tiny scar above his eye he looked capable of overcoming any resistance. But the officer was also a gentleman and was waiting for some sign to proceed.

She smiled and reached to the fichu that was tucked modestly into the neckline of her gown, then drew it slowly out, waving it like a flag of surrender before letting it fall to the floor.

He gave her a roguish half-smile in return and tore at the buttons on his coat, shrugging out of it, yanking his shirt over his head to reveal a chest that was broad and solid.

Her fingers itched to touch him. As he sat on the edge of the mattress to pull off his boots she fumbled with the closures of her bodice, eager to be free of it.

But she was too slow. He was already out of his clothes and grabbed her, tearing at the buttons, pushing the cloth away, shoving her stays and shift to the side and seizing a nipple in his teeth.

She arched her back and let him take her. His kisses were rough, hard enough to mark her, she was sure. The thought of hiding those love bites beneath a prim gown tomorrow made her wet with desire. She moaned into his ear, running her fingers through his hair, pressing his head to her to encourage him, spreading her legs to straddle him in invitation.

He released her to stare up into her eyes, then covered her lips with his. His kisses were deep and possessive, leaving no doubt in her mind what he wanted from her. She returned them, unafraid. Then she felt his hands, big and calloused, rough and yet gentle as he toyed with her body before settling into a rhythmic stroking between her legs that was driving her wild.

He paused and she moaned in frustration, then he began again, only to stop as she neared her climax, lulling her back to earth with gentle nips on her throat, only to take her back to a place that was a little more desperate than before. Finally, he tipped her over the edge with a single touch.

And while she shook, helpless, he filled her with one smooth thrust, leaving her gasping at his size and power as he moved in her. Her hands found his hips, clinging to him as he moved, steadying herself to meet him as he plunged into her. She belonged to him now. No matter what happened, she had been his, just as she'd dreamt.

She let herself go again as he shuddered in release against her. Then he held her in his arms, panting as they settled back to rest together.

Somewhere downstairs a clock chimed midnight. Boxing Day was over and she was a servant again.

The sweat on their bodies cooled them and she shivered, then glanced down to find she was still partly dressed, her crisp gown rumpled about her waist, the buttons scattered beneath her, poking her bare shoulders. The pinafore top of her full petticoat was torn half off her body and beyond repair.

What had she done?

A few moments ago, it had been nothing more than an erotic game. But now she could imagine the rush down the hall to get to her room. Suppose someone saw her, face flushed and clothes torn, running from the Major's room? Would they think he was a ravisher and her an unfortunate victim? Or would they see her as a seducer, eager to improve her position by providing services far beyond her duties?

Either one would be horrible. And what if the girls found out? They wanted their father to marry, but that did not mean they saw her as a candidate for stepmother. She should be ashamed of herself and not eager to snuggle back into the covers and begin it all again.

The Major looked just as shocked as she felt. He reached out and touched the ragged muslin of her petticoat as if he did not understand how it had come to be so. 'I will pay for the clothing,' he said, then glanced away, as if ashamed.

'That is not necessary,' she said automatically. In fact, it made things worse, calling attention to their carelessness and her wanton behaviour. She shrugged back into what was left of her garments, trying to make herself presentable for the short walk down the hall.

'You can borrow my dressing gown,' he said, reaching for the robe at the foot of the bed.

'No, thank you,' she replied and rose, walking towards the door.

'Lewis,' he said, then stopped himself and whispered, 'Charlotte. This is not over.'

'On the contrary, I think it is,' she said, hurrying to open the door and rush through it, shutting it with a soft click before racing to her room before the tears could begin.

Frederick stared at the closed door, wondering if he should go after her. He had behaved like a barbarian. And this, after the apology in the morning and the promise to her and himself that there would be no more incidents between them.

There was no defending what he had done, or the way he'd gone about it. There was some small consolation in the fact that she had been a willing participant. But now the sight of her fichu abandoned on the floor where anyone might find it made him feel even worse. He snatched it up and stuffed it into a bureau drawer, where it could remain until he could find a way to sneak it back into her room.

But how would he buy her a new gown without drawing attention to the fact? Slipping her the money to replace the garments he'd ripped was equally repellent. He might as well give her one of the bracelets that worm of a jeweller had been hawking. He didn't want a mistress. What use did he have for a woman who would tell him any lie that would keep her in jewels?

He wanted a woman who would be honest with him, even when he did not want the truth. Someone who understood his wants and needs almost before he could express them. A woman who surprised him with her beauty, her modesty and her ability to cast that modesty aside when he took her to bed.

He wanted her for more than just a single night. He wanted to live and die with her, to keep her always at his side.

The thought sent a surprising thrill through him, as the idea came to fruition. He had loved Charlotte Lewis as a friend while he'd been away. But once he'd seen her, he'd wanted more than friendship. What had just happened had been the inevitable result of his growing feelings and the lack of control that sometimes came with a long-awaited homecoming.

But what did she feel for him? Just now, she had given herself to him without reservation. But she had been refusing more respectable offers for months and was adamant that she did not want a repeat of her last marriage, or to lose another husband to war. Suppose she turned him down because of his red coat?

Worse yet, suppose she only accepted him because he was her employer? Maybe she'd felt she had no choice. That refusal meant losing her position. They would have to come to some agreement, but he did not want her assenting to a marriage that she did not truly desire, just for the sake of financial safety.

A sham union would not be enough for him. He had lived too

long alone to settle for a woman who did not love him. Perhaps it would be better to find a command somewhere far away, in a place where his injury did not hold him back. It would mean parting from his daughters again. But Jane would be leaving home in a matter of days. Eleanor would understand. If he left, she would still have Charlotte Lewis to care for her. She would be all right and he could return to loving them both as he had, safely and from a distance.

But that did not seem right, either. It was running from a fight and he had never done that in his life. What he needed was time to plan a campaign. And, since he could not sleep a wink with the delectable Charlotte Lewis lying just down the hall from him, he had all night to think.

Chapter Ten

Charlotte got little sleep that night, replaying the happenings of the past day in her head. How had they gone from agreeing that there would be no more kissing, to a violent tussle in the sheets and a shuddering release? And where were they to go next?

In the morning, she rose and dressed, careful to ignore the torn petticoat and buttonless gown wadded in the back of the wardrobe, an embarrassing reminder of her loss of control.

She moved the blue dinner gown to its place behind the other gowns as well. Putting on airs had done nothing but get her into trouble and she would not do it again. She was an utter failure as a chaperon if she secretly revelled in the things she was denying her charges.

And what was she to do if the Major called her into his office to give her another apology and tell her that what had happened was nothing more than an aberration of the Christmas season? What else could it be? He had said nothing about love or marriage when he'd carried her to his bed. He'd said nothing at all about anything.

If he apologised, she would accept it for what it was, a well-meaning attempt to make things right between them. But what if he offered for her, instead?

That might be almost worse than the apology. It might be just an excuse to keep her in her place, running the house as she had while he went back to the army. If he did not love her enough to stay with her, she would be left alone with his letters, just as she had been with Hiram. And eventually she might get that final letter explaining that something terrible had happened and she was a widow again. She did not want to risk her heart, only to lose it.

There was no avoiding it. She would have to go downstairs and see what he had to say. But when she arrived on the ground floor, he was not standing in the hallway, as she'd expected him to be. Nor was he in the study or the breakfast room.

The girls were there, as always. Or, at least, as they would be for one more day. Tomorrow was the wedding and, after it, Jane would no longer be her responsibility.

She gave them a falsely bright smile as she helped herself to eggs and toast. 'Where is your father?'

'Gone to the Horse Guard,' Eleanor said, rolling her eyes. 'And then to his tailors, probably to have a fresh uniform fitted.'

'I suppose it was too much to hope that he would be home with us for more than a few days,' Jane agreed. 'But at least he is staying for the wedding.'

'He is going back to the army?' Charlotte said numbly. It confirmed her worst fears.

'It certainly seems so,' Jane replied.

She sat down and chewed absently on her food as Jane began to talk about the menu for the wedding breakfast, wondering if it was too late to change the ham for salmon.

Charlotte had not known what she should do or say. But apparently, the Major had made the decision for her. There would be no further incidents between them because he would be gone again, after Christmas.

She felt a tear forming at the corner of her eye, ready to slip down her nose, and dabbed at it with the edge of her napkin.

'Oh, Mrs Lewis,' Jane said, offering her a handkerchief. 'Do not cry over me. I will always be your friend.'

Charlotte gave a shuddery sigh, glad of the excuse that the

girl provided. 'I am sorry to be such a ninny. I will be fine in a moment. But I think I must write a letter this morning, if you will excuse me.'

'Of course,' Eleanor replied. 'I am sure we can manage without you for a little while.'

She left her breakfast nearly untouched and went to the morning room with its little writing desk and sharpened a quill. She stared at the blank paper for a moment, searching for the words. How did one resign from a job one loved without assigning blame or hurting feelings? There was no easy way to do it. But if she meant to do what was best for herself, she could not stay here and allow things to go back to the way they had been.

It was not healthy to moon over a man one could not have, waiting eagerly for his letters and reading and rereading them, hoping to find a clue to his feelings. If he was leaving, so could she. It was the only way to free herself from hoping he might come back to her.

In the end, she scribbled out a few lines, stressing the need for a fresh start due to the changes in the household and the fact that her skills were hardly needed now that there would be only one girl to care for.

That was not true at all. Eleanor was as much trouble as any two other girls and should not be left alone. But perhaps Charlotte's absence would encourage the Major to remain in London to watch out for her. If so, her leaving was the best thing that could happen to this family and she would do it right after Twelfth Night.

She signed at the bottom, blotted the ink and folded and sealed the paper, writing the Major's name in fine script on the back. Then she took it to the study and set it on the desk.

She stared at it for a moment, to be sure that her mind did not change before returning to the girls who were celebrating the arrival of the bridal flowers.

Their scent was almost like perfume. But she'd had far too much of that this week. After taking one last sniff she turned away and lost herself in her other duties.

* * *

When the Major returned home, it was half past nine and the house had gone to bed early, to be ready for the big day tomorrow.

He had lingered at the tailor and then at a shop on Bond Street, obsessing over each detail of his purchases, though there had been little reason to. His mind was made up. He knew what he wanted and had no further input to give to the merchants.

Then it had been off to his club, where he accepted far too many drinks to congratulate him on his daughter's wedding and his own decisions for the future.

He should have come home earlier. He needed to talk with everyone, to explain to them the changes that were to take place, to receive the blessings of his daughters and to secure Charlotte's agreement. It was too late now, but perhaps, in the morning, before going to the church...

When he saw the letter on his desk, he recognised the hand immediately and tore at the seal and read. Then he read it again more slowly, searching for unspoken meaning in the few lines she'd written. If he could not stop her, she was leaving him and it was because of what he'd done.

The thought stunned him. He could not let her get away, now that he knew how to make things right. At least the letter said she would remain for the wedding and the rest of the Christmas season. He did not have to worry about her slinking off before he could speak to her.

There would be time tomorrow to change her mind. There had to be.

Chapter Eleven

The next morning, Charlotte arranged for a light breakfast to be brought to Jane's room, where she and Eleanor joined her to help with her toilette. She was already dressed in her wedding gown, an embroidered white muslin with a pelisse of dark green velvet that would look festive next to Jeremy's red and gold uniform.

'I do not know what I will do without you,' Jane said, staring at her in the mirror as the maid arranged flowers in her hair and took a curling iron to the fringe at her temples. She looked very near tears and was staring at her own reflection as if she did not know her self or her mind.

'I will always be there for you,' Charlotte said, trying not to think of a future without the Preston family. 'As you said to me yesterday, I will always be your friend, even if we do not see each other every day.'

'Do not be a goose, Jane,' her sister said from her seat on the side of the bed. 'You are only moving a little way away. It is not like you will never come home to visit. Mrs Lewis and I will be here, whenever you need us.'

She should tell them the truth. That she could not stand to be here any longer, to see their father so close and yet so far away.

But now was not the time. She would break the news after the wedding when everyone was not so emotional.

Jane was ready now and the sisters walked down the stairs hand in hand, Charlotte a step or two behind them. The Major was waiting at the foot of the stairs and, for a moment, their eyes met. He gave her an encouraging smile that made her wonder if he had read her letter. Was he relieved to be rid of her? Or perhaps he had too much to think about today to worry about a minor problem with the staff.

She forced a smile in return and then looked away. She would be happy today, for Jane's sake.

'You look lovely,' the Major said, staring between his daughters. 'Both of you.' Then he looked at Charlotte and the look in his eyes softened. 'Mrs Lewis, may I speak to my daughters alone for a moment?'

'Of course, Sir,' she said, going outside to wait in the carriage.

A few minutes passed and she wondered what he was telling them. He had looked very happy as he'd greeted them at the foot of the stairs. He had probably prepared some brief speech with a few words of wisdom for the new bride, the sort of thing that only his daughters needed to hear. It was a reminder that she was not really part of the family, no matter how she'd felt these five years.

Then the front door opened and he ushered the girls to the carriage, climbing in after them so they might begin their journey to St George's. The wedding was to be small, with no one but family there to witness it, and Charlotte supposed she was lucky to be included.

As the Major walked his daughter up the aisle a lump formed in her throat and she swallowed hard, fearing that it might be the beginning of tears. At least, if she were to cry today, she could blame it on the wedding and Jane's departure. It need have nothing to do with what had happened between her and Frederick.

In her heart, she savoured the name. To use it, even in silence, was an illicit pleasure, a chance to claim some small part of him before she had to let him go for ever. She took a seat at the front of the church, staring at his broad, red-coated back as he led Jane to the vicar and the ceremony began.

He stood ramrod straight beside his daughter, one hand protectively on her arm, the other resting on the pommel of his sword, as if ready to fight to the death to keep her. And then his moment came and, with a trace of wistfulness in his voice, he gave her to be married, stepping back as she turned to her love.

Then Eleanor took the bouquet Jane had been carrying and Jeremy took Jane's hand. As the vows were said, Charlotte thought of her own wedding, which had been in June in a tiny village church, and how happy she had been. Would she ever feel that way again? Perhaps it was her duty now to see to the happiness of others rather than focusing on her own.

The thought made her sigh, but she did it quietly, the barest whisper of air in the echoing stillness of the church. Then the ceremony was over and the licence was signed and they filed out of the church to make room for the next happy couple to be married.

They stopped in the portico where Jane turned back to them with a smile. 'It is time to throw the bouquet,' she said, waving the flowers at her sister. They had talked about this before, with Eleanor quite insistent that this was a tradition that her sister must keep.

'I am ready,' Eleanor said, holding up her hands to receive the toss.

Charlotte forced herself to smile, afraid to look at the Major as the bride prepared her throw. If he was upset by a simple kiss under the mistletoe, what must he think of this?

She would assure him later that the girl's fascination with marriage was harmless. It was still all a game to her. Her heart had never been broken and, hopefully, it never would be.

Then the roses were arching through the air towards them. Just before they reached her, Eleanor grabbed Charlotte by the arm and pulled her into their path.

She held out her hands in surprise and the bouquet dropped into them as if it had belonged there all along. She stared at them in dumb amazement, then looked automatically to the Major.

He was smiling back at her. 'Well, Lewis,' he said, 'what are we to do about this?'

'Sir,' she said automatically, 'I did not mean...' She looked to Eleanor, ready to hand the flowers back to her, where they belonged, but the girl stepped away before she could.

'I am far too young to be married,' she replied with a laugh.

'And you are leaving us,' he reminded her. 'Who knows what the future holds, now that you will no longer be working for me?'

Charlotte looked helplessly at the girls, who should not find out in this way that she was going. But they did not seem in the least distressed. Instead, they were smiling at her as if they knew something she did not.

The Major stepped closer to her, holding out his hand. 'If you are no longer working for me, I can ask what I want of you without fears that the differences between us will give you a reason to lie about your feelings. Charlotte Lewis, will you marry me?'

'Me?' she said, surprised. It was what she'd wanted to hear, but what was she to say?

'No other,' he replied. 'There is no other woman that I would rather spend my life with. And I will have a lot of time on my hands, now that I have sold my commission.'

'You are giving up the army,' she said. 'For me?'

'If you will have me,' he replied. 'I went out yesterday and had a wardrobe of clothes tailored and there is not a red coat or a bit of gold braid in the lot.'

'You are staying here,' she said, her face breaking into an amazed smile.

'And I had time to pick up a little something,' he replied, fishing in the pocket of his coat. He held out a ring set with emeralds and rubies. 'I saw it before Christmas and, even then, it made me think of you.'

'A ring?' she said, still unable to string her thoughts together. Not just a ring. One that would remind her of the Christmas she had found her love.

He reached for her left hand and pulled the glove off it before slipping the ring on her finger. Then he looked at her expectantly. 'You are not answering me, Charlotte Lewis. Do you have nothing to say for yourself?'

'Yes,' she said, laughing. 'Yes. I will marry you.'

'And do you love me, woman?' he boomed at her in a voice that would have made a soldier jump. 'If it is half as much as I love you, I might manage to be content.'

She laughed again and nodded, unphased by his tone. 'I love you,' she whispered. 'Since...for ever.' Then she looked to the girls, afraid of what they must think.

'Finally!' Eleanor said, clapping her hands together.

'We have always hoped,' Jane admitted.

'If we were to be allowed to pick the woman to be our stepmother, we would want no one other than you,' Eleanor agreed.

The Major pulled her close, lifting her off her feet as if she was a doll and kissing her on the lips. Then he reached up to wipe a snowflake from her hair. 'Come, everyone, let us get out of the weather. I understand there is a fine breakfast waiting for us at home. We will toast to the bride and groom and to the future.'

'To our future,' Charlotte agreed with a blush and followed her love, and her family, to the carriage and to home.

* * * * *

The Earl's Yuletide Proposal

Liz Tyner

MILLS & BOON

Dear Reader,

Christmas in the Regency could have meant a great deal to the staff of a large estate, enlivening them as they bustled around readying the household for the season. In fact, I wondered if perhaps the servants had more Christmas spirit than their employers, and I wanted to write a story about staff who truly looked out for everyone during the festivities, and perhaps had to guide others onto the right path.

My hero, Philbrook, needs that kind of guidance. He values duties and responsibilities, but he's been going through the motions of holiday traditions without attaching any importance to them—an easy thing to do when the first and foremost obligation of life is to see that people are provided for.

Sometimes we need help to assess things before seeing what truly matters, and I hope you find this story an example of assisting others, holiday spirit and love.

Liz Tyner

Dedicated to Bill, who helped create one of my happiest family Christmas memories on a Christmas Eve when temperatures hovered around freezing, and our riverbank campfire hardly warmed the rocks surrounding it.

Chapter One

'Lord Philbrook. Lord Philbrook,' Adriana called, holding the letter high, scurrying as fast as she could in her dress, hitching it up with her left hand so she could move faster. 'Stop. Please. Wait. You must…'

She gasped, unable to run any longer. She caught her breath, shivering from the raindrops pelting her with a mix of water and ice. She held the paper high while clutching her shawl to secure the covering.

If she had to charge at him and grasp him around the ankle to make him listen, she would. She knew how that would end— with him shaking her from his boot and giving her an austere stare that questioned her sensibilities.

He paused, looking over his shoulder with the merest glance until he recognised her, then he stilled as if turned into ice. Across from the vehicle a young man in livery peered over his bundle of mistletoe and a man in a tall hat watched from a distance.

Cheeks numb, she breathed in a blast of chimney smoke that teased her with a memory of warmth, but carried a stinging grit that she tightened her lips against.

Waving the letter again, she stepped closer.

He stared at her, eyes questioning, no longer frosted with ice.

'Lord Philbrook. You must read this.' Words forced into the air.

Then he appeared slightly gentler than the weather.

'Why are you—?' he asked.

'You must,' she said, ignoring the blast plastering a dampened curl against her face.

Hand trembling from the cold, she held the paper outstretched.

He took the missive from her, unfolded the letter and read.

'I had to stop you before you—before you—' She lowered her arm. 'Before your appointment for the Special Licence. Or I am to be sacked.'

Eyes tightening, he read the letter again. Then he studied her. 'So, I am sacked instead.' He laughed without humour and tossed the letter to the ground.

She jumped forward and lifted the paper, brushing the dirt from it. She'd already heard the contents and didn't want anyone else to peruse it. She was fairly certain one of the men watching would be too curious not to fetch it.

She turned to run back to Her Ladyship's, but Philbrook commanded her with one word. 'Stop.'

It would take a person much braver than she to ignore such a directive. She breathed in the stabbing air, turned and waited.

'What do you know of this?' he asked.

'It's a letter from Her Ladyship,' she said, trying to keep her teeth from chattering. She glanced at her shoes, feet hurting from the cold.

'Explain.'

'I did see her write the letter.' And heard her grumble on and on about the unfairness of it all, the injustice, the disgrace...

'My grandfather's dying wish was that I wed Lady Velma. He said it was important to have strength in a union and then he mentioned his wish that I wed.'

'She is forceful.'

'Why is she calling it off? Now?' The last word was delivered with such strength it made the cold winds around them gentle by comparison.

'She heard of your...' Then she swallowed. And swallowed again.

'My?'

'Your decreased fortune.' She whispered the words. Must she spell out her cousin's shallowness?

'My decreased fortune?' he almost shouted, eyes widening.

'Your reduced circumstances,' she whispered again, giving a sideways glance to his carriage. The cumbersome vehicle had been well constructed once upon a time and could have withstood a marauding army, but it was well out of fashion.

He looked at the carriage and then his gaze alighted on her again.

'My decreased fortune.' His tone had a deadness.

'Yes. I'm so sorry, Your Lordship.' She meant it, too. Her cousin, Lady Velma, was one of the loveliest women in society. No question about that. A frail swan of a woman. A delicate wisp who could have taken Bonaparte's army from him with little more than a sigh and a tremulous gasp, and if that hadn't worked, she would have taken him prisoner. One didn't go against Velma without expecting consequences.

'How does she know about my *decreased* fortune?'

Adriana took a step away at the sound of his words, unwilling to tell him about the letter Lady Velma had received. Unsigned, of course. From a concerned, caring person.

Likely.

He studied her, waiting.

'Well, I must return,' she said. 'Her Ladyship will want to know how you took the news.'

'And what will you tell her?' A shadowy smile passed across his face, but he appeared to be laughing at himself.

'That you appeared a bit gruff. Perhaps hiding your broken heart with valour. And—' She took another step back, but the distance never increased between them. She was shivering terribly now, not because of him, but because the wind was piercing. '—that you...' her voice strengthened '...bid me farewell, wishing her the best, and made your way into the carriage, grasping the door for support...'

'You'd lie?' His eyes almost twinkled. The twinkle. Oh, she'd seen hints of it before when he'd arrived to visit Lady Vel and she'd had to make an excuse as to why Vel was running behind.

Her knees almost gave way and it wasn't from the cold. In fact, she might have felt a burst of the sun, which had to have been blazing to have blasted through all that ice in the sky.

'I'd imagine it to be the truth,' she said. 'After all, she is your beloved.'

He half snorted a laugh. 'Apparently not.'

'You will recover,' she said, pulling at her shawl to try to gather some warmth. She supposed Her Ladyship would have been a good countess if he didn't upset her often. Cajoling her husband into giving her whatever she wanted. Spending her days taking care of her appearance. Being the most beautiful woman at any event. Making him proud.

He reached out and snapped the paper from her hands, the leather from his gloves brushing her cold fingers, sending a fresh batch of trembles inside her.

He could stand there and scowl in his greatcoat until night fell if he wished. She wasn't staying. She pulled her thin garment more tightly, hoping for a glimmer of warmth, and he suddenly seemed aware of her situation. For an instant, he didn't move.

She rather felt she was being dissected, one ravelling thread at a time, and coming up a few fibres short.

He shook his head, his tone mellowing into the warmest sound she'd ever heard. 'You're going to catch your death of cold if you aren't careful.'

The compassion in his voice was more in keeping with the man she knew. He'd never spoken harshly to her before. If Velma was rude to her, and he'd heard, he'd found a kind word to correct the situation.

'I must get back to Lady Vel,' she said, because she knew she'd catch a verbal thrashing if she didn't return to give a full report, including what he was wearing, how his eyes looked, what he did as he read the letter, the intensity of his sadness, and what his coachman did, and so on and so on.

'Come inside with me,' he said, taking her arm. 'You're shaking from head to foot.'

She could feel the pressure of his clasp, but no warmth from the touch, only the awareness of leather gloves.

'It's your choice,' he said.

It wasn't really her choice.

'I must get back. She's waiting on me.' And she hoped to have enough time to at least put on a dry dress so Lady Vel didn't complain of untidiness.

'No. You should not be standing about shivering like this.' Clipped, commanding words, with no expectation of disagreement.

And at that moment, she was tired of being icy and was especially tired of freezing while he stood in a greatcoat to his knees.

'It's December. Winter. Only two days before Christmas, Your Lordship. The sooner I get back and speak with Her Ladyship, the quicker I will be able to find a warm spot in the kitchen and thaw out.'

But he still held her arm. 'Go inside with me,' he said. 'You're not dressed warm enough. For indoors.'

The thought of a fire tempted her, but Lady Velma's blast of fury would be intense if Adriana didn't return immediately.

'Do you wish for me to be sacked?' she whispered, but staying with a grumbling Vel might be a worse fate than searching for employment. 'I know she is my cousin, but our positions in life are so different. My mother didn't marry a peer. She wed for love. If Her Ladyship gets angry, she will be ferocious. And I need to get things ready for Boxing Day.'

He studied her. 'Boxing Day? For servants?'

She nodded. 'But I must get back to Her Ladyship. She can be most determined when she makes up her mind.'

'Well, good,' he said. 'So can I.'

His eyes changed then. Softened. And he mustn't look at her like that. Because saying no to him was difficult enough when he was upset, but when he appeared kind-hearted, she could not refuse.

He glanced at his carriage. 'I don't want my driver being out in the weather any longer than he has to be.'

She followed his gaze. The servant had a big hat, a thick scarf around his neck, a coat, gloves, and looked to have a blanket around his legs. She shivered again.

'Do you have a concern with my vehicle?' He lowered his chin and his dark eyes held challenge.

'It appears warmer than I am,' she muttered and looked up at him, feeling her teeth chatter and noticing she was having trouble forcing her mouth to say the words.

He took in a breath that seemed to start so deep in his body she wondered that any air was left around her. And she knew he'd been asking her so much more than whether she had a *concern* with his vehicle. He was likely, possibly, perhaps, thinking of returning to Velma's and trying to rekindle her affection. If so, maybe he would allow her to ride with him if she wasn't offended by the elderly state of his carriage.

If he returned her in the vehicle, she would certainly get home more quickly and perhaps Lady Vel would reconsider the courtship.

'Then step indoors with me.'

He would have to cancel his appointment, she realised. He was so much more courteous than Vel.

'Thank you,' she said, deciding she would risk the fury she would find when she returned. Her toes were cold.

'I know you have had a terrible surprise,' she said, walking with him, forcing her lips to move, 'but really, I would not expect Vel to reconsider.'

'Well, I'm not.'

'Um…' She studied his face, minding her tongue.

Then he hurried her along. Once inside, she really couldn't tell it was much warmer and now her teeth were well and truly chattering.

He took off his hat and gave it to the man inside the door, and slid her shawl from her shoulders, the tips of his gloves grazing against her skin. It must be wonderful to have gloves that had never been mended.

He removed his coat and wrapped it around her. Suddenly she was covered, head to toe, in the light scent of shaving soap and masculine wool, and in a bundle of warmth. She no longer only imagined what it was like to have such warm clothing. The wool was caressing her.

'I am...' she whispered, shutting her eyes, savouring her instant with the coat. Surprised at the weight. She loved that coat. 'In love.'

'I had no idea.' He studied her. 'But you must get warm.'

'I will hold the coat while you finish with the clerk,' she said, her teeth still a little chattery, but she pulled her shoulders higher, the cloth brushing her cheeks.

It was fortunate she had never discovered the coat while he was courting Velma, or she would have had to run downstairs to give the wool a caress while he was speaking with her cousin.

'You don't want me to reconcile with Vel?' he asked.

Vel was her cousin and best for him not to know of how easily it was to pique her. 'I should not answer that question,' she said, hiding her eyes because really her thoughts were disloyal.

'I just want to be here a moment longer with...' she whispered, hiding her face so he would not see her savouring the unspeakable joy of his winter wear. 'This is wonderful...'

With her hands inside the coat, she snuggled it closer. 'Oh, goodness. I do not even know how you take this off to sleep.'

He blinked and his words were distinct. 'My butler wrenches it from my shoulders when I arrive home.'

'A brave man.'

Silence grew between them, but she didn't find it uncomfortable. He appeared to be studying his coat.

'And even with my carriage,' he said, 'it would not matter to you? Marriage?'

'Of course not...' And then she remembered her loyalty to her cousin. 'But I understand my cousin's... She is my family. And that means a lot,' she consoled him, but she shut her eyes and hugged the coat closer.

'Her Ladyship should have wed you for the coat alone,' she whispered. She meant to say the words to herself, but the warmth was the most delicious thing she'd ever felt.

'My tailor would definitely agree.' Not a hint of humour in his words.

'I should go now.' Yet she pulled the clothing close again,

raising her shoulders so that the collar covered her ears, warming her even more. 'But it's hard to leave...' She'd not been so warm since July.

He could talk about marriage all he wanted.

But she didn't want to hear another word about Lady Vel, even though he had mentioned an absence of feelings and the promise he'd made his grandfather.

Right now, that was not important to Adriana as she wasn't going to listen to him ramble on about his broken heart. She cuddled into the coat, pulling the wool tight around her ears, letting him talk about whatever he wanted. She was too busy thinking about the cloak of comfort around her to listen to anything he said. Wool was glorious. For once, she understood moths.

Then he paused and she knew she was to answer. What had he just said? Something like, 'Suitable for you? For the rest of your life?'

She heard a trace of compassion, but she wasn't really attending. Apparently, he had noticed her attention to his coat. It coaxed her to experience every thread and to enjoy the luxury of masculine warmth around her. She shivered with a whole new feeling. 'Of course,' she said. Goodness, the coat was more than suitable to warm her. It was exquisite. She did not know enough words to describe how it felt.

'If you're agreeable?'

'Yes.' She was always agreeable. Agreeable to everyone. She hid a sigh and tried to slip the coat from her shoulders to return it.

'Your full name?' he asked.

'Adriana Armstrong,' she said.

'You don't have a middle name?'

'No. Simple.'

'And your date of birth?'

She didn't see why that mattered, but she didn't care because she was going to hand over the garment and run home as quickly as possible. She told him the date, noticing he didn't even appear affected by the temperature, but it was warmer inside.

He turned to the man who'd let them in. 'Did you get that? We want everything completed at once. She's freezing.'

'Yes, Your Lordship. I will take care of getting things underway.' Bowing, he left.

She could barely walk in the coat and her fingers were tingling now. Just another heartbeat and she would leave, but he put an arm at her back and ushered her forward. And the air was warmer in the direction he was moving her. Ah, she could not refuse such an offer.

The man returned, his browed eyes seeming not to see her. 'He is ready for you, Your Lordship.'

Philbrook gave her what she supposed worked as a smile.

'Wait,' he commanded.

She snuggled into the wool. Really, she couldn't leave.

The coat was heavenly. Unfortunately, stealing it would be a capital offence. Staying longer with him was keeping her warm and she didn't care much about his broken heart, but she knew it wasn't based in love.

He'd been at the same gatherings she'd attended with Vel for years. While he'd always been kind and considerate, he'd never been one to hold long conversations with any of the ladies, though he'd danced occasionally and been entertaining before wandering on to discuss politics or projects with the others involved.

He studied her. Eyes appraising. Giving away nothing. Making her feel a little guilty for liking his coat, but it was a wonderful place to disappear into.

And she just couldn't remove the garment.

He started in the direction the man had taken.

'Surely you're not going to get the licence,' she called after him. Apparently, he didn't understand. 'If word of this gets out, she will not like it and will take it out on—'

He stopped and turned on his heel. 'I will *not* let her take this out on you. I'm getting the licence—if it is acceptable to you?'

'Yes. Of course. She will believe me when I tell her you continued on. But that money could be well spent elsewhere.'

He seemed to get taller and he looked down his most decidedly important nose. He didn't stop until he was standing in front of her, a tower of imposing strength. 'No. It will not.'

She could have easily given him about a hundred thousand

ways any funds could be spent better than on a licence to wed Her Ladyship, but there was no arguing with him.

'Well, I could be wrong.' She smiled, one of the ones she used when Vel needed to be coaxed to stop throwing things about.

Apparently, he was not as gullible as her cousin could be. He didn't make a sound, but she wondered that he was not making an ironic chuckle deep inside himself.

He left and in a few moments, the inner door was opened by someone. Philbrook returned with another folded paper, which he tucked into the pocket of his frock coat.

Poor man. Lady Vel would never marry someone who could not keep her in the finest attire.

She wrenched the coat from her shoulders, took one last lingering look at it, held it to him and said softly, 'With all due respect, you should reconsider this.'

'That remains to be seen, I suppose.'

He put the coat back over her shoulders, again covering her with securing warmth.

Who was she to argue with an earl? 'If that is what you wish, Lord Philbrook.'

'It is,' he said, smiling, or at least his lips moving, and his voice sounded a rich gravelly growl.

As they exited, she reached out, holding a hand for her shawl, and he waved the man away. 'I would like never to see that again. It's threadbare.'

'Of course,' the man said, taking the garment and exiting.

'You can't.' She turned to Philbrook. 'That's my precious wrap.'

'You will have one a thousand times better.'

'No. I can't. That one is precious.'

'That is a disgrace,' he said. 'You should never be about on such a cold day in such light clothing.'

She forced herself not to throw off the coat and rush after her shawl. But she could hardly run in such a coat.

'But—' she stepped to go after the employee '—I must have it.'

'You will have a new one.' Philbrook's eyes were stone and he ushered her out.

She would have to return for the shawl and it would be a distance out of her way.

After all, he was taking her back to Lady Velma's.

He helped her into the carriage—which wasn't really warm on the inside, but it protected one from the wind and precipitation.

He settled in and the carriage took off.

Oh, he was going to regret this when he came to his senses, she decided, noting the worn carriage seat. His coat was delightful, but she needed that shawl. Perhaps she could send a footman to retrieve it as they at least had warm clothing.

'I don't think the driver was listening,' she said, expecting the carriage only to move forward enough to find a place to turn around, but she noticed the vehicle wasn't changing direction.

She turned in her seat, looking behind her. 'He's going the wrong direction,' she said, bustling forward, perching on the edge.

'No. We're not. You need a place to stay until the marriage.'

He and Lady Vel were decidedly right for each other. Neither one listened to a single word of disagreement.

'We are going the wrong direction. You are not getting married to Lady Vel. At least not tomorrow. She may change her mind as she has some funds of her own, but you will have to do some crawling.'

'I do not crawl.'

'Fine. Don't crawl. Do as you wish, but I—'

'You are the one who isn't listening. You will have a new shawl. My aunt will chaperon until the marriage.'

The aunt wasn't the kindest person, but she wasn't the vicious crone that Vel claimed must have been uncovered from a cursed burial pit. She only seemed half that bad when Adriana had attended events at his house with Vel. Perhaps she would know someone in search of a lady's maid. Even though it would not be an elevation in status, it would be much better than working for a woman who enjoyed prodding her with a fan... Or a book... Or throwing them.

He studied her. 'Is there anything you simply must have from Lady Velma's?'

'I want my shawl,' she said.

'You will have one that is better than that pitiful rag.'

She struggled to remove his coat. 'I would rather be covered by that beautiful shawl than this oversized coat.' Mostly. His coat arrested her, but she wasn't keeping it even though it caressed her.

'You'll freeze.'

'Yes. But it's my choice.'

'Your freezing is not a choice when I am with you.'

She threw the garment into his lap and it rested half on her knees and half on his. The cold hit her again.

He raised a brow. 'You don't have to wear it. And I'm beginning to question whether you are as placid as you've always appeared.'

'Whether I am or not is none of your concern.' But she was getting herself in such a mess. She didn't have her shawl. She was getting further from Lady Velma's and she must hope her recounting of his mind-altering disappointment would soothe Vel somewhat.

She studied the coat and pulled it up around her, fluffing a corner of it his way, and then shared another bit of it. Outrage was one thing. Coldness another.

He understood and pulled it around them, tenting them with warmth.

Lady Vel had made such a tremendous mistake, unusual for her. But Adriana wasn't sure she was doing much better. She would somehow have to get a hackney to take her home and that would be costly. She'd also have to fetch her shawl on the way.

From the window, she recognised the path she'd travelled with Vel and knew it wouldn't be wise to return home without a vehicle and a wrap. She'd truly freeze.

The carriage was slowing in front of his town house. One with gables and large windows and which didn't even seem aware that it was a town house, but considered itself a mansion. In truth, she couldn't argue. She'd been impressed each time she'd attended an event with Vel at the home.

Several times Philbrook had even taken it upon himself to fetch her refreshments and once he'd even danced with her, jesting about changing their slow steps into a spirited country dance mid-song. She'd refused, as she knew he expected, but the exchange had made the dance more enjoyable.

Yet now he appeared so much more serious than he had in the past. He exited the carriage, taking his coat without speaking.

She raised her chin, took his hand and stepped out. He again wrapped the coat around her shoulders and she moved with him into the house.

Her chin, Philbrook's chin and the butler's chin were all in agreement—this might be the only butler in the world she didn't think she could cajole into helping her. She was going to have to go back into the cold on her own, but she must have a moment to think. Or to see if his aunt would understand.

Philbrook took her into a sitting room that had a case clock and a sofa that appeared sturdy enough to withstand two hurricanes at the same time, plus a snowstorm and drought—and Adriana sat. She intended to throw herself on the mercy of his aunt. Surely she was used to his ways and would be able to help her find her way home quickly.

He appeared to be lost in thought, but that was much better than hearing his fancies about marrying Lady Vel.

Then his aunt, a thin coil of hair atop her head like a coronet, strolled in, stamped her carved, over-tall cane on the floor and glared in a way that would have parted the seas if there'd been any.

'Aunt Bessie, I'd like to introduce you to my intended. Adriana Armstrong. We are going to get married tomorrow.'

'Pardon?' she said, taking a step to the side and shaking her head to try to clear her ears because she was sure she'd not heard correctly. 'We're not getting married tomorrow.'

'No more Lady Perfect?' The aunt interjected the question, waving a hand. 'Judging by her bedraggled look, I would suppose this might be Lady Imperfect.' She sniffed. 'You sure you're not trading a sow's ear for another sow's ear?' Her lips moved into a grim smile. 'Please take no offence, Miss. It's only a question. Someone has to keep the men in line.'

Adriana didn't move, trying to put the right meaning to the

words she thought she'd just heard. 'Did you say married?' she asked. 'Like wedded?'

'Yes.' He stared at her as if she were the one making outlandish statements.

'We're not getting married tomorrow. It's Christmas Eve.'

'Fine. The licence will not expire for a few days. We can get married on Christmas or Boxing Day or the day after if you'd like.'

'Christmas or Boxing Day?' She repeated the words and his attention passed to his aunt.

'Miss Adriana Armstrong,' he said. 'I'm sure you remember her. A relative of my former intended. We saw each other, the air tingled and we were instantly smitten.'

'With love?'

'We didn't question it.'

His aunt gave a dismissive wave in Adriana's direction and stomped closer to Philbrook.

'I've heard about this one. And seen her before. She's a companion to Lady Vel...from the impoverished side of the family. Velma's mother parlayed her beauty into a good marriage. This one's mother wasted her beauty.'

Adriana bristled. 'My father is a good man.'

The woman looked heavenwards. 'I suppose. And you have taken after him. Poor.'

'An honour,' she corrected.

'I'm starting to like Vel better,' the burial ground woman said. 'Vel is annoying, but she is the Earl of Lawton's daughter. I hope you weren't serious about the air sparkling, but if it did it was just with ice crystals. Not anything, um, good. Perhaps I made a mistake.'

The aunt obviously didn't mind that Adriana could hear the conversation. Adriana would have expected them to excuse themselves. But neither seemed inclined. And she felt her mind must have got lost in some kind of mental fog.

'It's past time I settled into a family life. And Vel was tossing me over because she thinks I'm impoverished,' he said.

'I know.' His aunt chuckled. 'I put that about. And it took

Vapid Vel long enough to get the message. Had to have it, um, spelled out for her. And told she had a wealthy secret admirer.'

So this was the person who'd written the letter Vel had received that morning, telling of the Earl's sad, sad state and hinting he was wedding Vel for her funds.

'Aunt.' His eyes darkened as much as hers. 'I should decrease your allowance if you think I am poor.'

The aunt took a step closer, glaring up at him, her posture challenging. 'And you still didn't get the message, either. I told you that Lord Weatherford's daughter was suitable. And Miss Wellston.' She tossed her arm out, palm upraised. 'And you bring home a cousin. Send the poor relation back.'

'I'm not sending *her* back. We've already received the special licence.'

That had been a special licence? How was that possible? she wondered. Everything had seemed so simple. Too simple for something as binding as a marriage licence.

The aunt put a hand to her chest and looked heavenwards, then emitted a low rumble. Next she narrowed her gaze at him. 'Even if I take her under my wing and dress her in the finest clothes and get her the best hairdresser, she'll still be a lesser cousin. You can't expect a miracle. She is not a blank canvas, but a dabbled one.'

'I'm not expecting a miracle. She'll be a good wife who doesn't demand every hour of my day. Besides, she thinks she's fond of me—'

'Your coat,' Adriana insisted, feeling her fog lifting. 'I'm fond of your coat.'

'Ha!' the older woman spoke over Adriana's words. 'She's fond of your title and all that goes with it. Nothing more.'

'His coat,' Adriana said. 'I like his coat. And his carriage is very comfortable.'

'That rolling heap of rust and bolts?' The old woman squinted. 'He needs a new carriage.'

'It has a strong roof and snug windows and doors,' Adriana answered. 'It's finer than many people have for a home.' She crossed her arms. This woman was as opinionated as Velma was.

The older woman's mouth was closed and she made a face as

if she were using her tongue to get something out of her teeth, but afterwards, the corners of her lips rose.

'It was damned insensitive of Vel not to have the courage to tell me herself,' he said to his aunt. 'This one at least showed up. She will be a fine wife.'

Adriana wanted to beg their pardon, even though she wasn't the person in the room who should be doing that—and explain that they were speaking about her right in front of her. But she kept her mouth closed. And wife? *Wife?*

'May I—? May I see that licence?' she asked, remembering his question about spelling her name. About her birthdate.

He reached into his pocket and took out the rolled paper and gave it to her. She saw her name. Spelled correctly. Her birthdate. And his.

'The name is wrong,' she said.

He took the paper from her and, with a sweep of his eyes, examined it, then studied her. 'You said you didn't have a middle name.'

She stared over the aunt's head and Philbrook didn't even see her. He didn't listen to her and he didn't see her. He saw a name on a special licence and that's all she was to him. He was over-tall, too confident by far, a man used to having his way as much as Vel was used to hers. He appeared slender, but he'd stood beside her and she knew that was an impression caused by his height. The carriage had dipped when he'd stepped inside.

He pivoted, facing the fireplace, and then Adriana noticed the painting above it. A boy, ten or elevenish, shoulder-length hair, a dark coat, fawn trousers, a stare that had all the confidence of the world, left fist resting against his hip, right hand lightly clasped on a table. She was fairly certain she remembered him wearing those clothes and he'd seemed so self-assured.

It truly didn't matter if he was in financial hardship or not. His funds couldn't be less than her own. His horses were well fed and his carriage driver was dressed in thick wool.

She had lived her last few years surrounded by wealth, watching her cousin luxuriate in a wall of perfume and flick crumbs of sweets from her lips with hands unmarked by calluses, and Adriana had enjoyed the awareness of riches, but realised her own mother had known the truth: that love was more comforting than an expensive array of jewellery.

Throughout the day, the servants commiserated with each other and with her. At night she slept in a tiny room in her even tinier bed and closed her eyes in a room surrounded by gifts the servants had lovingly made for her out of little more than scraps, but which felt more beautiful than any pearl or gold she'd ever seen. She could not leave them to step into a cold world. No wool could warm it.

'A misunderstanding,' she said. 'The licence should have— You weren't listening.'

'You gave me your birthdate,' he said. 'You weren't listening.'

'I surely wasn't.' She stepped closer and he held the paper so she could read it again. Yes, that was her name.

'What say you?' he asked, flicking his gaze over her.

She couldn't say anything.

'You should wed him,' the aunt answered for her. 'He's got that amazingly ancient carriage. Or I can keep you as a companion. Yes. My other one is getting above herself. Wants to see her grown daughter, as if that was necessary.' She tapped her cane.

Adriana lowered her eyes. She had been a companion to Lady Vel, her cousin, for five years since Velma's mother had complained of her daughter's rudeness to staff and hoped that Adriana could act as a peacemaker between Vel and everyone else.

She'd been pleased to have the employment and the reason had been the wonderful people she worked with. Leaving them would be too hard. And to work for his aunt would likely be no different than Velma's without the people Adriana cared for.

She had spent hour after hour anticipating Velma's wishes and ignoring her tempers. She had made the world around her cousin as peaceful as possible, much as she'd done when they were children.

When she'd heard of Velma's marriage plans, Adriana had wondered how her life would change, but Vel had planned to leave Adriana in charge of the house.

Philbrook interrupted her thoughts.

'Will you marry me?' he asked her. 'I suppose I should have made that question more distinct.'

She nodded. Yes, he should have made that part of the conversation stand out a little more. She'd heard of men getting down on one knee to ask a question of such import and now she knew why they did it. One needed to put some sort of physical punctuation around that query.

His aunt held her cane high and motioned Adriana her way. 'Let me show you my canes. My collection is the best in the world, I'd say. You won't find a speck of dust on them and I can use a different one each day of the year, but I prefer to coordinate them with my dresses.'

She was in a house of daft people. She might as well play along. She could make her escape later.

Philbrook took her hand, and she couldn't look anywhere but his eyes. It was as if Christmas carollers stood around her and suddenly burst into song after gazing at him and she couldn't blame them.

'That is going to keep you busy for a bit,' he said, seemingly unaware of the choir inside her, 'so I'll leave you two to get acquainted, and please let me know if you'd prefer Christmas Eve or Christmas Day for the wedding.' He kissed the air above her hand.

She didn't answer, but gave a shake of her head. Disagreeing.

He didn't seem to notice.

She wasn't the only one who didn't pay attention.

Chapter Two

After the aunt finished showing her row of canes lining the wall of her room, a servant appeared and whisked Adriana away.

'And if you need anything…' the housekeeper said, opening the door and standing aside. 'We've readied the rooms for you. Though of course we always leave the sitting room you'll share with the Earl just as he wants it.'

She stepped inside, blinking twice. A rectangular table with square bases on its legs sat at one side, with four chairs around it, all in a wood she was unfamiliar with. A mahogany cabinet with French curved legs was behind them, with some mismatched dishes inside, and on the top, an old hat hung from one of the knobs. A large room, obviously filled from very old furniture that had seen a lifetime or two of use.

Then the housekeeper opened another doorway. 'And this.'

This was a bedroom with a blue bedcover, a simple bedside table, a door which likely led to a dressing room and more space than her other room five times over. 'The room has been empty since Philbrook's grandmother died, I believe. And if you will step this way, Lady Velma.'

Even as she opened her mouth to correct the woman, it struck Adriana as sad that such a room should be unoccupied.

'The Earl's mother left years ago,' the housekeeper continued, 'and her sister was welcomed by the Earl.'

'I'm Adriana,' she said.

'Oh, my pardon. My pardon, Milady,' the housekeeper said. 'I must have forgotten.'

'No. I'm Adriana. Velma is...'

She could not say anything else.

Then she remembered the servants often knew more about what went on in a household better than the people involved. The servants would see all the puzzle pieces and were adept at forming their own conclusions. She might as well help them fill in the events.

'Velma was betrothed to the Earl previously. That has been discontinued. I merely delivered the news of the discontinuation and it has been such a blow to the Earl that he—he has—not shared the news with everyone yet.' She lowered her chin, her eyes, and her voice. 'So terribly sad.'

The housekeeper's mouth opened and she stared.

They left the rooms, almost colliding with a maid rushing to them carrying a tray of macaroons, the scent of the almond-based biscuits wafting her way.

She paused, staring at the tray, her mouth watered.

'Do... Do have some, Milady,' the hopeful maid said, holding the tray to Adriana. 'We made them for His Lordship's aunt, but Cook is preparing a second batch now.'

'Of course,' she said, for a moment adopting the manner of a woman who normally was called Milady. Treats were a weakness of hers and these appeared delicate, smelled of goodness, and called to her more strongly than her ethics did.

Taking one and feeling the lightness and the softness of the bite, she nibbled, then complimented the staff on the wonderful treat.

'I love Christmas biscuits,' she said. 'My favourite Christmas tradition.'

'Oh, no, Milady. These aren't Christmas biscuits. We make them at least once a week. Miss Bessie insists.'

'That must be wonderful. Like Christmas all year.'

The maid mumbled an agreement. 'I suppose it is.'

Before she finished, a screech sounded in the distance. Adriana recognised it and gathered her skirts and immediately ran to the noise, followed by maids.

As she scurried into the formal sitting room, Velma threw a wad of clothes in Adriana's direction, letting them scatter on to the floor between them, then she stomped on one of the dresses. Adriana saw her favourite garment.

'What—?' Velma shouted, eyes pinched and irises darkened into an apple-seed-sized glare. 'What do you think you are doing, sending for your things?'

'I'm so sorry, Your Ladyship,' Adriana said, arms at her side, shoulders tensed. 'I don't— I was… Um…um…'

A hand, feeling as large and strong as her back, steadied her and a baritone voice from behind answered, 'She no longer has to answer to you.'

Velma stamped a foot on Adriana's dress again. She snarled, 'I did not give her permission to leave. I gave her permission to send you packing. That was all.'

Philbrook stopped beside Adriana, clasping her hand. 'She doesn't need your permission. She is—'

'I am keeping her,' a shrill voice sounded. The aunt burst from her room, her cane moving at a fast clip.

'I'm taking her back,' Velma said. 'She is my companion and I did not give you leave to employ her.'

'We didn't employ her,' Philbrook said. 'She is—'

The aunt rapped her cane against his leg and his neck twisted when he peered at his aunt. 'Pardon?'

The aunt raised her cane as if trying to block Velma's vision of Adriana. 'She's no longer your concern,' the aunt said to Lady Vel. 'We're keeping her. I like her. Way better than you.'

Velma's mouth hinged open and seemed to lock briefly before clamping shut and widening again a little more normally. Vel turned to her, answered the aunt, but spoke to Adriana.

'She had better be home by nightfall,' Vel stated.

'It is entirely her decision,' Philbrook said. 'She's been asked—'

'Are you mad?' Velma said, ignoring Philbrook to again address Adriana. 'You cannot leave. You will miss Boxing Day and it is your favourite day of the year.'

Adriana held her breath. She hadn't known her cousin knew that.

'If you don't return,' Vel said, waving her palm from one shoulder to the next in a cutting motion, 'Boxing Day will be cancelled at my house. Cancelled. Terminated. Over. Done.' Then her voice dripped sweetness. 'Boxing Day. Gone.' And she made a fluttering noise with her lips.

'You can't do that.' Adriana touched the banister. 'You can't. The servants—'

'I can.' Velma's head bobbed sideways, then she tapped her finger to her lip. 'Mrs Ingalls, Perry, Enid, Miss Yale. Mannford. All without Boxing Day. So sad... But there will be another one next year. Perhaps...'

Vel bent at the waist, neck sticking out as far as it would go. 'Happy Christmas.'

And she turned, gave a kick to disengage Adriana's dress from her slipper and pranced out the door.

'Well.' A cackle. The aunt. 'Happy Christmas to Lady Velma as well.' She propped her cane against the wall, clasped her hands and raised them above her head. 'Crisis averted. A bad niece out. A potential good niece in. You don't have to thank me.'

His aunt took her cane and levered it if she were hitting a billiards ball, then left, singing. Adriana thought the song was about a-wassailing, but realised the aunt had changed it to *Here we go a-walloping.*

The sound of the carriage leaving echoed through the walls.

'Get that and have it taken care of,' Philbrook said, indicating the items Velma had kicked around the room.

She moved to collect her clothing, but his hand stilled her.

'I was not talking to you,' he said.

Two maids rushed out, gathering the dress and other items, and the housekeeper appeared at the corner and directed them. A horseback rider rushing through the streets shouting would have been more discreet. Servants would carry tales of this far and wide.

'I must have been—' Philbrook spoke under his breath.

'How did she know I was here?' Adriana wondered aloud.

'I sent a message to have your things sent here.'

That felt presumptuous of him.

'My apologies,' he said, turning to her 'I did not foresee this happening.'

'You didn't really know her,' she said. 'Just as you don't know me.'

'Would you ever act so?' he asked.

'I don't think so. I can't really see the purpose. Except for the drama.'

'You don't appear to be a person who likes drama.'

'No. I prefer peacefulness. At almost all costs.'

'It's better to see the truth, as I just did,' he said. 'I will see you at our marriage once you decide if Christmas Eve or Christmas Day will be better.' His hand left her back and the sound of his boots leaving clipped into the silence.

Another set of footsteps sounded.

'We'll make certain your clothing is freshened,' the housekeeper said.

Adriana didn't move.

'Are you...? Do you need anything, Milady?' the housekeeper spoke again.

'Um...yes.' Then she paused. 'Do you have a Boxing Day celebration here?'

'Of course, Milady. In this household we would not dream otherwise. The butler and I make certain that each staff member has a token of the Earl's appreciation. Everyone is assembled after breakfast and the gifts are disbursed.'

She wondered if she should have rushed after her cousin. This household was formal. Colder.

And Philbrook was marrying her to spite her cousin.

And Boxing Day at her cousin's would be cancelled.

Boxing Day. The one day of the year that she truly had Christmas.

Chapter Three

After she had finished dinner, alone in the room next to his aunt's, Adriana made a decision. She would follow her heart, just as her mother had told her to do.

She gathered her courage and slipped out the doorway, making the way to the rooms the maid had showed her, after retracing her steps a few times and getting a bit lost.

Finally, she found the familiar sitting room, and then exited it and stood in the hallway and rapped on the nearby door.

'Enter.'

He likely thought she was a servant. She didn't even have the courage to walk in when invited because it was his private rooms.

'It's Adriana,' she called out, trying to speak loud enough for her words to carry to him, but not to reach the servants downstairs.

He opened the door, standing even bigger than she remembered, or perhaps it was the shadows dancing around him making him appear commanding. The glimmer of a smile in his eyes and a spark of amusement past his lips reassured her.

'The maids rap soundly.'

Her heart thumped, forcefully reminding her it was beating.

But more important was the staff that she cared for and had spent the last five years of her life with and loved.

'I can't marry you,' she said. 'You're doing this to spite my cousin.'

His eyes, unwavering, studied her. 'Two betrothals cancelled in the same day,' he said, giving a chuckle she thought was directed at himself. 'That has to be a record. And probably will remain unchallenged for quite some time.'

He held out his forearm for her to clasp. 'Let's discuss it in the sitting room.'

She reached out, touching his arm with just her fingertips and thumb. She didn't think she'd ever grasped a man's arm who wasn't wearing a frock coat and she'd not realised an arm could be so sturdy. So much larger than her own. Alive. Her insides did a somersault and she swallowed, breathing as normally as possible.

He opened the door for her and she paused before going into the room, bolstering her strength. She couldn't leave her old life and step into another that she couldn't walk away from, particularly if it was as emotionless as the room.

The room truly was bland. Nothing like her cousin's room of flounces and ribbons and delicate furniture. Not even one sprig of holly. Or one red berry. Not even a nod to the celebration of Christmas.

Sad.

She had felt concern for Velma's servants because they'd had to arrange so many festive touches. Now she felt pity for the Earl's because they'd not been able to decorate.

She stepped inside with him and he softly shut the door.

Philbrook didn't seem so foreboding when they were alone. Just overwhelming and she wasn't sure that was in a terrible way. 'Did you really intend to wed me?'

He put a crooked finger under her chin, filling her even more with an awareness. 'Of course. I've been turned down before. This very day, in fact.'

'It's not…love.'

One brow rose. 'I have not had much luck with that emotion. I thought your cousin cared for me. And I have seen other sweethearts smile and I saw my title and fortune reflected back at me. In fact, your cousin seemed the least impressed by my inheritances than anyone I know. Except you.'

'She rarely is impressed.'

'The same as her cousin?'

'I can't afford to be.'

'Wed me and you can.'

'Was the proposal for revenge?'

He took her fingertips and briefly put them to his cheek before dropping them. 'You are caring. It was good fortune to me when she sent you as a messenger. And you were shivering. It was as if I'd never seen you before and I don't think I had, really.'

'You have to see my awareness that you appear to be a golden opportunity for me, but if you look around yourself and see the binding ties, obligations and rules your wife would be expected to adhere to, then perhaps the opportunity isn't as impressive as it might be.'

'You would rather live in Velma's household?'

'She enjoys a performance, but she's generally not that expressive.'

'We may grumble under the surface in my household, but voices never rise in anger now that my grandfather is gone. He loved a good commotion. Without him, it's easier to keep the volume lower.'

'Marriage is more than a simple combination of keeping voices low. It is a combination of families.'

'With the possible addition of children.'

'Of family,' she said. 'My parents are dear to me and I do not even know any of your family except your aunt. And people marry into each other's families, particularly if the husband has a home with relatives in residence.'

'Only Aunt Bessie.'

'Your mother?'

'She's not a close relative, I would say. We only see each other at events, Christmas and perhaps if she is running low on funds. She hates this house. Has sworn never to live here again. Prefers to live with my sister and her husband.'

'Not a close relative?' She almost gasped over the words. His mother?

'My aunt has always been a part of my daily life more than my mother. My mother might be gone for months, but Aunt was always nearby.' His words were strong, even if they were gentle, yet she sensed he wore a suit of armour over his heart. 'It was an arrangement that I would hope benefited all of us.'

She could see how he had so easily accepted distance in his life. The two people he'd been closest with had been a grandfather who was stern and overbearing and an aunt who carried a cane which she shook at people.

'Did you truly ask Vel to wed?' she asked, touching a hand to his arm, wondering if she read his intensity correctly.

'I was aware that my life was missing something. And my grandfather had requested it with his dying breath. It was just not the time to disagree with him.'

He clasped both her hands and stilled the world around them.

'Love never lasts,' he said. 'It's a false emotion, like a crate decorated with an over-tied bow. When you open the box, it's just an empty box.'

'My cousin isn't truly empty,' she said. 'You just have to look a little deeper to find her goodness most of the time. Though she does make mistakes regularly.'

'Would you consider me a mistake?' His lips turned up and he quickly added, 'Please don't answer.'

'Why me?' she asked. 'Because I am Velma's cousin?'

He laughed. 'The two of you do not favour each other. You've never created such a scene as I saw today from Velma. And I understand why she was so upset. She was scared of losing you.'

'We are family,' she said. 'We will always be family.'

'History...' one side of his lips tilted up '...has shown that family is not always the best ally.'

'At times, family is all we have.' And she had family. If she had to, she could return to her mother and father. They did not have much, but they would never turn her away.

She tried to read every emotion in his expression and see past the façade and deep into him. Yet it wasn't possible. Or was it?

'You said you weren't particularly close to your mother? I do remember seeing you with her when we were children.'

'Oh, she took me about on occasion. I was to be an earl and she was extremely proud of that. Reminded me of it often. Wanted everyone to know I was her son.' His lips turned up in a moment of whimsy. 'No one is very close to her as far as I can tell. Her sister, my aunt Bessie, is the considerate one though she can be outspoken, as you're aware of.'

'What about familial love?'

'It's a basic caring. Duties. If wed, we would each have duties and fulfil them to the best of our ability.'

They would both gain from a marriage, although perhaps she would gain substantially more. He would get a wife and she would get financial security for the rest of her life. She would never have to smile and pretend to go along with any tirades or ravings or some such, unless it was his, or his aunt's or his mother's or even more family members she'd not met yet. Instead, she would be expected to stand in the shadows and keep her opinions to herself.

The union did not sound so advantageous when put that way.

'I don't know that I can be a society bonnet.'

'You can always add a few frills and paste a smile on your face. You did it with Vel for years.'

'True. I make a special effort for her, but…' she crossed her arms '…that smile doesn't come as easily as it used to.' She was not giving a husband the same subservient smile she had given Vel to cajole her into happiness—and Philbrook had given away her wrap. Her wrap.

That was the sort of thing Velma might do. She'd not thought Philbrook that way.

She'd seen him court Velma and be most solicitous, although distant. In fact, while he'd waited for Vel, he'd seemed more gentle with Adriana and had hardly spoken to Vel when she arrived. He and Adriana had shared a smile between them at his patience when she had greeted him with the words that Velma would be along shortly. They'd both known the wait could be long.

Then she'd seen his reaction to a failed betrothal…and recover in his next breath. He said he didn't even believe in love—a false emotion.

'I thought Vel cared for being a countess and it would lead to a union of consolidated interests,' he added. 'Together we would have more power among the peers and perhaps that was what was important to my grandfather, but shouldn't be to me.'

'Consolidated interests?' Those two words whirled in her brain, forcing her to halt her musings and putting words in her mouth that she embraced. She interlaced her fingers in front of herself, palms down, swallowed, and spoke in her *Be kind to Vel* voice.

'It is with extreme regret that I beg your pardon, but I can't wed you and I will go to Vel and ask her forgiveness.'

A muscle in his jaw tightened.

'I believe,' he said, 'you must reconsider that. You don't want to live with a woman who behaves so badly.'

'She doesn't usually. Besides, it's been my home for years,' she said. 'And I want to fetch my wrap.' She could not believe she had parted with that dear garment. Her mind must have been truly frozen.

'That wrap—' he spoke the word as if it tasted of ash '—that you were wearing...'

'Yes. I miss it,' she said. 'It was a terrible mistake to let it go. I was just so cold. I just was not thinking at all.'

Now his eyes appeared to have taken on an internal ice blanket of their own and she strengthened her stance.

'I know it was not extravagant and a bit worn, but it was dear to me.' He had no right to diminish her apparel because it was not as costly as his own.

'You cannot,' he said. 'Velma acted like a child and the wrap was pathetic. You can't return to a life like that.'

'The wrap was lovely to me, my cousin is family and my home is my home.'

Chapter Four

Philbrook tried counting to five to control his temper, but he couldn't get past three. The poor woman was as intractable as her cousin. Must be an inherited trait. His aunt claimed often he'd inherited his mother's arrogance, his grandfather's pomposity and her own sweet nature—which he knew was not at all a compliment.

'Why?' He raised a brow. 'Why would you not consider an advantageous marriage?'

She took in a breath and let it out. Slowly. She studied the wall over his shoulder and he barely heard her. 'You tossed aside my clothing just as my cousin did.'

The thought that he would be considered the same as Velma speared into him. He took a step away, considering her words. He would never act as Velma had, but perhaps he had disregarded her feelings just as her cousin did. He must explain.

'No. I did not,' he said. 'The lowliest servant would not be allowed from my house in such attire. It is not controlling, it is caring.'

He firmed his lips, then stepped to the bell and rang it. Her little angry bee stare was not stinging him—overly. Then he put his hands behind his back so less of him could be stung. 'One moment, please.'

She was a bedraggled sort. Eyes the size of saucers when she wasn't trying to hide her wrath. If she'd truly been a bee, he'd have red welts over most of his skin just for insulting her pitiful wrap.

She was someone he wanted to put his arms around and protect. Such a shame she was attached to old clothing. Blast. She must have a fondness for faultiness. Vel. The wrap.

His carriage driver, Woodward, had once told him she'd even concerned herself after she'd noticed Woodward favouring a leg when the driver opened the carriage door for Philbrook to leave and checked on Woodward the next visit.

The little speck of a woman had tried to hire his carriage driver and told him that Velma's butler had agreed that the gardener could use a fine man for assistance. Woodward had insisted he wouldn't know a rose from a radish and later the grizzled old man had laughingly informed Philbrook of the encounter, but afterwards he'd always beamed when Philbrook had asked him how the garden was growing.

The memory caused him to reassess his view of her and he wondered if he should apologise. Working for Vel could not be all fun and frivolity based on what he had seen. And this woman wanted to wear a tattered cloth while returning to a floor-stomping shrew.

He might need to reconsider his attributes.

Or perhaps she was only happy when she was miserable.

A rap at the door sounded and the maid rushed in, shutting the door with a soft snap.

'Get Miss Adriana a wrap. Any cloak.' His eyes shut briefly. *'Hurry.'*

The maid's jaw dropped and she said, 'Of course.' She turned, grasped at the door, swinging it wide.

'No.' Adriana burst forward, stopping the servant. 'You do not have to get me a wrap. I need my old one.'

The maid searched his face, questioning, before she dashed from the room.

'I will be on my way,' Adriana said, stepping to the door.

'Please wait for the wrap.'

She hesitated, hand to the latch. 'I told her not to bring me one.'

'She will.' He had no question of that. 'I pay her wage.'

'It is not my wrap. I cannot take someone's wrap.'

'You cannot freeze.'

'I will hurry and keep warm by rushing.' The feminine eyes became bee-like again. And he'd never noticed before how lovely little bees could be. Those little stingers were only to protect themselves so the insects could create more sweetness.

'If you freeze,' he said, 'you'll be of no help to Lady Vel, although why you would return to a woman who stomps on your clothing concerns me.'

'Every occupation has its drawbacks.'

The door flew open again. The maid ran in with a shawl, holding it for Adriana.

'Thank you,' she said, smiling at the woman, taking it.

The maid gave a stiff nod and left.

He could see the debate in her regarding tossing it on the sofa and walking out.

'Keep it for now,' he said. 'Once we get your wrap, you can send it back with me.'

She moved to the door.

'I will have the carriage readied so I can go with you to make sure your wrap is collected.'

She hesitated and he suspected she was one heartbeat from bolting.

He indicated the window. The frigid weather.

'I can get my shawl on my own.' Her voice lingered in the air, softening it. He supposed it was her Vel voice and the thought caused his jaw to clamp.

Wide eyes studied him, with lashes long enough to sweep a lesser man under her feet.

'No,' he said. 'It's too far. It's cold. And I was going that way anyway.' To take her to Lady Velma's.

Adriana felt cosseted as he wrapped the borrowed shawl around her shoulders, filling her with a new warmth, and for just a moment they both lingered. She wondered if they were telling each other goodbye, perhaps spending a twinkling thinking about what might have been if they'd been different people.

She stepped down the stairs, passing the stone-faced butler who assisted Philbrook with his coat wordlessly, only the brush of fabric breaking the silence. Philbrook shook his head when the butler held out gloves for him.

They left the house and she could almost feel the demeanour of the butler following them. They got into the carriage, and she sat where the seat had been mended, noticing the scent of old fabrics and perhaps a hint of a cheroot.

Before they left, the driver, his countenance as solemn as the butler's, handed in a blanket. Philbrook took the covering to drape over her, surrounding her in a different household aroma.

In that moment, she completely understood why he liked the vehicle. Even though she'd not ridden in it as a child, it seemed to carry strong reminders of the past. The wheels would creak with the same sounds he'd surely heard as a lad. An envelope of memories just below the surface which didn't intrude, yet gave one a calming sense.

Or perhaps there was more to it. Perhaps it was the man sitting beside her who gave her the sense of security.

She glanced at Philbrook. He didn't appear to even see her, but then he darted a glance her way. The same one he'd sometimes given her at Lady Velma's. One of camaraderie. Distant, but somehow reassuring her that she wasn't alone. That he was giving her thoughts consideration even if they might have been behind different panes of glass.

She'd not known he was going to put the garment over her and truly it was thicker than her treasured one.

Admittedly, the shawl she wore now was luxurious, but Mrs Ingalls had knitted the other one for her. Even though the poor lady couldn't really see well enough to know if Adriana was actually wearing the shawl, Adriana would always step closer to her and hold out a side for her to feel. The clouded eyes would light up and Adriana's heart would glow.

For Boxing Day, Mrs Ingalls was getting a new shawl herself. Vel had purchased the wool, the servants had carded and spun the wool, and each servant, even the males who'd never touched a knitting needle, had been guided to knit at least a few stitches. Everyone in the house had had a part in it

Adriana had wanted Mrs Ingalls to have something each one of them had contributed to and made certain that it had happened in time for Christmas.

For Vel she was a relative and servant. For the staff, she was their leader, their confidant, their friend and the one person who looked out for their welfare. She made every person in that house have a better life—including Vel. And she loved them all.

Philbrook held one hand on his knee and used a thumb to rub the knuckle of his other one, a small scar running along the top of it.

'How did that happen?' she asked, pointing to the scar.

Momentarily his gaze widened a hair, then he studied the mark when he answered.

'I took Father's knife. He'd just passed on and the house was somehow different. I went to his dressing room, found his old knife, took it outside and decided I would cut down a tree. The knife slipped and I sliced my thumb. I was trying to hide what had happened, but I must have wiped my face, because Grandfather saw the blood and took the knife, and scolded me tremendously.'

'You must have loved your father dearly.' She wanted him to understand how he had felt love.

'Father was gone most of the time and Grandfather was a wizened old man who sat in a chair mostly and gave me lecture upon lecture.' He indicated the door. 'His. This carriage was his.'

'A reminder.'

'The carriage suits my size. And the springs. Best I've ever ridden in.'

'You don't think you have kept it the same to remind yourself of him?'

'It's larger than most. I like the ragged old seats because they're comfortable. My friends have spilled their drinks in it and I don't care. If there is a group, we take this one. Light for its size. My horses can pull it with no problem.'

'Not a memento?'

'No.'

'You don't believe you had a strong affection for him?'

'In the way one is fond of a wearied instructor. But the barbs were tiresome. After Father passed on, Grandfather believed he must be all things to me. And when Mother was with her father-in-law, a tug-of-war ensued. How was I to be schooled? Who was to have say over me? He insisted I live here and, as his heir, she really had little choice and so we resided here and she hated it. Hated it. And found reasons to be elsewhere.'

He rubbed his thumb. 'Although the three of us had the evening meal together when I was not away at school. A chance to stab at our meat, pound our vegetables and slice at our bread.'

'Sounds lovely.'

'Well, I may be polishing it up too much.' His mouth settled into a smile, yet his sight appeared to remain with his memories of the past until the carriage stopped in front of the structure where he'd purchased the licence.

He leapt from the vehicle and helped her out, taking her in to see the clerk who had taken possession of her shawl.

The clerk wrung his hands, insisting he had no idea where the shawl might be because it had been tossed into a crate of collected items going to the poor so they would have them before Christmas.

She didn't know what to do. The man in front of her had concern on his face. He leaned forward.

'We will do all we can to retrieve the item,' he said. 'I will find out where the poor are gathering and send—'

'Not necessary,' Philbrook said, 'I'll handle it.' He nodded a goodbye to the man and helped her outside, stopping just beyond the door.

'I'll see that a new one is made for you,' Philbrook said.

'I want my old one.' She bit her lip. She didn't want to tell Mrs Ingalls that the shawl had been tossed aside like a rag.

'It was a scrap.' He stood in front of her, speaking softly. 'I will have one made for you that will wrap you three times if you wish. Or you can take the one you're wearing.'

'Oh, I could not take this one.'

'Yes. You could. The servant will make another one.'

She hid her gasp. He had taken her shawl and now he was taking a servant's. A woman would have to spend hours knitting.

The driver had opened the door to the carriage and she didn't want him freezing, or herself—but she would give Philbrook a lesson in manners once they were alone.

His long strides put him in front of her and he waved the driver aside, gave quick directions and helped her up.

She stepped into the carriage and peered at him. 'I could never, ever take someone's shawl from them.'

'It's better than the one you wore.' He sat beside her.

'And now you are insulting my lovely shawl.'

'Lovely? Lovely?' He shook his head. 'It was pitiful. Ill fitting, and that's hard to say about a shawl. Looked like something stolen off a person who had no home.'

'You—'

She fluffed about in the vehicle and made certain he saw her response in her eyes.

'I will tell Mrs Ingalls that it went to a poor person who needed it badly. She will understand and her feelings won't be hurt.'

'Who is this Mrs Ingalls?'

'A member of the staff. She's— It was indeed an honour that she created it for me.'

'A maid? It's her job.'

She pressed her lips together firmly and inhaled slowly, thanking her good fortune that her cousin did not marry the barbarian. She turned. 'If I had a fan, I would tap your fingers with it.'

'Pardon?' he said. 'If you'd like to reprimand me, just hit me full force with a slap and I will not bat an eye. In childhood, my friends and I used to call it having a slap-out and I could handle it better than any of them. But don't punch me with a fist. The damage would be massive—to your hand.'

Her jaw dropped and she squeaked a breath. 'You are, quite frankly, very self-assured. Much like Velma.'

'The woman who jumped on your clothing and acted like a spoiled child?'

'One and the same,' she said. 'But at least she allows the servants to have a wonderful Boxing Day.' She hesitated and her voice wavered away. 'Or at least she did.'

'Boxing Day?' He perused her. 'It's a bit of a nuisance but understandable. The servants take care of it themselves.'

'*I* take care of it at Lady Velma's.

'You are, in a sense, her servant.'

'Yes, I am. So, Boxing Day is *my* Christmas. Everyone has a grand day and it has taken effort because it is very hard for some of the staff to keep secrets. In fact, I think the sharing of secrets, and the spilling of them, contributes to the joy of the day.'

She thought of the previous month. 'It really isn't only the day, but the time beforehand when we are furiously thinking of what we might plan and how we might surprise each other. And Boxing Day is the reward. The moment when we all chuckle together and share tales.' She touched his arm for emphasis. 'It is endearing.'

He appeared to be pondering the thought. 'But you could create that day wherever you are.'

'Perhaps. Perhaps not.'

'You would be in charge of the housekeeping staff at my house.'

'But they are a different staff. Not the ones I love. And it is their home, and for me to arrive and start upending things would be unnerving to them.'

'They are adults. They can handle it.'

'How uncaring.'

'You would not be unkind to them. And instead of having your own household, you prefer to stay with your cousin.'

'Better the...er...not-saint you know than the one you don't.'

His head tilted low to the side. 'I've never been called a not-saint before. At least to my face.' His eyes half closed. 'Many other things, perhaps, but not a not-saint.'

He put the scarred thumb to his chin. 'Is that a step above or below a not-sharp-tongued woman?'

Then she saw the little smile in his eyes and she did slap his knee with the shawl.

'That may bruise,' he said, rubbing the knee, and his smile increased. 'And the driver could have to help me into my house.'

'You are insufferable,' she said. 'Insufferable. If you worked at Lady Velma's, you would be let go.'

'I don't. And I was.'

'You were let go because Vel is—'

He raised a brow.

'Not a saint either. The two of you would have been…not perfect together.'

'But the licence is in your name.'

'Well. You could have spent those funds more wisely.'

'I disagree.'

The carriage rolled to a stop and he got out and helped her alight.

Then she took his arm and turned to the driver. 'I apologise, kind sir, but please wait for the Earl. He will be back shortly after he meets Mrs Ingalls.' She pulled at the shawl, and held it to the servant. 'And please return this to the maid with my heartfelt thanks.'

'Pardon?' Philbrook said, feet planted. 'I should not be in Lady Velma's house now. I am agreeable to the end of the betrothal.'

'You had best be agreeable to the end,' she said. 'It's in your own interest. There are plenty of mindless beauties to take her place.'

'Thank you. But I believe I will decline your invitation. I have found my beauty.'

She didn't know which invite he was declining, but she had had enough of pettiness over her attire. First, he gave away her shawl and then Lady Vel stomped on her dress. She was going to show him that she did have friends and good ones.

'It was not an invitation, Lord Philbrook.' She stared up at him. She clutched both hands on to his tree trunk of an arm, looked at his eyes, and held on. He took in a breath and slowly expelled it. 'I suppose, not-saint that I am, I should go with you.'

He took a step.

'Not the main entrance,' she insisted. 'Will your boots be able to step over the threshold of the servants' entrance?'

'I suppose I can limp across it.'

'If I need to drag you, I will do the best I can. I can get a footman to help.'

'I will manage. Thank you.'

She flounced to the outside stairs descending to the plain door mostly hidden by shrubs.

He followed along and she couldn't read his thoughts, but it didn't matter. He was going to meet dear Mrs Ingalls.

Opening the door, the familiar scent of Christmas baking spices wafted over her and took some of the irritation from her.

The door behind her clicked closed as he shut it. And in that moment, she realised she had dragged an earl into the realm of the servants and…perhaps it would be best for him to exit from the front steps. Or just exit. Immediately.

Chapter Five

'**W**hy, Miss Adriana,' a maid said, popping around the corner, 'I am pleased to see you. Lady Vel is in a prop—'

Then the maid's eyes halted on the Earl and she froze.

'We're just going to see Mrs Ingalls for a moment,' Adriana said. 'Is she polishing?'

'No. Cook needed peeling done.' The maid bobbed her head and darted away.

Adriana moved to the kitchen and opened the door. A trim lady, who wouldn't reach much higher than his elbow even with her mobcap on, looked up.

'Is that you, Adriana My Heart?' Mrs Ingalls asked when the door opened, her dim eyes lighting with the same warmth of the biggest fireplace. 'Talk had it that you were leaving us, but I knew better. My girl wouldn't leave me.'

'No. I couldn't,' Adriana said. 'But I'm sad to say I don't have the shawl you made for me any more. It went to someone who needed it badly.'

'Oh.' The brightness in her eyes dimmed. 'I've not enough yarn…' She squinted. 'Is that a man with you?' she asked.

'Yes.'

'My goodness me,' the woman said. 'Have you hired an-other footman?'

'I'm just on loan,' he answered. 'To make sure Miss Adriana made it home safely.'

'You have to watch her,' the older woman said. 'She is always trying to fit another member of staff into the house, but if the older ones don't like the new person, she just helps the new staff member find other employment, our Miss Adri—'

'Now, hush, Mrs Ingalls. Let's not—'

'And no one in the entire world can keep Lady Vel in as good spirits. Why, our life is a paradise compared to before. Well, compared to anything really. Miss Adriana is our best gift ever.' The older woman beamed. 'I'd never slept as easy as I do after she arrived and put things to order. My old eyes don't work as good as they once did, but she watches over me as if she thinks me her own grandmother.'

Adriana stepped over to give the older woman a gentle hug.

'She really didn't want to give the shawl away,' he said. 'She is a gem and an asset to any household. As you seem to be. She was torn to see it go.'

'No matter about the wrap,' the woman said, blushing. 'I'll be happy to knit her another, though I might need a bit of help from Miss Tuttle getting the threads picked out and getting the stitches started, and winter will be long gone before it's finished.'

She patted Adriana's hand. 'You're a dear one. I would not be able to make it without you.'

'You won't have to,' Adriana said. 'Everyone here is my family. I didn't grasp how much until today. This is my home. And no one can ever take care of me as well as you and the others do.'

'Don't lie to yourself, dear heart, you're the one who makes this home a joy.'

The older woman turned to Philbrook.

'We had a problem footman here when Adriana arrived, she suspicioned him out and, the next thing you know, he was gone,' she said.

'She doesn't have to send me on my way,' Philbrook said. 'I'll find my way out.'

He knew he was walking away from something he'd never

find again, but oftentimes life went its own direction and a person had to adapt or be unhappy.

'Nonsense,' Mrs Ingalls said. 'Adriana don't need to be looking after me all the time. Show the young man to the door,' she instructed Adriana.

He gave a respectful nod of his head to the older woman, then, realising she might not be able to see it, he said, 'I must thank you.' And he truly did.

Walking over, he took her fingertips, feeling the lines of time. 'It has indeed been an honour to meet you.'

He moved to the door.

'Goodness, Adriana, this one has a silver tongue and a golden voice. I don't think I've ever heard such a handsome voice.'

He stopped. 'This one?' he asked.

'Oh, yes.' She waved away his words and her own. 'Adriana has so many suitors that we have to shoo them away. Once a baron's son even sent her a note.'

'Mrs Ingalls,' Adriana said, gasping. 'The Baron's son was just thanking me for being so kind to his sister who was awkward at events.'

The older woman shut her eyes and shook her head. 'And she's such a dear one she thought that was all it was. But, of course, we couldn't talk her into sending him a nice note in return.'

'Well, he must have been wise if he saw her sweetness.'

'I have told her she shouldn't let her devotion to us keep her from living her life, but I don't say it enough.'

'I understand,' he answered.

'Your compliments have travelled straight to my head,' Adriana told them. 'I shall soon be expecting the floor to be brushed in front of me before I put each foot down.'

'Where is a broom?' he asked.

'Nonsense,' she said, laughing.

'Perhaps. Perhaps not,' he said, voice low, indicating she precede him to the doorway.

Mrs Ingalls waved them out and they moved into the hallway.

At the exit, he rested his shoulder against the door frame. Leaving would place her out of his life for ever. He knew that.

Few chances would occur for a happenstance meeting and she would not instigate them. 'If you wed me, there would always be room for Mrs Ingalls.'

'You are still asking?'

He held out a hand, palm up. 'Of course.' He studied her face. 'And I suspect you're still refusing.'

'I suspect you would be right.'

'But Mrs Ingalls approves of me.'

'She is fond of your voice.'

'Lady Vel will eventually wed and you need to consider what could happen then. I could provide a good home for Mrs Ingalls.'

'That is caring.' She took his hand and rested against him, curling into his strength. 'But she would be displaced,' she spoke with her head at his shoulder. 'It would be hard for her to navigate a new place.'

'I think you are the one worried about navigating a new place.'

'You might take in Mrs Ingalls.' She didn't respond to his comment. 'But there's Maud, and she's courting a footman here, and Mrs Ingalls loves her like a daughter. And there's Enid, and her fingers are getting stiff and Maud helps her as well.'

'I can take the whole household.' He would do it for her. He would do anything for her. Then he bent closer, lifted her chin and placed a kiss on her lips, her softness and femininity reaching all parts of him, and for a moment they just looked at each other.

Then he kissed her again before forcing himself to stop.

'I can find room for all the servants.'

'You only have so much space. It would be a tremendous upheaval for everyone. Everyone.' She touched his chest. 'Your aunt would react to a household of new servants. And the expense would be enormous.'

'You would stay here, with a woman who stomps on your clothing...for servants?'

'No. I would stay here—for my friends.' She took a step away and he saw the farewell in her eyes. Their first kisses would be their last. He could not leave her without presenting his cause.

'You would have your own household,' he said.

'I have one here.'

'You have Velma's.'

'She is my family and I am needed here. Everyone seems to depend on me. I truly feel like I solve the problems and make things go more smoothly.'

'You would always be able to do that at any home.'

'That isn't a reason to leave,' she said. 'I have the love and care that I have built up over the past five years.'

The moment was at hand to go.

A male servant stepped into the hallway and Adriana moved away from Philbrook, but before the servant walked on, his eyes assessed the situation, greeting her warmly, and giving Philbrook a glare he'd never received from a servant in his life.

He couldn't leave because he knew the moment he was out the door, that servant would return to make certain Adriana was still smiling and would be hoping to catch her attention.

'We need to talk privately,' he said after they were alone again.

'There is nothing you can't say to me that the whole world can't hear.'

'Yes. There is.'

She didn't speak, but debate flickered behind her eyes, until she appeared to lose the argument and advised him to wait.

Then she went to the room where the older woman remained and a heartbeat later she returned. 'We can use Mrs Ingalls's room.'

She'd asked permission of a servant.

In the little room, he first noticed the oversized chair crammed into a spot by the foot of the bed. Adriana moved to the shelf not filled with necessities but vases with holly sprigs and she rearranged the holly, although he could see no true change in it. A little glass bowl had some dried green in it and he wasn't sure what it was, but he supposed that was where the woodsy perfume originated from. A large, framed, flowery print hung on the wall with words elaborately written in red: *Shall I Compare Thee to a Summer's Day?*

The walls had so many samplers and drawings and even little

twigs connected with leather strips that he felt oversized, but he also felt something that he didn't understand. He could feel the spirit of the people Adriana loved.

She reached out and ran her fingers over a little box by the bedside, then she lifted it and twisted the knob. Music filled the silence.

'Mrs Ingalls was having trouble sleeping.' Adriana put the box back on the table, her voice a new music. 'Losing her sight and the frailties included was upsetting her. The servants and I collected our funds so that she might have the best music box we could get. At night, before she sleeps, she plays it. And if any one of the maids has a problem or a concern, she might slip down to the room, sit in the big chair and talk with Mrs Ingalls while she rests, then Mrs Ingalls plays the music when she feels all has been said, and the world is so much better.'

Adriana stood by the spindly chair, touching the wood as gently as if she touched a babe.

'I would have a sketch made of this room and every thread would be relocated.' He took her hands.

'You can't sketch our hearts,' Adriana said. 'If you moved a palace into a desert, it is a palace, but it is surrounded by dry land. Arid land. Where nothing grows.'

'You could make a desert a palace,' he said. 'With your presence.'

'No. I couldn't.'

But then, proving her words wrong, she kissed him. Shimmering blasts of her spirit melded itself into him.

She moved away too soon, reminding him again what a desert felt like.

'You could make the land verdant,' he said. 'Summer showers create beauty.'

'Vision is clouded by water and it might appear to be raining, but what if it turns out to be tears? And I will always be known as the one who took Velma's cast-off husband.'

He never wanted her to believe, or anyone else to believe, that she was second to Velma or anyone else. 'I understand.' And he truly did.

But he'd also realised something else in his life. It wasn't

love he'd not believed in—it was an Adriana. He'd not known
a woman like her existed. She was the only one who could provide a different life for him. Who could walk with him, joined
in purpose and meaning, and could give him an existence beyond any he'd otherwise feel.

'Can I hear the music box one more time?' he asked. He could
walk out of her life for ever—truly, it would be easy to find
someone who would stare at him with daydreams in her eyes
and be blinded by the pretty things he could get for her, the soft
words and the gifts recommended by the servants. But it would
be pointless to him. Because Adriana was the one woman in
the world who could give his life meaning.

She'd always been in the periphery of his life, showing kindness around him, yet his eyes hadn't truly opened to the treasure
she was until he saw her appearing so bedraggled and alone,
but she took the time to pick up a bit of refuse he'd thrown to
the ground. That was Adriana…doing what needed to be done
quietly and risking even more discomfort to herself. Her friend
had created a shawl for her and, no matter how tattered it might
appear, she proudly wore it in friendship.

She moved, twisting the music box's knob with a series of
clicks and releasing it. He listened, taking in the moment. Then,
when the tune ended, he stood, moved to the box and ran his
fingers over the maker's mark on it.

'You could be in charge of a mansion.'

A mansion in a desert. He saw the words without her speaking them. Not even if he were a duke or a king. She would not
be purchased.

'That's very kind of you to offer,' she said, softly. 'I will
consider it.'

Consider.

A kind way of saying goodbye.

'I must go,' he said. 'I have a very important errand to attend.'

He had to find a shawl.

He'd stopped on the way home to talk again with the clerk
and in the morning the servants searched the most probable
areas. The butler was co-ordinating their hunt and had made

arrangements for everyone to meet at a central location where he would make certain they could have tea and warmth.

They were to bring the owner back because anyone might claim to own a shawl for the high sum he'd offered to purchase it and he would need to inspect it. The servant would get a nice vail.

Philbrook's last hope for another chance to impress Adriana.

He'd not been able to keep from pacing. Finally, at midday, a butler knocked and stepped inside, leading a man with a hat missing part of a brim, and a footman presenting a tattered shawl out as if he held a pillow with a crown perched on it.

He'd touched the garment reverently and produced payment, and more.

Before the first man had time to exit, a second man and garment had followed and he'd discovered he didn't know exactly what the scrap had looked like, but he'd paid the man.

Then a third man arrived.

He was left with three faulty garments in his hands—he couldn't decide which was which. Adriana would have to be the judge.

Imagining stars of gratefulness in her eyes, he relished the happiness in her heart and his chance to see her again.

Moving to his carriage, his delight appeared contagious when the driver gave a jaunty nod after finding out where they were going.

After he arrived, strides long, he didn't go to the main door at her house, but the servants' entrance. Once inside, he found the area where Mrs Ingalls had been sitting and knocked. The older woman wasn't there, but a curious maid told him she would fetch Adriana.

He waited in the empty room, feeling a little sheepish for the three tattered shawls in his hands, but he really didn't know which one was the correct one. Even the wisest of men might decide on three separate gifts.

Adriana walked in the door, hesitant.

Every moment had been worth it, ten times over. He was in her presence again and truly felt he viewed her for the first time. He wondered if every moment for the rest of his life would be that way when he saw her and he knew it would. Adriana stirred something in him that had been dormant his whole life. Something he'd not known existed.

'I found Mrs Ingalls's shawl,' he said.

She moved forward and, with fingers outstretched but not touching the closest one, she said, 'This isn't—I've never seen any of those garments in my life.'

The air seemed to leave his body and he searched her eyes while he lowered the goods. Apparently, the shawl he felt so tattered was quite the fashion.

'Truly. I never have,' she said.

One faded shawl looked the same to him as any other faded shawl, but the disappointment hit him so deep in his chest he could barely breathe.

A blast of words directed at himself, but that he never said in front of women, whirled through his mind. He bit his cheek to keep from speaking them.

'Where did you get them? Did you think you could give me another woman's shawl? And these poor women...' She touched the fabric, accidentally touching his hand, jarring him with warmth to the bottom of his boots. 'The poor women will freeze,' she stated.

'I paid triple what they were worth.' He said the only thing that came to his mind. In truth, he'd likely paid more than three times their value. They were mere rags.

'That was kind of you,' she said, expression unchanging but then her eyes immediately brightened. 'Do you think...? Do you think they can be returned? I hate to think of the women being without their wrap so close to Christmas—and they might not have wool at hand to spin into yarn.'

'I can direct the clothes to be returned,' he said.

He wanted to say he wouldn't return to her. But he couldn't speak the words. They would be too true.

She saw the goodbye in his eyes.

She wanted the women to get their shawls back. She wanted them to stay warm.

She didn't want her life to change. The servants were her true family next to her parents. They had been together through Velma's tantrums. Through illness and celebration. Many had told her she was the daughter they'd never had, the sister they'd longed for, the reason their days had brightness in them.

Even Vel needed her.

'I must stay where I am.'

'I will see that they are returned.' His jaw firmed.

'I'm sure they will have a much better Christmas with the funds from the shawls—if you don't take the funds back.'

He separated each shawl, held it out, studied it and wrapped it over his arm, before giving her a glance she could not read.

'You will not ask for your money to be returned?' She didn't have any funds left to give him to replace the money he might take. She had spent it all on gifts for the servants.

'Of course not. It was my error.'

Her heart practically tied itself in a knot. He had done the right thing. He had made an effort.

'If you wait just a moment...' she thought of the abundant baking taking place in the house, and she knew many poor did not have ovens '... I can have some Christmas treats gathered for the families' children.'

He patted the shawls over his arm, giving her a bow. 'I will wait in my vehicle and you can have one of the servants bring the treats out. My driver will make certain the others receive them.'

He left, leaving chilled air behind. Her throat didn't want to work and neither did her feet, but she scurried around, finding the largest basket she could and assembling treats.

Then she collected two large buns still warm from the oven to give to the drivers. She ran out with the basket, the wind slicing into her.

He had a point. The servants treated her like a treasured guest. A friend. And they sheltered her. She depended on them so much. They cosseted her as much, or more, than she helped them.

Perhaps as she was so scrupulous about telling the truth to

others, she was telling herself the biggest lie of all. It was not just her taking care of them. They were taking care of her.

She stopped before reaching the carriage, staring through the window at a profile that appeared a continent away from her and perhaps he was.

The driver hopped down from the perch and she looked at the man, unable to say anything at first, feeling the loss and seeing the reflection of awareness in the driver's eyes. He was telling her she was making a big mistake.

'The two wrapped on top are for you and the other man beside you,' she said, lingering just a breath, not turning to the carriage to see if Philbrook was watching, knowing she had already said goodbye.

Without preamble, the driver jumped away when something caught his eye.

'Lord Philbrook,' the driver called out, scurrying to kick a wheel. 'Just aware. The bolts are sticking out. We can't risk leaving now. Just give us some time and we can fix it for you. And we should probably test it. Wouldn't want to send you to your maker so close to Christmas.'

He nodded to Adriana. 'Sorry, Miss. Don't want to lose a wheel or cause a horse to be lamed. It would be kind of you to let the Earl wait inside while we tend things. It'll only take a few— And it's so cold.' He shivered, an exaggerated move.

Philbrook stepped out, able to melt ice with his stare.

'It's fine,' Philbrook said, studying the wheel. His eyes raked the servant. 'I appreciate your concern, but the wheel will get us home.' He reached for the door.

Adriana touched his arm. 'You cannot risk injury. Or your life. Or cause the driver to have to work even more in cold weather. He could be frozen.'

His eyes had a hint of stone and steel, but then he blinked the coldness away and his voice was wry. 'I wouldn't want to risk the drivers' safety.'

'Please come back inside,' she said. 'You can wait in the kitchen. Mrs Ingalls will be there for company.'

She led him inside and, sure enough, Mrs Ingalls was in the room.

They spoke and Adriana could not stay. It would only make saying goodbye to him again hurt more. She was in her home. With her family. And she needed to stay there and not risk moving into a social world that would not accept her. To make a quick decision that would haunt her for the rest of her life. Being the recipient of yet another of Vel's cast-offs and everyone noting that she was the poor cousin he'd married in what surely was a moment of pity.

Adriana forced herself to leave. He would be gone soon and she would muddle on.

He was too much for her. Too much man. Too powerful. Too far above her in standing.

On the next floor, she stopped, watching his carriage from the window. The two drivers were just talking. Not fixing anything.

Vel walked up to her, looking out the window. 'What is that rickety rattletrap doing here?'

'Something went wrong with it. Philbrook is with Mrs Ingalls now, waiting while it's fixed.'

Velma turned away, shuddering. 'Can't believe I let him squire me around in that thing. But, oh, well, there'll be someone else wanting to be a countess as soon as they hear he's available again. He's just so blasted cold. Never wanted to kiss me.'

Then she left, leaving Adriana to keep watching the carriage.

Adriana kept staring out the window. The carriage driver took out a cloth and it appeared he was polishing a wheel. Then he talked to the other driver. One took a pinch of snuff. They really didn't seem overly concerned about the vehicle.

The vocal driver walked to the house and she watched until he was too close to view, then she turned away from the window, listening until she heard the carriage leave. Philbrook was gone and she still had the important things in her life. Her family.

She went to her room, reached under her pillow and pulled out the elaborate shawl she'd finished with thick yarn. The one they'd made for Mrs Ingalls. Adriana had wanted Mrs Ingalls to have the warmest shawl ever and the servants had called it a knitted hug.

She couldn't help herself. She put away the shawl and returned to the window. She peered out. The carriage was gone. All the Christmas spirit seemed to have left, squeezed out. Wrung out and tossed out into the cold, and trailing along after that vehicle which certainly wouldn't stop to have a few sprigs of holly be collected, mistletoe or a yule log.

It just irked her.

And it irked her that Vel had said she would cancel Boxing Day. In truth, Adriana would have found a way to continue it, but she couldn't leave the people she cared so much for. Especially to always be the second choice.

She had everything. Everything. And it was not causing a burst of happiness inside her as it usually did. Something had taken her peace. A few words and a proposal had caused her to doubt herself. And she shouldn't really. All was right with the world. Things were just as they should be. Although the house was quiet for Christmas time.

And she had been just the substitute for another and she would not live like that. It was one thing to work for Vel. It was another to be second place in a marriage.

She straightened her shoulders and decided she would go help Mrs Ingalls. Working hands strengthened the heart and head, as Mrs Ingalls would say.

When her foot touched the last rung on the step, she heard laughter. The servants must be celebrating early after all.

Then she walked into the room and heard a masculine voice say, 'I ate one a day until my mother found out and then she put a stop to it. Mother told me green persimmons never made anyone grow taller. But I got the last laugh when I finally outgrew the lad who'd had a jest on me.'

The servants were all standing around Philbrook and they were laughing. Laughing. They hesitated when she walked in, except for Mrs Ingalls.

'Didn't your carriage just leave?' she asked him.

'I suppose it did.'

'The driver wanted to make certain it was safe,' Mrs Ingalls said.

'And risk himself?'

'Oh, goodness,' Mrs Ingalls said. 'The driver is safe. It was just a bit of horse fluff caught in the spoke.'

The older woman studied Philbrook through dimmed eyes. 'I think he's sweet on me.'

'I am,' Philbrook said.

She knew they were jesting. Knew he was playing along with the dreamy gaze he gave Mrs Ingalls. But she was envious of that adoring, breathless expression.

'I would propose to you,' he said to Mrs Ingalls, 'but I have been turned down twice recently. I do not think I could take a third refusal.'

'You wouldn't have to,' Mrs Ingalls said.

The maids all blushed.

She felt as if her family turned against her.

Mrs Ingalls put her hand on the table and pushed herself up. 'I think we all have chores to do, don't we?'

The maids giggled and the footmen left with everyone else, and Mrs Ingalls crept around the table by Philbrook and pulled a sprig of mistletoe out of her pocket. 'I'll leave this with you.' She placed it in front of him, smiling. 'You need it more than I do.'

Then Mrs Ingalls made her way out the door, placing her palm on the wall to feel her way along.

'You have sweet-talked them,' Adriana said.

'Did I?'

Oh, he knew very well he had. The silkiness of his voice told her he agreed completely with her assessment.

'How did you get your driver to leave without you?'

'He did that on his own.'

'Truly?' The man had noticed her staring at Philbrook. Or the driver was trying to earn favour with his employer.

'I must be going,' he said. Then he narrowed his eyes and appeared in exaggerated thought.

'Is there something on the horizon?' he asked.

'Only Christmas and Boxing Day, as you well know.'

'Christmas?' he asked. 'I guess I must have overlooked it last year. Probably missed dinner that day, or the staff forgot to prepare our usual Christmas treat, a spun sugar confection over a pyramid of fried dough balls that doesn't consist of anything filling.'

'Sounds delicious.'

'Why don't you have Christmas dinner at my house?' he asked. 'You might have some ideas to make it more festive.'

'I always have Christmas with my parents. Vel is with her father's family so I use that as a chance to visit with my parents and my siblings.'

'May I join you?' he asked.

'It's Christmas.' She emphasised the word. 'A day for family.' She couldn't say anything else.

'I know.'

'Your family…'

'Aunt will understand.'

'Your mother?'

'Will complain no more than usual.'

'I don't know.'

'Your choice,' he said. 'It's all your choice.'

He waited and she noticed he still held the mistletoe cluster, giving the stem a little roll within his hand.

Then he put his free hand under hers and tapped it just enough that she lifted it. He put the mistletoe on her palm, his lips turned up and his eyes focused so intently on her that she blushed.

'You're welcome to hang on to that for use when I'm around,' he said. 'But really, you don't need it.'

'Neither do you,' she said, a dare rising in her body.

She ran the greenery up his sleeve and rested it on his shoulder.

'Which would you rather have?' she asked. 'A kiss or an invite to my parents'?'

'There's no reason not to have both.'

She could feel his gaze deep inside her, connecting her to him in a way she'd never known before.

'I will pick you up tomorrow,' he said, taking the greenery and holding it over her head. But he only brushed her cheek with his lips and moved his mouth so close to her ear she could feel his words. 'Your two lips work better than any Christmas tradition ever will to make me wish for a kiss from you.'

He finished by holding her close and his lips found hers, finally showing her what mistletoe truly meant.

He instructed his servants to have a good time. They were to be all smiles and frivolous. They'd stared back at him as if he'd instructed them to hop on one foot while doing their chores and in a way that was what he felt he'd done.

His butler had been affronted and he'd seen the man literally biting his lip. 'Merry, sir?' the servant had asked. 'I am. Every day.'

'We always give good wishes to the tradesmen who arrive at the house during the two weeks before a festive season.' The housekeeper put a hand to her chest. Upset. 'And we are careful to pass along a token of your appreciation as has been done since before your grandfather's time. We take pride in knowing this household runs as a well-constructed clock. When we are prepared for a bell before it rings, we give ourselves a silent salute.'

'Understandable and appreciated,' he said. 'Miss Adriana will likely visit on Christmas Day and I want her to see the reflection of the true happiness of my staff. She spends Boxing Day with her friends, but I would like her to see that the staff here has everything needed to have the best Boxing Day ever. No expense is to be spared. I want Cook's spun sugar sculpture supported by mounds of sweet balls of dough prepared, not only for the family, but for the staff. And I want Boxing Day to be an extravagant, pleasant event for everyone. Better than ever before.'

'Us?' the housekeeper had said, her voice ending in a squeak.

'Yes. I have been remiss in the past,' he said. 'And I want you to make this Christmas and Boxing Day superlative for you.'

They had stared at him. 'What needs to be changed?' the housekeeper finally asked.

'Everything possible, I suppose,' he said. 'More. Better. Bigger.' But time had been short, so he had rushed out to join the stablemen to find more holly, mistletoe and other greenery that might give the servants' hall a more festive air. He would show Adriana that his staff had the Christmas spirit.

And when he was returning home with a coach that smelled of a woodland and hardly had any place left for him to sit, he had more awareness of a Christmas spirit than he'd ever felt. Of what it truly meant. Of rebirth. Of the future.

And he knew the misguided path he had been on in the past had had one purpose. To bring Adriana into his life.

Chapter Six

Christmas dawned almost warm, sunny and bright. Adriana rushed to visit Mrs Ingalls and share a bite of breakfast with her and the other servants bustling in and out.

Vel was still abed after a late-night event her mother had planned suddenly so she could recover from the cancelled marriage plans. News of the broken betrothal had been broadcast far and wide as Velma's mother thought it best for any marriageable man to know her daughter was unfettered. The betrothal had, she announced to all and sundry, been merely a jest Velma had been playing on her and everyone else. She and Philbrook had had a laugh and remained friends.

Then the sound of creaking carriage wheels stopping caused everyone to quieten.

'I bet that is Lord Philbrook,' Mrs Ingalls said. 'Do you think he's returning to court Lady Velma?' she asked, all expression leaving her face, except innocence. 'Or is that the reason you didn't ask the carriage driver to prepare the vehicle for you to borrow and Cook lent you a wrap?'

'He's not returning for my cousin,' Adriana said, unable to keep the smile from her face as she rushed out the door.

His frail-appearing coach waited and she knew that she was tumbling forward into something that could be difficult to stop.

She went to the servants' door and saw him striding up the walkway, and her body responded with the feeling of potently spiked punch making its way throughout.

He whisked her to his carriage, and she gave direction to her parents' house. Inside, a wool blanket rested and he carefully unfolded it and wrapped her inside.

'Are you sure your fondness for the carriage isn't because it's a memento of your grandfather?' Surely he recognised his affection for his grandfather.

'It fits my size and is the most reliable vehicle I have ever seen, crafted by the best carriage maker in the world who was given all the time and funds he needed, according to my grandfather.'

'Your grandfather…'

'Was stern. Once he came in my room and saw my clothing scattered about before the maid arrived. But my chest swelled with pride when he said I was a man now and he appointed me a trusted valet.' He rubbed the scar on his hand again. 'Only this valet's duty was to see that I was trained to take care of my clothing and straighten my room. And he was to inspect it.'

'You were to take care of your room?'

'The valet would catch me gone and turn a shirt wrong side out, stuff my stockings into my pillow case, or wrap threads around my waistcoat. He's still my valet, but now he truly does take care of my clothing.'

'Perhaps you're fond of him?'

'After he sewed my shirt sleeves closed, I left a smelly fish under his bed,' he mused. 'Two days in a row. We both enjoyed that.'

'Like having a brother?' she asked.

'More like a favourite uncle,' he said.

'Well, I have brothers,' she said. 'Four of them and I suspect you're about to meet them. Prepare yourself.'

'I am,' he said, not looking concerned at all.

She bit the inside of her lip. Her family's home wasn't the fine estate of her cousin, Velma, but rooms above a shop where her parents worked.

She was anxious to see her family. When the carriage pulled

up to the shop, he appeared to be looking for a house and didn't seem to know what she meant when she indicated the rooms overhead.

The sight of her brother arriving at the same time distracted her and she stepped out of the vehicle.

'Auntie. Auntie. Auntie.' Suddenly she was surrounded by nieces and nephews and sisters and brothers and more hugs than she could count.

So much revelry burst around her she couldn't introduce him and she was swept into the shop as her family surged forward.

Her mother greeted her, handkerchief in hand, and gave her a hug before stepping back and dotting the handkerchief to her eye.

'We've missed all our family so.'

'Yes,' her father said, voice gruff with emotion.

'I would like to introduce you to—' She reached back, her nieces clutching her skirt, but he wasn't as close as she'd expected. She turned, realising he was standing, watching, no expression on his face, his thoughts deep inside himself.

'A friend of mine,' she said, fingers seeming lost in the air. She couldn't tell them he was an earl. Her mother would be overwhelmed to have a peer in the household. She had never even had her brother-in-law to tea. Only her sister.

'He must be a good friend if you risk introducing him to us,' her brother said, picking up his son and swinging him to rest on his hip.

'Now, be on your best behaviour,' her mother said. 'We have a guest.'

'I'm Edmond,' he said, 'as Miss Armstrong appears to have forgotten to introduce me.'

'Those your cattle?' her father said, indicating the carriage on the street below after she concluded introductions.

He nodded.

'Well, you must have grand employment,' her father said. 'If your employer lends you such a fine equipage.' Then her father knit his brows. 'Oh, are you a hackney? Don't believe I've seen that rig around here much, though.'

'I am partial to it, the cattle and the carriage,' he said, not answering the question.

Then the uproar continued and her mother sat them across from each other. And he seemed to be taking it all in, conversing enough to be sociable, laughing in the right places, yet, somehow, remaining apart from it.

And she was more aware of him than she was her family. She noted each flicker of expression, each movement of his head, sip he took, tilt of his lips. It seemed her happiness rested on her awareness of him.

Once in the carriage to leave, she told herself that his impression of her family didn't matter. She told herself the words again. It didn't matter.

The wheels creaked away, not moving with any speed.

'What did you think?' she asked, forgetting her statement to herself that she didn't care about his opinion.

'I liked them all, except that one little boy who bit my boot.' He shifted and peered at the scuff on his boot. 'Not my fault he didn't like the taste of leather.'

'He wanted your attention.'

'His yowl worked very well.' He laughed. 'And got everyone's notice.'

'Something like that always happens when the whole family is together.'

He clasped her hand. 'Thank you for inviting me. Now though, I would like for you to go with me to my family's house. Will you?'

'But...'

'I asked my mother not to leave until tonight. I told her that I hoped to bring someone I would like her to visit with.'

'I've seen her from afar. Just as I have with most of your family.'

'But you've never spoken with her, have you?'

'No.'

'You place a great emphasis on togetherness. On this season. On how well the servants are treated. I'd like you to see Christmas at my home.'

He clasped her hand and held it between them. 'If you don't want to do so, then I understand, but it would mean a great deal to me and I hope it would mean something to you.'

He spoke in such a way that she could hear the hope in his voice. Refusal was impossible to her. In fact, it seemed no one had ever asked her before to do something which sounded so important to them.

Even before she reached the entrance, she could see Christmas greenery overflowing the window sills.

When they walked inside, the butler wasn't there to take cloaks and Philbrook took his off and placed it crosswise over the chair, then helped her with her wrap and put it on top of his coat.

With the greenery in the windows and the two garments on the chair, the room felt in chaos and she felt a bit disarrayed herself.

Philbrook led her into the servants' area, then to a door which he opened. The staff had gathered inside the room and suddenly everyone's backbone straightened, except one older woman wearing a large apron. She was sitting, head forward, eyes closed, dozing.

A sideboard was filled with pies—currant, plum and mince that Adriana recognised. Sugar cakes thick with almonds. Biscuits with nutmeg sprinkled atop. A spun sugar golden web covered a tall triangle of cooked balls of fried dough.

Each collar was starched, each hair was in place and, except for the one asleep, shoulders were tensed.

The room appeared to have sprouted a forest. Enough greenery surrounded them that much of it was placed on the floor, One corner was stuffed with boxes and cloth bundles and paper parcels.

'Lord Philbrook,' the butler said and everyone jumped for space to stand and a maid tapped the sleeping woman's shoulder. She jumped awake, collected herself, gazed around and rose.

'Welcome to our Christmas celebration,' the butler intoned. Tree bark had more personality than the butler's face, but she noticed that he appeared to be communicating with Philbrook via eye movement and she caught the barest nod Philbrook gave him.

'We are just having the most festive of occasions.' The butler waved a hand around. 'Please join us if you'd like.'

The housekeeper, dark smudges under her eyes, pointed to the spun sugar confection. 'Oh, yes, and Cook has provided special treats for us.'

'So many gifts,' the butler said. 'What a joyous Boxing Day we'll have tomorrow.'

Palms patted together in soft applause and every face smiled.

'Thank you,' he said. 'Please enjoy your treats.' He pulled the door closed behind him, then stood outside the door, holding the latch. He examined her face.

'They couldn't all fit at the table.' She paused.

He should have had the butler do a test earlier. That was not his servant's mistake. It was his.

'When did you tell them to do this?' she asked.

'We started work yesterday. I gathered the greenery with the carriage drivers because we had so little time.'

'You gathered the greenery?'

'Yes. I would imagine they hardly got any sleep because by the time we returned with it, they all joined in arranging it as I'd asked them to do as a gift to me.'

'How early did they start this morning?'

'I'm not certain, but everything was perfectly in place when I awoke. I suppose you could ask them.'

He opened the door, hand remaining on the knob. Some of the servants stood, filling their plates. They realised she was standing there and a burst of smiles replaced all the tiredness.

'What time did you start working this morning?' he asked.

'Why, our normal time, I suppose,' the butler inserted and she could tell instantly that no one would disagree with him.

'My pardon that you are not having a superior Christmas,' he said. 'Hopefully Boxing Day will be better tomorrow.'

'But we are enjoying today so,' the housekeeper said, eyes darting from side to side, a stare instructing all the maids to agree. A chorus of voices concurred. 'And thank you for giving us the rest of the day to ourselves.'

'I appreciate your efforts,' Philbrook said, shutting the door after he spoke.

'Your servants don't even know how to relax,' she said.

'Yes, they do. It is just in a different style than you are used to. I have a stellar staff.'

'But you don't love them as much as I love the ones I live with.'

He raised a brow. 'It's not necessary for me to love them. It's necessary that their wages are given them and they are respected. They are staff.'

'That is heartless. And they probably care deeply for you.'

'If they were given the choice between receiving love or a wage, I think all my staff is sensible enough to choose the wage.'

She stared at him for a brief moment, then put her arm firmly around his and attached herself to his side, more secure than any pair of gloves he'd ever donned.

She tugged at his arm. Nothing moved but her feet, but then he let her pull him back into the servants' dining hall.

Again, the movement stopped.

'Everyone,' she said. 'Please tell Lord Philbrook what you think of him. One by one. I'd like to hear it.'

The employees' countenance outshone the sun.

'The best employer.' The butler took the lead.

'Efficient.' The housekeeper.

'The best employer.' A maid next to her.

'Precise.' The answers went around the table with each one speaking after the person standing next.

'The best employer.'

'Even better that what he said.'

'Upstanding.'

Philbrook raised a hand, stopping them. 'I pay their wages.'

'Yes, but there must be some affection between you.' She studied the faces.

'Oh, no, Miss,' the housekeeper said. 'He is an exemplary employer.'

She asked the butler, 'Does he not share a jest with you from time to time?'

'Of course not,' the butler said, huffing. 'He is an exemplary employer.'

The words thudded into the room.

'You'll get no argument from me,' Philbrook stated.

Servants stared at her. She could never live in a household so perfect. So austere. A home in which Christmas greenery appeared out of place,

'Very well,' she said, 'I hope everyone has a joyous Christmas and that your Boxing Day is relaxing.' She thanked them all for their well wishes and walked out with Philbrook, aware of how fortunate she was to have an assemblage of servants that she lived with and loved.

Suddenly it became more important to her than ever to understand Philbrook's thoughts and not just important for him. Important for herself.

He stopped when they were at the stairway and she had no option but to halt if she continued to hold on to his arm.

'Life is not about love,' he said. 'It's about duty. Love is like the spun sugar confection in the servants' area. It's a good treat, but it doesn't last long.'

'I like treats.'

'You may believe that.' He shook his head. 'But your actions prove they are not your first priority.'

She didn't respond.

'People are your first priority.'

'Love. I stand by it. And if what you say is true, it doesn't matter. Love and people go hand in hand.'

'Respect is important. Integrity,' he said.

'You can have them both.'

'Love causes men to be foolish. To leave their families. It's the height of self-regard with no thought to anyone else.'

'That's not love. It's selfishness.'

She peered at the greenery. 'I still believe in love,' she said, 'and Christmas.' It was true, she just didn't know if she believed you could decorate the world with holly and make it Christmas. Or you could put a wedding band on and have a marriage.

With her servants, the spirit of Christmas reached them all.

With her family, the gaiety stretched to everyone. And her parents genuinely loved each other. Affection filled their lives. It had been around her from childhood.

Perhaps his family had more of the Christmas spirit than he realised.

'You mentioned me meeting your mother,' she said. 'Is she still here?'

'Yes.'

From the distance in his face, she knew where he'd received his schooling on love.

Chapter Seven

When they walked upstairs into a small sitting room where his aunt sat, there was another woman who could be her mirror image—if it were drenched in cosmetics—perched in an opposite chair. Another difference between them was that the other woman's dress appeared more suitable for a fancy event and his aunt's, while fashionable, had nothing special to commend it. A huge platter of biscuits sat between them, some looking of fluffed egg whites, some of crisped flour, and some of nuts dipped in boiled sugar.

'Mother, this is—'

Immediately his mother interrupted. 'Lady Velma's cousin Adriana,' she said by way of greeting. 'I remember you from years past. And today my sister has been telling me about Velma's little dance on your dress. The two of you have always been close like that, I suppose.'

'We normally get on,' Adriana said and saw the disagreement in the faces around her. 'We do, even if we ruffle each other's feathers on occasion.'

His aunt Bessie lifted a biscuit, broke it two pieces and stared at her sister. 'She's better than Velma. You don't know how close we came to a disaster. I had to help.' She popped one half of the biscuit into her mouth.

The aunt rose, took the platter and offered the biscuits to Adriana. She shook her head, then his aunt walked to the door while carrying the platter, tapping the door facing with the side of her cane. She spoke over her shoulder. 'You could be right at home here, Adriana. My sister could make you feel as if you had never left Velma.'

'Well, I'm not enjoying this Christmas,' his mother said, directing her words at him, which held a bit of censure in them. 'The servants have been running through the halls almost like lost children, so befuddled and rearranging greenery after already having it in place. You know I can't stand the smell of woodsy things. I hate things being out of order just because it is December the twenty-fifth. We have eleven other months with a twenty-fifth. I'm sure Christmas could be better celebrated in the spring. Your grandfather and I were in complete agreement on that. For once.'

'Perhaps he was wrong.'

'Oh, it's totally unfair to expect servants to put out twigs, then expect them to clean up afterwards. If today is any indication of the normally superlative staff, I cannot imagine Boxing Day with the servants not working,' his mother said. 'I'll be happy to return home to my daughter's house. She understands that greenery is best left in the woods.'

She stood, gave a moment for everyone to appreciate her stature and perfection, then spoke to her son. 'Your aunt seems to believe the two of you are courting. I suppose it's true or Adriana wouldn't be here.'

'That is entirely up to Adriana,' he said.

'I am not at all surprised,' she said. 'Your grandfather is getting everything he wanted.'

'My grandfather wished for me to court Velma.'

She shut her eyes, let out a breath through her nose before raising her lids and said, 'No. He didn't. Why would you think that?'

'Because on his deathbed... With his last breath. He said he wanted me to wed... I nodded. I could not refuse him a dying wish, but it pained me to follow through with it.'

'That's a little cold to say that in front of Adriana, isn't it?'

'I understand a grandson doing his duty,' Adriana said, 'and wanting to carry on as his grandfather instructed.'

'Happy you do,' his mother said. 'I knew not to trust the old tyrant and I wanted to see how he would trick you. I was not surprised. Trying to control his grandson with his last breath. And Philbrook was so upset because his grandfather's illness came as a complete surprise.'

'It was a horrific day for me. I didn't realise he was dying until those very last moments and then he asked me to wed Velma.'

'Are you daft?' his mother said. 'He didn't say that.'

'He did.'

She put her palms to her temple. 'Didn't you hear him say cousin? *Velma's cousin?*' She gave a nod to Adriana. 'Pardon, the old goat never could remember your name and you were not around as much as she was.'

'He didn't even know me.'

'Yes, he did. Remember when you weren't very old and got mud on Velma's dress?' She chuckled. 'He saw it. He told my husband who told me. The old goat detested Velma from then on.'

Adriana put her fingertips over her lips. 'I shouldn't have done that. Mother was furious.'

'But you didn't tell on Velma. She pushed you into the mud and no one but my father-in-law saw it. Then you got up, covered in mud, told Velma you loved her and gave her a big hug, and he said she squalled like a little baby. He thought it so fitting.'

'I shouldn't have done it. I knew I was doing wrong. Mother was so embarrassed. Clothing was so dear and Velma could give away her dress, but we couldn't afford a new one for me. The stains didn't come out and I still had to wear it.'

'I wonder if you've not changed that much,' his mother said, glancing at her son. *'Pardon me, Velma, while I wed your betrothed. Love you dearly, Cousin.'*

'It's not like that,' Adriana insisted. 'It's not.'

'It's absolutely not,' Philbrook said.

His mother nodded, didn't answer and, with a roll of her eyes, disagreed as she left the room.

Adriana dealt with the thoughts bombarding her. To believe she was always getting her cousin's cast-offs was bad enough, but believing she was somehow using machinations to put her cousin behind her was even worse.

'I can see why you're not fond of love,' she said.

'But can you now see why I want to marry you?' he said. 'Why it would mean so much to have you near me? A woman strong from childhood. Who creates a warm home around her and wants to take care of the people she cares for. Who stands up for herself even when she does it in a calm way.'

Adriana didn't know if she could agree. Her thoughts tangled around what she had just discovered. She wondered if she was still getting revenge and calling it love. 'I should go home now. It's been an eventful day.'

He led her to his vehicle.

At the carriage, she stopped and greeted the driver whom Philbrook had waved away so he could open the door himself. The staff member gave her a respectful nod and climbed back into his seat, the carriage creaking its acceptance of the weight.

She needed to talk with the driver alone and she would find a way.

'I'd like to give Mrs Ingalls a Christmas greeting,' he said, when they arrived at her house. 'It would be remiss of me not to speak with her.'

Adriana and Philbrook walked into the servants' hall and Mrs Ingalls was sitting with her knitting needles. Her face glowed when she saw him.

'Did you get use of the mistletoe?' she asked him.

'Sadly, not as much as I'd hoped,' he said. 'I suppose it wasn't full strength.'

'Bah,' she said. 'You could put a dried twig over your head and I'd claim it was mistletoe.' Then she lowered her chin and glanced at Adriana. 'Any one would be wise to do the same.'

Adriana watched as Philbrook then took a holly twig from a small bough sitting on the table, and put it over Mrs Ingalls's head, and kissed her cheek. She chuckled and fanned her face.

'I suppose I must be going.' He twirled the twig and put it

back where he'd found it, then left, without giving Adriana more than the most proper and briefest of farewells.

The room felt more silent than any room she'd ever been in.

Mrs Ingalls locked eyes with her. 'You are making such an error,' Mrs Ingalls said.

'He was betrothed to my cousin. I did the right thing. Otherwise, I will be seen for ever as the one getting Velma's cast-off love.'

Mrs Ingalls pushed her hair back in place and adjusted her cap. 'I don't know. It doesn't feel to me like you're doing the right thing.'

'The right thing doesn't always make you feel happy at first. That's what the wrong thing does. The right thing makes you feel better later. The wrong thing starts out with the joy and leads to sadness or more of the wrong thing lying to you that the right thing doesn't matter.'

'Please stop over-explaining,' Mrs Ingalls said, waving her words away. 'That's what happens when you do the wrong thing.'

Chapter Eight

Boxing Day dawned with none of the fanfare she usually felt in her heart.

She knew Velma would sleep late and early morning was Adriana's time to use the carriage if she needed to go on any quick errands.

Her only errand was to find Philbrook's driver. She wanted to speak with him alone so she made arrangements to go to visit the man.

When she found him, he was even more grizzled than he'd been the day before.

'You did not want to leave Philbrook when offered employment,' she said. 'Why?'

'His wages is good. To me the only good garden is a hay field.'

She bit her upper lip. 'And why did you give him that folderol about the carriage wheel potentially being loose?'

'Well, if he was sweet for you, I thought you would make a better mistress than that...er... Lady Velma and you were kind enough to offer me employment. He could do worse. He has.' He rubbed his knuckles against his whiskers. 'He thought he was going to marry that other one, but he wasn't happy about it.'

'He tried to give the household servants Christmas off, but they ended up having to work twice as hard.'

'True,' he said. 'They were all so flummoxed. They feel he hardly has any Christmas at all and they wanted to make his Christmas special for him. And if he wanted them to pretend it was for themselves...' He shrugged. 'Whatever he wishes for, we wish for.'

'He seems so firm with them.'

'It's them that are firm with him. They want to be the absolute finest for Philbrook.' He tilted his head. 'That's the best man you'll ever find. If you have half a chance with him, take the opportunity and run with it, right to him. If I'm wrong, I'll spend the rest of my days growing them overgrown weeds called carrots.'

She considered the driver's words carefully. 'But he doesn't believe in love.'

The man's voice strengthened. 'He's a good man and it don't matter. He believes in doin' what's right and fair. He didn't get that from his mother or grandfather. He inherited those traits from his father and grandmother, and maybe a little part from his aunt. And maybe it's all just from his own thoughts.'

He chewed his inner cheek for a moment before continuing. 'And one other thing you got to think of: if he don't believe in love, maybe it's 'cause he never felt it. And you can be the first one he feels it with and with any children you might have. I'd take that wager. If you're wrong, you still get a good man. If you're right, then you get something only a few in the world ever have.'

She returned home, ruminating over the words the man had said. Her mother had always claimed love was the reason she was so happy in her marriage, but maybe it was their basic integrity. Her father was a good man and treated them all so gently that they all wanted to please him. Her mother was much the same.

When she stepped out of Velma's carriage, she turned and looked back at it, and realised it meant absolutely nothing to her. She couldn't have described it if she'd been asked.

But she could describe that old vehicle Philbrook drove. In fact, it gave her a feeling of warmth no other carriage had and perhaps it was because of the man who'd sat beside her.

A maid ran to her at the servants' entrance. 'Her Ladyship is calling for you. Hurry.'

Adriana rushed forward, then stopped and walked up the stairs at a normal pace.

After a quick knock, she walked into Vel's room.

'Were you at Philbrook's house this morning?'

'Yes.'

'Well, you can't take my carriage to his house any more and I don't want him being here. He is not welcome.'

'He is welcome in my world,' Adriana said.

Velma's eyes hardened. 'You are sacked. I mean it. I will have your things sent after you. But you must stay until tomorrow.'

She'd known when she said the words what Velma's response would be and she had known it would be the only way she could walk out of the situation she found herself in.

'I will leave now.'

'You can't until tomorrow,' Vel said. 'Today is Boxing Day. You must stay in case I need a handkerchief or a comb.'

'You will manage.'

Vel glared and crossed her arms. 'I will cancel Boxing Day. In truth. And I am going to tell that to Mrs Ingalls and everyone else. It is cancelled. Over. Done. No Boxing Day here this year because of you. And it is everyone here's favourite day of the year.' She peered at her closed hand and checked her fingernails. 'Or it was until this year.'

And then the little girl inside Adriana resurfaced. 'I love you. And I am leaving now. This is going to be my best Boxing Day ever.'

At Mrs Ingalls's room, she knocked and walked inside. 'I am leaving,' she told the other woman. She rubbed the side of her thumb. 'I will be with my parents. Please tell everyone to pick up the handkerchiefs with their initials and other gifts I have in my room.'

'You can't go now.'

'I can't stay,' Adriana said. 'I cannot. She is unbearable. And she sacked me.'

Mrs Ingalls said, 'Shakespeare mentioned that smooth are the waters where the brook is deep and I think that fits Philbrook. I believe you would rather have the still waters in your life and the substance of a man like the Earl at your side. Don't run from him. Run to him.'

She had to go. Even if she'd not been sacked, she had to leave because if she remained, she could not see Philbrook any more. Then she hesitated. 'But I can't leave everyone. And his house is too far for me to walk.'

Mrs Ingalls haltingly stepped to her and reached out. 'Don't fret about that now.' They clasped hands. 'You go on to your parents, dear one,' Mrs Ingalls said. 'We will send your things after you. You are more important to us than Christmas. We will be fine and it is vital to us that you are happy. That knowledge will be our celebration.'

In Mrs Ingalls's dim eyes, awareness shown through that Adriana's decision was the right one.

She ran outdoors and the sky wasn't spitting moisture, just gloom and the dreariness that only a cold Christmas season could add to a person. But she could almost feel the sunshine hiding beyond the clouds.

It didn't even matter that she was unlikely to get a hackney. All the drivers were as they should be. Home with their families.

The day remained overcast, but the clouds thinned some and the silence around her gave her a feeling of hope.

She was taking one step at a time to get closer to her future. She didn't know what it would be, but she was walking out of her cousin's shadow and into her own life.

Philbrook was late waking because he'd slept so fitfully. Immediately upon summoning his valet, the man had appeared with a note. Then, as Philbrook started eating breakfast, the valet said he'd fetch the carriage driver to speak with Philbrook because the driver had insisted he needed an audience with him when he woke.

Soon, the carriage driver knocked on Philbrook's door and

came inside the room, hat in hand, eyes shining with happiness. 'I had a visit from a dear lady this morning.'

'Does your wife know?' Philbrook asked.

'Not yet,' the carriage driver said, 'but the woman wanted to ask me about, um, er, a certain unwed man who may be a bit sweet on her. Wanted to know what kind of employer he was.'

'What did you tell her?' Philbrook asked.

'Well, I said he wasn't half bad. That she could do worse.' He stepped back to the door. 'And you could, too, as you well know.' Then he left, whistling 'Deck the Halls'.

Before the door was even shut, Philbrook's mother appeared in the hall and she grimaced at the tune. 'I must be leaving because my sister is warbling on and on about how lovely it is here and she knows I don't like this house. I don't know why she wishes to stay.'

'Did Grandfather really say that about Adriana?' he asked.

'I'm not sure. I think so.' She shrugged. 'But there is one thing I know. He would not have wanted you to wed Lady Mudbath.' She touched her bottom lip. 'But it doesn't really matter. It was the other one who always made you smile.'

'I didn't smile at her.'

'You may not have thought you did, but that's a better story to tell your children.' She shook her head. 'Son, you need to think of these things.'

She gave him a pat on the shoulder. 'Now take care of that crotchety old woman who lives in this house with you. The world needs more mean old women like the two of us and we need you. And you should think about adding an additional person to this household. One who has enough spirit to like that crotchetiest old woman who lives here. Don't let the opportunity pass you by.' She sighed. 'You'll likely never find another woman my sister can tolerate as well as Adriana.'

She left and he understood what everyone was trying to tell him. Everyone recognised it and he did, too. But it wasn't enough to recognise it. He needed to be willing to work for it and he would.

Adriana wanted him to love and he would find a way to unlock love with her.

He wanted a permanent love, not the nonsensical ones his friends told him about that caused them to turn their back on all they had committed to.

Instead, he wanted a feeling so deep and so intrinsic to him that it didn't feel like love but a part of himself.

None of the servants or his aunt let their feelings bubble to the surface, but it didn't matter. They were the people he needed in his life and who needed him.

But if Adriana needed someone in her life who demonstrated his love and that was what made her happy, then he would become that person. She was too dear to him, and to everyone else who mattered, to risk losing.

If Adriana wed him, then he intended to find a way to make sure his feelings burst into the world and shone so brightly that no one would ever doubt them. Because he wanted her at his side, day and night, and in his life—and carriage and family and everything else around him.

He smoothed the paper he had been clasping in his hand and smiled.

Chapter Nine

Her parents greeted her with welcome surprise and after a bombardment of questions that she really didn't have answers to, her nephew stumbled and bumped his lip and everyone's attention turned to him, and she was back in her family, almost as if she'd never left.

She'd hardly got seated when a wagon stopped in front of her parents' house, the vehicle stuffed with servants who all waved to her as she stepped out.

'Boxing Day was cancelled at Lady Velma's,' Miss Yale called out, laughing. 'So, we decided to have it here with you.'

Then she noticed a second wagon, with Mrs Ingalls sitting beside the driver, and the conveyance itself was filled with crates, sacks and what appeared to be hastily gathered clothing.

The wagon containing Mrs Ingalls stopped in front of Adriana and one of the footmen jumped to help the older woman exit.

'We also gave notice,' Mrs Ingalls called out. 'And then we were all sacked.'

'Well, it was hard to tell who was sacked and who wasn't,' Miss Yale said, 'so we decided it was best for all of us to leave.'

Adriana didn't know what to say. She couldn't think of anything.

'We couldn't stay without you,' Mrs Ingalls said. 'We just couldn't.'

'We can make pallets in the shop at night for all who won't fit in the house,' her father said. 'If these people care that much for you, then we cannot let them be homeless.'

'Well, I was hoping...' Mrs Ingalls had a wistful contemplative look '...that you might pass the problem on to someone else who can help us, as it is his fault.'

'Man about so high,' her father said, raising a hand, 'having a carriage that would likely fit my whole family?'

'That's him,' Mrs Ingalls said, holding out a sprig of mistletoe. 'And I brought this with me in case we found him here. Your daughter needs it much more than I do.'

'We have discussed it,' the butler said to Adriana. 'We decided you might need a nudge to go visit that certain man.'

'I'm freezing,' Mrs Ingalls said, pulling the wrap Adriana had given her closer. 'It's Boxing Day,' the older woman added, 'and we are all without work. Of course, we would do it all again...'

Her father waved them to the doorway. 'They are welcome to come in, but, Adriana, if they need that man to help them, I don't see what the problem is.'

'But...'

'You can't let them starve, or be forced back to Vel,' he said. 'Particularly not on their one day off in the year.'

'He'll take you to Philbrook's house,' Mrs Ingalls said, pointing to the driver. 'We decided it would be our gift to you.'

Philbrook didn't know what Christmas was, but he knew what it wasn't. A life without Adriana. He clasped the paper again and smiled.

'Vehicle at the door, sir,' his butler said, peering inside the sitting room. 'It's the woman who places so much importance on Boxing Day and staff. I can get the door, of course, but you could earn some hearty acclaim by telling her you gave me the rest of the month off.'

'Thank you,' Philbrook said, standing, still in shirtsleeves. 'But I believe I will just earn some good spirit by telling her we shared a jest and by greeting her at the door. Now, hand me a cravat.'

The butler laughed and fetched the neckcloth.

He threw on a waistcoat and the butler helped give the cravat a quick tie. Philbrook buttoned the waistcoat as he navigated the stairs.

Her eyes widened when he opened the door.

'You were expecting me to be here, I'm sure,' Philbrook said 'After all, it is the servants' day off.' He peered at her. 'I thought you'd be celebrating with the staff.'

She gave a slow shake of her head. 'They are with me—in a sense. They've left her. En masse. And moved to my father's house. And he is not wealthy. They must have jobs and I am here in anticipation that you might be able to help me find employment for them.'

'I had hoped you would say you were missing me and wanted to spend the day with me instead of the servants.'

'I've decided you are partly right,' she said. 'True caring is the measure of a person. I can't feed all the people I love—on love. Their stomachs would be empty.'

'How many staff members left?'

'All of them. Everyone. From the butler to the cook to the scullery maids to the footmen. And they wanted me to ask you for help.'

'I will find employment for the ones that do not fit into my household.'

'You probably will not need to,' she said. 'My cousin's parents will beg them to return. It's me the servants were trying to find a home for. And I knew it. They wanted me to come to you. All of them did. And they risked their livelihood in order that I might speak with you.'

He put a hand on her shoulder, the warmness of her reaching deep into his heart. 'You don't have to try to teach me about love. I understand now. I feel it every time I think of you. There is a belief that you should care for others as you do yourself and that is true for the way I feel about you,' he said. 'The staff who are around me feel a part of me and so does my aunt. And when I look into your eyes and see the compassion you have, I know you are quality beyond measure.

'I need you,' he continued. 'The staff needs you. We all need you. You created happiness in your residence. You have already made a difference in my home. Everyone has been mellowing, chatting about the efforts I wanted them to make for you.'

He reached into his waistcoat pocket, took out the note and gave it to her.

If you do not win Adriana you will be making the largest mistake of your life, though we are not sure you are quality enough for her. Our Boxing Day gift to you should arrive today: the sight of Adriana. If you don't convince her to wed you, we pity you.
Adriana's friends

'How can I win you?' he said. 'That is what it seems I must do.' He touched her cheek, warmness rushing into him.

'You have won me already,' she said. 'When you understood about my love of the servants and wanted yours to experience a day off as well.'

'Some people may say they fell in love at first sight,' he said, 'but I believe that I started to love at first kindness. And that is a feeling which stays with a person for ever.'

The day after Boxing Day, the wedding took place with the servants of both houses looking on. His aunt said she had no reason to attend, it was just paperwork to further the lineage. Though she felt she was responsible for the union, she didn't want to have to stand around and watch all that blasted happiness.

Velma sent a note, telling her the servants must be returned at once as she did not have time to find replacements, and Adriana had best not keep them because, if she did, Velma would have no option but to move in with Adriana. The servants agreed to return, but only on the condition they could visit Adriana regularly.

His mother had decided to stay one day longer and she felt

she was responsible for the union because her son would not have realised his true feelings if she hadn't told him his grandfather's wishes.

And Mrs Ingalls mentioned she was certainly pleased she had given Adriana the original shawl because it led to the proposal.

His staff basked in the knowledge that they had helped show the devotion they had for him and convinced him it was time for him to wed.

Both households celebrated their pivotal actions which led to such a happy event.

All the servants planned to return home except Mrs Ingalls. She'd said she was not leaving Adriana and a convenient room was prepared for her with all her possessions arranged just as she liked them.

Philbrook insisted he must give Adriana a present and she saw a multi-coloured shawl with extra thick yarn and wide spaced stitches wrapped over his arm.

'That's not mine either.'

'I know. It's a gift from my servants. When they understood that I had accidentally given away a shawl you liked, and that we were to wed, they spent last night making sure you had a gift from them that I could give you today.'

Their hands touched when he gave it to her and she ran her fingers though the fibres.

'Now we have three festivities to share,' he said. 'Christmas and Boxing Day and the celebration of our anniversary the day after Boxing Day.' He paused. 'No. Four. The rest of the year we can rejoice in our love.'

With that, he led her beneath the mistletoe and kissed her, his heart expanding more than he would have ever believed possible. Now he understood that the best kind of love was the feelings he had waited his whole life to experience and felt for his beloved Yuletide wife.

* * * * *

Lord Grande's Snowy Reunion

Elizabeth Beacon

MILLS & BOON

Dear Reader,

Juno, the heroine of this story, first appeared several years ago in my Yelverton trilogy. As she was surrounded by happy endings, I always felt that she needed one of her own one day, and here it is. Christmas is a time for family and love and second chances, and although her hero is haunted by war and guilt, if only he will let her, Juno can show him that true love really does conquer all. I hope you enjoy their snowy journey to happiness.

Have a wonderful Christmas and may all your hopes and dreams for it come true. Thank you for being the reason I have been able to do this wonderful job for so long.

Elizabeth Beacon

To all the historical romance writers past,
present and future—you lighten dark patches
and give us a good place to go when the
outside world feels sad and gloomy.
Love you all and long may you continue!

Chapter One

1819

'You can't ride to Chantry Old Hall with only a dog for company, Juno,' Lady Colby protested, '*and* the gardener says it will snow.'

Juno looked at the hazy blue sky and decided he was wrong. Just as well, as she *had* to be home in time for the worryingly early birth of her uncle's first child.

'I can join Sir Harry and Viola the rest of the way, but they will go without me if I don't hurry,' she replied, pulling on gloves as she sped down the path with Pard, her Dalmatian dog, at her heels and her godmother scurrying behind.

'It's easy to get lost in the hills, so they might go before you can get there,' Lady Colby argued.

'The innkeeper gave me good directions when I hired his best horse and Sir Harry will drive the carriage himself to get his wife there for the birth if he has to, so it's my quickest way home,' Juno said and pulled on the velvet jockey cap she wore for riding.

'He was wild to a fault until your aunt's sister and all those children tamed him, so I'm not surprised, but you're *not wed*, Juno—you can't attend a birthing.'

'I can pace outside the bedchamber with my uncle. Marianne and the Yelvertons stood by me when I needed them, so I must do the same for them. She will need all our support if the baby is too small to survive.'

When Juno's life felt shattered, just like her heart, Marianne had taken her in. She had been so kind and patient, helping Juno to pick up the pieces. At seventeen, her grandmother had planned to force Juno to marry a venal old man if he paid off the Dowager's debts, so she was left with no choice but to run away. When her uncle Alaric returned home from diplomatic duty in France, he was so furious to discover what his mother had done that he paid her debts one last time and publicly disclaimed responsibility for any more.

Juno now lived with her uncle and Marianne, but hadn't told them why she had refused another London Season. There was no point since she had loved and lost and it had hurt so much that she never wanted to experience such pain again.

'You *might* get there in time if the weather holds, but it would be so much better if you hired a carriage,' Lady Colby said.

'Not fast enough,' Juno argued and thank goodness they were in the stable yard of the inn so she could say a hasty farewell and ride away.

Uncle Alaric and Marianne were her family, but even they didn't know she had fallen in love before she ran from London. She had taken one dazed look at a handsome, dashing and hopeful Lieutenant Nathaniel Grange and lost her foolish young heart. Then he had marched back to war and taken her heart with him and the only way for her to escape a forced marriage was to run to Herefordshire where her former governess was living.

Uncle Alaric had been determined that Juno would have a better life, so he had employed Marianne as Juno's companion. He and Marianne had fallen in love, so some good had come of Juno's youthful troubles. And at least she was a strong and independent woman now and very happy to stay that way.

An hour later, Juno blinked snowflakes from her eyelashes in order to see the road ahead and Lady Colby and her gardener were proved right. It wasn't far to Sir Harry Marbeck's beloved home in the hills, but she wasn't going to get there and needed shelter from the storm. She fought panic before she saw high walls and a gate that was wide open. The lodge was shuttered, so she urged the horse into the avenue and prayed for sanctuary at the end of it.

Yes, there was a grand old house there, but it was shuttered and no smoke was issuing from its chimneys. For an awful moment she thought she was imagining it—she had heard of people losing their reason as they froze to death. She wasn't that cold yet and it looked real enough as the horse forged on to the stables. The first door she tried opened, but no reply came to her shouted greeting as she led the horse inside and Pard dashed ahead to make sure it was empty.

The place smelt of old dust rather than horses, but two stalls were strewn with clean straw for someone's return, so she led the horse into one while Pard rolled in the other and wind keened around the stout old building. They had a roof over their heads; she could snuggle in the straw of the empty stall with Pard and wait out the storm. Yet what if they were caught napping by whoever had left these stalls ready? And the deserted mansion was making her imagination run wild, so she had to be sure it was really empty before they settled down.

She shivered with nerves as much as from the cold when the back door opened easily and she stepped inside the mansion, feeling like the heroine of a Gothic novel. Best not think of the horrors waiting for them as they explored places they were not supposed to be as she crept past the dark, cold kitchens. Pard's toenails sounded loud on the flagstones as Juno pushed open the door between servants' quarters and grand state rooms, hesitating in the shuttered gloom.

'Who the devil are you?' a gruff bass voice growled at her from the shadows and she gasped in shock.

The sound of that voice had haunted her dreams for so long she felt the ground lurch under her feet as her heartbeat jarred, then galloped on in shock. *He* was here? But was he just one of those delusions she had been worried about? No, that deep, rich voice was so uniquely Nathaniel Grange's he really must be standing in the shadows waiting for her to reply and he didn't sound very pleased about her intrusion.

The echoes of his gruff demand died away in the dusty gloom and she was still silenced. A younger, freer Juno wanted to rush into his arms and feel them close around her again at long last. She wanted to feel fully alive again for the first time in so long, but then she remembered how long it had taken her to live well without him and stayed where she was.

'I thought you were abroad,' she said numbly and it was his turn for a shocked silence. Pard sensed the tension and growled belatedly, but she had no words to reassure him.

'Not now,' Nathaniel said as if that explained everything. 'And if you think he's a guard dog, best think again,' he added so coolly that she must have imagined he was as shocked as she was. Pard wagged his tail as if he thought the stranger wasn't a threat.

'Traitor,' she murmured as he sat and offered the wretch a paw. 'You have neglected this house quite shamefully,' she said as Nathaniel came closer and her heartbeat sped up again at the reality of him, here and seemingly all alone.

He had grown a great beard and his physique seemed even larger and more formidable than the youthful one she remembered so fondly. He was so unlike his old self she wished she had happened on almost anyone else. She had loved that boy so much and this man wasn't even pretending to be pleased to see her.

'You can leave if it offends you,' he said curtly and she felt tears threaten because he wasn't her Nathaniel at all. The past was dead and it wasn't safe to mourn it with him watching.

'I wish I had stayed in the stables now,' she said bleakly.

'They might be cleaner. I wish I had got my manservant to light a fire in the grooms' quarters before he took my horse to be re-shod.'

So you would have stayed there and not come bothering me, she thought up the words for him.

How she wished she had taken Lady Colby's advice and hired a carriage now. 'Give me a tinderbox and I'll light one myself,' she said with a sniff to let him know he was being a terrible host, but that was all.

'Even I am not that much of a yahoo, my lady,' he said.

'I'm not married,' she said brusquely past the mournful thought that although he had once sworn he loved her he must have lied.

'You didn't marry the fat old lord, then?'

'Of course I didn't! I ran away.'

'Nobody told me.'

'Why would they?'

'True,' he said. If she added up the hours they had once spent together, they should be strangers.

Yet five years ago she thought he was her one true love—the hero that shy Juno Defford never quite dared believe she would ever find until he found her hiding in the shadows one night in Mayfair. Now he was shrugging her off as if they had always been strangers, but she had learned to hide her feelings, too, so he wouldn't know how much it hurt.

'You have been away too long,' she said with a sharp look at the dust and cobwebs she could now see in the semi-darkness.

'I thought it was being cared for by my late uncle's land agent, but clearly I was wrong.' A pause and even he must have decided that brusque explanation wasn't one at all. 'My uncle and I argued last time I was here. He wanted me to sell out after my bill of divorce was passed in the House, but I thought it was better to remain in the army while the dust settled.

'I was an arrogant young puppy and thought I was untouchable,' he said as if talking to himself now. 'I was wrong and that stupid war with America they are now calling the War of 1812, although it went on longer, was more or less over by the time we got there. We were shipped back just in time for Waterloo so no time for home leave before the battle and then he died and I was…' He hesitated.

'Injured,' she finished the sentence for him. 'I saw your name on the list of wounded.'

And longed to dash to Brussels, but you had made me promise to wait for you to come for me, so I stayed at home and bit my nails, and you didn't come.

'Yes, then came the news of my uncle's sudden death and poor Dorinda's a few weeks later,' he said flatly.

She could weep for the bright and hopeful boy of nineteen she remembered—unbowed by his divorce from 'poor Dorinda' and three hard years at war in Spain and France. If only she had ignored his orders to stay away from him until the scandal of his failed marriage faded, how different their lives might be now. Except if it was only real love on her side it was best he had stayed away.

'Your former wife hated the military life and the country-side, but you were a soldier and your uncle's heir, so why did she marry you?' she asked boldly because she didn't have any-thing to lose and she had always wondered.

'Because we were both seventeen and too green to know the difference between love and passion. We were friends as chil-dren, so it probably felt real to her at the time.'

'I am sorry for your loss,' she said, wondering if he still loved Dorinda, despite her infidelity.

Juno would have followed him to war barefoot and unwed if he had let her, but had he mourned his unfaithful former wife so dearly he forgot her? He had stolen Juno's heart when he found her hiding from the lord she didn't want to marry and Lieu-tenant Grange was too kind to walk away from a girl fighting tears, so he stayed to joke her out of them. Then he kissed her to make it better and changed her world.

Had he been too kind to call a halt—was that how he had ended up married to his *friend*? She hated the notion history could have repeated itself, if he hadn't thought better of marry-ing Juno. She saw the closed expression on his once-open face and, once again, mourned the bright youth she remembered.

'Why were you out alone in a blizzard?' he asked and his turn to change the subject. 'And this fine boy is no protection so don't tell me you were not alone.'

'He usually is.'

'His instincts aren't working today, then,' Nathaniel mur-mured so softly she must have misheard.

'Do you have somewhere warmer where we can argue?' she

said as cold seemed to reach into her very bones and she knew it wasn't caused by the weather.

'The agent's house,' he said with another frown—maybe he didn't want her there either.

'It's very cold in here,' she said with as much dignity as she could find as her snow-wet clothes clung to her—no wonder she was shivering.

'Agreed,' he said and strode off into the gloom and she supposed he meant her to follow him. 'But where *were* you bound on such a day?' he asked without turning round.

'None of your business,' she said and scurried in his wake.

Chapter Two

Nate knew he was being an appalling host and to Juno, of all people. He was so shocked to find her here and so aware of her as a woman that his wits had gone begging. He was struggling with a mess of feelings which he had tried so hard to shut down since he had left her behind five years ago.

It was as cold as charity in here and so was he. Or at least he thought so until her voice shattered the silence and love, longing and sheer need almost smashed through the barriers he had built to stay sane. He couldn't blight her brightness and beauty with the dregs of the hopeful young fool she remembered.

Idiot, a remnant of the eager boy argued, *beg if you have to, but don't dare let her go again.*

But the boy was wrong. His arms might ache to hold her, but it was weak to want her to stare back at him with wonder and innocent, youthful passion in her bluest of blue eyes again when he didn't deserve it.

He had wanted the shyest debutante in town so badly five years ago that he had kissed her passionately and she responded like a flower in the desert to rain, so he knew he was a villain even then. He had still lived on the fire and sweet promise of her kisses until the horrors of Waterloo had slapped him brutally awake.

He had been nineteen and a selfish young peacock when he first met shy Juno hiding in the shadows at a *ton* ball, but he still knew more about life than he hoped she ever would. He had felt like a fully grown man, desperate to introduce her to the joys of the marriage bed as soon as he could put clear water between them and his first hasty marriage and divorce. Then he would try to convince her uncle that he, Nathaniel Grange, deserved to marry his niece and ward, but he had been wrong.

A year on Waterloo had taught him better. He led his men into hell time and time again, feeling like a butcher as they fell around him and he urged the remnants on, until he was wounded himself and was almost relieved to be dragged into a square with the wounded and dead. Even when he came back to consciousness in Brussels to find his faithful batman, Jackson, was fending off the army surgeons' saws and knives, the misery didn't end.

He got word his uncle was dead and a few weeks later found out Dorinda had died trying to birth a love child. He felt so sorry for that terrible ending to her wild, young life. Yet he could not weep or go home to Juno, who had taught him what real love felt like, because she deserved to marry a better man.

He had ruined Dorinda's life when they married too young and how could he have risked doing the same to Juno? He recovered from his wounds after Waterloo and sold out, but nightmares woke him screaming as he fought it again in his sleep and still everyone died. That was why he had stayed away and, while he was much better now, he wished he had stayed away a little longer.

Walking and riding through war-scarred Europe while working for board and lodgings had made life bearable until he beat most of his demons, but there wasn't much left of the gilded youth Juno had met five years ago. So, he must hope for a rapid thaw and watch her leave as soon as a way was clear. Then he would learn to live without her again and the less she had to do with him in the meantime, the better.

'The land agent's house is on the other side of the house,' he explained as every nerve he had tingled with awareness of her.

'Someone must have told him I am back, so he fled so fast he left some of his ill-gotten gains behind.'

'Slow down, Lord Grange.'

'Sorry,' he said. He hadn't used his title as a wanderer so it still felt like his uncle's, not his. 'I was so busy cursing the man I forgot my manners,' he lied. 'Best hold my coat so you don't stray,' he said and opened the door on the furious storm.

'Yes, sir,' she said as they stepped outside.

'Safe?' he gasped as he paused to get his bearings.

'Safe,' she confirmed with a sharp tug on his coat. 'Don't lead me into a ditch.'

No hysterics, just a reminder to keep his mind on where they were going. He felt bereft when they reached the agent's house and she let go.

'Where's your cloak?' he demanded testily, pushing the door open and trying to brush snow from her shoulders as she went past him.

'There wasn't time,' she snapped and reopened the door to let her dog in.

'Why?' he demanded, leading the way to the best kitchen Hodges had filled with luxuries from the main house. With what the rogue had stolen from the estate and years of servants' wages in his pockets, he was set for life. 'You could have frozen to death out there today.' She was stubbornly silent. 'Towels and blankets,' Nate said distractedly as he tried not to stare at the lithe feminine form outlined by her wet habit.

'Pard *is* very cold.'

'And you are not?' he said, gently pushing her into a chair by the fire because she would stand and shiver if he didn't.

'Don't manhandle me,' she said crossly. He wanted to kiss her bad mood away but, instead, he clenched his hands behind his back.

'You will only stand on your dignity if I don't and your dog is bred for the road, so stop fussing over him and worry about yourself instead.'

He marched out of the room, trying not to think at all as he ran upstairs to snatch his robe from the chair by the bed where he had slept last night. He remembered how she used to watch him with wonder in her blue, blue eyes and ached for her to do it again as he found those towels and blankets and wished he had staff to care for her every need. He felt he had failed her yet again.

Juno watched Nathaniel escaping her company with unflattering haste and tears stung, but she forced them back. Five years should have taught her not to care, but even the warmth from the range couldn't touch a coldness deep inside because somehow she still did and he plainly did not.

'You *can't* care,' she whispered.

She must not look for the charming young rogue who had sat out balls with her and made her feel so much that she didn't want to think about it right now. Pard got up from the mat by the fire to lay his head in her lap. 'It's all right, beautiful boy,' she murmured, 'or will be when we leave.'

'You must get out of those wet clothes,' Nathaniel said from the doorway and she knew he had heard.

'I have nothing to wear.'

'You set off in a snowstorm without any luggage?'

'Yes, but it wasn't snowing.'

'Someone must have told you it would, so why did you ignore them?'

'I am in a hurry.'

'Strong men die in these hills in winter so that's not a good enough reason.'

'I am alive and I'm not a man.'

'Obviously,' he muttered.

'Or accountable to you.'

'I'm sorry you think me overbearing, but it's for your own good.'

'Words that usually precede a lecture I don't want to hear.'

'I have no right to lecture anyone, but it was foolish to set out so unprepared.'

'My life, my risk.'

'What about his?' he said and Pard looked bewildered and whined.

'You just told me he was bred for the road.'

'This is life or death, not a game!'

'I know,' she said, 'but it's not Pard's fault, so stop shouting.'

'I'm sorry,' he said stiffly, but came over to fondle her dog and Pard licked his hand as if he thought Nathaniel needed comforting more than he did.

This close up, she saw a few white hairs in Nathaniel's beard and he was only four and twenty, so maybe Pard was right. She almost wished she had stayed in the stables and gone on remembering her passionate young lover instead of this austere great bear who obviously wanted her gone as soon as possible.

'Pass me a towel, please. My hair is dripping everywhere.'

'I wish I could provide a bath, but it would take too long to heat enough water,' he said and his concern nearly undid her.

'I have nothing to change into,' she reminded him, trying not to blush at the thought of being naked in the same house as him.

'You should have thought of that when you set off.'

'So you have said.'

'It bears repeating,' he said grimly.

'I told you, I am in a hurry.'

'Not good enough.'

Reminded why she was in such haste, she glanced out of the window at the relentless storm, feeling dejected and helpless. 'You aren't responsible for me,' she said blankly.

'Thank heavens.'

'Oh, go away,' she said, torn between wanting to stay here so he could infuriate her some more and the longing to be with her family.

'Take off your wet habit while I try to find you something to wear, then.'

'I can't sit here naked!'

'Wear this,' he said, throwing a vast man's robe on to a chair. 'I will go and see if my sister left anything wearable behind when she wed, although it would be outdated since she would make two of you nowadays, but anything is better than wearing a wet habit all day.'

'I'm not a lady of fashion,' she said, secretly relieved he didn't expect her to wear anything his late wife left behind since she would rather freeze.

'Then strip off those wet things and dry yourself while I'm gone.'

'Yes, my lord, three bags full, my lord.'

'And bolt the door after me,' he added curtly. 'Hedges might not be as far away as I'd like him to be and the locks haven't been changed yet,' he added.

She felt a fool for not thinking harder about such comfort here and neglect elsewhere. The land agent must have dismissed the servants, closed the house and pocketed all their wages. In Hedges's shoes she would run hard and fast, but he must be a fool to abuse such a comfortable position.

'Very well,' she said, following Nathaniel to the door. 'Be careful,' she said when she saw the storm was fierce as ever.

'That's rich coming from you.'

'Be reckless, then,' she said and slammed the door.

'Bolts,' his deep voice rumbled through the wood and she shot them into place so fast he should know how she felt, then she watched him dash away until his powerful figure was masked by snow and anyone would think he cared.

'Stupid idea,' she muttered softly and went back to the fire.

Chapter Three

Juno closed the shutters before stripping off her habit and everything else she had on. She put on Nathaniel's vast robe and it felt intimate against her bare skin, as if his touch was going places that no other man would ever see or touch.

'I must look ridiculous,' she murmured and rolled up the sleeves so her hands were free to reopen the shutters.

She sank back into the chair to stare moodily into the glowing fire. How silly to feel wrapped up in gruff care as she tried to sort the scent of clean man from something elusive and woody. If he hadn't spoken first, she might never have recognised him, but his voice had always been unique, as if an echo of it was lodged deep inside her to make sure she could never forget him.

It felt decadent to sit naked but for his robe with her long hair loose on her shoulders to dry. She must remember she was caught in a snowstorm with a man who had done his best to forget she existed. When she had first met Nathaniel she had endured her grandmother's contempt for so long that she hid in dark corners to avoid her icy disapproval as well as the man the Dowager Lady Stratford wanted Juno to marry. Why must she brood on the night they met? And thank goodness her grandmother lived abroad now and she would probably never see her again.

She glanced out of the window and knew it was too late to keep her uncle company as he paced and raged, worrying about his beloved wife and child. The snow had set in and she must pray all was well despite Uncle Alaric's despairing letter. She could picture him furious and frustrated not to be with Marianne and desperate for news as his thoughts turned gloomy. Was that why he sent out those hasty messages?

Juno sighed and envied Marianne's brother living close to Prospect House. He and his wife, Fliss, Juno's former governess, would have got there before it began to snow in earnest. Juno felt as remote from them as if she was on the moon and she might just as well be for all the chance there was of her getting home today.

Nate ran into the main house and shook snow off like a wet dog—just as well nobody was here to sigh at the work he had just made them. He smiled at the thought of Juno's dog shaking off snow much the same way and the house didn't seem as desolate now they were here. Servants would disapprove their lack of a chaperon and whisper Lord Grange couldn't keep his eyes off this unexpected guest. He couldn't bring himself to sincerely regret the emptiness of his poor house now she was here to share it.

He smiled at a fanciful image of Juno's dog dressed in a wig and spectacles and looking down his nose at unworthy Lord Grange as the only chaperon available. Nate ran up the stairs he had climbed so reluctantly an hour ago and strode past the rooms he and Dorinda once shared to his sister's old room. He sobered at the suspicion Hedges had been one of Dorinda's lovers, recalling how bare her old room was. He hadn't suspected why until he searched the agent's house for blankets just now and found Dorinda's discarded things in the attic.

Now he lifted the lid of a Spanish chest and smelt lavender and spices although his sister had wed a decade ago. Everything here had run smoothly when his uncle was alive, so something must have turned Hedges to fraud. Dorinda could have flirted and maybe more with the man to relieve her boredom in the country. She always thought each lover could be *the one,* until she found out he wasn't. Nate realised he wasn't that one and only just weeks after they married...

But what if Hedges blamed him for Dorinda's loss of interest? Nate felt a fool for struggling on with a dead marriage as long as he had. He should have admitted his uncle and sister were right to say it was a huge mistake to elope when they were both so young—better to end it cleanly before more damage was done. In the end Dorinda had begged him to. She had left a trail of disappointed lovers behind her for Nate to pick one rich and cynical enough not to be hurt if he was sued for criminal conversation with another man's wife, so Lord Grange could get a bill of divorce through the House on his nephew and ward's behalf.

He shook off the past and worried about Juno instead, as he searched for warm clothes to fit her. He was surprised his sister, Ella, had left so many behind when she wed. Maybe she thought she would spend more time here than she had. Meanwhile Juno was naked but for his dressing robe and he must not linger on such a heady idea. He scooped up warm gowns and a winter riding habit, knowing she would leave before her habit was dry if it stopped snowing.

The idea of her perishing of cold if it started again made him shudder and swear to do anything he could to stop her. If he stayed away from the agent's house, she would feel more secure and might not try to outwit Mother Nature again today. He would hand over his sister's clothes and sleep in the stables to let her know she had nothing to fear from him if she stayed.

He would wrap himself in guilt and horse blankets, sleeping in the stables where he and Jackson had inspected the chimneys and decided it was safe to light a fire. That way she couldn't leave without him knowing and the road from the village must be blocked or Jackson would be back by now.

Thanks to Hedges squirreling away luxuries at the agent's house there was enough food and firewood to prevent them freezing or starving. He had planned to live there while the chimneys were swept and this lovely old place had the grand clean it needed. He cursed the damage Hedges had done to it as he found a valise to pile undergarments, gowns and a warm shawl into. Where was Ella's old cloak? He found it then braved his dressing room, looking for the heavy military one he had sent home when he sold out.

Glad of it now, he hurried to the garden door, worryingly eager to see Juno again. After running through the snow again, he knocked on the door of the agent's house and waited a minute before hammering on it anxiously. He was about to shout and maybe batter it down when the bolts were drawn back and Juno opened it at last.

'I was asleep,' she admitted, blinked her sleepy blue eyes and yawned.

He felt his heart lurch and had to stamp about pretending to remove all the snow he could from his boots. She looked as if she had just got out of bed and he was desperate for it to have been his. He was a man, so of course he wanted her, but a painful sort of tenderness at the sight of her heavy eyed and undefended made his heart seem to turn over in his chest so he dared not look again until his defences were stronger. She could have *died* today. Imagining her freezing to death in some windswept corner if she hadn't found his forlorn old place made him stifle a moan of protest.

He wanted to grab her and hold her, feel her heart beat and reassure himself she was unharmed. He knew where that might lead and refused to rob her of future choices. She was very different to the shy girl he remembered. He guiltily missed the shy adoration she had once watched him with as sleep receded and she dared him to laugh at the vastness of his robe on her when that was the last thing he felt like doing.

'Along with your fierce hound?' he said, fussing the dog that seemed far more pleased to see him than she was.

'He knew it was you,' she said and scurried back to her chair by the fire as fast as his trailing robe allowed. He would never be able to wear it again without feeling she was wrapped in it with him and that wasn't the right way to think when she was blushing as if she had read his mind.

'Are you warm yet?' he said, trying not to notice she was tucking her bare feet into his robe as if the sight of them might arouse the beast in him.

'Yes, thank you,' she said politely.

'Shall I light a fire in one of the bedchambers for you to change by, or would you prefer me to see if your horse is missing you while you do it here?'

'I only hired him this morning, but I suppose he could be missing his friends.'

'You were in such a hurry you hired a job horse?'

'He's not one of those and it was urgent,' she said and frowned as if reminded she still needed to be somewhere else.

'He's not worth risking your life for,' he protested.

'Who isn't—the horse?'

'No, the man you ignored a raging blizzard to get to.'

'What, Sir Harry?' she said and blinked as if still fighting sleep, so had she been dreaming of the damned rogue behind Nate's back?

'Harry Marbeck?' he asked, past jealousy and bitter hurt. 'He's married.'

'To my aunt's sister Viola,' she snapped and glared as if he was despicable and he probably was, 'whom he loves dearly.'

'*Harry's* in love? He swore he never would be, nor marry.'

'Then he has learned some sense.'

'Well, I never,' he said. So much had changed since he left maybe impossible things were possible after all. Maybe if he was a very good baron for a very long time he could deserve to tell Juno that he had always loved her and always would, even if he would never deserve her. Wild Harry Marbeck hadn't deserved his Viola either, but she had married him anyway. Yet Harry had always been a good man at heart and Juno was better off without an idiot like Nate Grange.

'How far is it to Chantry Old Hall?' she asked.

'A couple of miles as the crow flies, three by road.'

'It might as well be fifty,' she said with a mournful sigh.

'Why?'

'I must get home and Sir Harry and his wife will hasten to Herefordshire now so I wanted to beg a ride.'

'I thought your uncle's principal seat was in Wiltshire,' he said. Relief she was desperate to be with her family, not a lover, made him sound clumsy and uncaring and she clearly thought so, too.

'He hates Stratford Park so he and Marianne have bought a near ruin not far from her brother's manor.'

'Hasn't Stratford got enough houses already?'

'Marianne likes creating order from chaos and he likes to help her. He was very bored living in grand houses and playing the dutiful Viscount.'

'I suppose you are going to tell me they are in love as well,' Nate said wearily.

'Of course.'

'Anyone else?'

'Marianne and Viola's brother, Darius Yelverton, who married my former governess, but you don't know them so never mind their love story.'

'Darius Yelverton? There can't be two with a name like that and he was a captain in the light infantry with a sister who married one of his sergeants. The poor fellow was killed at the Battle of Badajoz.'

'Yes, that was Marianne; she is married to my uncle now.'

He heard the defiance in Juno's voice so his shock was showing. Hard to imagine dignified and aloof Lord Stratford marrying the widow of an artillery sergeant, but Nate envied their passionate marriage. It must be passionate for Stratford to have wed her for love, so nobody was safe. Except Nate, who didn't feel worth loving and what if he bored Juno as easily he had Dorinda? Juno deserved to wed a good man with an innocent heart, not a weary fool trailing scandal and tragedy behind him. He might bore *her* when the ink was hardly dry on their marriage lines as well and that was a disaster he couldn't contemplate.

'Yelverton and your governess are in love as well?' he said.

'Very much so.'

'Whatever *is* the world coming to?'

'A better place.'

'I can see how your uncle's marriage connects you to Yelverton and Marbeck, then, but not why you are in such a hurry to reach Stratford's wreck in the country.'

'Former wreck,' she argued absently.

'Stratford can afford the best care for his wife in childbed, so why were you taking an appalling risk to get there in weather like this?'

'You wouldn't understand.'

'I might.'

'You are not close to your family.'

'I was when my sister and I grew up here,' he argued. 'Our uncle and aunt made sure we had a happy childhood.'

'Your uncle died soon after his wife, though, didn't he?'

'A year and a half later.'

Nate had doubted his uncle's will to live after his beloved wife's death, but he still did not sell out and come home. He thought he was saving his uncle more gossip about his own unhappy marriage, but perhaps it was really because he was too much of a coward to face it himself.

'A heavy blow for you and your sister,' Juno said gently.

'Aye,' Nate said bleakly. He was such a cold fish it was no wonder she was silent. It hurt to feel, so he had locked his emotions down so tightly he felt as if he had grown a hard shell around them and was still too much of a coward to break it. When he left her behind five years ago, he had intended to come back and marry her, but after his last battle it had seemed kinder to stay away.

Chapter Four

Juno didn't know whether to pity Nathaniel or be furious he was pretending not to care. She pitied the fierce feelings that drove him from a home he clearly loved. Why did he think it was a weakness to feel much at all nowadays?

'We were discussing your relations,' he said stiffly.

'You were. I was trying not to.'

'I'm not a gossip,' he snapped.

'They still won't want your pity.'

'You think me such a weeping willow?'

'No.'

'Then tell me why you are so desperate to get to your uncle's former wreck in the country and maybe I can help you.'

'How?' she said, glancing at the relentless snow outside.

'Using some common sense would be a good place to start.'

'Love trumps it and I love them even if you think me a fool for doing it.'

'Not for loving. For not looking after yourself.'

'Then I'll tell you if you promise not to scold me any more.'

'I promise to try,' he said with a rueful shrug.

'Please do. My uncle and aunt were overjoyed when she realised she was increasing earlier this year as they had resigned themselves to it never happening.' Juno stopped to remember their stunned joy when they finally realised why Marianne had been so out of sorts. 'The baby is due at the end of January, so I was visiting my godmother before Christmas instead of after when I got a message from my uncle to say Marianne's pains have begun. The babe may be too small to survive and if she dies it will break his heart, so I must get home in a hurry.'

'Love matches look a bad risk to me.'

'I have seen them in action and they seem a risk worth taking,' she said, trying not to mourn the one they could have had if only he had cared enough for her.

'So-called love fooled me into marrying a woman who could never love one man,' he said cynically.

Her heart bled for the boy who wed a girl who couldn't be faithful if she tried, but if he couldn't see that wasn't love it was as well he didn't come back to marry her. Knowing he was waiting for her to get bored and stray as well would have been worse agony than living without him.

'As one risk didn't pay off, you will never take another?' she said and he avoided her eyes.

'No, I won't.'

'Then I pity you. Love is the finest emotion one person can feel for another.'

'I don't want anyone's pity,' he said as if she was rasping his pride raw.

She raised her eyebrows to say she doubted he was immune to all human emotions and maybe that sparked his temper, or perhaps he was trying to prove a point as he swooped in and kissed her. Fire shot through her and his mouth was so yearning and tender on hers she couldn't pretend to be outraged.

'Hmm,' she murmured instead, 'more.'

'You don't know what you're asking,' he said shakily, but lowered his head to meet her eager lips with such ardour it felt familiar and new and even more wondrous than it was before.

He still held back, his mouth teasing and not as intense as she wanted. She sensed fierce needs fighting to get out, but he would not lose control of them. There was a tremor in his hard muscle to say it cost him an effort to raise his head and meet her gaze. His eyes were dark and stormy, and maybe there were too many dreams in hers, but she couldn't look away.

He kissed her again, as if he couldn't help it, but didn't sneak his tongue into her mouth to dance with hers as he had in shadowy corners of *ton* ballrooms five years ago, with all those people so near as he taught her about delicious pleasure in his arms. The emphatic burn of need deep inside her was familiar, but she had wanted more for so long that his control made her angry.

'I *do* know,' she argued fiercely. 'I know I want *you* and you showed me how.'

'You were so young, I shouldn't have,' he murmured before kissing her again as if he couldn't fight such powerful needs alone.

'And you were such an old, old man,' she teased when she could. 'Touch me,' she murmured with a breathy sigh.

She wanted his big hands gentle on her naked skin, wickedly arousing in secret places only ever eager for him. Sensual promise burned in his dark eyes as he tugged the knot in the robe's belt free and wild excitement leapt inside her as the soft stuff parted, She gloated at the hard flush of colour burning his cheeks as he eyed her naked body and she felt breathless and so hotly needy. The way his pupils flared, then contracted as she gazed up at him without shame, felt delicious.

She was proud of the womanly body he eyed with such hunger and settled her shoulders into the cushions to flaunt her aroused breasts. She wanted sheer need to drown his scruples so he couldn't help but love her fully and freely at long last. Thrilling heat coursed through her at the very thought of him deep inside her and she wriggled against the cushions to demand he do something about it right now.

'I can't,' he murmured, despite watching her half-prone body so hungrily she knew he was lying. He most definitely could, but he didn't want to. 'I would have to shave this off first,' he said, running a rueful hand over his beard as his eager eyes roved her body and her nipples went pebble hard and never mind his confounded beard. 'I would scratch and burn you, here,' he murmured, trailing a wondering finger around the tightened areola of one nipple. He gently flicked the startlingly responsive tip of the other and made her gasp as heat shot through her so fiercely she moaned for more, but he had already moved on.

'And here,' he added huskily as he trailed his caressing finger down her flat stomach and stopped just short of the dark curls hiding her sex. Fierce longing threatened to blaze out of control as the breath stalled in her lungs. She rasped in more as his fingertip settled on yearning skin for a pulse-thundering moment.

'Especially here,' he said huskily, his gaze so intense as he nearly touched her most intimate secrets and the wild ache at her feminine core scorched so hotly she writhed against the cushions in desperation and without an iota of shame. She wanted him to join with her, to forget beards and beds and everything else but finally becoming lovers.

'You want to kiss me all over?' she murmured softly. It sounded like bliss to her, so why didn't he just get on with it?

'All of you,' he confirmed huskily, 'everywhere.'

'Then why don't you?'

'If only I hadn't grown a beard, I could show you so much pleasure without despoiling you, but I did so I can't.'

She closed her eyes to shut him out as bemused wonder faded to utter loneliness. *Despoiling you?* How dare he say so? She had felt such magic, such sweet need for him as her lover at long last and he could say that?

'And we don't want you *despoiling* me, do we?' she snapped because fury was better than hurting so much she didn't want to think about it.

'No,' he said so coolly she wanted to kick him.

'Go away, then. Keep my horse company; wander your poor old house brooding, but I must change now and you are confoundedly in the way.'

She jumped to her feet as if impatient to don his sister's clothes while she still ached for him, but refused to beg or cry over more shattered dreams. Frustrated desire might be burning and twisting inside her, but she would *not* be ashamed or humoured with half-measures. She had learned to live alone when he left her last time. So she tied the belt of his robe to hide the womanly curves he had gazed on with lying hunger and stared out of the window at more snow and an early dusk.

'Give me time to pack my valise again and I'll leave you alone for the rest of the day,' he said so expressionlessly she wanted to yell and scream and force him to admit he was devastated and lonely, too.

Make him stay—show him how good being your lover would be, bad Juno urged.

But Lord Grange was impatient to be gone and she had endured enough hardship for one day.

'I'm sure the horse will be glad of your company,' she said and bent to comfort a bewildered Pard.

'My fault,' Nathaniel said guiltily.

She closed her eyes to fight the tears. He was taking blame now and it felt worse than not *despoiling* her. 'That's almost as bad as saying it's for my own good.'

'It is, but I'm still sorry.'

'Are you, my lord?' He was silent. 'Just go, Nathaniel,' she said wearily. 'Worry about your poor old house because I can take care of myself.' He still didn't move, but she had to make him go somehow. 'I will leave food in the hall and a pot to cook it in,' she added, wondering why she cared if he starved. 'No doubt you learned how to during your wanderings abroad.'

'No doubt,' she heard him murmur as the door shut quietly behind him.

Moments later she heard him pile firewood on the back porch so she didn't have to fetch it in. Blinking back tears, she changed into his sister's old clothes as more logs thumped on the floor outside and he wouldn't look so there was no point in closing the shutters when he already seen her all and walked away.

You bungling idiot, Grange!

Nate trudged through the snow with a cooking pot in one hand and a valise in the other. His body ached with frustration and his heart felt so sore he wanted to rub his chest to soothe the ache, but knew it wouldn't help. He felt bereft and so lonely he wanted to go back and beg for her warmth and all the wonders she had just offered him. Even if she ached as well and cried the tears she had refused to shed in front of him, at least she would wake up free of him tomorrow.

He closed his eyes, torturing himself with a picture of her stiff with pride as she watched him go and the pain in his heart said *you fool*. Yet if Juno ever told him *she* had made a mistake and didn't love him it would break him, so he was a coward and decided not to risk it. He stood still in a new squall of snow and let the cold creep over him so he could stop thinking about Juno warm and naked and wanting the unworthy lover she had stumbled across in a snowstorm and so utterly desirable and...

Oh, damnation take it, Grange, just stop torturing yourself!

War should work; the last grim battle when he was so dazed by smoke and gunfire he was deaf and half-blind by the end of it and there was his best reason to stand here in the snow. It chilled him down nicely until he got to the stables and saw the fine horse Juno had hired and had to curse her reckless bravery. The thought of her thrown off in an icy wilderness made him want to stamp back to hold her close and love her with every last inch of his shaking body until he was convinced she was safe and properly warm from head to toe.

Juno was so bold, brave and magnificent, and fantasies of making love to her had haunted him for so long he should be able to fight them off better than this by now. Yet his fantasy Juno was still a girl; the real one was every inch a woman and why the devil did he kiss her?

Nate climbed the rough stairs to the grooms' dormitory, trying to think of anything but Juno, deliciously warm and heavy-eyed as she lay naked in that chair and wanted *him*. It took every scrap of willpower he had to push away and not take until they were sated and bound together for life.

He could be making love with her right now if not for Dorinda's ghost whispering, *Be very sure Juno won't tire of you soon after the wedding as well.*

At the time he didn't know why he couldn't be as disloyal to Dorinda as she was to him, but maybe it was the idea of Juno, a woman so loyal, strong and brave, that stopped him. He had never deserved her and now she was breathtaking—all elegant limbs and slender curves and dark hair long enough to touch her neat derrière when she sat in that confounded chair and he wanted her so much how could he *not* kiss her?

Everything else had faded from his mind when he saw heat and need and something more in her gaze that he didn't want to think about now. He felt as if he had killed his own men as well as the enemy in battle. He had seen things he never wanted her to know a man *could* see. He had failed to love his wife enough to stop her straying. So, yes, he was tempted by Juno naked and wanting him, but maybe the only worthwhile thing he had ever done was to leave her free to find a better man. Even if she hated him now, at least he hadn't ruined her chances of marrying that better man one day.

It was nearly dark inside the stables and he remembered the tinderbox in that pot of Juno's as he fumbled for a lamp in the tack room and luckily the glass had kept the mice from eating the candle. He finally managed to get it lit and safely closed, but nothing could keep his thoughts from Juno long and he hated the thought of her riding away in the morning if a thaw set in. She was such a fascinating and contrary woman he felt the stark ache of frustration bite again.

So don't keep thinking of her naked, then, you fool.

He needed more distractions and climbed the rough stairs to the loft where the stable boys and unwed grooms had slept. It should match the comfort his horses would enjoy if he still had any. He frowned at the thought of all the fine ones Hedges must have sold, but if he sat brooding about the villain he could freeze to death.

He drew up imaginary plans to house the stable boys and grooms in far more comfort as he searched for the kindling and logs the lads had chopped for a fire none of them was here to enjoy once Hedges had purged The Grange of all servants except the ones who served him. Nate hated the man for pretending to be acting on His Lordship's orders when he closed the house as if the people meant to care for it didn't matter.

His forlorn homecoming had forced Nate to realise how much he loved this place, but he had to make up fantasy bloodlines to fill the empty stables next to distract him from aching for Juno. She was more important than a house or this land and if only he was a better man she would feel like his true home.

He added a new forge and indoor school to train riding horses to his plans, then ran out of ideas and stared into the fire he had managed to light in the cold hearth. He might as well give in to memories of Juno when he almost thought he deserved her, because nothing was big enough to stop him thinking about her tonight.

Chapter Five

Young Juno was the magic he didn't deserve when he found her in the shadows that first night. She distracted him from his woes, enchanting him with unexpected humour and her deep-down courage and integrity. He had been amazed nobody else noticed how lovely she was under the shyness, but she was never shy with him. That first night he had kissed her because he was free at last and why not? She was utterly delicious and watching him adoringly.

You young cockscomb, he accused the younger self who enjoyed her adoration and thought he deserved it.

Then he went away, left her facing such horror alone that he wanted to howl a protest at the thought of her running from a forced marriage at a heartbreakingly young age. The acute danger she had faced because of her own grandmother's coldness and greed made him feel so sick the thought of making a meal from the food Juno packed into the pot turned his stomach. The marriage that wicked woman intended for Juno was no more than legalised brutality.

He thought of Juno saying *I ran away* and of course she did, but what a useless fool he had been to leave her with no choice but give in or do just that. He had thought he was being so noble, sailing away from the temptation to make her his and brave her furious uncle's wrath afterwards. Putting an ocean between them so that his second marriage would not seem the reason why his first had failed felt like a fine sacrifice to that arrogant boy. If he could go back in time, he would break the smug idiot's nose and order him to wake up and realise he was just a heedless young fool.

He should have sold out as his uncle had wanted him to. He was always less than Juno deserved, but she had wanted him so he could have worked hard to become better. And now it was too late, wasn't it? They should probably marry because they had been marooned here alone. The idea of marrying Juno felt wondrous and he wouldn't even need to say he loved her, but he had killed the chance she would accept him for mere propriety's sake when he stood back from fully loving her.

He stared at the fire and waited for dawn, knowing his nightmares would come back if he slept with *I ran away* pounding in his ears. He pictured all the horrors a lonely girl running across England faced as he shivered in a room unheated so long it would take weeks to be truly warm, thinking he deserved every cold second of the long night ahead.

Juno had spent the night in the chair by the fire because lying where Nathaniel had slept last night was impossible. She must have dozed since Pard's loud sighs woke her when the fire burned low and he was cold. Uncle Alaric said she spoiled him and he was right. Reminded of the true reason she was sitting brooding while Nathaniel was probably doing the same elsewhere, she prayed Uncle Alaric and Marianne were both safe and not grieving their longed-for baby. She felt guilty because although she was desperate to see them, she wanted to stay here with Nathaniel as well. There was more between them than he was willing to admit and she wanted to know what it was before she left.

Suddenly she heard manly stamping about outside the front door to let her know he was back from wherever he had spent the night. She should leave him to shiver, but yawned and stretched cramped muscles instead and went to let him in.

'Good heavens, Nathaniel! What a difference,' she gasped as

she took in the sight of him clean shaven and even more handsome than the young man she once knew.

'I need a barber,' he said, sheepishly smoothing his dark locks. 'Luckily there were sharp scissors and a razor in the kit I left here, although it's so long since I used one I had nearly forgotten how.'

'You still need new clothes and a valet,' she told him with a critical look to pretend he didn't make her heart race even faster without the whiskery disguise.

'I need maids, carpenters, grooms, a butler and a housekeeper more,' he said ruefully.

'And they would have to get here,' she said as they went back to the kitchen.

'True, drifts will be blocking the roads, so staffing this place must wait.'

'Do you think I could walk to Chantry Old Hall?' she said hopefully.

'No, it's too far and the snow is too deep.'

'There must be some way to get home now it's not snowing.'

'You wouldn't get a hundred yards on foot today.'

'How do you know?'

'Because I know how deep the snow is and up here, we sometimes get cut off for weeks in winter.'

'I am stuck, then?'

'Yes.'

'For how long?' she asked and he shrugged.

'Until the weather changes or we dig our way out. It's early for such a heavy snowfall so it *might* turn to rain.'

'Or stay on the ground until Christmas.'

'Yes,' he said and didn't look as worried as he should be.

'What sort of Christmas would it be with your house closed and me desperate to leave?'

'But we would have each other, Miss Defford,' he said with a soulful look and a hand on his heart like a stage Romeo. She knew he was trying to cheer her up and didn't want to be touched by his playacting.

'Idiot,' she said with a reluctant smile. 'Be serious, Lord Grange.'

'Very well, then—Jackson, my former batman and travelling companion, will persuade the villagers to dig through the snow so he can get here quickly since he thinks me helpless without him.'

Juno nearly asked why when Nathaniel was so self-sufficient. 'What shall I do when they get here?' she asked instead.

'I thought you would be delighted to see them.'

'They will be shocked I was trapped here with just you.'

'When they see my makeshift quarters in the stables and yours in here, notice your dog is large and might be fierce if provoked, they will marvel at our joint strength of character and propose me for sainthood.'

Pard wasn't very fierce yesterday, but Juno hadn't resisted Nathaniel's kisses. Now she didn't know what to make of the man hiding under that great beard. How would she feel if they had kissed until his control snapped so they woke up this morning as lovers? Wonderful, she decided defiantly—she would have been fully, urgently loved by the only man she ever wanted to make love with, but she didn't feel like that now.

'Make love to me before they get here, Nathaniel,' she blurted out impulsively. Where was her pride, for goodness' sake?

'How can I?' he said huskily.

'Since you shaved off that ridiculous beard the excuse it will scratch me won't wash and men and women have been doing it since time began.'

'Don't joke about it, Juno,' he said so huskily he must feel something, even if it was only embarrassment.

'I was never more serious in my life,' she argued and wasn't prepared to lie that she felt nothing when he touched her, even if he was.

'I could get you with child,' he told the wall on the other side of the room as if every word must be paid for. 'I couldn't hold back once I was inside you,' he added, gazing at the kitchen clock this time and it had stopped.

'And you wouldn't want that, would you?' she said bitterly.

'Not for you, not like that.'

'Oh, well, there is nothing else to be said, my lord.'

'I would have to marry you first,' he shocked her by saying anyway.

Her breath stalled and her heart raced, but he still refused to look at her, so she knew it was only his conscience talking. 'Perish the thought,' she said flatly.

'Don't,' he said, putting a hand on her shoulder as if he wanted her to look at him. His touch scorched her skin through his sister's old clothes, but she couldn't watch him pretend it was what he wanted. 'Don't dismiss us, Juno,' he added, so hoarsely he must feel something. *Yes, that embarrassment you were just wondering about.* 'Marry me.'

'Why?' she countered so warily he took his hand away and she missed it so much she shivered.

'We suit one another,' he said as if it was a good enough reason and a frozen silence argued otherwise. 'We wanted each other when we were not much more than boy and girl and it hasn't gone away. I'm not worthy of you, but we could have a good life together—be two halves of a better whole than I shall ever be without you.'

But don't expect me to say I love you, she added in her head, mourning the boy of nineteen who'd said it so easily she had believed him.

He wouldn't have left her so lonely and for so long if he meant it, though, would he? She refused to wed him now for the sake of their reputations if the gossips found out Lord Grange was alone with Miss Defford for a day and night. 'I ran away from being a *suitable* wife five years ago,' she said bleakly.

'Don't compare me with that randy old goat.'

'Why not? He wanted me for much the same reason.'

'No, he wanted a shamefully young wife to get an heir on. Don't lump me with him, Juno—I can't endure it if you truly think there's nothing to choose between us.'

'Very well, then, I won't,' she said with a sigh. Not even to protect herself from more hurt could she compare young, vigorous Nathaniel Grange with the elderly lecher who had made her life a misery five years ago. 'I always wanted you as fervently as you wanted me,' she admitted.

Probably more so, her inner pessimist added.

'He wanted me, willing or no, and unwilling excited him so I ran and kept running after my purse was stolen and I had no money for the next stage. I walked twenty miles to the town where my former governess was staying and hid whenever I heard anyone coming rather than risk him catching up with me.'

'Tell me!' Nathaniel barked as if she had left a crucial part out of a report to a superior officer.

'I just did.' She couldn't tell him she had been terrified throughout that endless-seeming journey and so wretched and confused about him as she ran she wasn't careful enough with her purse so every penny she had was stolen too easily. She could not let a slavering old man do things she longed to with Nathaniel, but *he* went away.

Love wasn't supposed to be that hard for girls just out of the schoolroom, yet it felt starkly real for her as she sheltered from a storm in a remote barn all night and dreamt how wonderful life would be if Nathaniel was there with her. She pitied her young self, so lost and alone, wishing she could tell her she would make a good life without him. Yet now Nathaniel was here, independence didn't seem quite so wonderful.

'What a damn fool! I knew Stratford was in Paris, yet I didn't sell out to protect you from the cur,' Nathaniel said as if he hated himself for it now. 'My uncle and sister begged me to when Boney abdicated, but I wanted to escape the scandal when Dorinda begged me to divorce her so we could both be free. I thought you were safer with an ocean between us—hah! Safer?' he barked as he paced. 'You would have been safer in a bear pit than with that disgraceful lecher and your stone-hearted grandmother.'

'I survived—indeed, I found out I could look after myself so there was no need for a knight to ride to my rescue.' She saw him wince as if she had stuck a knife in him and at least he felt *something*, even if it was only guilt.

'I couldn't marry you so soon after my divorce, the tabbies would have eaten you alive,' he said bleakly.

'You could have if you loved me,' she said coolly.

That was the real hitch in her grand love affair—he had been so desperate to marry his *friend* Dorinda he had eloped with her, but he had put an ocean between himself and Juno rather than do the same with her. He could have married her, but he didn't want to. He could have done so, then taken her with him if he did, so how dare he offer to now they had been forced together by the snow?

'How well do you think that would have worked?' he said. 'Whispers would have done the rounds I only rid myself of Dorinda to marry you and you were too young and vulnerable to be pilloried like that. Indeed, your uncle would have put me in the stocks himself and told the mob to throw stones if he hadn't killed me first.'

'Either you weren't brave enough to face him then, or you only wanted a few stolen kisses from a green girl—I vote for the latter.'

'No, I thought you would have met a better man than me by now and married him instead,' he said stiffly.

'Why would I put myself back on the Marriage Mart after I had escaped it? Why be ignored or mocked until I hid in dark corners with bored libertines and let them fool me about love all over again?'

'Ah, don't, Juno—you would have learned how to cope in time. You are a fine and fiery woman, and some lucky and untainted young man would have snapped you up if only you had let him meet you.'

'How do you know?'

'Because you are magnificent. The promise and strength under your shyness was the reason those silly little cats persecuted you when you were too young to realise what they were up to. They knew you would outshine every single one of them one day without even trying.'

So magnificent you don't want to make love with me even when I all but beg you to? I don't think so, my lord, she thought starkly.

'Thank you,' she said out loud.

Chapter Six

Nathaniel sighed as if she was being contrary and Juno wanted to scream at him for being obtuse. 'You still haven't told me exactly what happened after I left,' he said.

As if it mattered now. 'I escaped the room my grandmother locked me up in when I refused to wed a lord who promised to hand over my dowry if she made me marry him. I picked the lock and crept out of the house one dark night, paid for a seat on the Dover stage because I knew they would expect me to flee to my uncle, then I went the other way to ask my former governess for help until my uncle came home and I was safe again.'

'You must have been so frightened,' he said shakily, as if imagining the fear and danger of that frantic journey. *You have no idea,* she thought with the desperation of it sharp in her memory and missing him every step of the way had made it worse.

'Not as frightened as I was of marrying a man I detested.'

'Brave girl,' he said.

'No, I was terrified. I expected him to catch up and force me up the aisle with my grandmother's consent until my uncle rode to the rescue and I was safe at last.'

'While I crossed the Atlantic pretending we had never met,' he said as if he was furious with his younger self for leaving her so alone and maybe she still was, too. 'Because I wanted to keep my hands off an innocent girl that I should never have dallied with in the first place.'

'You went because of me?' she asked and horror outran hurt at the idea he thought it was just dalliance.

'What if I had stayed and bored you as soon as the gloss and passion of being married to me wore off and you were stuck with me for life, Juno?'

Never, I would never have been anything but enthralled by you, Nathaniel, the old, besotted Juno protested silently.

But there was such a gulf between love and passion it felt pointless to say it out loud. Only love was big enough to bridge the void and she refused to let it be one-sided.

'And, yes. I went because of you,' he admitted. 'I had to give you space to be certain I was what you wanted and how could I ruin your life as I did Dorinda's with my blind passion and impulsiveness if I was not?'

She would have argued no, it was really love if he had given her a chance back then. 'I was so afraid for you,' she admitted shakily instead.

'Don't you know the devil looks after his own?'

'You're not his and I know you were wounded at Waterloo so stop being flippant.'

'I recovered though, didn't I?'

'Did you, Nathaniel? I wonder.'

'Enough to know I wasn't good enough. I couldn't watch *you* turn away from me with bored eyes, Juno. I would have wanted to kill any man *you* loved instead of me.'

She tried not to be flattered by the difference he made between her and his former wife, then saw the insult in his words. 'You thought *I* would flit from man to man like your precious Dorinda? I *loved* you, Nathaniel. How dare you make my decisions for me. I can make my own mistakes, thank you very much. You look like the worst one of all right now and don't you dare touch me, I couldn't bear it.' She paused and took a deep breath, but he didn't try to and didn't speak either. 'I'm not a pale shadow of your wife. How dare you think I would follow her example?'

'Of course you're not like her, but when Dorinda married me

she swore she loved me and I must not leave her behind when I went off to fight. She got hysterical every time someone even mentioned my commission, but she was bored within a week so I must have been a poor husband. I dragged her off to Spain and let her suffer the privations of life on the march and she hated every rough billet and missed meal and the smells and dirt and everyday dangers.'

'Yet she begged you to take her with you.'

'She had no idea what life was like on campaign and it made her miserable.'

'So miserable she slept with your commanding officer? And you didn't know what it would be like either—at barely seventeen you were a boy and no doubt you thought it would be a grand adventure.'

'I was still her husband and who told you she did that?'

'I forget, but her lovers were hardly a secret.'

'She wanted me to divorce her, but I was too stubborn to admit we had made a terrible mistake when we eloped so she could go to war with me.'

'It was her mistake as well.'

'Both our mistakes, then, but a very good reason to make sure you were certain about your feelings for me.'

She wanted to rage at him for lumping her with Dorinda, but felt so sad he had taken the blame for the failure of his marriage when Dorinda sounded like a spoilt brat who only wanted what she should not have.

'The lack was in her, not you, Nathaniel,' she said gently. 'It was beyond me why she wasn't content with such a fine and handsome young man even before I met you and afterwards I hated her.'

'Why?'

'Because you hid in the shadows with me to avoid the gossips and, though you pretended to be merry and teased me out of my misery, your eyes were so sad I ached for you and hated her for making you feel less than you should be.'

'It was mainly my pride that was hurting.'

'Poor boy,' she said softly and, looking back at how young

he had been, she did pity him and even found a little of it to spare for poor, dead Dorinda.

'Say idiot boy rather and you'll be closer to the truth.'

'Because you married her?'

'Because she had grown so lovely, I was flattered when she said she loved me. We were so hungry for adult adventures we mistook youthful urges for far more.'

'And she *was* very beautiful,' Juno admitted reluctantly.

'Nowhere near as beautiful as you are,' he said and looked as if he meant it.

She wanted to believe him, but couldn't manage it. 'Everyone said how lovely your wife was and she must have been to lure the boy you were into a hasty marriage. I know I am not a beauty, so keep your empty flattery, my lord.'

'It's not flattery, but I'm not a boy now and can resist temptation if I try hard enough now.'

'You didn't yesterday.'

'You have no idea,' he said and closed his eyes as if trying to shut her out.

'You kissed me and walked away, so it wasn't much of a temptation, was it? You were dallying with me again, weren't you?'

'No, I didn't walk away because I don't want you; I did it because I do.'

'True intimacy requires emotion and you don't want to feel any for me.' He was stubbornly silent and she sighed and shook her head. 'I absolve you from any duty you may feel to the girl I was five years ago and the woman I am now, Lord Grange. I will not marry you for the sake of my good name or yours.'

'I don't have one so do it because you want to,' he urged her.

'And know you are waiting for me to be as big a lightskirt as your late wife? No, thank you; I won't walk in her shadow.'

'You're nothing like her.'

'I know, but you don't.' Tears threatened when he stayed silent and confirmed her worst fears, despite his hot and hungry kisses yesterday. 'Go away, Nathaniel. Do what you always do and leave me to fight my demons alone,' she said coldly.

He looked offended, bowed stiffly and did just that, the great, stupid ox. She heard the door slam behind him and let out a shaky breath. She wanted to sit and weep for the young girl who had fallen so deeply in love with the wrong man five years ago, but it would be a waste of time and tears. Instead, she found a handkerchief, blew her nose and refused to cry any more tears for Lord Grange.

There were plenty of kind and sensible men in the world and it was high time she found one and married him. She might even be glad she had met Nathaniel again in another decade or so now she knew what a mistake it was to go on dreaming of him loving her back.

She opened the window a bare inch to grab some snow from the sill to cool her sore eyes, so the wretched stuff was useful for something. Pard must have followed Nathaniel outside and he needed a walk, but she missed him. Nathaniel obviously liked her pet's company, but she wanted to stay cross with him so how dare he be human? Finally, she was as neat as she could be without a maid, so she drank a cup of the finest China tea and felt almost ready to face the world.

If only the chimneys in the main house had been swept fires could be lit and it would start to come alive, but there was old soot and jackdaw nests to make it too much of a risk so she couldn't be busy in there. She found the boots he must have brought over for her and she wasn't inclined to be grateful as she followed Nathaniel's tracks through the deserted kitchen gardens to see if the horse was still happy.

It wasn't actually snowing at the moment and if only Nathaniel had come home after his uncle died this place could have been neatly tended and smoke would be rising from the bothy and hothouse chimneys. A gaggle of indoor and outdoor servants would be sweeping the paths clear of snow and she hoped they would laugh and throw snowballs because she wanted Nathaniel to be a good and kind employer. It felt wistful for her to have this image of being at His Lordship's side as they joined in the fun. Silly idea, she informed her inner dreamer and shut the door on the walled garden where nothing was stirring except the odd hungry bird, then marched to the stables, careful not to walk in his footsteps this time.

Her skirts were wet, but the horse seemed happy, and Nathaniel had groomed and mucked him out. So, she closed the stable door behind her and wondered what to do next. Building a snowman seemed childish and having a snowball fight with dignified Lord Grange impossible, and he was right about the depth of snow. She could wander through what was left of the pleasure gardens or follow his footsteps and force her company on him, since raiding his late uncle's library for a book didn't appeal and there was nothing else to do. The agent's house was warm and comfortable, of course, but Hedges's malice seemed to linger in every stolen luxury he had squirreled away there so she didn't want to go back yet.

It made sense for her to know where Nathaniel was. They were alone here so she would track him down and go away before he noticed her. His footsteps led around the back of the big house and, as his legs were longer than hers, she had plenty of exercise jumping between them. The wind had piled snow across the lane leading down to the village and she was glad of the path Nathaniel had already cleared, then she rounded a bend in it to see him digging snow as if he was desperate to get away from her. She should take the slap and go back to the agent's house, yet he looked so lonely striking at a drift with an old wooden spade although Pard was digging happily at his side.

Chapter Seven

'You will wear yourselves out,' she said softly.

Pard wagged his tail, but Nathaniel stopped digging and didn't turn to look. Why hadn't she gone away as she had promised herself she would when she tracked him down? Hope, she decided bleakly as it faded and every time he rejected her it hurt more.

'That's the idea,' he told the wall of snow in front of him before facing her with defended dark eyes.

His newly shaven face was so unfairly handsome in the full light of day her heart thumped at his sheer masculine beauty and her breath went shallow again. Did he feel as exposed to her gaze without his beard as she had when he rejected her brazen offer of her body yesterday? She doubted it and turned away.

She had better look for that book after all because she needed to escape from a snowy world where nothing was as she wanted it to be for an hour or two. Her long-cherished fantasy of them being reunited and free to love was only ever a fantasy and he didn't share it.

'I'm sorry I was so forward yesterday and just now. I embarrassed you,' she said stiffly and only because it was cowardly to retreat without saying her piece. She must face facts even if they were painful and painful they were when he looked shocked at her mentioning her unladylike behaviour.

'I'm the one who should apologise,' he said austerely.

'Better forget it happened, then,' she made herself say despite the blush burning her cheeks. 'We can go our separate ways and pretend to be strangers if we ever have to meet again, my lord,' she added coolly.

'Ah, don't, Juno—I could never forget you.'

'However hard you try?'

'I had to last time; I was married and divorced before I was even of age.'

'I would have risked anything, done anything to be with you five years ago.'

'Then why won't you marry me now?'

'Because you have a guilty conscience and don't love me.'

'We can't wipe out who we were five years ago or even now, so of course I feel guilty about wanting you as fiercely as I did.'

Past tense, Juno, remember that.

And guilt felt such a flimsy reason for marriage.

'Forget the past; worry about getting us out of here in time for me to be of use to my family,' she said.

'I was a rogue and you were innocent when I kissed you in the shadows back then, Juno, so how can we pretend it never happened?'

'I kissed you, too, so stop being so damned noble that you set my teeth on edge.'

'And they are such nice teeth as well,' he said with the sudden smile that reminded her why she fell headlong in love with him five years ago.

Even his mane of overlong dark hair suited him ridiculously and maybe his mouth was sterner than it used to be and no longer had a quirk of laughter waiting to break free, but he was even more devastatingly handsome. Yet the years since had drained the hope out of him, and she mourned it with a sidelong glance. He would be irresistible if he ever got it back, but he had grown into his boyish looks even if he lacked the old edge of humour to make him less austere.

He had always been able to make her go weak at the knees

and it seemed unfair that he still did. She scooped up a handful of snow and threw it at him because he was so infuriating, and she was proud of her aim until his snowball hit her throwing arm and of course she had to retaliate. Battle raged and Pard barked delightedly, dashing between them, then digging at the drifts so eagerly most of the snow he dug out flew back at her and she shook it off as best she could.

Nathaniel laughed so hard she redoubled her efforts to cover him in as much snow as she was and suddenly there he was— the laughing, reckless young man she had fallen for so hard five years ago. Joy at the sight and sound of the man he was meant to be threatened to make her dream impossible things again. So, she fought their snowball battle even harder to stop herself saying any more foolish things.

'Pax,' he said at last as she paused for breath and she eyed him warily. 'Pard is worn out,' he added innocently, yet his dark eyes gave him away and of course he wasn't as innocent as he was pretending to be. She looked from his face to her dog panting happily at his new friend's side.

'Hmm,' she said dubiously and was quite right since Nathaniel's next snowball hit her in the face.

'Oh, no, I'm so sorry,' Nathaniel said and strode over to brush snow from her hair and even her eyelashes. 'I didn't mean to do that,' he said huskily, his touch so gentle it warmed her despite the cold snow she shook off her face. She felt her stern hairstyle fall down and must have looked flushed and dishevelled as she blinked up at him.

'I hope you weren't a sharpshooter,' she said shakily.

'No chance of that,' he said ruefully and outlined her brows with his index finger before running a shivery line down her nose and over her mouth, then lifting her chin to persuade her to meet his suddenly serious gaze. 'I feel something deep and real for you, Juno, I always did,' he admitted gruffly, but he didn't look very happy about it so she refused to be flattered. 'But I don't deserve you now any more than I did back then.'

'Did I ask you to, Nathaniel?' she argued softly.

'I would have to be a better man to do so now, though, wouldn't I?'

'You could be good enough as you are if you really wanted to be.'

'Ah, don't, Juno,' he whispered painfully, yet he soothed another shivery line along her jaw, as if his fingers had a mind of their own. 'Please don't tell me you have been waiting for me to come home.'

'I fell deeply in love with the wounded boy you were at nineteen, Nathaniel, so why wouldn't I? And please don't say there wasn't a scratch on you because we both know that's a lie.' She cursed the hurt his late wife had put in his dark eyes, the sad quirk war made in his sensitive mouth when he wasn't trying to hide it with humour.

'Aye, it hurt,' he admitted roughly. 'Dorinda used to say she loved me as much as she could love one man, but it was impossible to settle for just one.'

'She didn't try very hard,' Juno said, feeling cynical again.

'I realised that when I met you, but it was already too late, if only I had had enough sense to know it.'

She wished she hadn't made him serious and sad. He deserved to be the carefree young man he should be, the one who had laughed and thrown snow and enjoyed Pard's company. That man was worth fighting for. 'Why do you make excuses for her?' she asked him.

'Because it was my mistake, too,' he said wearily.

'Was I one?'

'No, you were the wonder I didn't deserve.'

'Yet as I fell in love with you when you were so newly divorced from your late wife, half the guilt is mine.'

'No, you were an innocent—a lovely, lonely girl I should have left in peace as soon as I realised your dark corner wasn't empty.'

'I think you were too kind to do that.'

'Kind to myself, then, and not you.'

'Ah, but I was so lonely, Nathaniel, so bewildered by the world I was pitchforked into so suddenly I couldn't catch my breath. *You* didn't judge me tongue-tied and unworthy of effort like other men and I was always at ease with you. Everyone else thought me such a mouse there was a rumour doing the rounds

I couldn't talk properly and was only pretending to be shy, but I wasn't a mouse with you.'

'What silly young puppies they were and why would you want to know them?' he said and she had to smile because he was younger than most of the gentleman who had ignored and avoided her during her first and only Season.

'When they spoke to me my mouth would go dry and I couldn't think of a single thing to say, yet I could talk to you.'

'Perhaps because you couldn't see me properly in the gloom.'

'No, because you made me feel better and the rest didn't matter.'

'You weren't shy when I kissed you.'

'I grew up in one glorious moment when you kissed me. I was my true self and it was such a lovely surprise not to be the one everyone seemed to think me, so no wonder I kissed you back.'

He chuckled at her remembered astonishment, but sobered too soon. 'I still kissed you in dark corners, then ran off to war. My true self is the worst of rogues and you were wasted on me.'

'No—only think how I would have felt if my first kiss was forced on me by an avid old man, Nathaniel. It would have put me off kissing for life and knowing how it should be gave me courage to run when saying no didn't stop him insisting he was going to marry me whether I wanted to or not. I couldn't let him do the things we did and more, so please stop pretending you bent my life out of shape. You showed me how a kiss should be. I didn't want him spoiling it, so I ran and I'm glad.'

'I could kill him.'

'You would have to stand in line after Uncle Alaric, Darius Yelverton and Sir Harry Marbeck.'

'Why haven't they done so yet?'

'Because I asked them not to.'

'Why?'

'Partly because they have wives and families who would have to flee to the Continent to spend time with them if they were caught duelling and what sort of life would that be for the people I love?'

'*I* don't have a wife or much family.'

Ah, but I love you anyway, her inner Juno insisted, but she told her to be quiet.

'You are nothing to do with me, Lord Grange.'

'Exactly, so nobody will know why I challenged the...' She reached up to stop him saying whatever he was going to call the fat old rogue and Nathaniel confused her by gently nibbling at her fingers with mischief in his dark eyes. Her heart felt as if it was going to turn over with frustrated love for the stupid great oaf.

'I don't want you to have to leave the country before you have hardly got your feet over the threshold because you recklessly fought a man who isn't fit to wipe your boots on,' she said huskily. 'Promise you won't shoot him or do any of the other things I know you are thinking of doing to him, Nathaniel?'

'He should pay for what he tried to do to you, Juno, even if it was with the help of your stony-hearted grandmother and I can't fight her,' he said with such fury in his eyes she felt as if a cold hand had closed around her heart.

She smoothed out the frown from his dark brows with a tender smile she hoped he was too busy being furious to notice. Distracted by seeing his face in the full light of day this close up for the first time, she realised his eyes were a deep moss green, not the dark brown she had always thought.

How strange they had only met in semi-darkness until now, so she hadn't known such an important thing about him. What a luxury to see him with the brightness of reflected snow and the sun trying to peep through a veil of cloud. It did finally break through and shone lovingly on his raven-dark locks to turn them blue-black. She tried to stamp an image of him so alive and unique on her inner eye so she could gloat over it when they had to part again.

'Haven't you heard that the best revenge is to live well?' she said shakily.

'You don't though, do you?'

'I am loved and useful,' she argued. 'I help Uncle Alaric and Marianne to rescue young outcasts as they once did me. I have a purpose in life and a family who love me, so of course I'm happy.'

'Not as happy as you should be. You should not have to do it all alone, Juno.'

'My choice,' she said with a shrug and turned away from his gaze because it had been his choice to leave her solitary when he didn't come home and marry her.

'My blame,' he argued softly.

'Don't think I haven't noticed you didn't promise what I asked,' she said rather than go over the same ground again.

'As long as he stays out of my way, I will stay out of his.'

Chapter Eight

'Not good enough, Nathaniel,' Juno said and held his gaze with a challenge to tell him she wasn't going to let him evade making her that promise.

'He hurt you,' he protested with a fierce frown.

'Not really. I hated being a debutante and evading his unwanted attentions was the push I needed to flee the *ton* and break from my grandmother's control.'

'I hope you aren't trying to say he did you a favour.'

'He did in a way, but he also wed a widow twice my age later that summer and they have a son, so I don't want them to suffer for his sins.'

'Yet the innocent often suffer for the guilty,' he argued.

'For the last time, I am not a wide-eyed innocent. I was very happy to love you when you weren't nearly as cynical as you are now. Promise not to go after him, my lord. I won't get out of your way until you do and my feet are confoundedly cold.'

'Not until you take it back. You *were* an innocent until I came along and...' He tried to say whatever he was going to about his not-quite seduction of the girl she was to his boy, but she clamped her hand over his mouth to stop him again and it could be habit forming.

'Don't you dare say you nearly *despoiled* me,' she said

fiercely before she took it away and tried not to let him know the feel of his mouth under her fingers made her forget how cold it was for a heady moment.

'That stung, did it?' he said with a wry smile.

'Only like a serpent,' she said and turned her head away to refuse to let him laugh her out of that promise. 'Promise me,' she challenged a nearby pile of snow and the cold air.

'I have already promised not to seek him out, but if he says one wrong word about you in my hearing, I won't be able to keep my hands off him.'

'You give with one hand and take away with the other.'

'Apparently I'm good at it, but I'm also human, Juno. I won't promise not to react if he tries to blow on your reputation when his should stink like rotten fish.'

'My uncle dealt with him when he got back from France.'

'I suppose he would.'

'He did, so why don't you trust him to silence the repellent old toad?'

'I suppose I should.'

'Make me that promise, then.'

'Nag,' he teased, so she raised her eyebrows and tried to look superior. 'Ah, very well, then; I promise not to kill him.'

'Or force a quarrel on him so you can wing him in a duel?'

'That as well, if he stays away from me and mine.'

'I'm not yours, though, am I?'

'No.'

'So?'

'Away from you as well, then.'

'And?'

'I won't seek him out if he does so, that's all I can promise.'

'I suppose it will have to do.'

'I almost feel saintly,' he said and how could he think he was cynical and not worth loving when he made her heart flutter and warmth rush through her when they were standing on packed snow and her toes were nearly frozen?

'I wouldn't go that far,' she cautioned.

'No, and it's even colder now the sun has gone in again and you have snow down your neck thanks to my clumsiness.'

'And Pard's paws must be so cold now he has stopped throwing snow at me.'

'Despite being a man and supposedly beyond needing a meal in the middle of the day I could eat for my country,' he said, although she knew he would have gone on digging for hours if she hadn't interfered. What that said about his need to get to the village as fast as possible and hers for him not to she was unwilling to think about too closely.

Once he abandoned his digging and followed her back to the agent's house for a hearty luncheon of potatoes baked in the range, good strong cheese and pickles followed by sweet apples and yet more smoky China tea, Juno hoped for so much from the rest of the day. Instead of sitting with her and wiling away the day as she wished he would, Nathaniel spent it splitting logs and shovelling snow from the paths to the stables and main house.

By the time he finished it was nearly dark, so she hoped for a long winter evening in his company instead, but he took the meal she had cooked while he was busy away to eat in the bleak loft over the stables. She sat in the best kitchen of the agent's house, missing him while she nibbled at her meal without much appetite. He *had* only wanted to marry her to prevent a scandal, then, and she would choose scandal over a loveless union with the man she still couldn't help loving every time.

Pretending to read a book she found in the late Lord Grange's library to pass the time, until she realised it was upside down, she sighed and shook her head at her own stupidity, then let Pard out one last time and banked up the fire before going upstairs to bed. She would try to sleep in the one Nathaniel used on his first night here and what a miserable homecoming that must have been.

If she'd accepted his dutiful proposal earlier today, His Lordship might be with her in this lonely bed right now. She had no doubt he would give her great physical pleasure and she longed to bear his children nearly as much as she ached for him, but not as a duty to her good reputation and his title and lands. But, oh, if only he had waited to meet her instead of marrying Dorinda!

Would a shining youth like dashing Lieutenant Grange have sat out any dances with Juno when they did meet if he wasn't so recently divorced? If he hadn't once eloped with a flirt and brought their marriage to end, he would have been too busy bedazzling more sociable young ladies on the dance floor in his dress uniform. He would not have had any time to spare for shy Juno Defford who hid in gloomy corners. With all those eager young ladies competing for his attention he would never have noticed her at all.

Dissatisfied with her gloomy conclusion, Juno thumped the pillow and wished she had stayed downstairs with Pard. At least there she could listen to him sleeping and watch the quiet glow of the fire. She sighed and closed her eyes again to lie in the dark and try not to think of what might have been, but when she finally drifted off to sleep, she dreamt of Nathaniel as eager and urgent for her as she was for him and what a fine fantasy that was.

It seemed like only minutes later when Pard barked downstairs, so Nathaniel must be out there since Pard sounded excited and not alarmed. She pulled her borrowed gown back on, thankful she had slept in her underclothes, but feeling dishevelled and sleepy as she ran downstairs to let him in and find out why he was knocking so urgently.

'What's the matter?' she asked as soon as she pulled the bolts back. She felt scruffy, when he was as neat as if he had the valet she had twitted him about yesterday and had slept in a fine feather bed, not a stable.

'Good morning, Miss Defford,' he replied coolly, but shadows under his eyes said he hadn't slept as well as she first thought and she was fiercely glad. 'I can hear Jackson and his troops in the distance.'

'Oh, I see,' she said and supposed she did since his ordeal was nearly over. 'I will tidy myself,' she said and went to do so before joining him in the best kitchen.

'I'm sorry,' he said as she walked back in, looking as elegant as she could in his sister's old clothes.

'What for?' she replied distantly, hoping he wasn't going to propose again.

'Being alone here when you arrived so your good name isn't as spotless as it should be.'

'It wasn't spotless to start with, not after I crossed England on my own five years ago, but I never felt as lonely then as I do now.'

'Oh,' was all he said stiffly and they walked to the main house several yards apart. 'Is it my fault?' he asked at last.

'Is what your fault?'

'The loneliness?'

'No,' she lied. 'I expect most women of two and twenty are lonely now and again when they lack a husband or lover.'

'Never mind them—I'm interested in you.'

She shot him a sceptical look. 'So interested you left these shores five years ago and didn't bother to find out if I had married or not when you came home?'

Pard came running up to tell them strangers were on their way and he was here to protect her, so at least she could make a fuss of him and hope she and Nathaniel had nothing left to say to each other because she didn't want him to propose again. It was as cold in the main house as it was outside, but she agreed to wait in the ladies' withdrawing room as if she was only visiting while Nathaniel went to greet Jackson and the villagers and warn them a lady had been forced to take refuge here by the storm. She opened the shutters and uncovered a chair to sit in solitary splendour and wait for her audience like a stray princess.

Jackson turned out to be a small man who exuded energy and by the time it was dark Juno had a maid and mattresses were being aired for her and the master of the house and his man. Jackson had theirs carried up to Lord Grange's unsuitable quarters above the stables as soon as they had been swept and dusted and mopped to his satisfaction, as even he could not magic up a chimney sweep to make it safe for fires to be lit in the main house. As the capable man began to exert control over his master's kingdom, Juno wondered where Nathaniel was, but he turned up at twilight cold and weary and said he had walked down the hill and the lower he got the thinner the snow cover became so they could probably leave tomorrow if it didn't snow in the night.

'*We* can leave?' she asked him with haughty look to argue with that word.

'I can't let you ride on alone, so don't even think about doing so.'

'I am perfectly capable of getting home without your permission.'

'Just as you did the day you set out without any luggage in a blizzard?'

'As I would have if not for the freakish weather you have up here.'

'Of course, it must have been balmy and quite calm down on the Severn Plain and a magic carpet will waft you home without any need to worry about mud or changes of horses or your comfort and safety along the way.'

She wanted to argue her life would be wonderfully easy the moment she got away from here, but knew the roads would be muddy and busy when it was just over a week before Christmas, even if the snowfall was negligible elsewhere. Goods must be got where they were needed for the festive season, travellers would be on their way to family or friends for a solemn Christmas Day churchgoing and eager celebrations after and he was right about her disastrous journey here.

'I know it won't be easy,' she admitted. 'I intend to hire a coach at the next posting inn so there's no need to twit me about riding alone since I know it was folly.'

'True, but you did it for love,' he said as if he understood she loved her family even if he thought she was a fool to risk so much to get home.

Chapter Nine

'My uncle's carriages are still in the carriage house, imagine my surprise, but since all his horses have been sold, I can't lend you one of mine,' Nathaniel said with the bitterness of that loss in his deep voice so he must be really tired.

Juno hated the idea of Hedges getting away with such a heavy blow to Nathaniel's power and pride, but he wouldn't want a man to hang even after stealing the vast amounts the rogue must have taken when his back was turned.

'There's no need for you to worry about me when your house needs putting in order so badly. I'm glad the villagers know it was Hedges who closed it down and put them out of work so he could pocket their wages. You will now have plenty of willing hands to help you restore it back to its former glory.'

'The Grange waited so many years for me to come home that a few days won't make much difference and you're not leaving without me so you might as well resign yourself to my company,' he told her a bit too firmly.

'I can look after myself.'

'As you did on the way here? No, I'm coming with you even if you pretend we are strangers all the way home.'

'We *are* strangers.'

'Liar,' he said softly and, confound the man, he was right—

he wouldn't feel like one of those if they lived apart for the rest of their lives and what a horrid idea.

'You don't want me,' she argued with him anyway.

'Not true.'

'Don't, Nathaniel,' she said, 'and don't you dare propose again.'

'Why not?'

'Because I won't marry you for less than love and you don't believe in it.'

'Don't you love me any more?' he said almost as if he was teasing, but she refused to be joked into the marriage bed even if she still did.

'Irrelevant,' she said stonily and refused to weaken.

'Pretend I'm a cousin or a hired escort, then, but I can't stay here while you battle snow and mud and everyone who will try to take advantage of a lady travelling alone.'

'Hmm, maybe you can be my coachman?' she said slyly and was shocked to see he was taking her flippant comment seriously.

'Excellent idea,' he said smugly. 'Then I can make sure you are not driven into a ditch by a hired one who has taken too much brandy to keep out the cold.'

'I wasn't serious. You're a lord; you can't drive a coach and four.'

'I can, you know; I'm a devil of a fellow. I can drive anything from mule cart to coach and six thanks to my travels and I doubt anyone will recognise me muffled up to the eyes on the box. The more I think about it, the more it looks like an excellent idea, so well done, Miss Defford.'

'Will you stop being so infuriating?'

'Sorry, I was born this way.'

'Indeed you were,' she said between gritted teeth and wondered if she could slip away before anyone was up tomorrow, but it was not the sort of weather for stumbling about in the dark and she didn't know the way. 'My uncle will know you are no coachman,' she cautioned.

'Therefore he will be on my side next time I propose to you.'

'Remember the stocks you said he would have put you in if he knew you had kissed me so often before I fled town five years ago?' He nodded. 'Well, he will throw those stones himself if he finds out you did it again and I won't marry you.'

'You won't tell him I kissed you, then or now,' he said confidently.

'No, I won't,' she admitted with a gusty sigh—he knew her too well.

'Then stop trying to evade my company. I shall stick to you like a burr until you're safely home and then we shall see.'

'Yes, you will see I managed perfectly last time I travelled alone and can do it again,' she muttered, but he must have heard since he frowned and shook his head.

'No, you didn't. You survived and you're not going alone this time,' he said as if that was it: Lord Grange had spoken.

'I won't marry you if you ask me in front of my uncle and half of Herefordshire.'

'That could hurt my lordly pride,' he said as if she might pity him and give in.

'I have told you no often enough for it to be your own fault.'

'Even if you turn me down in front of the entire county and this one as well, I intend to get you home safely, so stop wasting your breath.'

'You could be a complete whipster for all I know.'

'Luckily for you I'm not.'

'So you say,' she said, but he was irresistible in this mood and if only he had it more often they would already be lovers. Laughter fitted the young man he should be so much better than the morose mood he was in when she arrived and was it really only two days ago? It felt as if her whole life had changed since she set out in such a hurry, but it hadn't. Reminded how urgently she needed to get home to find out if Marianne and her baby had survived the birth, she decided to give in and cope with Nathaniel's proposals of marriage purely to stave off scandal when she got there.

'You are a very contrary woman,' Nathaniel told her and it felt better to argue with him than dread bad news when she got home.

'Says the most contrary man I have ever encountered,' she said crossly.

'I will ride behind you and make you conspicuous if you don't accept my escort,' he carried on as if she hadn't spoken.

'My new maid says she can stand whatever the weather throws at us after working on the farms since the old lord died so I won't be alone.'

'She won't protect you from mud and bullies and greedy landlords, so give up, Juno. I'm coming with you even if you take half the village with us.'

'Why?'

'Because you are far too lovely to be safe on the roads. While a maid and a dog won't scare the wolves away, I can.'

'I suppose so,' she said reluctantly. He *was* big enough to put off any man thinking of taking advantage of her or Jessie. Riding to Chantry Old Hall over the hills was one thing, travelling main roads in the cold, mud and bustle was quite another.

'Be ready to leave at first light,' he said. Common sense argued get home as fast as she could and she didn't want to say goodbye to him yet anyway.

'Have I ever told you how infuriating you are?' she said.

'I think we were too busy kissing each other to spare enough breath last time.'

'Don't say that. Someone might hear you.'

'Someone is very welcome to.'

'That would suit you very well, wouldn't it, my lord?'

'It would, my Juno, it most definitely would,' he told her with a mock leer that made her want to laugh again, but she couldn't afford to.

'I was wrong. You're not infuriating, you're maddening, and I still won't marry you.'

'Shame,' he said as if he knew she wanted to, but couldn't trust her heart to him twice unless she knew he truly loved her back.

She wasn't sure she could live without him for the rest of her days anyway. Even if he never said *I love you* she could have his children to love. Maybe mutual interests could be enough as long as she had them with him. Or would it be torture to feel more, love more and always be disappointed when he didn't love her back? If she had never seen Uncle Alaric and Marianne so happily in love, she might accept half-measures, but she had so she must not. Yet the thought of spending the rest of her life without him hurt so much as she went to bed alone again that night to be haunted by those stupid dreams of what might have been if the Fates were kinder.

Jackson and Nathaniel were a formidable team. The newly appointed stable boys had walked Juno's horse to the village the night before, then set out as soon as it was light next morning to very carefully lead the horses down the hill. Juno tried not to be sad she was leaving a neglected old mansion that could easily have been home if Nathaniel truly wanted to marry her. Where the lads stopped to wait for them with the horses there was only a dusting of snow already melting, but it still took all day to reach Worcester, so they had to stay the night.

There hadn't been a carriage to hire on the way there— *'What with it being so near to Christmas and all, my lord*—so Juno had pulled her jockey cap down and kept her head bowed whenever Nathaniel claimed she was his sister. She just hoped none of her uncle's neighbours were on the roads to argue, but everyone seemed far too busy getting where they wanted to be for Christmas to bother much with strangers. She took dinner and breakfast in her bedchamber with Jessie and made sure they both stayed out of sight as much as they could.

Being lodged so close to the cathedral reminded her it was not very long to Christmas Day now and joy would soon break the austerity of Advent. If Marianne and Uncle Alaric's baby had not survived, it would be bleak for everyone at Prospect House. Juno was desperate to find out now they were so close to home.

By the next morning Nathaniel had managed to borrow a chaise and four from an old army friend who lived in a smart town mansion on the outskirts of the city, then he did as he had threatened to and tooled the horses himself, claiming he had promised his friend he would before he agreed to lend his prized team as well as his smart new carriage.

They changed horses in Broadley and Nathaniel took one look at Juno's set face when he tried to suggest they stay the night and accepted her curt refusal. She was tense as a bowstring and trying so hard to be hopeful as they got closer to her home and all the reasons not to be piled on her shoulders.

By the time Nathaniel turned the team into the now-smooth drive twilight was falling. The instant he pulled up his team Juno wrenched the carriage door open and jumped down without waiting for the steps to be lowered. Nathaniel tossed Jackson the reins and leapt from his perch, almost beating Pard in the race to catch up with her.

'Hold up, my Juno,' Nathaniel whispered encouragingly as he put an arm round her waist when she stumbled in her hurry to get to her family. He must be so weary and cold after driving over muddy roads for so long, yet he was supporting *her*? No wonder she loved him, she thought hazily but never mind that now, she needed to know what had happened to Marianne and the baby.

Chapter Ten

'Oh, my goodness, Juno, here you are at last. Where on earth have you *been*?' Miss Donne stood on the steps, scolding as Juno dashed towards her with a complete stranger holding her up. 'We have been so worried about you,' her governess's own former governess said with a sharp look from Juno to her unlikely coachman and back to wonder if they had reason to be concerned.

The noise of their arrival brought grooms running from the stables to attend to their horses and Marianne and Uncle Alaric's latest group of waifs were peering out of the windows of a cosy sitting room where Miss Donne must have ordered them to stay or they would all be out here as well.

'It snowed. We were stuck,' Juno explained tersely. 'What happened?'

'Well—' Miss Donne said, then broke off when Jackson and Jessie appeared behind Juno. 'Maybe you should go first,' she said as if all sorts of mistaken ideas were scurrying about in her busy head.

'Lord Grange; this is Miss Donne, my former governess's former governess and a very dear friend of the family when she is not stalling.'

'How do you do, ma'am?' Nathaniel said with such an elegant bow Miss Donne looked pensive.

'Penelope, Percival and Persephone Parker, Angela Randal and Sophia Black are the ones watching us from that window as if we are exhibits at a fair,' Juno added impatiently. 'And now...?' she said to Miss Donne with a hard look to say stop drawing out the agony.

'Juno! At last.' Fliss Yelverton ran down the steps to hug her former pupil so Nathaniel finally had to let her go.

'Please, Fliss, just tell me what's happened,' Juno begged.

'You might not believe it, I'm still not sure I do,' her uncle's voice interrupted from the top of the steps and he didn't *sound* broken-hearted.

'Believe what?' Juno said impatiently.

'Two of them, Niece.'

'Two what?' she snapped before his words sank in and wonder took the place of acute anxiety at long last. 'Two *babies*?'

'No, ostriches,' Uncle Alaric said, then shrugged to let her know he was still in shock. 'Of course two babies—twins.'

'What sort?' she managed to say.

'Oh, you know, the usual,' her annoying uncle said with a broad grin. 'Two legs, two arms, the right bits in the right places.'

'Which bits?'

'Well, really, Juno! One of us should have taught you better than that,' Miss Donne scolded and chivvied them up the steps so they could start to get warm and at least see each other's faces in the brightly lit hall.

'One of each,' Viscount Stratford told Juno with a very proud smile as soon as the door was shut behind them. 'My Marianne has done it again; she has given us an instant family to go with our first proper home. She's a woman in a million,' he told Juno with a wide gesture at the fire burning in the hearth and polished panelling reflecting the candlelight where it wasn't covered in greenery or bright berries and China oranges and knots of ribbons in red and gold ready for the Christmas season.

'Oh, Uncle Alaric, I'm so pleased for you both! And now I

have *two* little cousins to boss around, and a boy and a girl as well. Clever, clever Marianne.'

'It was a joint effort and you'll be more aunt than cousin, love, but if you think you're being introduced to them in that state and without an explanation of where you have been first you had best think again.'

Fliss just smiled as if she hadn't stopped since the Defford twins were born safely. Even the sight of her former pupil dressed in clothes a decade out of date and accompanied by a mysterious lord couldn't stop her delight that Alaric and Marianne had a family of their own to spoil now.

'We *do* need baths, a warm fire and something to eat,' Juno said, hoping to put off the explanation her uncle demanded.

'You do,' her uncle said silkily and eyed Nathaniel frostily.

'Lord Grange was kind enough to drive me home after I was stranded at his house while trying to cross the hills to Chantry Old Hall in a snowstorm,' she said, hoping Nathaniel's travel-worn state would soften her uncle's stern gaze.

'Lord Stratford,' Nathaniel said with an elegant bow in return to her uncle's curt nod.

'I didn't know you were back in the country, Grange. I hope you will take your responsibilities more seriously now you are finally home.'

'I will, although I have hardly had time to get the full measure of them yet.'

'You were home in time to meet my niece though, weren't you?'

'Indeed, I had that privilege,' Nathaniel lied stiffly.

Juno wanted to bang their heads together for acting like a pair of stiff-legged dogs getting ready to fight for dominance. 'His Lordship rescued me from a blizzard and insisted on seeing me safely home as soon as it was safe to travel,' she said to try and stop them doing something stupid to one another.

'What the devil were you doing riding alone, Juno?' her uncle demanded sharply.

'Trying to get here as soon as I could after reading your dour letter and it was barely seven miles to Chantry Old Hall so it should not have taken long.'

'It might not in the summer, but you could have died from exposure in a storm as fierce as the one Harry and Viola described as they dashed down their hill ahead of it to get here in a hurry.'

'What did you expect me to do, sit in my godmother's house twiddling my thumbs while we waited for your next gloomy message? Begging a place in their carriage was the fastest way to get here.'

'I should never have sent one to you as well,' Uncle Alaric said, clearly embarrassed about his panicked despair for Marianne and their unborn child when he sent them.

'The babies were born a month early nevertheless,' she said, feeling anxious again as twins were usually smaller than single babies so premature ones must be tiny and so vulnerable.

'Probably not, according to the midwife; she thinks they were barely a fortnight less than full term and we are a pair of nodcocks who can't add up. Apparently twins often come early since there isn't enough room in there for both of them, if you see what I mean.'

Juno smiled and shook her head. 'Oddly enough I do, but you really aren't very good at explaining your instant family to the one you already have.'

'I'm not, am I?' he said, forgetting to be suspicious of Nathaniel in his overriding joy at being a father. 'Marianne wants to be up and about again, but the doctor forbade it for at least a week, although I'll lay you odds she won't stay there for Christmas.'

'I would not take them, but that's why I'm here. I can order a household nearly as well as she can now, so she has no excuse to be up and doing too soon,' Fliss said.

'You had best go and tell her so again, then, and explain why there is such a fuss down here before she gets up to find out for herself,' Uncle Alaric said with an anxious glance upstairs.

'I wish Darius was here,' Fliss said wistfully, 'she might listen to her brother.'

'She might,' Uncle Alaric said doubtfully.

'Where is he?' Juno asked.

'Playing host to Sir Harry and Viola at Owlet Manor since a

houseful of guests would only make Marianne more likely to ignore the doctor's orders.'

'I will take my leave, then, Your Lordship, Mrs Yelverton, Ma'am,' Nathaniel said and Juno was amazed he had been a silent spectator for so long.

'As you have only just returned home you cannot have made arrangements for the Christmas season, Grange, so I hope you will come back and join us for ours,' her uncle said, sounding so smoothly chilly Juno shivered on Nathaniel's behalf. 'You have done us a great favour by giving my niece shelter in her hour of need, then seeing her safely home, so we really must insist on sharing our celebrations with you to say thank you.'

Nathaniel bowed silent assent and Juno shivered again at the manly glare the two men exchanged under cover of being painfully polite to one another. It made her feel furious with both of them, but Nathaniel was gone before she could tell him so and her uncle was far too pleased with himself to listen to her reproaches when he came back inside from seeing his unexpected visitor off in every sense of the words.

The twins were delightful, when they weren't crying, or hungry or smelly, which their doting mama accused one or the other of being most of the time. Marianne was so besotted with them she was even jealous when Fliss, Juno or their father whisked a twin off to be changed. Juno supposed it was the privilege of the wealthy to have nannies to do the bathing and changing and one she would gladly enjoy if she ever had a baby herself, but best not think about that now.

It promised to be the most joyous Christmas season the Defford family had experience in living memory, with two healthy and usually happy babies sleeping in Lord Stratford's dressing room, since their parents refused to banish them to the nursery. Yet Juno missed Nathaniel so badly it was hard to be as happy as she should be. She even missed him pretending to be immune to deeply felt emotions and every day had expected a letter to arrive saying Lord Grange would be unable to join them for Christmas after all.

* * *

By the day before Christmas Eve, it still had not arrived and she almost began to believe he would turn up as ordered.

'You're so sad, Juno,' Fliss said when she found her in the still room where she was hiding from all the excitement.

'No, I have a headache.'

'It wasn't a question, my love. Something happened when you were lost in the snow and I know you don't want to talk about it, but I love you too much not to try to. Are you pining for Lord Grange?'

'Of course not—he's the most infuriating, stubborn, wrong-headed man I have ever met. I don't miss him and I never have.'

Oh, curse it, her tongue had run away with her and now Fliss knew more about Juno and Nathaniel Grange than she wanted her to.

'Ah, so I was right; you two *have* met before.'

'We were barely acquainted five years ago,' Juno said and what a loose tongue she had today.

'A few minutes can be long enough,' Fliss said and maybe they were for her and Darius, but there wasn't going to be a happy ending for Juno.

'Not for him.'

'Tell me,' Fliss urged quietly. 'You know I will keep your secrets and Darius has always understood that, so please don't accuse me of telling him in advance.'

It was a relief to shut the door on the rest of the world and tell someone who loved her the secret she had kept for so long.

'So you loved him five years ago?'

'Yes, I couldn't help myself. He lit up my world.'

'That's a hard feeling to lose and now I know why you were so sad and quiet the year we three were busy finding our own particular Yelvertons to love. I thought there was more to it than your grandmother's appalling behaviour and the shock of escaping from that awful old man on your own.'

'I missed Nathaniel so much, Fliss. I hated thinking he might be killed so far away and I would be the last one to know.'

'No wonder you didn't want another Season in town and

were set on making a life alone, but why can't you be happy with Lord Grange instead?'

'Because he wasn't here; he didn't come for me after Waterloo or when his ex-wife died, so he can't have loved me. He wouldn't make love to me last week either and that proves it.'

Juno didn't blush and Fliss didn't pretend to be shocked. They were not pupil and governess any more, but two adult women who knew too much about love and life to bother with false modesty.

'Men are such stiff-necked idiots when they decide they are not good enough—or rich enough—for us, as my daft love convinced himself he wasn't for me; as if we care about such things as long as they love us back and never stop.'

'He doesn't want to, Fliss. He thinks I would grow bored with him just as his late wife did, but she was a fool and he's all I have ever wanted. I love the great gruff idiot, but he doesn't even want to love me back.'

'Prove to him he's an idiot then, fight for him.'

'I already have, but she's won, Fliss. His late wife's ghost whispered *Look what happened when we married for so-called love* and he listened to it. I hate her for making him doubt himself and he just won't see that I can't help loving him. I would have stopped long ago if willing it away would work.'

'What fools men can be, Juno, love,' Fliss said and held Juno when she finally let herself cry for the young love that she had kept a secret for so long.

'Oh, Fliss, why does love hurt so much?' she wailed for a desolate moment, then heard herself being melodramatic and gave a watery chuckle. 'Because it *is* love, I suppose, and that is always a risk.'

'Very young men can be hurt so badly, despite their manly defences, Juno,' Fliss said gently, 'and Lord Grange had to protect himself from his wife's infidelities at such a young age he must have been hurt more than most of them can imagine. I don't know him, but I can tell he feels something powerful for you and don't look at me as if I don't know what I'm talking about. He wasn't acting like a man who doesn't care when he brought you home. He hardly took his eyes off you the entire time he was here and Alaric tried very hard to capture his attention with his stiff-necked comments and suspicions.'

'Truly?'

'When he turns up in answer to your uncle's lordly summons, ask who else was here but you and your uncle that day. I'll lay you long odds he has no idea.'

'He only wanted to marry me to avoid a scandal when news gets out that we were stuck in his snowbound old house for two days and nights without a chaperon.'

'He's made a fine mull of things, then, hasn't he? I know he has strong feelings for you, whether he wants to admit to them or not, Juno.'

'I won't marry him to silence the scandalmongers.'

'I don't think you will have to, but I shall cross my fingers and hope he has looked into his heart since he left you here to stew.'

'That's just what he has done, isn't it? The conniving wretch.'

'Now I think he's rather a clever wretch since it seems to be working.'

'It's all right for you to think so since you're not in love with him,' Juno said grumpily.

Chapter Eleven

Nathaniel arrived on Christmas Eve looking fine and fashionable and quite unlike the gruff bear she first met again at The Grange in the snow, or the weary travel-stained giant who drove here last week. Juno's heartbeat skipped at the sight of him looking as close to a model gentleman as he could manage in such a short time.

He also looked very serious and a little nervous when Uncle Alaric bade him welcome, almost looking as if he meant it. Nathaniel looked ominously like an honourable gentleman come to propose marriage to a lady he had compromised and somehow Juno had to stop him doing that again.

She had already weathered a thundering scold after confessing she had refused Nathaniel's dutiful offer of marriage to save her good name. She could tell she wasn't forgiven for that refusal yet when Uncle Alaric told Nathaniel he was very welcome with a sharp look in her direction. He had changed his tune, hadn't he?

Juno sighed when they went off together pretending gentlemen didn't have time to eat between breakfast and dinner by way of the kitchen. She didn't eat much of her own luncheon since she couldn't force it past the tightness in her throat. Fliss had gone home to spend Christmas Day with her brood and

Viola and Harry had done the same thing. Juno ate with the children and Miss Donne, who claimed someone must keep the children occupied, so she might as well stay and do so since everyone was so busy with the babies.

Miss Donne obviously didn't need her help, so Juno wandered out into the winter garden trying not to feel lonely and rather forlorn. Here and there faint signs of new life were showing—primroses and violets were starting to grow and a robin sang from the top of an ancient holly tree.

It had been dry all week so she sat on the steps in front of the summer house and wondered why it wasn't a winter house. With nothing else to distract her she let out a pent-up breath and tried to compose her thoughts. It was the Defford twins' first Christmas and she had to hide this edgy tension somehow, so maybe being still for a while might calm her enough to act as if Nathaniel was a chance-met acquaintance.

'What a heavy sigh,' the man himself said so close by she wondered how such a big man could move so silently. Her heart was beating so fast she couldn't think of anything to say when he swirled his heavy old army cloak off his shoulders and gestured for her to sit on it before he joined her. 'It's too cold for us to shiver on opposite sides of the garden,' he said with a smile in his eyes that made her heart threaten to turn over and it ought to know better by now.

'You will be cold without a cloak.'

'I hope not,' he said and looked as if he was the one with an attack of nerves this time. It softened her determination not to listen to his latest offer of marriage. 'For a man who hates to waste words, your uncle can be very eloquent,' he added ruefully.

'What has he been saying?' she said warily.

'Nothing I haven't told myself ever since I left last week and he's right: I am a coward for not risking being hurt again. You are the opposite of Dorinda in every way I can think of. I love you, Juno. I have loved you from the moment I first laid eyes on you pretending you were quite happy in your hiding place. My life had a purpose again and that was to persuade you it was safe to love me. No, please don't interrupt; Stratford says I need to clear my slate and he's far too terrifying to argue with when he's intent on protecting his beloved niece.'

'But you only ever needed to say you still love me, Nathaniel. It's all I ever needed you to say, but you didn't when it mattered, so why should I believe you now?'

'Because I have been a fool for such a long time?' he said wryly. She was so tempted to give in to the leap of joy in her heart, but she hardly dared trust her own ears when they were desperate for the words.

'That's true,' she said.

'I'm trying to be humble, Juno.'

'Oh, is that what it is?'

'I am a fool,' he said doggedly. 'I loved you, but I thought we needed to wait until the scandal of my divorce had died down so I could court you in form.'

'I would rather you had just loved me,' she said.

'Maybe later,' he said and his dear eyes were full of emotion at last and his pretending-not-to-be-sensitive mouth was smiling wickedly and this felt real.

'Maybe,' she whispered and her world had suddenly turned the right way up again. She saw love and heat openly in his darkest of green eyes at last. Had the daft great bear truly loved her all along? A cold and lonely place inside her warmed and settled, even if he was an honourable great fool to have stayed away so long.

'Where was I?' he said shakily, as if he could hardly believe happiness was within touching distance either and didn't want to risk ruining it.

'Being a fool,' she reminded him.

'Ah, yes, I dreamed of you all the way across the Atlantic Ocean and back. On the eve of the Battle of Waterloo I sat in the rain and mud and all I could think of was how much I missed you.'

'While I was nibbling my fingernails to the quick worrying about you and then you were wounded—' She stopped, because seeing his name among the wounded had been the worst moment of her life so far. Never mind having to flee her grandmother's wicked plans for her, that was the day she knew something important inside her would die if Nathaniel failed to recover. He silently reached for her hand as if he had needed her as much as she had him. 'I ached for you,' she said simply.

He gave her the wry grin that always made her heart race. 'Me, too,' he said, then seemed to go into himself as he recalled that terrible time again. 'I saw things at Waterloo I can never forget, Juno. My men fell around me before I took that bullet and I will only admit to you how glad I was to be excused from the slaughter. I could not come home to you when I had such nightmares and dark moods it would have been a kind of hell to live with me.'

'As if living without you was not,' she said. His emotions were so fiercely felt it must have hurt him to hold them inside and wander the Continent until some of the horror receded. 'I wish you had let me share it, Nathaniel; love isn't just for the good days, or it wouldn't be love.'

'How could I offer you shouts in the night and a husband who couldn't tell the difference between remembered horrors and his own wife if I had dared to sleep next to you and risk fighting the enemy again in my dreams?'

'Ah, my love, you have suffered so much, but I would have said yes to any and all of it. I would have gone with you on your travels if it helped you fight your demons. I would live anywhere with you rather than be so lonely again without you.'

'Oh, love, you humble me,' he said shakily. 'Did you really miss me so much?'

'Only as if I lost half of myself and nothing felt quite real without you.'

'Me, too, as if I had lost an arm or a leg.'

'Ah, my love, you are such an idiot to have left us both so lonely for so long and I'm not sure you deserve me, but I will love you until my dying day and don't you dare go away again.'

'What would my life be without you, love? I know I don't deserve you, but will you marry me anyway?'

'Oh, very well then, as we love one another I might as well.'

'Ah, at last—you are showing some common sense, my love. Tomorrow will suit me and the Reverend Yelverton assures me he has one more Christmas marriage left in him so it might as well be ours, since he and Mrs Yelverton are staying at Owlet Manor and I have a special licence burning a hole in my pocket, so will you marry me in haste, love?'

'I don't have a wedding gown or any of the things brides are supposed to have like guests and attendants and bride cakes.'

'You will have me and I'll have you. What else do we need?'

'Nothing,' she said blissfully and he kissed her until words faded away and only feelings mattered.

It was such a happy Christmas Day after all and Juno loved every minute of her scratch wedding. She wore the deep red velvet gown she had been keeping for the day without realising it was perfect for a Christmas wedding. Her uncle gave her away; Fliss and Darius were their witnesses and Jackson Nathaniel's groomsman.

'I love you, Juno Grange, so much I can't find words for how happy you have just made me,' her groom said as they walked down the aisle together as man and wife.

'And I love you, despite your poor vocabulary and shameful tardiness, my lord,' she teased and smiled blissfully back at him.

'You're never going to let me forget that, are you?'

'No, a wife needs some advantages, what with this being such an unfair world for us females.'

'You will never be less than my equal, Juno,' he promised solemnly and then his wonderful smile broke out again and he halted her for another kiss.

'It's all very well for you two billing and cooing like lovebirds, but the rest of us want to be in the warm again,' her uncle said from behind them, but everyone knew it wasn't the cold making him impatient; he wanted to be with his beloved family on this day of days. So Reverend and Mrs Yelverton, Darius and Fliss went back to their Christmas dinner and the bridal party sped off for Prospect House, where Marianne and the babies and their rescued waifs waited for their Christmas dinner and a wedding breakfast combined and Juno wondered if the dear old house had ever witnessed such a joyful Christmas as this one.

A year later

'Happy anniversary, Lady Grange.'

'It is, isn't it?' Juno felt so loved and contented when her husband's warm arms pulled her back against his great body as he caressed her baby bump, feeling their child kick, and his deep hum of happiness said more than words about his state of mind. 'I thought last Christmas could not be bettered, but I was wrong,' she added dreamily.

'Just over a year ago this house was cold as charity and so was I, but just look at us now, my love. Look what you did,' Nathaniel said.

'Look what we did,' she corrected and snuggled even closer into his warmth and strength. 'It is very fine now, though, isn't it?'

'Nowhere near as fine as you are, my lady,' he murmured in her ear and she snatched a quick look around them to see if anyone else had noticed, but amid the chaos and chatter of a large family Christmas everyone was too busy, or maybe too tactful, to watch their host and hostess very closely.

'I was cold, too, Nathaniel, cold and lost and now...' Words failed her for a moment as sheer happiness made tears threaten and that would have him in a fine tizzy now she was so big with child. 'Now I have you,' she said huskily, 'and the Bump,' she added with a rueful smile as her hand joined one of his on her great belly.

She felt dreamily content as she watched the children her family already rejoiced in chase the twins, who were determined to explore every inch of The Grange's spotless great hall decked out with evergreens and gilded fruits and warmed by the vast Yule log that was only the latest one to burn on the hearths to make sure it was warm enough for the babies.

'I feel even more of a fool for staying away and making you lonely as well now we have all this, love,' Nathaniel told her.

'Don't, we were too young to live well with this much love. We both needed to grow up a little to realise how precious it is.'

'I certainly did,' he said dourly.

'No, you needed to heal.'

'What I really needed was you, if only I had been clever enough to realise it.'

'And now you have me,' she said with a purr in her voice, 'in every sense.'

'Behave yourself, my Juno,' he said with his body telling her how happy it was about all those senses.

'I don't think it's me we should worry about right now,' she said.

'No, you will have to stay where you are to hide my delight in my wife and our coming child while we talk about snow-storms to cool my ardour.'

'I don't think that will help much,' she said, memory of the one that had forced them together again making her feel a little too delighted about him as well.

'I think it's time you had a nice rest, given your condition and the strain of playing the perfect hostess.'

'What's your excuse?'

'Love,' he said and it worked.

* * * * *

Their Convenient Christmas Betrothal

Amanda McCabe

MILLS & BOON

Books by Amanda McCabe

Harlequin Historical

The Demure Miss Manning
The Queen's Christmas Summons
"His Mistletoe Lady"
in *Tudor Christmas Tidings*
A Manhattan Heiress in Paris
"A Convenient Winter Wedding"
in *A Gilded Age Christmas*

Debutantes in Paris

Secrets of a Wallflower
The Governess's Convenient Marriage
Miss Fortescue's Protector in Paris

Dollar Duchesses

His Unlikely Duchess
Playing the Duke's Fiancée
Winning Back His Duchess

Matchmakers of Bath

The Earl's Cinderella Countess

Visit the Author Profile page
at millsandboon.com.au for more titles.

Amanda McCabe wrote her first romance at sixteen—a vast historical epic starring all her friends as the characters, written secretly during algebra class! She's never since used algebra, but her books have been nominated for many awards, including the RITA® Award, Booksellers' Best Award, National Readers' Choice Award and the HOLT Medallion. In her spare time, she loves taking dance classes and collecting travel souvenirs. Amanda lives in New Mexico. Visit her at ammandamccabe.com.

Author Note

Welcome back to the world of the St. Aubin sisters and their matchmaking adventures! I am so excited to be here again. One of my very favorite spots to visit is Bath, which is full of Regency atmosphere with its beautiful honey-colored buildings, elegant crescents and glorious gardens. Having tea, listening to the chamber music and people watching at the Pump Room is glorious! I love to imagine Ella and Mary there, scoping out matches, gossiping with their friends—flirting with their romances.

I also love it because of its echoes of Jane Austen. Even though she really disliked living there, to me it seems like a place where her characters could belong. My favorite of her books (maybe because it was the first I read?) is *Emma*, and I always giggle at Emma's terrible judgment in making matches for her friends and planning their lives. I started to wonder—what if someone like her was *good* at seeing who belonged with whom? What if those ladies could actually make their way in the world by helping others find happiness? They don't expect, or maybe even want, that happiness for themselves, but of course it finds them. This is how the St. Aubin sisters came into being...

I hope you enjoy their world! And look out for Sandrine's story, to come soon...

Prologue

Bath, England,
1817

Charles Campbell had no right to look so very handsome.

Mary St Aubin half hid behind the table of cake and sweets at her sister's garden wedding breakfast to stare without being seen as silly. She did *feel* rather silly—she was not known to be shy at all, with her love of parties and people, which had great advantages when making matches at the St Aubin and Briggs Confidential Agency. Yet ever since she'd met Charles Campbell at an assembly, each time he was near she turned into a blushing, tongue-tied miss.

But really, who could blame her? she thought as she looked up and up his long legs in buff breeches, then across his broad shoulders perfectly outlined in a dark blue coat. A strong jaw and dimpled chin above a simply tied, snowy cravat, pinned with an amethyst thistle. A blade of a nose, sharp cheekbones, sun-browned skin and vivid, bright green eyes. His dark hair, a bit too long for fashion, waved across his brow, carelessly swept aside. He was perfect.

He chatted with the bridegroom, their old friend and neighbour and now Ella's besotted husband, Frederick, Lord Fleetwood, and Fred's stepmother Penelope Oliver, laughing in the sunlight. The golden happiness of the day cast a glow over everyone, and Charles was no exception. She could have vowed that all the light was gathered only on him.

She hadn't been able to cease thinking about him for days. They saw each other often in Bath. At teas and garden parties, dances, cricket games, at the shops where he was accompanied by his young ward Adele Stewart. She had dared to try to get him to dance once, only to be turned away laughingly, but they often talked and walked together, and his scent of bergamot soap and sunshine made her dizzy with delight.

Ella sometimes mused on finding him a suitable wife through the agency. There were whispers of unhappiness in his past, a youthful marriage that somehow went awry. Sometimes she saw such shadows across his face when he thought no one was watching, and she longed to go to him, to make him laugh as the old Mary would. The Mary who went to parties and was careless of much else. But now Ella was leaving, and Mary was in charge of the agency and its future. She could not impulsively run to handsome gentlemen and hug them.

And they said he was returning to his estate in Scotland soon, leaving Bath. It made her so sad to think of never seeing him again, not having his presence to watch for at parties, not hearing his laughter.

She studied him carefully, as if she could memorise him for the greyer days ahead. The way he brushed his hair back, tilted his head as he listened to conversation, a small crease between his eyes.

He suddenly turned—and caught her staring, too late for her to run away. His smile widened, that dimple appearing in his chin, and she almost melted. To her shock, he excused himself from Pen and Fred and started across the garden, towards Mary, his steps lazy and long, his smile never fading.

'Miss St Aubin,' he said, his deep, chocolate velvet voice touched with a Scots brogue. 'What a splendid day for a wedding.'

Mary made herself smile carelessly in answer, trying not

to be nervous, not to blush and stammer. 'Indeed it is. Perfect, just as Ella deserves.'

She glanced at her sister and new brother-in-law, holding hands as they moved among their guests, smiling into each other's eyes as if they saw nothing else. Mary turned and strolled in the other direction towards a garden maze and was surprised and quite pleased when Charles went with her.

'They are a lovely couple,' Charles said. Mary thought he sounded wistful, his eyes unreadable as he studied the newlyweds. Did he think of his own lost wife? Her heart ached at the thought.

'Yes. They always have been, since we were young and ran through the woods together like a pack of wildings,' she said with a laugh, hoping to make him smile. 'Those were fun times! My father, being an ever so respectable vicar, was quite in despair of our manners. But he never needed to be so with Ella, she was always so perfect. So caring and unselfish.' Mary thought of all the times Ella had comforted her, reassured her, soothed her, laughed with her, and soon Ella would be gone.

Charles must have seen something of her thoughts. 'You will miss her,' he said simply.

Mary blinked up at him. He did always seem to *see* her every time they talked. Saw what she did not say. 'Yes, I shall. She has been like a mother to me for so long, as well as a friend. But I am overjoyed to see her so happy now. She above everyone deserves such love.'

'Doesn't everyone deserve love? That is what Penelope says your agency does—finds everyone their best match.'

'Yes, indeed,' she said, surprised he knew about the agency. 'Especially people who, for one reason or another, have—shall we say—extraordinary needs. Want a little something more, more understanding, perhaps. We can give a bit of assistance in finding their other halves.'

'Very intriguing.' As he listened to her carefully, watched her unwaveringly, she felt her confidence grow. She forgot to feel flustered around him and just saw—well, saw *him*. 'You must meet such fascinating people.'

'Oh, yes! There was a botanist who wanted someone to share

his love of his hothouses, a historian who married a novelist who wrote medieval stories, people who are shy or have too many cats or too large a house. Everyone has a tale to tell, hopes and fears and dreams.' She told him about a few more of their more interesting clients, revelling in his laughter, his attention, which never wavered.

She looked out over the wedding party, the guests, the cake and the ribbon streamers, heard the laughter. It was a wonderful day, one for friends and hope.

'Do you ever wish for such agency assistance for yourself?' he asked, his head tilted in interest.

'No, not at all,' Mary answered. And she did not. The work was what she loved, what she craved, and she couldn't bear the thought of losing it.

Mary often thought of those awful days when her mother was dying. How she was just a child but would sit beside Mama and bathe her brow and hold her hand, listening to her murmured words as Ella and the nurse hurried about looking for medicine and clean towels. As her father sat in his library, unable to cope with what was happening to his own family just above his head in the room that smelled of camphor and sweat. Mary thought if she held on to her mother tight enough, she couldn't leave.

But then her mother opened her eyes and whispered to Mary, 'My dear girl. My beauty. I see myself in your eyes now, your passion and longing for merriment, and your anger. At your father?'

Mary couldn't bear to nod, to tell her mother of her real anger towards her father for abandoning them at this moment. She blinked back the tears and tried not to show those terrible feelings. 'I shall curb my passion, Mama, I promise!'

Her mother shook her head. 'No, never do that! It's what will make your life an adventure, my darling. But do not trust in men. Trust only in yourself. Your father—his work has always come first. I understood that when I married a clergyman. You must follow a different path. Promise me!'

Mary, frightened, shaken, had no idea what another path could be, yet she had agreed. What else could she do? And then her mother was gone.

Mary had only Ella after that, their father disappearing into his work more and more. Work and family did not seem to mix, Mary thought. Ella had sacrificed so much to be both mother and sister to Mary, to love and raise her. Then they had their own work, and Mary loved it. The agency gave them both what they needed...craved—security and control in a world where both were in such short supply. Just as their mother had said.

Mary had once cherished romantic dreams, it was true. She'd read poetry and fantasised about fair maidens and rescuing knights, about eternal love. Those faded away in the real world, and whenever her old self beckoned, she pushed her back. She couldn't feel that way again, couldn't take that risk.

But when she was near him, she was tempted indeed. 'I like to help others. We could certainly be of assistance to *you*, if you needed it.' She swallowed hard, wondering why she had said that. Helping him find a match was the last thing she wanted to do! Yet, she had told him the truth—she liked to help people find their happiness. If he needed that help...

He looked appalled. 'No, I am not good husband material, I fear. I must concentrate on my estate right now and on helping Adele.'

'Of course you are husband material!' Mary cried.

He was the most husbandly man she'd ever seen.

His dark brow quirked as he looked down at her. 'Do you think so?'

'Yes, of course. You are—are...' Handsome. Dreamy. Strong. 'You have every quality we look for in our clients. I promise you, ladies would clamour for your attentions.' Just as she did. 'You are as handsome as a medieval knight, kind and charming.'

He reached for her hand, holding it lightly on his palm as if it were a precious jewel. He stared down at it, his eyes darkened, and she found she could not quite breathe.

'How *douce* you are, Miss St Aubin,' he said quietly, roughly. 'I doubt anyone has ever seen me quite like that before.'

'How could they not?' She couldn't bear to go on. She went up on tiptoe and impulsively pressed her lips to his, longing to know what he tasted like, what he felt like. His lips were warm, surprisingly soft, and he tasted of champagne and strawberries. Warm, so warm, so inviting.

Shocked at herself, she stepped back, staring up at him. He looked just as surprised, his green eyes wide, lips parted.

'I will take that wonderful feeling all the way back to Scotland with me,' he said hoarsely.

Mary wanted only to sink down into the grass and disappear. Now she would never, ever be able to forget him!

She had no idea what to do, so she spun around and ran away. Surely she would not ever see him again.

Chapter One

Bath,
December 1818

'Mary! If I come in here to find you working late again, I shall—I shall…' Eleanor, Countess of Fleetwood, paused on the threshold of the offices for the St Aubin and Briggs Confidential Agency, and stomped her satin evening slipper.

Mary St Aubin put down her pencil to laugh at her sister. Ella had always been so sensible and soft-spoken, angelic in her steady temper and always, always responsible. Never one to stop someone from working or ever stomp her foot.

Over a year of marriage to her darling Fred seemed to have changed all that. She was still the kindest heart in the world, but there was a lightness about her now, a glowing happiness, a constant smile. It was wonderful to see. Now it was Mary, the one who used to always be ready for a lively dance or a game of cards, who was constantly working.

'You shall—what?' Mary said. 'Send me to bed with no supper, as you did when we lived at the vicarage?' Their mother had died so young, leaving Ella in charge, raising her sister and looking after their disorganised father.

Ella stooped to greet Miss Muffins, their exuberant terrier

puppy, who lived with Mary now in the rooms above the office across from the Abbey. Miss Muffins rolled around wildly, leaving traces of pale fur on Ella's velvet evening cloak. 'I would do just that if I thought it would do some good!'

'And I would go.' Mary sighed as she scanned the close-written lines of the account book. 'An early night sounds heavenly after trying to fathom these figures all day.'

Ella frowned and hurried across the room past cabinets filled with files detailing patrons seeking their perfect matches, past pale green brocade-covered settees and armchairs, marble-topped tables holding silver vases of white hothouse roses. Every detail meant to create a sense of serene and happy romance, of a prosperous business. She ignored the view of the Abbey outside the windows draped in yellow silk, the dark blue purple of night drawing closer. 'Is it so very amiss, then?'

'I am not sure what is happening.' The agency, once so busy when Ella and their friend Harriet had been in charge, with a waiting list of patrons who had come to them seeking their perfect spouses, had grown quieter in the last few months. 'We've had fewer new patrons lately. Since you and Harry both wed, and Harry went to live in Brighton, I think. Perhaps I am simply a terrible businesswoman!'

'That is certainly not true. Look at all the couples we have helped! All thanks to you and your intuition! You are so good with people, so good at reading what they need deep down inside.' Ella leaned over the desk to study the ledger. 'It must be a slow time of year, that's all. With the Christmas festivities approaching...'

'It's not that. Christmas has always been rather busy for us before. All those cosy thoughts of family, plum puddings and carols at the pianoforte while the domestic hearth crackles and children open their gifts.' She tapped the end of her pencil against the parchment. 'I think I might have an idea.'

Ella studied Mary carefully, as if she could see past any words to Mary's deepest worries. Mary had never been able to hide from her sister. 'What is it, then?'

'It was something Lady Anstruther said to me when we met at the Pump Room, on our morning visit to see the newcomers to town and pretend to sample the waters. Everyone goes there, you know, in Bath! I was so hoping she would seek our help for her niece. She had concerns about our "knowledge of such delicate subjects." Just gossip, of course, but after that I noticed a few other people who had expressed interest in a match avoiding me. It is my...lack of knowledge of marriage, I am sure. Marriage of my own.' Mary was not used to people avoiding her. She loved parties, conversation, loved her work.

'How perfectly absurd of them!' Ella cried, making Miss Muffins bark. 'You have been the only reason the agency was heard of at all. You are so good at listening to people, so gifted in seeing what they need in a match. Where would the Martin-Bellinghams be without you? Lord and Lady Langham? And dozens of others.' Ella stomped her foot again. 'Perhaps I should come back to the offices for a time. Just to help you a bit.'

'No! You're not often in Bath now, and when you are, you should enjoy yourself for a change. You have Fred and the twins, and Moulton Magna, to look after, and you've been looking forward to Christmas there this year.'

Moulton Magna was Fred's grand but rather ramshackle earldom estate, and it needed Ella's elegant, steadying hand as it revived after Fred's father's long years of neglect. And the twins, Annabelle and Edward, were crawling and too adorable for their mother to miss.

'I shall simply find a way to persuade patrons to return to us, I am quite determined on it. They shall know they can trust me, even with you and Harry gone.' She closed the ledger and pushed it away. She would not worry Ella, not now when her sister was getting all the fine things she deserved. She had always worked too hard, sacrificed too much for Mary. 'Now, where are you going this evening in such a beautiful new gown?'

Ella still looked much too concerned, but she smiled brightly, as if determined to match Mary's own determined cheerfulness. She gave a little spin, making her emerald-green gown, embroidered with delicate gold leaves and beaded vines, twirl and sparkle in the lamplight. 'It's from Mademoiselle Sandrine Dumas's shop, of course! Is she not terribly clever?'

Mary nodded in admiration. Mademoiselle Sandrine had

opened her shop in York Street only a year before and was already the sensation of Bath. Everyone coveted one of her creations, which were more than mere dresses. They were dreams, of colour, texture, sparkle. Just as Mary knew how to match a couple, Sandrine knew how to bring out any lady's real beauty, her essence. She had done several wedding gowns for agency patrons, and Mary could only hope they would have more to send her soon.

'You shall be the envy of everyone there. Are you going to the opera, maybe?'

Ella tsked. 'It's Penelope's soirée, of course. I came to see if you would come in our carriage, but you're not even dressed.'

'Pen's party! Oh no.' Mary slapped her hand over her eyes. Penelope Oliver was Fred's stepmother and Mary and Ella's dear friend, who had recently married her true love Anthony Oliver and set up home with him in a grand townhouse on Greenleaf Street. This was her first party in her fine new drawing room.

'Never say you forgot. Oh, Mary. You have certainly been working far too hard if *you* are forgetting social engagements! You used to enjoy a party more than anyone else.'

'Especially for friends like Pen. We haven't even seen her since she returned from her wedding trip to Italy!' Mary had indeed always loved a party, loved being around people, hearing them chatter, swirling through a dance. She had never been made to be buried in ledgers, yet there she was. She had to prove herself, both in her own mind and to their patrons. But maybe part of that was socialising with them. 'I shall just change my gown at once, Ella, if your carriage will wait for a few moments.'

'Of course it can wait. I'm meeting Fred there, and he won't even notice I'm late once he starts a card game with Anthony.' Ella eyed the file cabinets.

'And no working while you wait! I forbid it. The agency is mine now.'

Ella laughed. 'I was only going to take a tiny peek. See who is new, who might like who. Who might—well, you know...'

'Who might suit *me*?' Mary asked wryly. She'd seen Ella watching her with a speculative gleam in her eye and suspected

Ella's matchmaking skills might be moving closer to home. 'Ella, you know we do not use patrons to make matches for ourselves.'

'Yes, I know,' Ella sighed. No one would ever trust them as matchmakers if it was suspected they were only working for themselves. And Mary had no interest in marrying anyway; the agency took up all her time and attention, her affection. She had to focus on it. 'Even if they might wish for us to match them with *you.* So many of our patrons have mooned over your golden curls, my dear sister! Is Mr Overbury still in the files?'

Mary nodded sadly. 'Indeed. I have offered him any number of introductions to fascinating, lovely ladies, but he says none of them would suit. Too tall, too petite, too brunette, too poetical, too lacking in poetry, too sensible, too flighty.' But she and Ella both knew that was not Mr Overbury's problem. His problem was that he had conceived a great infatuation for Mary herself. He followed her about at assemblies, sent her poetic love letters. It had been thus ever since he came to the agency many months before. 'Surely you are not saying I should accept his suit just to get him out of our books!'

'Oh, no, never Mr Overbury. He does have a fine fortune, but those waistcoats of his! But, well, someone better. Someone you could truly care for as I do my Fred. Maybe you are right that—that...'

'That my spinster state, when you and Harry are so blissfully wed now, might really be having an effect on our patrons? That a matchmaker who can't match herself isn't trustworthy? Sadly, yes, maybe so.'

Ella squeezed her hand. 'You must never think of marrying for the sake of business. But for yourself, dearest, you might just...'

'Might what?'

'Find someone to be with. I've never felt so *right* since Fred and I married, never so exactly where I should be! To be seen and loved for ourselves—it's blissful.'

Mary shook her head. Ella did indeed deserve every blissful moment she had. But Mary had spent her life managing *other* people's lives, other people's romances. Did she sometimes wish for such a thing herself? Certainly she did. It made her rather wistful to see Ella and Fred laughing together, staring into each other's eyes as if nothing else existed. Sometimes the sleepless nights seemed terribly quiet and dark, and sometimes she wished she had someone to advise her, help her. But only with someone who truly understood her, saw her, someone she could understand and help in return. After being responsible for herself for so long, it was frightening to think of relying so much on someone else! She could only give in to that for the strongest of loves, for someone who loved and needed her. And Charles, after being married before, after having his own life, surely couldn't love her in that way.

She glanced out the window to the snowy evening, and for an instant she saw not the chilly evening but a warm springtime day, cheering Charles on as he ran about the cricket green, his long, lean legs swift as a panther. Kissing him in that garden…

Perhaps she had dared to dream that *he* might be that understanding man. But it was not to be. Charles Campbell had gone back to Scotland after that golden spring, so she had heard, and he was there now only in the dreams she saw late at night, when work and the rush and bustle of the day had given way to silent hours. She imagined him then, the sunlight on his hair, the feel of his broad shoulders under her touch. The way his lips tasted. It gave her such pangs to think of him now.

She shook her head. Distraction would be very good right then and a party just the thing. Even if Pen's husband *was* Charles's cousin, and she might hear of him there.

'I shall go change my gown now. I just wish I had a Mademoiselle Sandrine creation to wear!' Mary pushed back from the desk, a bit stiff after sitting there so long, and gathered up her shawl, dislodging Miss Muffins from where she had parked herself on the fringe. 'I promise, Ella, you do not need to worry about me. I shall find a solution to our business troubles, and the agency will soon be busier than it ever was!'

Chapter Two

'You think I should *what*?' Charles Campbell gaped at his cousin Anthony over his hand of cards, not sure if he should shout or laugh. Or if he had even heard the man correctly. He'd thought everyone had given up trying to see him wed, considering him an old eccentric hiding in his Scottish castle.

In the end, he didn't laugh *or* shout. That wasn't like him, he always tried to be calm and rational, to weigh possibilities and make the most sensible decision. He had to do that ever since he'd become guardian to a young lady who needed his help. If he merely proceeded slowly, the clock would tick down to Anthony's wife's soirée, and he wouldn't have to converse over cards with the man any longer. 'Interesting idea, Anthony.'

Anthony laughed and laid down a card. They had known each other all their lives, since they were in leading-strings with Charles's mother being sister to Anthony's father, and they knew each other too well. 'Of course, Charles. I am serious. What better solution could there be? Adele needs a mother to shepherd her through Society now, and you need a companion. You've become much too solemn and bearish lately.'

'Can you blame me?' Charles said. He gestured to a footman for another glass of wine. He very much feared he would need it if matrimony was to be the subject that evening. 'I wasn't such a fine hand at marriage the first time. No lady deserves such unhappiness.' Charles seldom thought of his youthful marriage now, and never spoke of it, but it always seemed to lurk there in the back of his mind, the terrible way it ended, his mistakes.

Anthony nodded sympathetically. 'Of course I remember Aileen. But you were so very young! And most ladies are not like her. She was filled with restlessness and dissatisfaction from the very beginning. You would be more careful in your choice now.'

Would he? Or would a new wife be just as unhappy with him? Charles wouldn't take that chance. 'Nor are most ladies like your own excellent wife. We can't all be so fortunate with our hearts.'

Anthony beamed, a veritable ray of sunshine as he had been ever since he found his Penelope again after long, lonely years and became a devoted husband. 'Pen is an angel, it's true. I'm the luckiest man in the world.'

'And you think we should all be just as happy in our own domestic arrangements, yes?'

Anthony laid down another card. 'Certainly! Why not? My own days were so quiet, so lonely before, and now life is filled with possibility, with glorious moments. I care about you, cousin, about all our friends, and wish nothing but such happiness for you all.'

'And you are a good man to have such kind wishes for everyone, Anthony, which I know are most sincere.' It was true; Anthony had always had a tender heart, a generous soul, matched by his new wife. It was no surprise they wanted to spread the glow of domestic bliss far and wide. But Charles knew too well that could never be for him. 'But there is only one Penelope in the world. The rest of us are out of luck.'

'Pen is just as worried about you as I am. We know you have your hands full with Adele. It cannot be easy to suddenly be a father figure. And to such a—a lively young lady.'

Charles laughed. It was true that Adele Stewart, his kinswoman and ward, was very *lively*. She read a vast amount of romantic poetry and expected life to be just like in those pages. If it was not, then she would *make* it so. And now she fancied herself in love with one of the most unsuitable lads possible.

Peyton Clark, a penniless rogue, whose uncle it was said had cut him off because of his bad behaviour. Charles had no idea what to do next, and a lady's hand on the tiller for a while would be relief. A lady who knew what it felt like to be a girl, what to do to safeguard one so heedless and romantic as Adele.

Charles feared, though, that his judgement was as clouded in its own way as Adele's. He had once thought himself so in love with Aileen, he was blind to the truth, blind to how unsuited they were. If he tried to choose another wife, he would probably only make matters worse.

'You and Pen are truly the best of friends, Anthony, and I'm grateful for all your concern and advice lately.' Pen had indeed tried to help as much as she could with Adele, taking her to modistes, arranging matters for a London Season, listening to her. It kept Charles somewhat sane. 'It was all manageable when we were in Scotland, but sadly we couldn't stay there forever. Adele needs friends, distractions. Scotland was too quiet, too chilly, and she seemed happy in Bath last year. She must...'

'Must marry one day. And so should you, Charles. There are many lovely ladies in Bath!'

'I'm sure there are. Pen and Lady Fleetwood have introduced me to several at the theatre and Pump Room in the short time since I returned.' Yet he had not seen the one lady he most wanted to meet again, Mary St Aubin, of the golden hair and dimpled smile. Mary, who had haunted his dreams since she pressed her lips to his in that garden. 'If I must marry for Adele's sake, it will have to be a quiet, responsible-minded, sensible lady to make up for my misspent youth.'

'Charles...' Anthony started to protest, but then had to shrug ruefully, for just as he and Charles had known each other all their lives, he knew Charles's youth *had* been misspent.

Drinking too much, cheap pubs, illegal gaming halls. Trying to escape from the coldness of his family, his upbringing, to push down the longing for a life, a purpose, for someone to understand him. He knew that was what that behaviour had been about, really. All culminating in his marriage to Aileen, a young lady he'd known for years, as she was their neighbours' daughter, but who he had not truly known at all in the end. He would not make that sort of mistake again.

'That was all a long time ago,' Anthony said quietly.

'Not so very long ago.' Music floated into the small sitting room where they were playing cards, signalling the party must be beginning. 'Adele needs a steady hand, and I need...' What did he need? He knew all too well what he *wanted*. Had wanted ever since he glimpsed her across the Assembly Room dance floor, her golden hair shining like summer sun, her laughter sweeter than the waltz music. Mary.

He was of no use to a lady like Mary. He had too many responsibilities on his shoulders, a niece to guide through the Season, a cold estate in Scotland. Too much to make up for—his rakish youth, his mistaken marriage. Aileen had been a bit like Mary—always dancing, always laughing—until life with him rang that out of her.

No. He was better off on his own, with no one else harmed by his choices. If he did marry again, it would have to be to a sensible, pragmatic lady who would understand the parameters of his life, the limits of what he could give. What he could truly do. His heart was guarded now, as it should have been all along. Mary St Aubin was too full of heat and mischief, and she deserved a place to expand and bloom like a summer rose.

Charles glanced out the sitting room window at the snow lightly flurrying against the purplish sky, the graceful pale stone walls of the elegant square. Summer felt like a long distance away.

'I declare even your excellent Penelope couldn't find a lady who would have me,' he said lightly, folding his cards.

'I wouldn't place such a bet. She and her friends are most renowned for their skills in the matchmaking arena.'

Charles was intrigued. 'Skilled in finding ladies for desperate gentlemen? You do shock me.'

A dull red flush spread across Anthony's face. 'Not like *that*, you old rake! They make marital matches. And are very good at it.'

'Many bored ladies in Society like to try to throw their friends together, I'm sure. It can't always work. It all seems so...random. As if a lady knows a single man and a single lady and nothing else about them, so they must suit. Not that Pen would do that...'

Anthony shook his head and leaned across the table to whisper, 'When I met Pen again here in Bath last year, I found out that Lady Fleetwood and her sister, along with Lady Briggs, who is now the Marchioness of Ripton, ran a sort of agency, matching people who were having troubles meeting suitable partners in the usual way. People who...wanted something more out of their marriages. Compatibility, love even.'

'An agency? Like a business? Lady Fleetwood and Lady Briggs? And...' And Mary? Mary making matches. Was that why she'd kissed him in the garden? Testing him out for her ledgers? How strange. How intriguing. 'And Miss St Aubin?'

'I know it sounds most peculiar, but they do so many people an excellent service. The Confidential Agency does nothing so vulgar as advertise, of course, or put out signs on their doors. They are strictly by referral, past patrons giving letters of recommendation to those in need. Whispers at the Pump Room or the Theatre Royal to a friend who might need a tiny push in the right direction. Bath is filled with those seeking their perfect partner, you know.'

'How extraordinary.' And it was. Charles could feel his already considerable admiration for Mary grow even more. She ran a business! A strange one, to be sure, but a business. Another reason she would not want to marry someone like him. When Aileen ran from him, he thought he saw why she would do that, why he could not make a lady a truly good husband. He'd never seen happiness and family contentment with his own parents. How could he give that to someone else? Especially not someone as strong and independent as Mary. 'Did they introduce you to Pen?'

Anthony shook his head. 'We had already met years ago, you know, before she married the late Lord Fleetwood, and finally discovered each other again here in Bath. But so many others owe their happy marriages to this agency. Including Lady Pennington, who will be here tonight. She used to be Miss Evans, remember, the rich merchant's bluestocking daughter? Everyone said she would only be married for her money, before Ella and Mary found Lord Pennington and his studies, and she fell quite in love. Now look at her! Happy, studious and doubly rich, as Pennington had his own fortune. They say they have a new scientific laboratory at Northland Park. I supposed we'll see it for ourselves at their Christmas house party this month! They found Miss Evans someone just as rich and dotty about studies as she was. They saw the match straight away.'

Charles sat back in his chair, startled at the thought that Mary could do such things, wave a magic wand and make perfect matches. He was certainly impressed by her, by her ingenuity and by her energy for such work, but he was not sure such fairy-tale magic could be real.

'You know, Charles,' Anthony went on, 'I am sure they are exactly the ones you should be talking to about your—your conundrum.'

'My lack of a spouse is hardly a conundrum.' And Charles was sure they were exactly *not* the ones he should talk to, even if it was. He could never speak to Mary about the truth of his past, of his marriage. 'As fine as the St Aubin ladies are, my needs are quite small after such glittering matches as the Penningtons. I wouldn't want to bother them.'

'They would never be *bothered*! They are friends to us. Lady Fleetwood has been so busy with Moulton Magna of late I'm sure she's not at their offices much, but Miss St Aubin is. Pen has been helping her a bit. She's a wonder at organising and such.' He looked awestruck at his wife's filing ability, just like everything else about her. 'She will be here this evening. And at Lady Pennington's house party. Plenty of time to seek her advice, casually.'

Mary would be there in that very house that very evening? He felt a rush of something like panic, as if he were a boy again. Yet there was also excitement, longing. 'Miss St Aubin is to be here?'

'Certainly. She's been too busy to go out in Society much of late. Must be so odd for her, she did love to dance.' As he certainly did not. She would never want to see him again if she had the displeasure of dancing with him! Even as that would give him the excuse to touch her, be close to her, he knew he could not inflict his dancing on her. 'But Pen persuaded her that the festive season should be shared! Shall I have Pen talk to her about your situation?'

'No!' Charles snapped too loudly. Anthony looked startled, and Charles felt terrible for his loss of control. His childhood had been filled with his father's sudden rages, his mother's distance; he didn't want to do that, didn't want to give Adele that sort of home. Another reason he shouldn't marry again.

'No,' he repeated calmly, considerately, and laughed. He shuffled the cards as if he hadn't a care in the world. 'Let the ladies enjoy their parties. Pen is right, Christmas should be shared. I will work out my own small troubles. No wife required.'

Anthony looked unsure, as if he wanted to say more, but Penelope came in just then, her bright blue star-embroidered gown shimmering around her. She looked rather harassed.

'There you are, Anthony!' she cried, straightening a chair, twitching a drapery. She paused to kiss her husband's cheek and studied the cards on the table. 'The guests are arriving, and you and Charles are hiding away in here. It looks like you lost terribly, by the way. Why didn't you play the ten of hearts there?'

'Pen!' Anthony said with a laugh. 'You can't let everyone know what a terrible card player I really am.'

'Well, now you can escape your bad cards and come with me to greet the guests.' She kissed him again and went to check the chairs at the next table. 'What were you and Charles speaking of, then?' She sounded suspiciously casual, as if she guessed the matchmaking nature of their talk.

'Nothing at all, I fear,' Anthony said, giving her a long glance.

'How is Adele?' Charles asked, hoping to distract them. Adele had been getting ready for the party with Pen and was hopefully staying out of trouble.

'She is very well and looks so pretty in her new frock. I let her borrow my hairdresser, and she was so excited to try the new style. How lovely she's growing! And so charming. I'd love it if she could play the pianoforte later. The heather breezes are so good for her. She will be quite the diamond of the Season this spring.'

'And unsuitable romances seem to suit her, too, I fear,' Charles muttered.

Penelope frowned. 'She harbours some unsuitable tendre? She hasn't spoken of it to me, but I suppose I have seen her looking at Mr Clark...'

''Tis just a young lady's poetic fancy, soon vanished, I'm sure. I shouldn't mind so much if that fancy found a more harmless object than Clark, though.'

'I am quite sure there is a quick solution,' Pen declared. 'I shall give it some thought tonight. And keep a close eye on Adele during the dancing, of course. I fear it is so easy to make a misstep at such an age, one not always easily recovered from.'

That was exactly what Charles feared. Adele needed help, and so did he, to navigate such rocky shoals as a first Season.

A footman stepped into the doorway, and the music from the drawing room was growing louder. 'The first carriages are arriving, Mrs Oliver,' he announced.

'Thank you,' Penelope said. 'Shall we, my darling?'

The happy couple swept out to their party, arm in arm, leaving Charles to his thoughts. And his thoughts were all of Mary St Aubin, her quick elfin laughter and bright hair. The joy she brought when she was nearby.

Suddenly, as if summoned magically by his thoughts of her, he glimpsed Mary St Aubin through the crowd. The light seemed to gather only on her, bathing her in a sparkling glow. She laughed, her face alight, her golden curls bouncing, and he couldn't look away.

He hadn't seen her in some months, so he'd often told himself she couldn't really be so beautiful as he remembered. But in truth, she *was*, or even more so, like sunshine breaking through a grey Bath sky. How he wished he could save her up, save how she made him feel, for another dark day!

He drifted behind the gathering, still watching her. She accepted a glass of wine from one of the crowd of gentlemen around her and gifted the man one of her jewel-like smiles. She chatted and laughed, her honey-brown eyes glowing. Charles was enthralled by her, by the glow of the cloud she seemed to walk on. Enthralled, bewildered and—and jealous. He watched her smile again at one of her admirers, the curve of those rose-pink lips, and he found he longed to taste them. To see if they were as sweet as he remembered from their too-brief, much-remembered kiss.

'Uncle Charles? Are you quite well?' Adele asked, and it was as if he were suddenly shoved off his delicate cloud of Mary dreams. Cold reality closed around him again.

Laughing a bit at himself, at his moment of folly, he turned to his niece. Adele studied him with a most bemused expression on her pretty face. He remembered her as a toddler, when she would frown fiercely at the world around her as if trying to understand its every puzzling scrap. Now she did the same, though from the bright blue eyes of a young lady about to leap out into the unknown.

He smiled down at her and took her arm to draw her closer, a wave of protectiveness washing over him. 'I am quite well, Adele. Why do you ask?'

'You did look rather peculiar just then. As if you'd swallowed some wine the wrong way.' She looked around the party, twisting her lace fan in one hand. He wondered if she looked for her suitor and knew he had to distract her.

'Pen wanted to know if you might play the pianoforte, maybe before the dancing begins,' he said. Pen had only mentioned it in passing, of course, but he knew she wouldn't mind if Adele sat down at the instrument at all. She was very talented, her musical skills so expressive. She deserved so many fine things in life, more than a rake like Clark could give.

'Play?' she cried, startled. 'But I need to find my friends! I did promise I would...' She seemed to remember herself, remember to try and be discreet, if Mr Clark was indeed what she looked for. 'Of course I can, if Aunt Pen asked.'

'You are so accomplished, my dear, everyone asks for your Scottish airs at every gathering lately.' That was very true. Adele had so many admirers, if only she would look around. Just another reason he would never let her throw herself away on someone most unworthy of her artistic gifts, her kind heart, her pretty face and fine manners.

As he turned to lead Adele towards the pianoforte set in the corner of the drawing room, he glimpsed Mary one more time. She was so beautiful, so dangerous to his serenity of mind. He couldn't think of anything else when she was near.

She was a glorious distraction he certainly did not need.

Chapter Three

Mary always thought parties really should start with some sliver of excitement, some frisson that anything could happen in the next hours. Especially for a matchmaker! The thrill of watching two people dance and thinking 'Hmm, maybe...' watching two people laugh together. It gave it all such a sparkle. She greeted Pen and Anthony with a laugh, and urged Ella and Fred to go and dance, shocking as a husband and wife dancing together would be!

She carefully studied the crowd around her. The swirl of colour, the men's dark coats against the ladies in their pastel pinks, sky blues, pure white, amethyst, green. The shine of jewels in the candlelight, the laughter and chatter blending with the swing and twirl of the music. The sweet scent of hothouse roses and winter greenery in the air, along with fine perfumes. It was all very pretty, as Pen had excellent taste, but as always what really happened at the start of a party was not frisson but—ever so slight boredom. Oh, not at Pen's parties, really. She knew how to blend music, conversation, decoration to perfection. Yet it was all very much of a sameness those days. The same people, the same talk. And Mary had once so loved parties!

Now she felt a bit lonely as she took in the happy crowd around her.

'Some wine, Miss St Aubin?' she heard someone ask, and turned to find Mr Sillerton standing there, impeccable in a finely cut green coat and perfectly tied cravat pinned with a large cameo, his brown hair swirled into the latest style. She had tried once or twice to gently steer him towards an agency match, but he seemed happy as a single gentleman, as a pseudo-suitor to Mary. But he had sent her a few marriage-minded friends, and she needed all the help she could find.

'You quite read my mind, Mr Sillerton,' she said, and took the glass from his gloved hand with a smile. 'It's become quite the crush this evening.'

'Mrs Oliver is a hostess par excellence, it's true,' Mr Sillerton said, gesturing at the growing crowd around them. 'Her food and wine, and definitely the intelligent conversation of her chosen guests, is far above average in Bath! But I fear this town has become rather dull this season. That last play at the Theatre Royal was so very lifeless! And the quality of dancing at the Assembly Rooms abysmal. It's a fine thing Lady Pennington is having her Christmas house party to carry us away from it all. They say Northland Park is superb!'

Mary nodded and secretly hoped she would meet new clients there. Maybe they would be lurking under the mistletoe, waiting for their ideal partners. 'Indeed. I'm very much looking forward to it.'

'Lord and Lady Pennington were a product of your fine agency, were they not? You clever girl. They are a scintillating pair, and poor Miss Evans looked so unpromising at first.'

'Yes, they do seem quite happy together,' Mary said, proud of their finest match yet. 'I am of the hope there will be many more such people at their party in need of a soupçon of assistance.'

'I fear all the men are in love with *you*, our fair Miss SA, and won't be set on lesser lights. Much like my own pitiful self!' He clutched at his heart through his fine cream brocade waistcoat. 'This party is a mere salve to my heartache.'

Mary laughed, glad she had friends who could amuse and distract her from thoughts of Charles Campbell.

Was it a sign that marriage had been mentioned so often of late as a solution to her problems? It was true that the right alliance could set straight many things in one wave of a vicar's hand in benediction. Her business would be seen to be in safe, *married* hands. She'd always known what she *should* want, a husband and children, a house to look after. Yet what she liked was her work. It was most satisfying to see the happiness she could help create for others, to make her own way in the world after a childhood in which she and Ella were dependent on their scatter-brained father. A husband would not like his wife working outside her drawing room.

Yes, indeed; a husband might be a nice thing to have. Useful. And a family such as Ella had now looked wonderful. But she knew few households were blessed with such real love and understanding as Ella and Fred, and Pen and Anthony, possessed. Mary couldn't fathom marriage without such a meeting of hearts. She let herself be distracted by a few gentlemen clustering around her, offering wine, a dance, a stroll about the room.

The music of the dance had faded, and she heard the strains of a soft song instead, an air on the pianoforte. It sounded most enticing, and she drifted towards the sound of it from the instrument in the corner of the drawing room. She nearly bumped into a petite, slim figure draped in pink silk on the way, the wine in her glass jostling. She glanced down, and recognised Mademoiselle Sandrine, the modiste.

'Oh, Mademoiselle Dumas!' Mary cried. 'I do beg your pardon. How lovely to see you again! And how charming you look.' She studied the pink gown closer, admiring the slashed sleeves revealing puffs of beaded white satin à la Renaissance. Sandrine was often invited to social events by her favoured patrons, as all ladies in town hoped to engage her. And, being French and mysterious, she was considered most fascinating. 'That must be the very latest in sleeves.'

'Of course! My business depends on such things,' Mademoiselle Sandrine said with a laugh, her bell-like voice touched with a Parisian accent. Though she wore spectacles, and seemed not at all ashamed of that fact, she was quite pretty, with dimples and flashing brown eyes. But behind those lovely eyes lurked something like a shadow, a sadness. Mary wondered where it came from. Something in the lady's past, some grief? 'Now that we can see all the latest French fashions, we are spoiled for choices in our silhouettes.'

'I do wish there was time for me to have such a frock made up for Lady Pennington's party.'

'Oh, I shall be there, too! I'm so looking forward to getting a glimpse of that laboratory. I'm sure I could make up a new gown for you before then, if I have the correct fabric in my stock.'

'Could you really?' Mary gasped. Perhaps an ultra-stylish ball gown or walking dress would catch some attention for the business. 'You are an angel, Mademoiselle.'

Sandrine laughed again. 'I am merely a very hard worker, much like yourself. But this music—now, *that* is angelic. Such expression!'

Indeed it was. A song full of expression and light and shade, no mere succession of keys as young ladies' playing so often was. This was music with feeling and talent.

Mary went up on tiptoe to peer through the crowd gathered to listen to the music. To her shock, she saw it was Adele Stewart, Charles's niece, who played. Her head was bent, strawberry-blonde curls dangling over the keys, as if she saw nothing else, her brow furrowed with emotion. Yes, it was definitely her. And if Adele had returned to Bath, then surely...

A man stepped forward to turn the page of the music, and she saw it was really Charles. Suddenly back in Mary's own town, in her life, real once more. Everything else grew blurry around her, reality sharpening only on him, and she couldn't quite breathe.

She'd thought she could forget him when he was far away in Scotland, that he would fade from her thoughts and memories. That hadn't happened as of yet; she remembered him in the dark of night, when all was quiet. Thought of his sea-green eyes, crinkling as he smiled that warm chocolate smile of his, thought of how his touch sent tingles all through her, how his kiss swept away everything else in the world.

But she'd been sure he *would* fade, given time, as all impossible dreams did. As a girl, she had been romantic, dreamy; as a woman, she had to learn to be practical.

Now, there he was again, no dream but all too real. And even more handsome than she remembered. Not like a fashionable fairy-tale prince, but so very *real*. Maybe it was the Scot in him that gave him such an air of freshness and vitality, even when he stood still. That spark of humour and raw energy that hummed about him. That small hint of danger, like a hardened warrior off the battlefield, relaxed and smiling but liable to leap into action again at an instant's notice.

Mary pressed her folded fan to her lips to keep from laughing. She was surely too old now to indulge her young, poetical self, yet here she was, being so terribly fanciful! Making him into the hero of a novel in her own mind.

He glanced up, and with no warning, his gaze met hers. Something seemed to sizzle and crackle in the air between them.

Mary inadvertently took a step back, nearly treading on someone's train. She wanted to run, to hide from that green gaze that seemed to see everything, but she was hemmed in by the crowd with nowhere to go. And she really wanted to run forward, as well, to catch his hand in hers and stare and stare into his eyes forever.

'Who is that?' Sandrine asked. Her gaze narrowed as she studied Adele's gown, a creation of cream and gold that shimmered like autumn leaves in a breeze. 'I think the dress is one of mine, but I don't remember them.'

'Mr Campbell and his niece Miss Stewart. They left Bath not long after you arrived and must have only just returned. Perhaps Penelope loaned her the gown, it suits her very well.' Sandrine's creations were the envy of the town, transforming their wearers into rare beauties in colours and trims that enhanced their own lovely qualities. She was especially sought after for wedding gowns, though Mary wouldn't think Adele was quite ready for that. 'They live in Scotland, but he is Mr Oliver's cousin. I'm sure they must be here for Christmas.'

'A handsome family indeed,' Sandrine murmured. 'That gown looks well on her but doesn't quite fit correctly in the sleeves, *n'est-ce pas*? I just got a bolt of spring-green muslin that would suit her hair very nicely...' She wandered away, murmuring about silks and laces.

As Mary watched her go, trying to pretend Charles was not mere feet away, she felt the hard press of a stare from somewhere in the crowd. She finally saw Mr Overbury watching her, and when her gaze met his, he started towards her.

Mary pivoted on her shoe heel and slipped back into the press of people in hopes she could vanish before her unwanted suitor found her. She'd once found Mr Overbury amusing, fun to talk about poetry with even, but the more she talked to him, the more she entertained his visits to the agency and tried to find him a wife, the more he pressed closer to her.

To her vexation, though, the people she *wanted* to pay attention to her, potential patrons of the agency, seemed to see right through her! They nodded to her but would not approach for conversation. She chatted a bit with the Morleys, a couple who'd formed their attachment through the agency when everyone in Bath had said they were quite doomed to single life because of their obsession with taxidermy. They were kind, but even they only wanted to ask after Ella, sing her praises as a superlative matchmaker.

'And now her own match is to an earl! So fitting for her!'

Ella's marriage to Fred, and her semi-retirement from crafting matches, seemed to have enhanced Ella's professional reputation while everyone seemed to forget that Mary had also worked to build their business.

The crowd grew once again as the dance music struck up. Mary turned towards the doorway of the sitting room set aside for cards, hoping it would be a bit quieter, have a space for her to take a breath. Perhaps she would even find a game herself. She was rather keen on whist and hadn't played much lately. Not since that game with Charles at the Assembly Rooms. She remembered peeking over the edge of her cards to see a man coming to their table, so tall and powerful, clad in a fashionable, conventional evening coat of dark blue superfine, but he might as well have worn a kilt and carried a broadsword, he seemed so arrestingly of another time.

Yes, she could definitely use a quiet game to clear her head.

But she realised her mistake right away. Charles Campbell stood near the fireplace, quite alone—and still more beautiful than a man had a right to be. Months in his windswept Scotland seemed to have made him even more gorgeous, carving his sun-bronzed features into a Greek statue, making his eyes even brighter.

It felt as if someone had kicked the breath from her, just seeing him there in life and not in her daydreams.

He was watching something across the room, and she thought maybe she could back away and dash off before he approached. She was too slow, though, too caught up in the sight of him, and he suddenly began towards her. A slow smile spread across his lips, making her knees tremble.

She couldn't run away now. She made herself smile merrily, as her party-loving self would once have, and went to meet him. She held her hand out, arm straight, as if she could keep him far enough away. Another mistake. He took her hand, and heat shot through her whole arm straight to her heart.

'Mr Campbell,' she said lightly, her inner self all in tumult. 'How nice to see you again! I didn't know you had returned to Bath.' *Liar.* Truly, she'd thought of little else but him since she first saw Adele at the piano and realised Charles must be in Bath, as well. She'd daydreamed about him, thought about him in her bed at night, doodled his name in the margins of ledgers and then furiously scratched it out.

'Only recently, Miss St Aubin. I fear Adele is of an age when she needs a great deal more society than Castle Campbell can give her.'

'That is your estate?' Blast him, but even the name of his home sounded romantic and rugged!

'Yes, near Dunfermline. It's an old place, maybe a bit draughty and out of style, but with views from the ramparts for miles...' He sounded most wistful, and Mary wished more than anything she could see the place, share it with him.

'And I daresay you miss it very much,' she said softly. She imagined him there, striding the heather-covered hills, his hair tousled in the breeze. Holding out his hand so she could walk beside him.

He smiled, a bright too-quickly vanished flash. 'Aye, I'd happily spend all my days there. Adele deserves more, though. She needs far more people to hear her talent at the pianoforte, for instance, than just me and the servants.'

'Oh, yes, I heard her playing when I first arrived. She is very talented, such charming expressiveness, so much understanding of the emotions of the music. She is certainly accomplished, as well as pretty.' Mary glanced around the card room, remembering what she'd heard about each gentleman there, whether he was single, what his estate and character were. 'She should have her pick of suitors here in Bath and in London. And once she's settled, you can return to your castle, yes?' She thought of him vanishing into the Scottish mists again, never to be seen, and felt a sharp pang at the idea. Not that she should feel that way; he could never be closer to her than he was right then, anyway.

A frown flickered over his brow. 'I do fear she may have—well, I think perhaps...'

Mary had seen such an expression on worried parents' faces before. 'Has she perhaps formed a...less than ideal attachment?' she asked gently.

He swallowed. 'Have there been whispers?'

'Oh, no, not at all. Not that I have heard, and I must stay abreast of all the talk of the town.' Usually she did, though she feared not so much lately. But she did still hear murmurs and giggles when there was forbidden romance to be seen. 'I have just seen such things before, with parents and their impressionable young daughters. Are you concerned? Is this *parti* pestering Miss Stewart, pressing his attentions? I could have a quiet word with her, give her advice on seeing such unwanted admirers off without a fuss.' She just wished she could do that herself, with men like Mr Overbury. Some suitors would not be put off with gentle hints.

Charles smiled down at her. 'That is very kind of you, Miss St Aubin. I'm afraid it may be—well, that is to say...'

He did look adorably flustered, which made him seem even more handsome. Mary tried very hard to focus on his words, his conundrum and not on the way his hair tumbled over his brow. 'I see. It's a bit more complicated, then.'

'Rather, yes. I left her with Penelope, but I think I should go find her now. Would you walk with me?'

Anywhere. 'Of course.'

He offered her his arm, all perfectly proper and correct, yet she did not feel quite so proper when she touched him. The warmth of him against her hand made her want to throw herself at him and seek his kiss, like a wild creature! Somehow she managed to just walk with him at the edge of the room, slowly, just like an ordinary evening. She hoped her polite smile did not tremble.

'What is amiss with your niece?' she asked.

He frowned. 'I fear she is in love with someone quite unsuitable. Well, she says it is love, but certainly it is not.'

'I see. That sounds worrying, of course, but not so rare. Young ladies do fall into infatuations sometimes, and it always seems to be with the most terrible rakes. It usually passes. Who is this man?'

'His name is Peyton Clark. He is heir to his uncle, but they say the old man has tired of his antics and cut him off, or very near to it. He cannot support a wife, either financially or emotionally. I do not know how to persuade her that parting from him is the best thing for her.'

'Hmm, yes, I see. I have not heard of this man, but I know his type all too well. You are right to be concerned, and it does you credit as a guardian.' She scanned the floor and saw Adele twirling along the line of the dance with a young man. 'Is that Mr Clark with Adele now?'

'No, thankfully. I believe that is a Mr Bellingham.'

'Ah, yes. New to Bath. Grandson to a duke. Quite the scholar, they say, very interested in ancient Minoan culture.'

Charles laughed. 'Now, why doesn't Adele find herself someone like that? Connections, intelligence.'

'And quite nice, from what I hear. But young ladies of a poetical turn of mind, and I do seem to remember Miss Stewart was quite a reader, seldom have yet learned to be sensible. I fear I speak from some experience.'

He glanced down at her, his dark brow arched with interest. 'You were…poetical?'

'In my sad youth. I fancied myself quite the Mrs Brereton. Do you know her work?'

'I do not. But I sympathise. I was once sure I was destined to be a poet myself and grew my hair ridiculously long as I strode about the hillsides endeavouring to look tragic.'

Mary laughed as she imagined such a scene. 'Did you indeed?'

'Oh, aye. I was tiresome beyond belief, Miss St Aubin. And it took me some time to come to the realisation that a career as a poet requires the ability to write something more than just somewhat intelligible business letters. I had no Byronic turn of phrase in my fingertips.'

'Oh, poor Mr Campbell!'

He gave her an exaggerated pout that made her laugh harder. 'I know. To have my youthful dreams crushed so cruelly. My *da* said it was beyond time I ceased stalking over the hills like a bogle and applied myself to my duties.'

'I am quite sure you have many other talents beyond literature.' Kissing, for instance. Ah, yes, she remembered he was quite good at that.

'My *da* said my only true vocation was in gambling and whisky bottles.'

Mary was shocked. Her own father, the vicar, would never have said such a thing! And Charles didn't seem at all the soused sort. 'How untrue! I am sure he doesn't think so to see you now.'

Charles watched the dancers, his expression very far away. 'Perhaps he would not. I hope he would not. He passed away many years ago, and I fear that was when I realised he was entirely correct. I had a duty to the estate and its people, to my family.' He smiled at Adele as she swirled past with Mr Bellingham. 'Adele is the one who inherited any artistic talent in our family. I'm sure it came from her mother. Elspeth was a gentle soul who loved to paint and sing, just as her daughter does.'

'I did love hearing her play earlier. So beautiful, so full of emotion and imagery. Few people truly feel the music in that way. She seems far out of the common way of accomplishments! And so pretty. If you needed help finding someone, you are welcome to come to the agency. I could...' She fell silent, as she realised Adele could easily find a nice young man all on her own, if she could just learn to trust herself to see to her future. Mary wanted to help, not as a matchmaker but merely as a friend.

'You think you could make her a fine match. One high in Society?'

Mary was flustered. She had not thought Charles would care about such things, as so many parents did. 'Of course I could try. We do sometimes have titled gentlemen come to us, even a poet or two.' Or at least they once had. She would need to find such patrons again. That was what she needed to concentrate on, not Charles's green eyes and broad shoulders. 'But someone like Adele has no need of such assistance. If you wanted a titled match...'

'I want only her happiness, her security. And I'm not sure she is in no need of assistance.' He suddenly stood very straight, a determined look on his face. 'I have been told she is, in fact, of need of a lady's help in these matters. A mother figure. I try my best, try to do as her mother would have wished, yet for a man on his own...'

Mary suddenly realised what he spoke of—marriage. Not for Adele but for himself, to give Adele a mother. 'You—you seek a wife.' She had not meant to blurt it out so plainly. Images flew through her mind, of Charles arm in arm with a veiled lady as they marched down the aisle. A lady who was certainly not Mary.

Charles shook his head. 'Not really. Perhaps. I fear I am too set in my ways. I don't know many people. Penelope does say...'

The music for the next dance set ended, and couples changed places on the dance floor. She saw Adele claimed by another young man who led her to their spot, even as the girl studied the room for someone else. Probably her unsuitable Mr Clark. 'Well, I always think dancing is the perfect way to meet and observe new people.'

He nodded decisively, as if she had given him some assignment he must carry out. 'I quite agree. Would you do me the honour of this dance, Miss St Aubin? You could help me learn to observe, tell me what you know of the people around us.'

'I would be happy to assist, Mr Campbell.'

He offered his arm, and she slid her gloved hand over his

sleeve, feeling the tense flex of his forearm beneath her touch, the strength of him. The solid warm reality. She was going to dance with *Charles*! It would be painful to show him eligible ladies, talk of his prospects without her, but she would at least have this moment to remember, to imagine when days were too dismal. That was surely something.

They took their places in the figures of the dance, yet Mary thought he looked rather…odd. Haunted maybe.

'I fear I should warn you,' he said tightly. 'I am not a good dancer. At all.'

Mary laughed. How could he not be? He moved with such an easy, athletic grace, a man who was obviously accustomed to walking and riding. And she had seen him play cricket, the flex and taut power of his back under his shirt, the swift, loping stride of his run. She shivered. 'I am sure that cannot be true. But such a hint of modesty in a gentleman is most commendable.' She often said that to men who came to the agency, a gentle hint to rein in the boasting a wee bit. Not that she had ever heard a whisper of boast from Charles.

He laughed, too, that rough, whisky-dark sound that made her feel so very hot and cold all over. 'This is no modesty, I fear, but *treowth*. I do well enough riding, and luckily can walk straight down a lane without disgracing myself falling over, but when the music begins I sprout two left feet.'

'Mr Campbell…' The music began, a lively polka, and she couldn't say any more. He took her hand and they spun away. At first, it was giddy fun, and made her laugh as the lights of the room blurred around her. But soon enough she saw all too well what he meant by 'two left feet.' He nearly sent them careening into another couple, not once but twice, and got his foot tangled in her skirt. By the time the music ended and he escorted her to the edge of the floor, she was out of breath and dizzy.

'I—you were quite correct, I fear,' she said breathlessly. 'It is not modesty.'

He grimaced. 'I did warn you, Miss St Aubin.'

'Indeed you did. But most ladies need a bit more than a warning.'

He laughed ruefully. 'They want to be swept around the floor, feeling lighter than a cloud.'

'That is one way to open a small door to a lady's heart.' And his smile was another, that self-deprecating quirk to those sensual lips. A lady would forgive much for that.

She glimpsed Mr Overbury making his way through the crowd and knew she had to talk quickly. 'Mr Campbell, may I speak freely?'

'Oh, I do count on it, Miss St Aubin. I'm a rough Scotsman, you know, delicate hints fly right over my thick head.'

Mary very much doubted that. Not much seemed to get past him. And his head was very pretty.

'Tell me, then,' he said. 'If such a hopeless dancer as myself came to your agency, would you turn him away forthwith?'

Mary laughed. They would have ladies pounding down their door if he was a patron. 'Not if they were otherwise suitable, of course not. We are here to *help* people. It's what I enjoy the most about my work.'

He studied her carefully, until she could feel her cheeks turning warm. She had to resist the urge to flap her fan. 'I can see that. You have a kind heart, and you have built a very useful business.'

'Well,' Mary whispered, 'I do think—I would recommend dancing lessons. Dancing is indeed one of the finest ways to become acquainted with someone. It's a chance to stand close, to have a quiet word together. We do have dancing masters we vouch for, along with painting teachers, French and German speakers, elocution tutors. Not that you need those, I'm sure.' She studied him again, the sharp angles of his elegant, powerful face, his sensual lips. 'Are you interested in lessons? Or perhaps a tutor for Adele? Our agency's services...'

She paused. What would she say if he did want to hire the agency for more than help with dancing? Could she find it within her to help him make a match with someone else?

'Adele is already a fine dancer. She's just in danger of being disgraced by her clumsy uncle.' His gaze swept over the crowd, and she wondered if he sought a lady he found beautiful.

And she saw that Mr Overbury, who had been providentially

halted by a group of his friends, was headed her way again, scowling at Charles as if jealous. If only he had reason to be, she thought with a sigh.

Charles went on. 'I really should become a passable dancer if we're to move in London Society circles. And Adele deserves to find a good match. If I can help her in any small way...'

'With dance lessons?'

'Aye. But I would rather—well, that is...' He hesitated.

'Yes?'

'I would rather no one know of my faults on the dance floor.'

Mary smiled in understanding. '*I* know. And I certainly do not think less of you.' On the contrary. It made him seem even more endearing to her.

'Exactly. Could I engage you, or if you prefer your agency, to assist me with a lesson or two?' He smiled at her hopefully.

He wanted to dance with *her*? Mary sucked in a deep breath, trying not to feel such excitement at the thought of having her toes trod on by him again. By being close to him. 'You want me to teach you to dance?'

'Just a lesson or two. To show me a few simple steps.'

'Dancing is an art! To become skilled, one needs many lessons.'

'Many?' He frowned. 'I don't plan on dancing so very much. Card rooms at parties are much more suited. I just want to not disgrace my family name by barrelling over all the couples on the floor.'

Mary was temped. *Very* tempted. Surely it could do no harm to dance once or twice? To help out a—a friend? 'I shall think about it. Perhaps you could help *me* with something, as well?'

'Certainly. Just name it, Miss St Aubin.'

She was tempted again, this time to demand a kiss as payment. But she knew better. She was older than Adele and meant to be wiser. She had to guard her heart. 'See that man over there?' she whispered, and nodded towards Overbury. He was searching the crowd with a most determined look on his face. 'Could you just take my arm and steer me away from him?'

Charles scowled at the man. 'Is he pestering you?'

'No, I wouldn't say that, exactly.' Yet she would. 'He wishes for the agency to find him the perfect wife, and he decided long ago it was me.'

'One can hardly blame him for thinking that,' Charles said, casting her an admiring smile that made her feel terribly warm all over. 'But surely he knows a gentleman should never press his attentions on a lady once rebuffed. I shall speak to him.' He started to stride off, his face dark and thunderous. Mary wondered how Adele's Mr Clark wasn't yet scared away.

She grabbed his arm. 'No, no. I do thank you for being my white knight, but I am sure Mr Overbury will soon find a more suitable *tendre* and forget all about me.'

He frowned doubtfully, but Mr Overbury did seem rather halted in his tracks. 'If you are certain...'

'Of course. Let us just walk over there for a moment and try some of those ices.' She did not need a scandal for the agency if two men argued over her in a ballroom. But she had to admit, she felt rather glowing and satisfied to have had a defender for a moment. Especially if it was Charles.

Penelope came to them through the crowd, a worried frown on her face. 'Oh, Charles, I fear Adele slipped out of my sight for a moment, and now I cannot find her! I thought she was dancing with that nice Mr Bellingham.'

Charles's laughter turned in an instant to taut watchfulness, chagrin. 'No, Pen, it's my fault. I never should have asked such a favour of you when you have much to do as hostess. I will go in search of her. She can't have gone far. Is Clark here, then?'

'I—I don't know. He could have slipped in,' Pen fretted.

Mary thought they seemed more worried than they should. Just because Adele has a pash of sorts, she *was* at a party and could be with any number of people. 'Are you sure she has gone off with this man in particular?'

'No, but one of the footmen thinks they glimpsed someone rather like Mr Clark earlier. I just thought...' Pen shook her head. 'How silly of me!'

'I'm sure she's close by. Come on, I'll help you find her,' Mary said, and led the way through the room.

They finally glimpsed Adele near one of the windows, standing with a man whose back was to them. He touched her hand,

and she smiled shyly. A smile that faded when she saw her uncle stalking towards her. The man hurried away, and Adele stared after him.

'Adele,' Charles said, 'I thought I asked you not to talk to that man again.'

Adele set her chin stubbornly and fussed with a ribbon on her sleeve, not looking at her uncle. 'It's a party! Am I not meant to speak to anyone? How unfair you are, Uncle.'

He opened his mouth as if to argue with her, which Mary knew would go nowhere. She shook her head at him and smiled at Adele. 'Will you walk with me, Miss Stewart? We can discuss the new fashion in sleeves, I am not at all sure about them.'

Adele nodded, still refusing to look at her uncle. Mary took the girl's arm and turned in the other direction, hoping she could distract her while Charles calmed himself. She had once been young herself; such infatuations had to be handled carefully. Grown-up infatuations had to be, as well, she found the more she was around Charles.

Charles watched Mary and Adele as they strolled across the room, arm in arm. At last, Adele smiled, a tiny quirk, but it was there. He felt the warmth of relief and gratitude for Mary's words of reassurance, the way she helped Adele now.

He'd been racked with worry over his ward ever since they came to Bath, and she seemed to drift further and further away from him as he struggled to understand what she was going through. He marvelled now to see how easily Mary understood, knew how to speak to Adele, speak to her as a young lady, a person, at a difficult moment that left him baffled. He was not used to such emotions—not even his own.

Mary just understood. She listened. She even laughed at how terrible a dancer he was and made him laugh at himself! That was a failing he couldn't show anyone, only her. When he looked into her eyes, saw her smile, he would trust her with anything.

And she was so very beautiful. Achingly so, with her sun-gold hair and those dimples set in peachy, creamy skin. Even the way she walked, slow and easily graceful, was lovely. She made him feel so many things he'd thought forgotten in the mists of time. Things like laughter.

Penelope came to him and took his arm, urging him to stroll with her as Mary and Adele were lost to sight through the crowd. 'Mary St Aubin is a wonder, is she not?'

Had Pen read his mind? Seen his infatuation? He looked at her sideways, trying to read her expression. 'She is very kind, yes.'

'Certainly she is that. She is also pretty and full of fun. You could use that very much.' She squeezed his arm. 'Don't worry, Charles. I am sure between us all we can steer Adele, and you, in the right direction.'

'Do you think so? I am a hopeless case, but Adele is young.' And he could not fail her, could not fail Adele's mother.

'It's not easy being her age, on the cusp of grown-up life but not there yet, so uncertain. And with her parents gone, as well.' Pen shook her head sadly. 'If she had an aunt…'

Charles laughed. 'Are you going to urge me to wed again?'

'I don't mean to be a nuisance, my dear! But to have someone to share life with can be sublime. To share worries and joys, have someone to help and advise us, to be with us in the dark of the night. Yes, it's wonderful.'

'Not always,' he said, thinking of Aileen, their quarrels and unhappiness. The way she had run away rather than stay by his side a moment longer.

'You must find the right one, just as I did with my Anthony,' Pen said. 'Third time was the charm. The Confidential Agency could be of help, if Mary herself won't have you.'

'No, not the agency,' he said, more sharp than he intended. He could not ask Mary for that. 'No, I should not wish to trouble them, they must be busy.'

Pen frowned doubtfully. 'If you say so. There are many other ways to meet suitable ladies, especially in Bath. The Pump Room, card parties, garden fêtes at Sydney Gardens…'

'I am quite well just as I am, Pen, I promise.'

'Are you?' she murmured.

He gave her a teasing grin. 'Am I such a pitiable figure, then?

Am I in my dotage now and need friends to find me a kind lady to wheel my chair about?'

Penelope laughed. 'Certainly not! I had two older husbands myself, and you, our Scots *gaisgeach*, are nothing of the sort. But having someone to confide in, talk to, laugh with—and, er, other things, of course.' Her cheeks slowly turned pink, making him chuckle.

He then pictured Mary and those 'er, other things,' saw her in a firelit bed, her golden hair tumbling down over her naked white shoulders, and his laughter faded. He feared he blushed a bit himself. 'If it comes to that, Pen, I know where to look. And to find a wife, as well, but I shall not.'

'Do you know where to look, though?' She scowled at him impatiently. 'Sometimes, it is all right under your stubborn nose.'

Chapter Four

Mary often thought of the Pump Room as a sort of second office for the agency. Everyone came there, newcomers and old Bath residents alike, mingling under the chandeliers, partaking of the vile water, chatting, watching. She could meet anyone there, perusing the guest book, taking tea, getting caught up on all the gossip. One of her very favourite parts of visiting the rooms was definitely *not* trying the waters herself, but seeing a happy couple or two who had formed their match with a sprinkling of her help.

She stepped into the Pump Room the morning after Pen's soirée, ducking out of the grey drizzling day into a haven of pale green and cream and gold, of sparkling chandeliers, soft harp music. People strolled by the long tables dispensing the water and along the windows draped in green taffeta, so civilised and ordinary. She waved at a few people she knew, including Mademoiselle Sandrine, who of course had the finest ensemble in the whole room. Mary took a cup of tea in lieu of the water and went to examine the arrival book.

'Miss St Aubin! How delightful to see you here,' she heard a cheerful voice call, and turned to Lady Pennington, née Miss Evans, one of the agency's greatest successes. Her father was a wealthy merchant, new money, and her mother had determined that her daughter would raise them up in Society by marrying well, no matter what the daughter herself thought. And the daughter only wanted her studies, her own interests! Once there had been a thought to match her with Fred, one of Mary's few mistakes. But now all were happy.

'Lady Pennington! I would have thought you would be at Northland Park, preparing for your house party.' They lightly kissed cheeks, and Mary admired her gown, a walking dress and spencer of amethyst velvet trimmed with glossy sable that matched her small hat. Lady Pennington had been a most questionable dresser under the supervision of her mother, all orange bonnets and bright green pelisses with feathers, but now she was quiet the model of style.

'We leave tomorrow. The staff there is so frightfully efficient, I fear there isn't much for me to do except be in their way.' Her husband, tall and lanky with shimmering golden hair, came to her side, and she beamed up at him as he took her hand. 'We have been so eager to hear Dr Farnon's lecture on the botany of Brazil this evening before we leave. Will you be attending?'

Mary smiled. The Penningtons' scientific interests did rather make her feel wooden-headed, but it would be lovely to see their fine home, see their happiness. 'That lecture does sound fascinating. But I confess, what I am really looking forward to is your party! I haven't had the prospect of such a very merry Christmas in some time.' She remembered the festive season when she was a girl at the vicarage, before her dear mother died. The music, the scent of evergreen boughs and spiced wine, laughter. Family.

'Well, I do hope no one will leave our home without having a great deal of fun. We're so eager to share it,' Lord Pennington said. He saw one of his scientific cronies in the crowd and left his wife to stroll about the room with Mary. They walked beside the windows, looking down on the baths below, steam rising from the waters into the cold air.

'I do hope our guests will enjoy themselves,' Lady Pennington said. 'My parents always had such a lavish celebration. Ours will be quieter, more in an old style, I think, but still merry. Cosy.'

'It sounds perfect. And Northland sounds like a splendid setting for it all.' Northland Park was a grand estate, not far from Bath, which had been first built in the Elizabethan era, but had been sadly abandoned for years. The Penningtons had been working since their marriage to restore its grandeur.

'And a perfect setting for romance?' Lady Pennington said teasingly.

Mary wondered if she had noticed how she looked at Charles, and felt that terrible warm blush coming back on her again. She wished she had not worn the high-necked pelisse! It was too hot in the Pump Room by half. 'Whatever do you mean?'

'I mean, after all you did for me and my William, how splendid it has all been since we married, I want to help as many people as I can find just such a contentment. So I have invited a person or two who I think might like to be happily wed and need a bit of help. As I did.'

'Oh, Lady Pennington. How kind of you to think of them, and of my agency. I should not want to intrude on your party, though.'

'How ever could you? You are the dearest of friends, you helped me when I needed it most, and now I want to help you if I can.' She looked rather concerned as she took Mary's arm. 'Your agency is a great benefit to those of us who are a bit out of the common way, and who wish to find a sponsor who is the same. I wish to see it prosper. It *must* prosper!'

Something in her vehement tone caught Mary's attention and concern. 'Have you heard any whisper that it might not prosper?' she asked carefully.

Lady Pennington smiled gently. 'I just think your work is so very important. I hope you can help out a few friends you'll meet at my party, that's all! Oh, look, there is Lady Hanson. What a splendid hat! We must speak to her and find out who her milliner is.'

Lady Pennington hurried away through the crowd, and Mary trailed after her, trying to keep smiling, to hold her chin up. Were people watching her now, shaking their heads with pity?

That poor St Aubin girl...the last one unmarried! How can

she expect to make fine marriages for others if she hasn't one herself? they might say.

She glimpsed Penelope and Adele across the room, near one of the tall windows, and wondered with a jolt of bright excitement if Charles was there, too.

As she drew nearer, she saw they seemed to be having some sort of disagreement. Adele looked on the verge of tears, waving her lace-gloved hands as Pen shook her head. Mary glanced over her shoulder, wondering if she should retreat before they saw her, but it was too late. Pen caught a glimpse of her, and a smile transformed her expression. She nudged Adele, who also looked up and smiled at Mary, her eyes still glistening with anger or sadness.

'Mary,' Pen said, 'how lovely you look today! What a beautiful pelisse. Mademoiselle Sandrine is so clever.'

'Yes, indeed. She is a wizard of taffeta and beads!' Mary answered, trying to match Pen's determined merriness, to pretend she'd seen no quarrel. 'They do say she's begun rather specialising in wedding gowns, as well, that her beautiful creations bring luck to any bride.'

'And so they would,' Pen said.

'Well, Uncle Charles refuses to let me order a gown from her for myself, even though Aunt Pen's dress looked well on me at her party,' Adele said with a pout. 'He says not until I am older! How cruel he is.'

Mary gave her a sympathetic smile, though 'cruel' was one of the last words she would use to describe Charles Campbell. *Handsome*, of course. *Rugged. Swoony.* Was that last a word? No matter, he certainly made her want to swoon when he was nearby. But cruel? No. Pulchritudinous. Yes, that was another one...

No. She wouldn't start sighing like a love-struck schoolgirl right here in the middle of the Pump Room! She had decided firmly on focusing on her work, not on good-looking gentlemen who didn't know how to dance.

'Mademoiselle Sandrine's designs *do* tend to be rather sophisticated, but I'm sure you will be able to order her creations soon enough,' Mary said. 'And this dress you're wearing is quite delightful. That shade of green suits your lovely hair so well.'

Adele glanced down at the skirt of her pale green walking dress. 'Do you think so, Miss St Aubin? Truly? I hoped that— well, that *someone* would admire it, but he—that is, *they*—are not here…'

Mary exchanged an alarmed glance with Pen. Charles had said Adele was caught in the web of an unsuitable infatuation, but she did seem to dwell on her doomed romance rather a great deal. Mary saw that it needed to be nipped in the bud. 'But I do see so many admiring glances coming in your direction, especially after everyone heard your exquisite gift for music last night,' she said, trying to keep things light and encouraging, to make Adele smile and perhaps see how many possibilities were out there for her. 'And how fortunate I am to see you both today! I was just speaking with Lady Pennington about her Christmas house party, and I know I'll see you there. I'm so excited to see the estate after they've done so much work on it in the last few months. They say it is quite a showplace.'

'It should be a most merry Christmas,' Pen said. She squeezed Adele's arm. 'And I'm sure we can persuade Charles to let you have a new frock or two for the occasion! You will be the diamond of the party.'

Adele smiled, but it looked rather sad. Mary felt for her, remembering too well how it was to be so young, so full of yearnings that couldn't be understood or fulfilled, confused and unsure but wanting so much to rush ahead. She'd seen how Ella had sacrificed for their future, to take care of Mary, and realised that was what life was about, not about romantic dreams. When she met Charles, though, those old fantasies had come rushing back. It must be even harder to be young, to be stumbling along blindly in life, with no mother. Mary remembered that, too, but at least she'd had Ella. And she couldn't let Ella down now by losing their business. 'You must tell me what you plan to order. I confess I am rather worried that my own wardrobe will not be worthy of such an occasion…'

She managed to distract Adele with chatter about fashion, and left her with Pen and a few others while she went to fetch them some tea. As she studied the crowd around her, she heard a whisper from the two ladies in line ahead of her.

'That Stewart girl,' one of them said, catching Mary's attention with the mention of Adele's name. 'She should have a care, showing such favour to a man like Peyton Clark. Have you heard that his uncle declares he will cut him off, his behaviour has been so bad? Someone should counsel her about the company she keeps.'

'Poor girl, I do feel for her,' the other lady clucked. 'What can one expect from a girl who has lived in Scotland?'

Mary felt a flash of anger on Adele's behalf, then fear. Maybe Charles was not overreacting, if Adele's partiality for Clark was already seen. She hurried out of line to look for Adele, hurrying through the crowd so quickly she tripped over her hem and started to fall, right in front of everyone. Someone suddenly caught her arm before she could make a cake of herself, and she gasped.

She peeked up and saw it was Charles who held her. Charles, who looked down at her in concern.

'Do forgive my clumsiness again, Miss St Aubin,' he said, in that Scots burr that never failed to thrill her to her very toes. 'I've been too long from civilisation, you see.'

'Not at all,' Mary said, and was deeply chagrined to hear how breathless she sounded. She had promised herself to treat him with only politeness and professionalism, and not get carried away admiring his glorious eyes and handsome shoulders! Now here she was, not moments later, sighing over him right in the middle of the crowded Pump Room.

To be absolutely fair, though, he was staring as well. His expression was rather thunderstruck, and time seemed to hover in stillness. Mary started to wonder if she had a smudge on her nose and automatically reached up to check. The teacup she held rattled in its saucer.

'Here, let me take that,' he said, and reached for the trembling cup. His fingers slid over hers as he took the cup, warm and strong.

'Thank you. I just need to return to Pen, I promised her some tea. I was just talking with her and Adele.'

'Shall we go find them, then?' he said. 'I did tell her I would catch up with them as quickly as I could, after I saw to some business this morning. I fear Pen will start to feel like Adele's gaoler.'

'Of course.' They turned and strolled the other length of the room, Mary trying to ignore the eyes that watched them. 'Adele really is such a lovely girl. Such a sensitive heart.'

Charles smiled wryly. To her surprise and delight, a dimple appeared just above the carved line of his jaw, making him look so young, so adorable. 'Perhaps *too* sensitive. I fear I indulge her novel reading and poetry writing, there isn't much else to do at Castle Campbell, and she's convinced she must have just such a tortured love.'

'I well remember such feelings at her age. I pity her. It can be so confusing, so overwhelming, and when we are young we have no experience to tell us how quickly it passes! Especially a young lady who feels so deeply, as I suspect Adele must.'

'She takes after her mother in that. Elspeth was also a kind, romantical soul.' His eyes were shadowed by sadness as he thought of Adele's mother. 'I would never want to crush that out of Adele. To sympathise with and understand others is surely a great gift.'

'It can be, yes.' Mary thought of her work, of the satisfaction she gained in helping people find their happiness. Maybe Adele needed similar work. 'But without a leavening of good sense, it can be a danger, as well.'

'That is what I fear.' He suddenly raked his hand through his hair in a frustrated, quick gesture. 'Oh, Miss St Aubin. I'm afraid I am failing her mother. I promised I would take care of their daughter, but I am an old bachelor who only knows how to run an estate in remote Scotland. Manoeuvring through Society, shepherding a young girl through its perils, is beyond me, try as I might.'

'I can see that you care a great deal for your niece. She is fortunate to have you looking out for her. But it's true that steering her through a first Season will be no simple matter. You must know the other families, especially their sons, know which parties to attend and which to avoid, what to converse about, how to entertain.'

'That's another thing I fear. Pen and Anthony are a great help, but I don't wish to monopolise their time and energy with my own problems. They are still newlyweds. I'm not sure what to do at times.'

'Does she seem serious about this Mr Clark, then?'

Charles frowned. 'She says so, and I do often catch her sighing and writing unfortunate poetry rhyming with his name.'

Mary couldn't help but smile at the image. 'Bad poetry. Oh, dear.'

'Indeed. But I can't tell if it's a *tendre* or...'

'Or a fantasy. Yes. I'm sure that when she can make more friends her own age, meet more young gentlemen, this will fade. In the meantime...' But assuring words failed her. She was worried about Adele. It was so easy to make a mistake at her age, to take a wrong step that led to a great fall. She would have to make enquiries about that Mr Clark.

'It's that meantime I worry about.' He stared out the window with a faraway expression, as if he didn't see the snow, the passing people at all, but a bleak future. 'You say you understand her feelings. Were you in love when you were her age?'

Mary laughed, thinking of her youthful flights of fancy. It was obvious when she stood next to him that they were not all quite behind her, not when the lemony scent of his cologne, the sight of the curl at the end of his hair, made her giddy. 'It was not all that long ago! But, yes, I fell in and out of love all the time back then, as much as I could in our little village. I even wrote poetry! I had Ella to look after me, and nothing went beyond that secret poetry. I certainly have learned prudence, learned to use all that I have seen of human nature at the agency to read people in a somewhat deeper way. Adele will do the same.'

Charles studied her closely, and Mary had that sensation he always gave that he could really *see* her, see beyond her easy smiles to the worries she held deep inside. 'I confess I'm quite curious about your youthful *amours*, Miss St Aubin. Were they much like Adele's dastardly Mr Clark?'

'Not at all. There was not much scope for dastards in our vil-

lage! And for all Mr Clark's seeming failings as a suitor, I admit
he does have a rather nice face and lovely golden hair. I liked
that sort of thing, too. But they were local farmers and squires,
perhaps a visiting poet or two, that's all. I sought an intelligent,
curious mind and kind understanding as well as blond curls!'

He tilted his head, still watching her. Seeing her. 'And if you
were to choose a suitor now, would you seek those same qualities? Intelligence, kindness and golden hair?' He ran a hand
through his decidedly dark hair.

'I—I'm not sure,' Mary stammered. 'I never intend to wed
myself. I have my business to attend to, and seeking love for
others brings me my greatest happiness now. I help them find
their perfect matches.'

A muscle flexed in his jaw. 'I, too, have vowed to never marry
again. I was a poor enough husband once.'

Mary felt the cold touch of sadness as she watched the dark
cloud drift over his handsome face. Had he loved his wife so
very much, then, that no one could replace her? 'I am sorry. It's
a loss to the ladies of Bath.'

He gave her that crooked little smile that made her breath
catch. 'I am sure they are heartbroken. But I was a terrible husband, I wouldn't inflict that on anyone else. I never imagined I
would have to act as a father to a young lady, either.' He glanced
around the room, as if suddenly remembering they were not
alone at all but in the midst of a watching crowd. 'Should we
find Pen? I fear this tea has grown quite cold.'

'Yes, certainly,' she murmured, though she couldn't forget
his words. He would be a terrible husband. She was beginning
to worry that she could not agree.

Charles poured himself a brandy to take away the taste of
the vile Pump Room water and listened as Adele ran up the
stairs and slammed her chamber door. All the way home, she
cried and declared him 'the cruellest man *ever*' for not understanding her love.

He shook his head as her footsteps pattered overhead, and
took his drink to the window to study the scene outside, the park
across the street, the people hurrying past the honey-coloured

buildings as rain threatened again. Yet he didn't really see the clouds, the chimneys, the nodding flowers in the park; he only saw Mary St Aubin's face as she laughed up at him in the Pump Room, her face glowing like summertime. Her laughter making him want to laugh, too, making him feel young and free again.

He hadn't felt that way in a very long time. Or—ever, really. That sort of happiness, of fun, could be quite addictive.

He frowned as he tried to remember his younger days, that heady time when he first met Aileen and was so sure in his recklessness and headstrong heedlessness that he was in love. That he could never make a mistake.

Then he inherited his father's estates and had to grow up in a great hurry. The days of running around town from dances to dinners to horse races with Aileen were over, and by then he had begun to tire of it anyway, to long for something more. He hadn't been able to see the cracks, the uncrossable crevice between them. Aileen did not like the serious Charles. She wanted a rake, a rogue, a person he could no longer be. He longed for a wife to help him, make a life with him, work beside him, someone he could help in return. He couldn't go back.

He frowned now to remember those dark, confusing days, that time when he could not be what his wife wanted. It had long kept him from marrying again, even as he knew he might have to.

And there had been no other lady to capture his fascination. Not until Mary and her golden laughter.

Mary, who liked the social life of Bath, he knew that from what Pen had said, from what he'd seen in Mary's smiling ways in the card room, on the dance floor. A cold castle might not suit her, might make her unhappy as Aileen had been. He feared he could no longer trust his judgement.

A crash sounded overhead, and he winced. He also doubted his judgement in matters of parenthood. He saw too much of his old youthful infatuation now in Adele, and he ached for her. Young love was not the merry thing poetry said it was, it was perplexing and painful, and he could not persuade her it would pass. He could only try to protect her until it *did* pass. And he seemed to be fumbling badly with that.

'*Baw,*' he muttered, and tossed back the last of his brandy. He couldn't sort out matters of the heart as easily as he could an account sheet for his estate, and that was a shame. He could only enjoy Mary's company while he had it, and store it up for the return of cold, lonely days.

Chapter Five

'I don't like the look of that sky, Miss Mary,' her maid Daisy clucked as she helped her into her warmest pelisse. 'Are you sure you should go out today?'

Mary glanced out the window. It was indeed a grey day, but then it always was at that time of year in Bath. The pale, watery yellow sun had not made an appearance from behind the clouds for hours. But she longed for a nice long walk to clear her head after a sleepless night worrying about Charles and what she'd heard from enquiries about Mr Clark. 'I won't be long, Daisy. I did promise I would call on Mrs Heston and her son today.' Mr Heston wanted to wed but was painfully shy, and Mary needed every client she could find for the agency. If a house call was required, she would do it. 'I'll take Miss Muffins with me.'

The terrier perked up from where she hid under a chair and wagged her tail at the promise of a walk. Daisy snorted and handed Mary her hat and gloves. 'Fat lot of good she'd be if it snows. She'd be buried in a drift right off with those short legs.'

Miss Muffins huffed at the insult.

'I doubt it will snow more than a few flakes. This is Bath, after all! Rain, certainly. Snow, probably not.' Though Mary was really not sure. There *had* been more snow than usual lately. But she had to go. 'I'll return by teatime, Daisy.'

She took up Miss Muffins's lead and left the cosy confines of their home and office. The day was quite dark and grey as she made her way out of town towards her potential client's house. She passed a row of cottages, a half-timbered inn, a farmhouse gate. She tried to think only of her patrons but found her thoughts turning more and more to Charles, as they had much too often of late. 'Focus, focus,' she whispered as she made her way towards the house.

By the time she left, she felt rather optimistic about the possible patrons and matches she could suggest for them, and quite pessimistic about the weather. She glanced up into the charcoal-coloured sky, the snow that was starting to fall around her, as she and Miss Muffins hurried back the way they had come. Daisy was quite right, she should not be walking alone with snow coming harder, faster every instant. She'd gone too far from her patrons' house to turn back and was too far from her own home. Miss Muffins whined and pulled back on her lead, no help at all.

'Miss St Aubin!' she heard someone shout, the words almost carried away on the wind.

From the fog and swirling flakes emerged a curricle. A solid, strong figure wrapped in a blue greatcoat sat high on the seat, like a bird of prey swooping down from the snowy sky.

'Miss St Aubin, there you are,' a man said, in a rough Scots brogue. A very *familiar* brogue. 'Blast it, but I'm glad to find you. Here, get in at once.'

'Mr Campbell?' she gaped. Indeed it was, she saw as he leaped down and hurried around to her side, his eyes glowing jewel-green in the gloom. 'What are you doing here?'

'Pen called on you, and your maid said you had gone out, and she was worried about you in this weather. What were you thinking, woman?'

Mary almost laughed at his abrasive tone. She really rather liked being called *woman* in that tone. 'I had to meet with someone for the agency. I couldn't disappoint them.' Or lose their possible custom, even for snow.

'Well, come along, I'll see you home.' He swung her up into his arms as easily as if she weighed no more than a leaf and held her safe above the frozen ground. He settled her on the seat, Miss Muffins on her lap, and urged the horses ahead again. The snow swirled so heavily now she could barely see ahead of them. She could only lean against him, feel the heat of him as her protection against the storm.

Soon enough it became clear they could go no farther. 'There's an inn just ahead,' she called near his ear, above the howl of the wind. 'I saw it when I was walking out. We could stop there for an hour.' And then she would be alone with him at an inn. She knew it couldn't be helped, but her mind was awhirl with images of what could happen at inns.

She shook away such thoughts and gestured to the old half-timbered building as it came into view through the haze.

'You're right, I think we should rest here a while, wait for the weather to clear,' he shouted over the whine of the wind. 'It's not far back from here, but with this visibility...'

Mary peered into the swirling white ahead of them and nodded. She was certainly nervous at the thought of being alone with him, of guarding her feelings every moment, but she saw the sense in this suggestion. He drew to a halt in the small courtyard of the inn and was helping Mary down from the carriage seat when the door squealed open. A square of welcoming amber light spilled out into the gloom.

'Sir! Do come inside right away!' a woman called. 'Were you caught unawares in this storm? Frightfully sudden it was.'

'Indeed. I'm very glad we found the haven of your establishment when we did,' Charles answered. He took Mary's arm in his strong, sure grip, even as her legs wobbled and she feared she would fall. He led her towards the welcoming light of the door, keeping her close.

The landlady, plump and red-cheeked, clucked over their frozen state as she ushered them into a bright common room, warm with firelight and scented with dried herbs hung from dark old ceiling beams. If they had to land in an emergency harbour, Mary thought, this was not so bad at all.

'Well, now, you and your wife just sit down by that warm fire and I'll fetch you some hot negus. My manservant will see to your horses,' the landlady said. She waved at a maidservant.

Wife. How ridiculously thrilling that sounded, Mary thought. She'd spent so long telling herself she would not marry, that she would never rely on anyone else! Surely that flash of excitement was merely the thrill of playacting, nothing serious. A real marriage, a real attachment, would be too dangerous to the independence she'd nourished. She gave a little cough to cover her absurd delight and glanced around the room with its benches and tables, a few men playing cards and drinking ale, the maidservant who took her damp pelisse and cooed over Miss Muffins. How delicious to think they all considered her to be Mrs Campbell!

And Charles did not disabuse them of this notion. 'How kind you are, madame. I was afraid to have my lady out in this weather any longer.'

'And right you are.' The landlady poured out the steaming mugs of warm negus. 'I do have a private parlour where you might be more comfortable,' she said, scowling at the card players until they looked away. 'Nothing grand, I fear. We usually have just a few travelling merchants, some farmers going into town, who stay here, but sometimes we do have gentry on their way into Bath who use the parlour, so it should be comfortable. There's also a small room adjoining where I can send in some warm water for washing.'

Mary glanced at Charles, whose hair was tousled over his brow, a smudge of dirty snow melted on his sharp cheekbone. She feared she looked even more dishevelled after her walk, a positive ragamuffin. She started laughing and bit her lips to try and stop herself. She was quite afraid if she started laughing at their predicament, she would never stop.

Charles, too, looked very much as if he wanted to laugh. It felt all too cosy, too comfortable being with him then. As if they could read each other's thoughts. 'You're very kind, madame, thank you.' he turned to smile at Mary. 'If you want to wait here a moment, my dear, I will go make certain the room is ready. You can warm yourself here.'

'Of course, my darling lambkin,' she teased. She waggled her fingers at him as he followed the landlady down a corridor, then cuddled Miss Muffins close and sipped at her negus.

How fun this could be! If they had to be trapped in the snow, this was the best way to do it. And she would get to be, had to be, alone with him. If she could trust herself, which she wasn't at all sure she could when it came to him.

After a while, she decided she would find him and order some food. The maid directed her to a small chamber at the end of the corridor, and she gathered up Miss Muffins and made her way towards the door.

'Mr Campbell, I do think—' she began, and then froze in her tracks, her words fleeing.

The door to the small washroom was open, and Charles stood there, a towel in his hand, his hair damp and tousled. His face seemed even sharper, more sculpted in the firelight. And his shirt was quite discarded.

He did not look like the marble statues that were thus far her only reference for the male form. They were smooth, nonthreatening, pale. He was burnished gold in the firelight, his skin rippling and satin-like over taut muscles. A pale pink scar was puckered over one shoulder. She could not look away, couldn't move at all, could only stare as her heart beat loudly in her ears. He was—he was *beautiful*.

Mary spun around, closing her eyes tightly. But the image of him was still there, bare skin golden in the firelight. 'I'm so sorry!'

She heard the rustle of fabric, the whoosh of the towel being tossed over a chair. 'Perhaps, under the circumstances, you should call me Charles,' he said, his voiced filled with chagrin *and* amusement. 'Especially as I'm meant to be your husband for the day.'

Mary giggled, seeing every bit of the absurdity of their situation. 'Then you must call me Mary. Or wife o' mine.' She dared turn back around. 'Oh, you shouldn't put that back on yet or you will catch the ague, and this won't be as much fun anymore.' She looked around the small room and found a grey blanket folded over an armchair. 'Here, wrap up in this, and I'll put this shirt by the fire.'

He hesitated, and she wondered if he would squeal and cover

up like a shy maiden. He didn't seem at all the sort. He smiled, lazy and heated, alluring. 'If you're sure.'

'There is no sense in anyone becoming ill because of missish manners. I'm not so prim as all that, I hope, and no one can see us here.' There was nothing to fear—except her own feelings. That shivery awareness of his every movement.

She fetched a blanket and wrapped it around his shoulders, trying not to lean into his heat and hold on for dear life.

'Is that painful?' she whispered, and before she could stop herself, she lightly touched that puckered scar along his shoulder.

His shoulders tensed, and his face took on a sharp, wary, watchful expression. 'Not at all. It's quite old. A souvenir of my misspent youth. I fear I was not always so very respectable.'

She was most intrigued. The maidservant arrived then with a tray of food, and she couldn't ask. She went to the small mirror hanging on the wall by the door to distract herself, trying to smooth her tangled hair. He looked like a Greek god in dishabille, and she looked like a street urchin, red-cheeked with cold, smudged and tousled. It was not fair at all.

But there was little enough she could do about it at present. She went to sit in the chair beside his and sliced a bit of ham and cheese for their plates. 'Will you tell me about your youth, then?' she said.

He laughed but seemed to hesitate. 'I'm not sure it's so very interesting. And it would be a long tale.' Miss Muffins came to sit beside him, staring up at him with adoring eyes. Mary feared she was just the same.

She glanced out the window, which was blanketed in swirling snow. 'I think we have time, and I do love a good tale. I promise I'm not so shockable, Mr—Charles, I mean. I can't be in my sort of work. I hear so many things at the agency.' Like about Mr Clark, which she knew she had to tell Charles in turn. But right now she only wanted to hear about *him*.

Miss Muffins fell asleep, and the only sounds for a moment were her little snores and the popping of the fire. It was so warm in there, so cosy, and it felt all too *right*. Too much exactly where she should be, where she longed to be.

'Now that sounds far more interesting than my mundane stories of a rather ordinary youth of sowing wild oats,' he said.

Mary laughed. She wanted to know all about his wild oats, wanted to know everything about him. 'I will give a story for a story, then.'

'Very well. Sounds like a good bargain.' He stared into the crackling red-gold fire for a long moment. The blanket slipped off his shoulder, revealing the pink line of the scar against his firelit bronze skin. 'I fear it was a duel over a widow whose affections I was sure were mine alone. I was quite mistaken, but being a hot-headed youth, I could not just laugh it away as any sensible man would. So we fought.'

'And what happened?' she asked breathlessly.

'He left me this, and I left him a nicked wrist, and that was that. I was quite bored with the widow by then, and never fought a duel again. Though I nearly did over a curricle race one summer afternoon, when I was sure my competitor cheated.'

Mary deeply envied that unknown long-ago lady who had duels fought over her like a queen in a knightly tale. Envied her that Charles felt so deeply he carried the scar to that day. What would it be like to be the object of his passion in that way? 'Was the lady grateful for your gallantry?'

He grimaced. 'For a time, yes. Then she married a viscount, and I went on to win a carriage race to Brighton.'

He told a few more tales, voyages to Italy, sailing the Channel, the wild Highlands of his homeland.

'But I think it's you who owes a story now, Mary.'

She sighed. 'I am sure I have nothing to compare to duels and Italy and carriage races! I've always wanted to travel, ever since I was a child and read *La Vita Nuova*. I would sketch what I imagined the Roman ruins looked like, the hill towns of the Cinque Terre, the gondolas of Venice. I thought of the ringing of ancient bells, the smell and warmth of it all. It would take me away from the vicarage for a while.'

'Ah, yes. I remember Pen said you were a vicar's daughter.'

'And a great trial to my good father, I was!' Mary said lightly, remembering the narrow corridors of the vicarage, the constant callers, her father's closed library door. 'Especially compared to Ella, who was always perfect and did just as she should. Our mother died when I was quite small, you see, and Ella took on so many duties in our household. Our father was so distracted by his work. I was always reading poetry and wandering off to daydream in the woods. Except for the time I spent at school. I liked that so much! New friends, tea parties. But that didn't last so very long, and then I was back to reading in the vicarage linen cupboard, which was the only truly warm spot in the place.'

She closed her eyes for a moment, remembering those lonely days. She had decided long ago not to marry, not to divide her attention between the agency that was so important to her, Ella and their independence, and a husband and home. She'd seen such things could not mix, not really. No matter how much she might long for a hearth of her own, a place to belong. She'd managed to push down those longings, bury them in work.

Until she met Charles, that is. Then those old dreams haunted her all over again. She had to remember her resolve.

'You wanted a wider world,' he said quietly.

'Yes, indeed. Like Italy! Or sailing the seas, exploring Persian souks, watching the horse races in Paris, all sorts of things.'

'I admit I read too much poetry myself as a child,' he said, and Mary nodded as she remembered what he said about writing terrible poetry and wandering the hillsides. 'Perhaps that was what led me astray when I left home and went to school, then to university at St Andrews! I wanted to be someone different than my father thought me. I just didn't quite know what.'

'It's funny, I always thought you did rather look like a poet,' she said, her heart aching at the sad wistfulness she saw on his face when he spoke of his father, his childhood. She glanced away, worried the wine had loosened her tongue, and soon she would be reaching out to smooth back that tempting stray lock of his hair, touching his face and feeling the roughness of his afternoon whiskers against her skin.

He gave her that quirky smile that always made her breath stop. 'Did you indeed? A poet?'

'Certainly. You aren't quite like all the Bath gentlemen, you know. Your hair, which could use a trim, but I hope you will not do such a thing. Your accent.'

He laughed ruefully and ran his hand through the damp waves of his hair. The blanket slipped a bit on his shoulder, making his skin gleam golden in the firelight. Mary took a deep sip of wine.

'I did try penning a verse or two, as I told you,' he admitted. 'But I fear my talents in literature, much like dancing, lay only in appreciation. Not that ladies in my younger days cared about terrible rhymes, as long as I could mention their sky blue eyes.'

'I am sure they didn't mind a jot,' Mary murmured. What would he say in a poem about *her*? She feared she'd never know.

'But I, too, longed for escape when I was young. Life at Castle Campbell was never what you'd call "lively," despite its history of battles and sieges and such. There is only farming, herding, a small village nearby, seeing to tenants. The sky is always grey, the hillsides thorny. I love it now, but back then I wanted life and noise. So as soon as I could, I ran and ran, and kept running—until my father died, and I had to take it on as my own. Then Aileen happened...' His words faded, and he looked very distant. 'Like you, I had a lonely childhood. My parents didn't much like each other and spent time apart as much as possible, neither of them often in the same house as me. I knew Aileen for a long time, and she was so beautiful, so vivacious. I thought in her I might have found a partner, someone to build a life with, you see. It turned out not to be that way.'

Mary thought building a life with Charles would be a grand thing; she couldn't quite believe a lady would run from such a blessing when she had it. Just because Mary had decided long ago not to marry herself did not mean she couldn't see the appeal, especially with a man like Charles. But she could see in his eyes, in their distant expression, in the small frown on his lips, that it hadn't worked out the way he hoped. 'It did not?'

He laughed wryly. 'Not at all. A partner in building a home, a quiet life that really mattered, was not what Aileen wanted. She longed for parties and theatres, a city filled with admirers, and who could blame her. She was young, we both were. I learned prudence and care. She did not.'

Mary nodded and turned away from him to stare into the flickering flames in the grate. She saw that Charles, like herself, would not easily give away his heart. He'd learned caution, as she had. And that meant they could not be right for each other. 'Then what happened?'

'Adele appeared, and I had to become fully respectable and dull. Aileen would have hated that.'

Mary would never, ever call him dull. They stared at each other in the firelight, amid the silence that grew and expanded and echoed, wrapping them both in some spell. He understood her feelings, her loneliness, and she understood his. How she longed for more in that moment, longed to give him everything, know everything about him! She stood and hurried to the window before she could act on it and reach out for him.

'I think the snow is slowing down,' she said. 'Surely we could make it back to town before nightfall.' She hated to think of the scandal if they did not! And yet she wanted, so very much, to never leave their warm nest at all. To always be just with him, like that, forever.

He came close to her side. Too close, for now she was wrapped in his heat, his delicious scent. She only wanted to be closer and closer. 'I wish we didn't have to leave so soon,' he said, his accent rough and deep. 'It's so peaceful here, so…'

'Yes,' Mary whispered. It was indeed peaceful. Even the rush of her emotions at being near him felt right when they were there, a part of the world as natural as the snow.

She glanced at him and couldn't turn away. She was sure she would never be able to again, and her heart would tear in two when she was forced to walk away.

As Mary St Aubin stared up at him, her caramel-brown eyes wide and glowing pink lips parted as if she wanted to speak but could not. As she stood so close to him he could smell the sweetness of her lavender perfume, feel the silken brush of her loosened hair against his skin. It was intoxicating. Dizzying. She glowed like an angel, and he very much feared all his hard-won control was slipping beyond his grasp.

It had been a great mistake to be alone with her. He'd known it all along, ever since the instant he saw her looking so forlorn, trudging along the snowy lane. All his rescuing knight instincts had come rushing out as never before. Yet what could he do? He could never have left her alone in the snow or driven through the blinding fog until he wrecked the carriage and they both froze. He was obviously a fool where lovely Mary was concerned, but he hoped he wasn't *that* great a fool. And he would never, ever put her in danger.

Now the silence in that small, intimate room, the warmth of the fire against the cold outside, wrapped around the two of them like a shimmering ribbon that bound them together. Held them close, so close there seemed not even a breath between them. She gazed up at him with those summer sunshine eyes, her lips parted as if she felt just the same as he did, had the same longings to touch, to kiss, and he remembered what it was like when they first met. And how it was when they parted.

He did want her with that all-burning desire, wanted her beauty, her grace, her springtime perfume, her innocence and intelligence. He wanted to kiss those soft lips, taste her strawberry-like essence, feel her slim, graceful body against his, hear her gasp his name. Blast it, he wanted her in his bed! He was just a man, after all, one who hadn't had a woman for some time. Surely that was all this could be—nature.

But even as he told himself it was mere instinct, a man and a woman, Charles knew that wasn't true. It wasn't 'nature'; it wasn't just *any* attractive woman. It was this woman. Mary. It was Mary who tormented him with being so very close and not touching.

He didn't just want her touch, the rush of physical satisfaction. He didn't want to just make love to her, though—curse it—he definitely wanted *that*. Just as much, he wanted her comfort, her wry humour, her quick sense of observation and wisdom about the world around her. He wanted to hear the silver bell music of her laughter, to *make* her laugh. He wanted her body, her kiss, but also—could it be? He wanted her friendship. He couldn't have both. Mixing friendship and passion could surely only lead to temporary reprieve from the cares of life, from old memories. Once the flame burned away, one could be left with a warming glow, but it always seemed to him that it ended rather in cold ashes. He couldn't bear that with Mary. He couldn't take that chance and see it end as it once had when he realised he'd been a fool for what he thought was love with Aileen. If he saw the coldness of contempt, disappointment, in Mary's eyes, his heart wouldn't quite recover.

And that made her very dangerous indeed to his equilibrium.

'Charles?' she said softly, and it was as if someone shook him awake out of a dream. He was afraid he'd been staring at her like a love-struck lackwitted lad, and he laughed at himself.

A little puzzled frown creased between her eyes, and he longed to kiss it away. His adorable, confused angel.

'I'm sorry, Mary,' he said. 'The snow must have set me in a *dwam*.'

'A *dwam*?'

'A swoon, a trance.'

She sighed as she gazed out the window again, fraying but not breaking a bit of that shimmering ribbon of creation. Her pale, perfect cameo profile glowed against the greyish light. 'I did think maybe the snow was slowing a bit, but now it looks as thick as before.'

How he wished the snow would just go on forever and ever, leaving the two of them right where they were, alone together in their own magical spell. But he knew very well it could not last, would never last, and soon enough they would go their own ways. He noticed her shiver and guided her over to the warmth of the hearth.

'Come, let's sit by the fire again, you're cold. There's some more spiced wine, and this bread and cheese.'

She smiled at him, a sudden radiant burst that made him ache to grab her against him, hold her so very close they could never be parted. 'I'm not sure more wine is a good idea. I feel so fuzzy-headed already. But I will have one more drop.' She took the glass, and in return picked up his shirt from where it warmed by the fire and handed it back to him. She turned away as he dressed, her hair sparkling in the light, and he hated how cold it was when she was away from him.

Dressed once more, he sat down across from her at the fireside and poured out the last of the wine. As he passed the goblet to her, Miss Muffins suddenly leaped up into his lap and flopped down with a happy sigh.

'She likes you,' Mary said. 'But then, I suspect most ladies do.'

'Not at all. Adele declares I'm an ogre with no romance in his soul, who wants only to cruelly separate her from her one true love.' He tossed back the last drops of wine as his real-world troubles came back on him. 'If only I really did have a tower where I could lock her up until she's safely betrothed to someone suitable. That would make things so much easier.'

Mary laughed, and there was that bell music again, brightening everything around him. 'It would solve many problems in the world, I'm sure. But then the land would be so cluttered with towers.' She sipped at her wine and told him the gossip she'd heard about Mr Clark, that he had no money of his own, and the uncle he depended upon was on the verge of disowning him for his unruly ways. That he had pursued more than one heiress before. He was truly unworthy of Adele.

'But there may be a simpler way to help Adele than locking her up in towers,' she went on. 'Well, simpler but perhaps not *easy.*'

Charles nodded. When it came to helping Adele, he was very glad to have Mary on his side. To no longer feel so alone. 'I'm eager to hear any advice. I only want to be a good guardian.'

'Another suitor, one just as handsome as Mr Clark, but also respectable and suitable in your eyes, might do the trick. If we could find someone to sweep her off her feet and away from Mr Clark, then...' She snapped her fingers, as if conjuring a match from magic.

Charles felt a spark of hope as he looked at her shining eyes. 'Then she would forget him!'

'Hopefully. Of course, it might be his very lack of suitability and respectability that has her so fascinated right now. Feeling as if she must fight against authority, which is you, to win her love can feel exhilarating. I've seen it so often in poetry-minded girls.'

Charles was enthralled by how Mary looked when caught up

in her professional work, her matchmaking. Her eyes sparkled, her hands danced, her toes tapped. He longed even more to kiss her, to feel that sparkle flow into him. 'The *Romeo and Juliet* feeling. I see what you mean. But you have seen a sufficiently alluring Prince Paris come between them?'

'I have, a few times. The trick is finding just the right one, and making sure he feels deeply in love with Juliet. Er...with Adele. And she can never, ever suspect we had anything to do with it. It must appear to be all her own discovery, her heart. There will be a greater selection of princes once she's in London this spring, and she will be so busy with the Season itself. Adele does seem the sort who would very much enjoy shops and galleries, dances and teas.'

'So we must keep her distracted until then?'

'That's the tricky bit.' She chewed thoughtfully on the edge of her thumbnail, staring into the fire as if it might have answers. 'I will look through the agency's files to see if we have any suitable young men. I fear, though, that our client list is a bit—well, not quite as robust as it once was.' Her expression shifted, turning rather sad as she glanced away, and he wanted to fix it for her, repair anything to make her smile again. 'And there is Lady Pennington's Christmas party. Adele will surely enjoy that, and who knows what gentlemen might appear on the guest list.'

And Mary would be at the party. A few days to be with her in the country amid a festive party. That was enticing—and alarming. 'I hope so. As you can see, Mary, I need a great deal of assistance in this Adele endeavour. You're so good with her, making her feel listened to, understood, while I am an old bear who keeps fumbling about the harder I try. I'm sure she would listen to your advice if you would agree to spend time with her at the party. Maybe talk to her all about the delights waiting in the Season, but not for ladies already married to rakes with no fortune.'

Mary laughed again. 'I am not entirely sure *anyone* can turn a young lady from thoughts of forbidden romance.' She tapped at her chin thoughtfully. 'It is so hard that young ladies can so easily ruin their whole lives before they even get a chance to fathom the world around them.'

Charles wondered as he studied her face, her faraway little frown, if that happened to her. He wanted to harm anyone who had ever hurt her. Before he could stop himself, he reached for her hand. Her fingers were soft, warm, so small against his, yet they held so very much. He felt the danger crackling around him, but he raised her hand to his lips and pressed a lingering kiss there, breathing deeply the scent of her perfume.

He glanced up to find her watching him with wide eyes and parted lips, as if captured by the starlit moment just as he was. 'I—I think maybe the snow really has stopped now,' she whispered.

Charles feared his heart had utterly stopped, as well.

Chapter Six

'But I love him! And he loves me. Why can we not be happy? It is so unfair!'

Charles closed his eyes and tried not to sigh as he listened to Adele's wails. It had been going on for an hour, though it felt like days, and yet neither of them seemed able to make the other understand. 'Adele, you must be reasonable…'

She gave another frustrated shriek, and he opened his eyes to see her flop down on a chaise and kick her feet. Sometimes she reminded him so much of her mother—a calm, graceful, grown-up lady—and sometimes she seemed to need leading-strings again. He loved her so much and wanted to scream along with her with his own frustration.

How he longed for Mary, her understanding, her serene smiles, her humour. When she was near, everything seemed brighter, steadier, more hopeful. Easier.

'It is so unfair,' Adele sniffled. Charles's heart ached to see her so unhappy, so lost in uncontrollable feelings she didn't know what to do with. He also laid awake into the night envisaging someone, something, he wouldn't let himself have. His feelings were his own to manage, but surely he could help Adele? Surely he could control her life as he could not his own, could make it turn out right for her?

'I thought the purpose of going to London was to find a husband,' Adele went on. 'Wouldn't it be easier if I married now and saved us the trouble? I know you would rather go back to Scotland.'

She wasn't wrong there. He did rather want to go back to Scotland. Things seemed simpler there, with the crisp wind carrying the smell of heather, with the duties he knew and understood, where there was no lady with melting caramel eyes and tempting laughter. None of this guardian business that always caught him on the wrong foot. But more than that, more than anything, he wanted Adele to be safe.

'Because Mr Clark doesn't have the income to support a family,' he said. He did wish Mary was there, she always had a better way of stating bald, unpalatable facts. 'And his reputation...'

'He is not like that now! He loves me, and he says that's all that matters. And *income*! Who cares about such trifles when there is *love*?'

Charles struggled not to burst into laughter. 'Oh, Adele. Love, especially that of someone entirely unreliable, won't put a roof over your head. It certainly won't buy those Mademoiselle Sandrine gowns you love so much. I promised your mother I would protect you.' He knew he sounded like his own father, and he hated that, but he knew it couldn't be helped.

'I wish *you* would fall in love! Properly in love. Then you would know how it feels. The agony of it all.'

Agony. Charles thought of when he first met his wife, Aileen, how young and wild he was, how he couldn't stop thinking about her. Yes, he had been foolish once, too, had not been able to see that lust wouldn't make a marriage. It wouldn't last. At least he'd had other occupations, and Adele did not. 'I do know how you feel. But we all must learn practicality one day, my darling. You really are so young. You have to consider your future.'

'I am sure I will never feel differently about him,' she protested. 'Time will change nothing.'

'Then waiting a few months, going to London, will make no difference.'

Adele gave one more frustrated shriek. She jumped up, ran out of the sitting room and slammed the door behind her.

Charles went to stare out the window at the leaden grey sky, suddenly so tired. He had begun to feel like a trained parrot, bleating the same lines to Adele all the time and never getting through to her.

I wish you would fall in love! she'd cried.

He imagined Mary, walking in the sunlight, smiling up at him, taking his hand. Making everything just as it should be, only with her presence. Yet he could not fall in love again, could not see that light in Mary's eyes fade.

He had to go and get ready for the night's assembly, though, and he found the only thing that made him want to go there at all was the prospect of seeing her again.

Mary climbed down from her carriage at the Assembly Rooms and studied the pillared portico, the golden light spilling from the windows and doors as guests eagerly flocked inside for a respite from the winter's night. She usually much enjoyed her evenings there, enjoyed seeing friends, considering potential matches, having a game of cards, dancing in the elegant pastel ballroom beneath the sparkling chandeliers. Tonight, she felt even more excited—she might get to see Charles again! She longed to store up every glimpse, every word.

She swam her way through the crowds on the stairs, joined the river of people flowing into the ballrooms, waves of bright silks, pale muslins, waving plumes—and no Charles yet. She took a glass of lemonade from one of the refreshment tables and studied the dancers, amusing herself by making imaginary matches among them.

She glimpsed Ella and Fred dancing, swirling past in a golden haze of happiness as they smiled up at each other. So unfashionable to dance with one's own spouse! But they looked so very happy, no one who saw them could care about fashion. She imagined dancing with Charles like that, moving as one across the floor, eyes for no one except each other. Then she remembered the truth of how he really danced, and she laughed to picture the rest of the couples lying on the floor under the onslaught of his two left feet.

Suddenly, as if summoned by her daydreams, he appeared

through the crowd. Taller than everyone else around him, he seemed to dwarf them with his presence. He was dressed in elegant black and white, but she would much rather he wore a blanket again...

No, she told herself sternly, and waved her fan a little faster. She dared peek at him again and realised Adele was beside him, looking fidgety and distracted as she scanned the crowd, and Charles was frowning.

'Mr Campbell,' Mary said, ever so polite and proper. 'And Miss Stewart. How charming you look! That shade of blue does suit you.'

Adele dragged her attention from the room, and gave a little curtsy. 'Thank you, Miss St Aubin. It's not from Mademoiselle Sandrine, of course, but I did like the lace on the sleeves. If only I *could* have one of her gowns! So artistic, they would suit my own nature so well.' She slid a reproving glance at her uncle. 'I am hoping she can make some of my wardrobe for London, if I must go,'

'And my pocketbook hopes she will not,' Charles said, grumbling through a teasing grin. Even Adele had to give a grudging smile, and Mary had to restrain herself from beaming at him, letting all her feelings pour out of her at his feet.

Mary laughed. 'She is expensive, I daresay, but worth every shilling. She is much in demand. We are fortunate she set up shop here and not in London. But you do show fine taste in choosing that lace, Miss Stewart. It is exquisite.' She took a step closer to Adele, hoping to find a way to distract her from looking for Mr Clark. 'Are you very much looking forward to the Season? I am sure you will find much to delight you there.'

Adele shrugged. 'I am looking forward to the shops. And the museums and galleries, the concerts. I do love music so much. I long to see the Tower and the Elgin Marbles.'

'And looking forward to making new friends?' Charles suggested.

Adele frowned. 'I have enough friends, I think. And one *great* attachment, if only *someone* would listen to me.'

Charles exchanged a long glance with Mary, and she gave her head a little shake. Best not to let such little outbursts take on greater importance, she tried to tell him through her arched brow. She tried to turn Adele's thoughts of 'attachments' by pointing out other gowns, fine jewels, commenting on the music and soliciting her opinion on the orchestra.

As Adele joined the dance and Charles was engaged in conversation about agriculture in Scotland with a group of gentlemen, Mary drifted away to study the crowd. She noticed a mother and her daughter, Lady and Miss Tuckworth, who had made some enquiries about the agency but committed to nothing yet. Mary had rather hoped they would engage her; Miss Tuckworth needed a new coiffure but seemed quite sweet, just the sort of young lady who would suit a young man on Mary's files.

'Miss St Aubin,' Lady Tuckworth said with a sweet, sweet smile, treacly sympathy in her tone that made Mary's teeth ache. 'I'm so happy to see you out and about this evening. We must discuss dear Tabitha's prospects.'

Miss Tuckworth looked as if her 'prospects' were the very last thing she wanted to discuss. She stood behind her mother as if she wanted to hide there, twisting her gloved hands in her yellow-striped skirt.

'I would be happy to, Lady Tuckworth,' Mary said, hoping for one more on the agency's books. Tabitha Tuckworth was exactly the sort she most enjoyed assisting. Like Miss Evans turned Lady Pennington before her, she seemed someone who would bloom once away from her family. Perhaps Mr Heston, who Mary had called on the day of the snowstorm, would do? 'If you would care to make an appointment to call at the office, or I could come to you...'

Lady Tuckworth tilted her head, that sweet, pitying smile still in place, the feathers in her hair nodding. 'I am afraid, Miss St Aubin, that, competent as I'm sure you are at some aspects of such a business, I have some...concerns.'

Mary glanced at Charles, hoping his own conversation meant he could not hear her. She wouldn't want him to think she could not take care of herself! That she could not manage her business. 'Concerns, Lady Tuckworth? I'm sure I can address any reservations you may have. We do have many letters of recommendation.'

'Yet surely most of them came from when Lady Fleetwood and Lady Briggs were in charge of your files? And they are both so very well wed now. A testament to their skills.'

Ah. She *was* the problem. Mary's spinster state. She had feared some potential patrons might think that way—that a lady who cannot find her own match surely couldn't make one for anyone else. Something must be wrong with her! But Mary knew she could see what others needed in romantic attachments far more clearly because she was not blinded by her own emotions.

Not until Charles, anyway. He quite blinded her to all else but him.

'You are so young, Miss St Aubin, and passably pretty,' Lady Tuckworth said. 'You have accomplishments. Dancing, French. If you still cannot make a match for yourself, how can you do so for others? How can you move in the proper Society for making connections?'

'Lady Tuckworth,' Mary said through gritted teeth, trying to keep her smile pasted on. *Passably pretty*, indeed! 'I assure you the agency has many connections, and I have the experience to...'

Lady Tuckworth's head tilted so far Mary feared those feathers would topple her quite over. 'I am just not so very certain...'

'There you are, my dear,' Charles suddenly said. He appeared at her side and took her arm in a loose, gentle clasp. Mary stared up at him in amazement, trying to ignore the warmth of his touch through her glove, the way he smiled at her, bright and dazzling. What on earth was happening? 'I have been looking for you everywhere. Such a crush tonight, don't you agree, Lady Tuckworth? Miss Tuckworth?'

Tabitha and her mother gaped at him, just as Mary was sure she did herself. Tabitha blushed and simpered a little.

'I—yes, indeed, a crush, Mr Campbell,' Lady Tuckworth stammered. 'You are acquainted with Miss St Aubin?'

'Acquainted?' Charles beamed down at Mary, while his widened eyes begged her to play along with whatever he was doing. Her heart pounded so hard she feared the whole assembly could hear. 'We are betrothed.'

'Betrothed?' Tabitha squeaked, a spark touching her for the first time. Perhaps, like Adele, she read romantic poetry. 'How very sweet!'

'Sweet. Yes,' Lady Tuckworth said doubtfully.

Mary froze. Was this a dream? Surely it had to be. For he could not have just said…

That they were betrothed.

'It is quite the secret for now,' Charles said, squeezing her arm. 'Smile,' he whispered to her, and she felt her lips do that automatically. 'You are one of the first to know. I am quite sure we can count on your discretion before the official announcement. We simply could not wait to pledge our troth to each other. We are perfect together.'

Mary knew very well that Lady Tuckworth had not an iota of discretion in her. She beamed at them now, starry-eyed with romance and possible gossip.

Mary tried to keep smiling, to act like this was all quite normal, but she feared her face might crack with it. Had Charles suddenly gone mad? What was happening here?

'Oh, Mama,' Tabitha sighed. 'How romantic it all is!'

'Indeed,' Lady Tuckworth said. Her fan beat hard with the force of her curiosity. 'Well, I must offer my felicitations, and my apologies for misjudging you, Miss St Aubin. I must see about making an appointment to discuss dear Tabitha.'

'You are so kind, Lady Tuckworth. Now, if you will excuse us…' Mary managed to say.

'Of course. Lovebirds must have the chance of a dance!' Lady Tuckworth trilled.

Mary grabbed Charles's hand and marched him through the crowd to find an empty sitting room off a corridor just beyond the main staircase. She ignored the stares that followed them. Behind the card room, she found a small, silent storage chamber, the boxes and crates shadowed hulks in the moonlight and snowshine from the windows. She pulled him inside and slammed the door behind them.

'What were you thinking?' she gasped, whirling back to face him in the shadows. 'Telling her we are *betrothed*.'

There, in that silvery light, he looked like magic. A Scots

warrior, a powerful poet, his hair shining, his green eyes glowing as he watched her warily. But she had to remind herself he was a madman.

'I fear I wasn't thinking,' he said, his brogue thick, his expression heart-meltingly chagrined. He ran his hand through his hair, as he so often did when he was baffled. She would not think about how adorable it was right then. She would *not*. 'I just saw your face when she said you couldn't be trusted to make matches, and I—I wanted to help you. Something in me knew I *had* to help you.'

Mary pursed her lips as she remembered him rescuing her from the storm, carrying her to the inn, a gallant knight in shining armour. Was this all that was happening now? He thought to save her from gossip with that gallantry? That dear, infuriating man! She was quite dizzy with confusion.

'But now she'll tell everyone we are engaged, and then—then we'll have to deny it, and no one will ever trust me to make a match!' she whispered. She covered her face with her hands, overwhelmed. 'Oh, Charles. I know you had the best of intentions, and I…'

I love you for it.

Oh, no, no, no. She could not love him, never love him. His heart had been lost over his wife and her betrayal; hers was locked up against loneliness and temptation, locked up beyond her work. She had to focus on what was important: saving the agency. Never love. A love he couldn't have for her.

'I am sorry, Mary. Truly, deeply. Bringing you distress is the very last thing I want to do. You're good at your work, and to hear her say such disparaging things—I was just overcome with anger.'

She took her hands down and studied his face. His gloriously handsome face. Oh, why couldn't this be real? 'What are we going to do now?'

He smiled at her, that lazy, teasing smile she could never quite resist, and came to take her hand. She *really* could not resist that. 'Mary. Is it really such a terrible thing?'

'To get married?'

'Maybe not actually get married, but to let people think we might?' he said hopefully.

'Whatever do you mean?' she said. It was much too tempting, too alluring, to think of being betrothed to him in any form at all. Especially if it involved some mischief of them against the rest of the world.

'You need to be seen as someone who knows how to make a match. I need someone to help me with Adele. It could be fun, couldn't it?' he teased, his fingers warm on hers. 'We can break it off later. I can break it off and be seen as the villain who could not appreciate a rare treasure. Just until we achieve what we need to.' He squeezed her hand, and she felt not so alone now. She seemed to have a partner in crime, and it was so wonderful. So frightening.

'But what of *your* reputation?' she asked.

He laughed. 'Mine? Never fear, I have faced gossip and disapproval before. I am sure I will have a fine match for Adele by then and will just go back to Scotland. I don't mind if there's some tutting about me after that.'

She studied him carefully, searching his eyes. It was crazy, wild! And maybe, just maybe, it was an idea with merit.

She shook her head. Oh, no, she was being tempted by *fun* again! Maybe even by a deep, secret wish to pretend he was hers, just for a time. What if her heart tumbled away then? What if she could no longer resist him, no longer resist how she felt? She couldn't bear to pick up the pieces of a cracked heart when they parted.

But there was that fun. That mischief. She'd almost forgotten that part of herself, and now it called out to her like a siren song! Of course her heart was in danger, how could it not be when he smiled at her like that? But he held out a way to salvage the agency, the thing she and Ella had worked so hard to build, the thing that was like their family now. This was all false. Playacting. She knew that going into the scheme, surely she could manage it. Surely she could just enjoy his company, store up a few memories and laugh while doing it.

Surely it could work. Couldn't it?

'Maybe it could work,' she began, and laughed. 'Or at least we could have some fun while we go to perdition!'

Charles felt quite like his old self as he walked home from the assembly, having sent his carriage home so he could enjoy the brisk wind on his face, the movement easing his restlessness. The sense of carefree mischief, of fun he carried—he barely remembered what that felt like! At least he had it for a moment, while the golden glow of Mary's laughter carried him forward like a cloud. He had to relish it before the reality of that night's mischief closed in, and he had to unknot the cord of a false betrothal. He'd almost forgotten what it was like to be impulsive, to follow something just to see where it could lead. To give in to the instinct to save a fair maiden, especially when it was Mary St Aubin.

He wanted, needed, to protect her and Adele. He would do anything to see them safe. Mary loved her agency, and he could help her keep it. Surely that meant more than any danger to their emotions? Surely, knowing this was a joke, that it would end, meant they could see their way clear to the finale. And he dared admit to himself, he would do anything to spend a little more time with Mary. To make her laugh.

He paused at the top of a steep, hilly lane to study the flickering lights of the town spread before him, flickering little spots of amber that beckoned through the winter night. It all looked so different because of Mary, and he glimpsed beauty in the cobbled streets and high walls he'd never seen before. The world seemed so wide, so filled with possibilities. Maybe it wasn't real, maybe it would end, but in this moment he felt only excitement at the thought of seeing her again.

He thought of how she'd looked at the party, her bright hair shimmering, her fan sweeping as she studied the gathering with shrewd eyes and laughed at it all. How it felt when she touched him, sparks flying from her fingertips. He'd never wanted to kiss a woman more, to taste her, touch her. The curls and coils of her beautiful hair beckoned, and he'd wanted to draw the pins from those curls, let them stream down over his hands so he could feel their softness. Feel if they were truly as warm as the sun on his skin. To kiss her neck, breathe in her perfume...

'You're daft, man,' he muttered to himself, and laughed. Surely he should attempt his youthful poetry again; it was the only way he could even begin to capture the essence of Mary in words or thoughts. But he knew he could not, because she was truly all feelings.

He raked his hand through his hair, leaving it standing on end. He couldn't remember how to woo a lady at all. Not after his marriage, years trying to forget. How would he even begin to decipher how to make this thing with Mary real? Persuade her that maybe they could actually be good for each other?

Couldn't they? Or maybe he truly didn't have romance inside him now. Nothing to offer her. Nothing to find within himself.

When he held her close, he was sure he'd never wanted anything more. All cares vanished, and there was only her. When he was alone, he didn't know anything at all. Not any longer.

He started walking again, soon running along the lane, his arms outstretched as if he could leave his worries behind. He had a betrothal to plan!

Chapter Seven

'You did *what*?' Ella and Penelope chorused, their eyes wide, teacups frozen in their hands as if they were in a choreographed scene at the Theatre Royal. It would have been funny if Mary hadn't been shaking with nerves.

She glanced at Charles, who stood beside her in Penelope's drawing room. He smiled as man engaged should. Only Mary could see the twinkle of mischief in his eyes.

Right after the ball, she'd realised the great flaw—well, *one* of the great flaws—in her impromptu bargain with Charles. It wasn't just Lady Tuckworth and her sort who would hear of their engagement, and Lady Tuckworth certainly wouldn't stay silent for long. Their own families would certainly find out, and that's what happened. Ella had run an errand before leaving Bath for Moulton Magna and heard a whisper of it.

Charles had suggested to Mary they might confide in their families, but she had feared what might happen if they did, urged that they wait, just a tiny while. She didn't want Ella to know how bad things had become at the agency, didn't want her to feel she had to leave her family at Christmas and tidy up the mess. Mary would fix it first, she had to. And deep down in her most secret heart, she wanted to have these moments with Charles, these secret little moments together. Just for a while.

Charles gently took her hand and gave it a gentle squeeze, helping her feel steadier, more sure this craziness just might work in the end. She'd recalled their meeting at Mollands, the way he made her laugh, made her see brightness around her again, and she had a box of her favourite violet creams tucked into her reticule, a present from him that showed her he remembered, too. He was with her in this—for now, anyway.

'You are *engaged*?' Ella whispered. She carefully placed her delicate cup on the table, delight replacing shock on her face. 'Oh, Mary! I did not realise the depth of your feelings for Mr Campbell.'

'Or his for you,' Pen added.

Mary peeked up at Charles. He looked rather expressionless for an instant, as if he were as unsure as she was how to convey 'depth of feeling,' but then he squeezed her hand again and smiled, as dazzling as a summer day.

'It's marvellous, truly,' Pen said, and clapped her hands.

'Marvellous,' Ella echoed, but she did not sound quite so sure. She glanced between Mary and Charles, a tiny frown between her brows, and Mary felt the pierce of the most awful pang of guilt.

'It is not, well, *official* official yet,' Mary said. 'We aren't having the banns read or applying for a special licence. We're just…seeing how this feels. For now.'

'But I am sure we'll hear wedding bells soon!' Pen said. She jumped up and rushed to hug both Mary and Charles. 'You are both such wonderful people, you deserve all happiness. You deserve each other. We shall be one great family.'

Mary hugged Pen back, yet deep down she felt quite the wretched creature for letting her dearest friends believe their tale. Yet she was sure it was a necessary evil. She had to save the agency and see to Adele's future happiness. Surely it would all be well in the end?

'What a merry Christmas we shall have,' Pen said.

Ella also hugged Mary, embracing her extra close. Mary felt the prickle of tears as she thought of all Ella's care for her, how much she wanted to make her sister proud and happy. 'Shall we just take a turn about the room, my dear?'

Mary glanced at Charles, who nodded, though she feared he looked as doubtful as she felt. Pen chatted up at him, drawing him away and leaving Mary alone with her sister. 'Of course.'

Ella linked her arm with Mary's, as they had so very many times, and they strolled by the windows in the meagre sunlight, looking down at the crowds hurrying past towards the shops, the outline of the Abbey in the distance against the flurries of snow.

'I had no idea you had such fondness for Mr Campbell, Mary,' Ella said. 'You must tell me everything!'

Mary glanced over at Charles, at the way the light turned his glossy hair to the darkness of midnight, carved his cheekbones and the elegant blade of his nose into a classical sculpture. It was true no one would wonder at her feelings for him; she just feared they were becoming all too real and would bite her sharply in the end. 'I wasn't so sure myself. I suppose I couldn't quite put it into words, even in my own mind.'

That part, at least, was so very true. Whenever she was with Charles, or thought of him, which happened far too often, her emotions whirled around like a rainstorm, leaving her tossed about, confused, giddy. 'As we said, we are merely seeing how matters progress right now. Long engagements can be good.'

'That sounds wise. Remember all the patrons of the agency we might have advised thusly? One must be very sure about marriage, it's all for one's future. Mr Campbell's a fine man, of course, handsome and well mannered, connected to so many people we care about. But—you *are* truly fond of him, I hope? That is the only thing that really matters.'

Mary thought of how it felt when Charles touched her, kissed her, the flames that roared and crackled, sizzling over her whole body, all her thoughts. The way everything else vanished when he was near. She thought of his pale, pure green eyes, how he looked at her as if he wanted to devour *and* protect her all at once.

'Yes,' she whispered simply. 'I am fond of him.' And, oh, it was the truth! The honesty of those words hit her too hard. She was fond of him; she relied on him now, more than anyone else, and she worried all her care over the years, her independence, was crumbling away. Had she made a mistake? Should she turn back?

Yet it seemed too late. Ella gave a relieved smile, and Mary couldn't put a burden on her again. 'That is all I could want for you. You deserve all the very best, Mary my darling, and I've prayed you would find happiness such as I have with Fred.'

Mary nodded, remembering how Fred and Ella looked at each other, as if they were the only people in all the world and saw only each other. 'I don't think it is quite like what you have with Fred. But I am very happy right now.'

That, she found to her surprise, was also true. She *did* feel happy, lighter, more optimistic than she had in a long time. Having a partner in mischief was—fun. She felt quite like the old Mary again.

She would not think of where it would all lead. Not yet.

'You'll tell me if things do change, won't you?' Ella took Mary's hand and looked into her face searchingly, earnestly. 'I'm always here for you, Mary, no matter what. I want to know how you're feeling.'

'And I am always here for *you*, Ella,' Mary whispered. 'You have always been the best thing in my life, my safe port. What would I have done without you?'

Ella blinked against a sudden brightness in her eyes, and Mary feared she would start crying, too. 'I am so proud of you, Mary, truly.'

Mary hugged her sister tightly, hoping deeply that the pride would still be there when this ended. 'Oh, now you have made me a complete watering pot, and that will never do!'

Ella took out a lace-edged handkerchief and dabbed at her eyes before doing the same to Mary, gentle and motherly. 'Not on such a happy occasion.'

'You must go and celebrate a wonderful Christmas at Moulton Magna with Fred and the twins, and not worry a jot about me. I promise I will let you know the instant anything changes.' Such as the ending of a faux betrothal. Mary's heart ached a bit at the thought.

'I must be the one to organise your wedding breakfast! Once you decide on where to wed.' Ella tucked away her handkerchief and took Mary's arm again to continue about the drawing room. 'You shall have such fun at Lady Pennington's party. I want a full report on her lovely new home.'

'Certainly. Every carpet and painting and Christmas pudding. She was one of our great agency successes!' And it was to have more such successes that Mary was doing this, she reminded herself.

An hour later, Mary and Charles escaped Pen's house and stepped out into the crisp breeze of the grey-sky day, snow drifting lazily over their heads. 'Do you think they believe us?' she whispered as they hurried away. He offered his arm, and she slid her hand over his elbow, leaning close to his warmth.

'They seemed to,' Charles said, but she thought he sounded rather doubtful. 'Ella did look at you rather piercingly at times, she knows you so well.'

'Indeed she does,' Mary sighed. 'I wish we did not have to humbug them so, they care about us both so much.' They turned down a cobbled lane towards the gates to Sydney Gardens, quiet now in the cold day. They could walk there and not be overheard.

'They did appear terribly happy at the thought of a wedding,' he said.

'Who wouldn't? Lace and orange blossoms and cake, what's not to like?'

He slanted a glance down at her, shadowed beneath the brim of his hat. 'You've attended many weddings, I'm sure.'

'A fair few. The good thing with agency couples and their nuptials means they are nearly always happy and excited to begin their lives together. It's a very jolly way to spend a morning! Not like some other wedding processions I see, where everyone looks so grimly determined.'

'I know just what you mean,' Charles muttered, studying a shop window they passed with a faraway expression she wished she could read. Did he think of his own first wedding? Of the ghost that haunted his heart, stood between him and giving his love away once more? Then he smiled again, shaking off whatever wistfulness had passed over him, leaving Mary aching to comfort him. 'Shall we walk in the gardens for a while, then? I think the snow is ceasing.'

'I'd like that.' She longed to just walk with him, laugh with him, forget about work and schemes and everything else, as she only could with him.

Sydney Gardens was indeed wonderfully quiet and peaceful, with the pathways dusted with glittering snow, the fountains silent. But a few passers-by did rather stare, and Mary worried the secret was now out.

'After your great experience of such events, what would you want for your own wedding?' he asked lightly.

Mary laughed. 'Oh, I do like planning parties and such! When I was young, I would hide at the back of my father's church and watch him preside over weddings. Like many little girls, I would imagine myself as a bride, what I would wear, how I would feel...' Her words faded as she recalled that dreamy girl she'd been, the visions she'd had of clouds of romance, brightness and fun. Now she thought she didn't want to belong to anyone or have them belong to her, to rely on their happiness for her own. She'd seen such things go awry as often as they'd gone well at the agency. She'd seen her mother leave her behind, seen her father bury himself so far in work he couldn't see his children. Even Ella left in the end, though for the best of reasons, Fred and the children. Nothing in life was within control. A lady had to depend upon herself.

Yet she was so tempted to lean on Charles, confide in him, hold on to him, and that was dangerous.

'You never wished to wed, then? You would surely be an expert at it all.'

Mary laughed wryly. 'Never an expert, no. I am good at helping others find mates, seeing what would make them happy. But I grew up seeing how lonely a match can be when it's not exactly right, or when something terrible happens.' She thought surely he could understand that, after his sad marriage, and she dared to tell him a bit of her truth. 'My mother died when I was a child, and my father could not bear it. He buried himself in his work, and Ella was left to help me. I saw that one can only really rely on oneself in life.'

The glance he gave her from beneath the shadowed brim of his hat was strangely sad, and Mary feared he pitied her. She could never bear to have Charles, of all people, feel sorry for her. 'But,' she added lightly, 'I do enjoy a fine wedding.'

'What would be your dos and don'ts for a wedding, then?' he asked.

Mary made herself laugh lightly. 'I should be a wedding planner, then, as well as a matchmaker? I think I would be rather good at that. I do so like to *organise*.'

'And I hate it,' he said, with a dramatic grimace that made her laugh more. He did always make moments so much more fun. 'I am a great shambles, as Adele likes to remind me. I lose things in my office all the time, forget appointments, neglect social obligations.'

'It does sound as if you need a tidier-up,' Mary said.

'Indeed I do.' He gave her one of his crooked little smiles, the ones that made her heart thunder so, and she wondered suddenly if they *could* be a good match. She could run his castle; he could make her laugh. They could kiss all the time! And it could be...

No. It couldn't be. Running away never seemed to solve problems for anyone, and it would mean leaving behind her work or, worse, handing it back to Ella. She deserved a happy life with her family, which was why Mary needed Charles's help now. It didn't matter how much she'd like to see his castle, see the place that made Charles—Charles.

She turned away and stared hard at the icy fountain, imagining its cold in her own heart.

'Now, my advice for weddings...' she said. 'I would have Mademoiselle Sandrine make my gown, of course. She should make every Bath bride's gown.'

'Mademoiselle Sandrine? Oh, yes, the modiste. Adele is always saying I should let her order gowns there.'

'And so you should! Her creations are amazing, more than mere ribbons and fabric. They are created to suit each woman uniquely, make her feel lovely. It's also a joy to visit her shop. So inviting and elegant. I would definitely get my wedding gown there, if I required one, so I would feel like a—a confident empress on my day!'

Charles laughed, the sound so deep and rich, like summer sunshine. That's what he always made her think of, summertime. 'An empress? I picture you more as a fairy queen, I think.'

Mary shivered with a sudden golden glow at such words. He thought of her in that way? It sounded so fanciful, so...romantic. 'A fairy queen? I'm sure I feel too prosaic for that.'

'You, Mary? Prosaic? Never! You are all dances and merriment.'

She felt the heat of a blush stain her cheeks. Those extraordinary eyes of his—green as the sea one minute and deepest, most mysterious jade the next—looked at her with such intensity she could feel the shaking of it all the way to her toes, in every part of her. He seemed to see *all* of her, as no one else ever had.

She dug her nails into her gloved palms to keep from leaping on him right there on a public pathway.

She looked away to the silent fountain of a Grecian goddess. If only she could stay as cold and emotionless as her, distant from the world and its dangers. 'I am sure Mademoiselle Sandrine could make a fairy queen gown, too. One with tulle and lace and maybe silver spangles. Flower wreaths.' Ah, yes, she could picture it, floating and ethereal, drifting her through a flower arch like a cloud. And she could picture Charles there, too, tall and powerful, smiling at her from an altar...

'There would be roses and lilies,' she said quickly, trying to distract herself from thoughts of his smile as he held out a hand to his bride. 'So I suppose it would have to be in summer. An arch around the church porch all white and pink! A bouquet of rosebuds tied with more pink ribbon, rose petals scattered by little girls into the air. And green, of course, emerald ivy leaves...'

'To match the fairy queen's emerald crown?' he teased.

To match his eyes. 'Exactly. And a wreath of roses. No bonnets with veils! I would want to see everything that happens. Only a few guests, people who truly care about the match. That's the best luck at a wedding.' And her family had grown small, too, with no parents to weep with joy and wistfulness. There was Ella and Fred, and she knew they would be the ones crying with joy for her. She pushed away that pang of guilt that always came when she thought of Ella. 'But there would be more! At my father's cold church, the ancient but quite adorable Mrs Fristle played the organ. She'd been doing it for simply decades, and though she sometimes let others play for Sunday services, she insisted on doing it herself for Easter and weddings. She always played "Gentle Patience Smiles on Pain" for some reason, one wouldn't have thought it quite right for a wedding, but it wasn't an event without it.'

He laughed. 'So you would have the estimable Mrs Fristle play that song?'

'Oh, no, she passed away years ago, I'm afraid. But maybe that song in her memory. And some Mozart! I do love Mozart.' She suddenly realised it was *Charles* she pictured at the altar, his smile, his glowing eyes. His hand reaching for hers. She shook her head hard, reminding herself this was only a fantasy, a game. She couldn't have such feelings, and even if she did, he could never return them. She had to rein in her imagination, that was all.

'And what about the wedding breakfast?'

She peeked up at him, wondering if he teased her, but worse, he looked terribly serious. Almost as if he, too, pictured a wedding where they held hands.

'Oh, more guests than at the church, of course, for I would want quite an enormous cake,' she said, trying to keep it light and dreamy. 'And there would be salmon mousse and white soup and mushroom tarts. A flower-bedecked carriage to carry the couple away at the end. Somewhere simple and quiet...'

She looked up at him, and he stared back at her as if they both envisaged what might happen in a quiet cottage after a wedding. She turned away, warm-cheeked, flustered.

'But we need only concern ourselves with managing an engagement,' she said with a nod. An engagement that needed to look convincing.

'Indeed,' he said with a little cough. 'Lady Fleetwood and Pen know now. I shall have to tell Adele before we go to the Christmas party. Hopefully it will distract her from Mr Clark.'

'I do feel so dreadful for deceiving them now,' Mary admitted. 'But if I am to save the agency...'

'And if I can keep Adele safe and happy...' He nodded. 'But I do understand. I feel the same.'

'We should decide now how to get out of this in the end, without hurting anyone,' Mary said. She did fear now *she* would be the one hurt when she couldn't be with him, see him anymore. It was looking more and more as if their impulsive scheme was a danger to her. 'A broken betrothal could obviously look bad for the agency.'

'I shall make it look entirely my own fault,' he said, determined and stony. 'You can declare you could not bear to live in a quiet, cold old castle in Scotland when so many here need your help.'

'Yes. Indeed. I could not.' She pictured a medieval fortress of a place, grey and tall against the heather. Strolling the ramparts arm in arm with him...

No. Focus on the 'grey and cold,' not the 'cosy with Charles' bit. 'And I could say what you suggest, that the agency and its patrons need me,' she went on. 'It would be a source of gossip for a few days, but then hopefully the glittering new matches I make would erase any doubts. I just need to prove myself. But I'd love to know what your home is like, really. I only know such places from novels.'

They stopped at the edge of the slushy river, and Charles studied the water with a most thoughtful, faraway expression on his face. 'It's a harsh beauty, aye, but the most profoundly true beauty. In the mornings, the mist comes up and wraps around the old stones of the house like...like shreds of grey lace. Such mists have come upon the castle from its earliest moments, the same as what we see now, and in those moments I feel close to all my family that has come before me.'

Mary could just envisage it, morning light trying to break through the fog, casting gleams and shadows on the walls, grey and silver and purple. 'It sounds wonderful. My own family...'

'Yes?'

'Well, it was just me and Ella for so long, I don't know about any other family at all, really. To see things as my ancestors once did, know that we are connected—that would be wondrous.'

He reached out and gently touched her hand, as if he recognised her bittersweet feelings at such a thought. 'And when the mist vanishes into the daylight, you can see the hills all around, silver and amethyst with the heather. You could wind some in your hair and be a fair lass indeed.'

Mary laughed. 'I should enjoy that. It's been an age since I made flower chains for my hair!' She had a vision of dashing up the hills with him, the sharp green scent of it all intoxicating, flowers wound around them. But that would never get them what they had vowed to find together, solutions to problems they had right here and now. It would not erase the past or the present and all that came between them. 'But what shall we do now, to make people think our betrothal is real?'

'We could quarrel at an assembly,' Charles said after a moment's thought. 'And then make up!' His green eyes glinted with mischief, making her laugh. It almost made the magical Scottish mist vanish from her mind. Almost.

'And you could sing beneath my window at night!' Mary cried. She started to feel herself rather enthusiastic for the theatricals. 'No dancing, though. But for now, we must look engaged. You must take my hand often, as if you can't help yourself.'

She impulsively grabbed his hand, and immediately realised her mistake. Even through their gloves, she felt the strength of him, the heat of his fingers. Yet she could not let him go. Those sparkling, shimmering bonds she'd so often felt between them seemed to tighten around her, pulling her close to him.

'And I could press your hand to my heart.' He matched his words to action, taking her hand and holding it close over his coat. She could feel the steady rhythm of his heartbeat there. 'And kiss it, thus.'

Staring into her eyes, he raised her hand to his lips and pressed a lingering kiss to her fingertips, warm through her gloves. It was all she could dream of, all she longed for, and all she couldn't have in reality. He smelled of lemons and sunshine, and she felt like soaring up into the sky on a cloud. All heat, excitement, fun.

There was a laugh in the distance. Mary was startled, dropped to the cold, hard ground from that shining cloud. She suddenly felt the chilly wind again. She broke free from him and stumbled back a step. She stared up at Charles, stunned, dizzy. He stared back.

'I—I think we need some rules,' she said hoarsely. She could still feel him, taste him, even as they stood apart, not touching at all.

'Rules?' he muttered.

'Yes. If we are to keep up our show.'

He smiled, slow, lazy, and she had to hold herself back from throwing herself against him again. 'I would say anyone who just saw us would think we were engaged.'

Mary couldn't help but giggle through her daze. 'That is the problem. We must maintain control, if we are to preserve the story of our betrothal—and its breaking off. And control over *ourselves*.' She nodded. Yes. She had to simply control herself and her impulses.

And that had never been her strong suit.

He straightened his coat, picked up his hat from the ground where it had fallen in their kiss. 'What rules would you suggest?'

'Well…' She tried to organise her swirling thoughts. 'No kissing. That should be number one.'

He frowned. 'Where is the fun in that?'

She pursed her lips to keep from laughing. 'So, rule number two. No fun.'

'Ach, now you're just being daft. I barely remember what being betrothed is like, I was quite young and callow the first time, but I am sure it was not *fun*. It should be!'

'A real engagement, yes.' Though she *was* having fun, she was startled to realise. She loved thinking of rules she wasn't sure she could keep, loved seeing his teasing little smile, loved having a scheme. A secret. 'But it is Christmas, and we're going to a party. I suppose there could be *some* amusement. But not too much.'

'Just a tiny bit.'

'A tiny bit, yes.' She tapped her finger on her chin, planning.

'So, rules. No whispering in dark corners. No walking alone in the evenings. I will help you dance, but no enjoying it. No twirling about.'

'I think I can safely promise not to enjoy dancing. I could never keep up with a fairy queen's light step.'

'And no flirting!' she cried. She felt such a terrible, happy little glow when he called her that.

He clapped his hand over his heart. 'I vow I never flirt. Not now. I am an old, responsible, stodgy bachelor.'

'Now you are the one being daft. No one would ever call you stodgy.'

'So, what about holding hands? I assume that's allowed.'

Mary reached out and tentatively touched the tips of her fingers to his, waiting for that lightning strike. The more she touched him, the more she craved it. 'Maybe. But not like this!' She wrapped her fingers around his tighter, clinging on as if she were drowning.

He smiled down at her, slow, sensual, and wrapped his other hand over her fingers, holding them together. '*Och*, Mary, you are *delichtsome*. Like—I don't know. Fireworks. Fizzy champagne. I've never known anyone quite like you.'

Mary smiled. *Delichtsome* sounded quite a wonderful thing to be. 'I thought you never flirted now.'

'I don't, but you bring it out in me. The old me. You make me remember how bright the world once seemed.'

And he made her see he could be the storm in her heart and the shelter from the world, just the same. It was sorely, deeply tempting. 'So, shall we agree to have just a little fun being engaged, then?'

He raised her hand to his lips for a lingering kiss. 'Some fun, it is. And a few simple rules.'

'It's a bargain, then.'

After all, how hard could pretending to be engaged really be? Terribly hard, she was afraid. The more time she spent with Charles, the more she cared about him, and the more you cared about someone, the more there was to be lost. She dreamed of love, of a life with someone like Ella had, but the reality of it was frightening. It was better to be alone than unhappy with the wrong person. And Charles, after his marriage, after his youthful follies did him false, could never return love, surely. After all the fun and laughter, that would be too painful.

She glanced up at him now, at the way the pale sunlight sparkled on his hair, the half-smile on his beautiful lips. Surely with only a false betrothal, there was no risk, nothing to lose. But she feared she was about to step foot off a cliff into an unknown blue-sky future, and she shivered.

The string of little silver bells on the shop door sang out a joyous welcome as Mary stepped inside Mademoiselle Sandrine's shop the day after her discussion of rules with Charles. As always, it felt like an oasis of serenity and elegance, of lightness and brightness against the winter day, against a sleepless night thinking of Charles, and she let out a deep breath as she looked around.

Everything—from the gilded letters on the small sign on the door to the pink-and-blue pastel floral of the carpet, the scent of rose pot-pourri and lavender in the air, the blue satin draperies at the bow windows, and the frescoed ceiling of goddesses and cupids on clouds—seemed ineffably, perfectly *French*, in the old regime way. Just like Sandrine's musical accent, her perfect way with stylish accessories.

The blue brocade chairs and small marble-topped tables holding porcelain trays of tiny pastel cakes, the attendants in their blue dresses and crisp white aprons waiting on patrons, told everyone they could expect nothing but the most fashionable and tasteful there, and the gowns on a few mannequins dotted around the floor confirmed it.

Mary felt delighted as she studied a pale lilac and white striped walking gown, with a matching pelisse trimmed with swansdown. A ball gown of creamiest, heaviest satin that glowed. A display of gloves fanned out on a glass counter, blue, pink, butter yellow, snowy white. She longed for all of it, every single bead and embroidered flower! She wondered what Charles would think of her in that sophisticated dancing dress of burgundy silk and lace, daringly cut low over the shoulders...

But no. She was not there for herself that day, not there

for something to entice her 'fiancé,' even if she was terribly tempted. She was there on a mission.

Mademoiselle Sandrine herself appeared from behind a blue velvet curtain, which Mary knew led to the studios and offices that produced such magic.

Like her shop, Sandrine was the perfect image of elegance and calm. Tall, slender, clad in mulberry silk with an embroidered shawl draped over her shoulders and a neat chatelaine at her waist, her dark hair twisted in an elaborate chignon at the base of her swan-like neck. Everyone in Bath hoped for gowns created by her, yet it was true no one knew much about her, knew anything about her life in France or why she came to Bath. The mystery just seemed to make the gowns more enticing.

'Mademoiselle St Aubin,' she said with a smile, 'how lovely to see you! Have you come to look at some of the new fashion plates for springtime? I just got a lovely book from London. There is much to suit you there.'

'Oh, you are a wicked temptress!' Mary said with a laugh. 'I do love the springtime frocks the best of all. The bright colours and light fabrics.'

Sandrine nodded. 'It is my favourite, too. But I have your gown ready for Lady Pennington's party, as well. We shall look at that book, then I'll wrap it up for you. Do you have time for tea or maybe some chocolate?'

'Yes, thank you,' Mary said. She was in a hurry to return to the office, to making matches. Everyone who had arrived that morning had wanted only to ask about her engagement!

'Sophie, fetch the tea, *s'il-vous plait*, and those new cakes from Mollands,' Sandrine said to one of the blue-clad assistants, and led Mary to two chairs set in a cosy little window nook, near a display of—what else?—a wedding gown of palest sky blue silk overlaid with organza, a matching veiled bonnet on a stand beside it.

As Sandrine poured the tea and offered some of those luscious little cakes, Mary studied the fashion plates. She smiled at a very stylish tartan pelisse, thinking of Charles and his Scottish castle.

'These are indeed very *a la mode*,' she said. 'I especially like this spencer with the braid on the sleeves, so cunning, and this organdie theatre gown.'

'And that, perhaps?' Sandrine said, rather slyly, as she gestured to the tartan. 'It is called the Auld Alliance. For the friendship between Scotland and France, of course, though I am not sure a Parisian lady would wear such a fabric. Which is too bad, this dark green is beautiful.'

Mary frowned. Were rumours of her engagement already flying around the crescents of Bath? 'Why would you say that?'

Sandrine laughed. 'Oh, *mon ami*! Bath is a small village, isn't it? And people do like to whisper and confide here in the shop. That's the point; this is a safe space for them. A tiny bird told me you and a certain handsome Scotsman are secretly betrothed.'

'Not so secretly, I see,' Mary murmured.

'The bird brought her baby chick with her to order a new gown in this pale green taffeta. She said you especially advised it once at your agency.'

'Ah. Lady Tuckworth, I see.' She *had* advised the green for the Tuckworth girl before, when they asked her advice in attracting a style-minded gentleman. Funny how only now did they think of her advice.

Sandrine made a locking motion at her lips. 'I am silent on my sources. But is it true? He is so very handsome! Like an—an ancient warrior. Defending his castle from the Vikings, leading his knights into battle…'

Mary laughed. 'Yes, yes, I see what you mean.' And she thought exactly that when she looked at Charles, that he didn't quite belong in their modern world. She studied Sandrine and wondered if she should be jealous. Other women would admire him, certainly, and Sandrine was very beautiful. Very mysterious.

'We are—fond of each other,' Mary admitted. Such lukewarm words for the burning emotions she felt when he was near! 'But we have not called the banns yet. In fact, he is rather the reason I'm here.'

Sandrine clapped her hands, looking terribly gleeful. 'You wish to order a wedding gown! And maybe a little trousseau?'

Mary glanced again at the frothy wedding gown on the mannequin, the pearl-edged veil, and sighed. 'If it comes to that, of course. There is no one else I would trust more with such a creation. But today I wanted to see if you might have something that would suit Miss Adele Stewart, his niece. She is about to have her first Season.'

'Ah, yes, Mademoiselle Stewart. Such a pretty young lady, and her playing at Mrs Oliver's was so enchanting. She came here one day with Mrs Oliver, I remember, and seemed truly wistful over that display.' Sandrine nodded to a gown in the other window, a pale pink and creamy white muslin trimmed with satin roses. 'Yet she did not order anything.'

'She says Mr Campbell won't let her. That she is too young. Yet you might have noticed she did borrow one of Penelope Oliver's gowns for the party, and looked so beautiful. I'd like to help her gain some confidence before she goes to London, and how better than with one of your perfect dresses.'

'Hmm.' Sandrine tapped at her chin, her eyes narrowed as she seemed to go into herself where there were visions of every lady's perfect gown. She got up and looked through a tray of ribbons, a rack of lace shawls. 'This one, maybe?' She held up a white-on-white embroidered shawl and shook her head. 'Not quite right. The frock in the window is a good start, but I want to do something just a bit different. A bit unique.' She turned to a rack of rolls of jewel-like fabric, rich satins, delicate silks, ethereal muslins, and got caught up on a pink chiffon embroidered with slightly darker roses. 'This as an overskirt! And a wreath at the shoulder. Young, spring-like, just like her.'

'Yes, perfect!' Mary exclaimed. The colour would be delightful on Adele, taking her creamy skin and red-gold hair and making them positively garden-like. 'You always do have just the right garment for each person.'

Sandrine swirled around the chiffon in a blur of sunset-pink. 'Just like what you do, Mademoiselle Mary! You find each person their perfect match, the one who will make them stronger, braver, even more themselves. And then they come here for me to make their dream days complete.' She sat down across from Mary again and smiled. 'I'm glad to hear you have found your own dream.'

'What do you mean?' Mary asked cautiously.

'You and Mr Campbell. You and your sister have helped so many people through your agency, you deserve your own happy ending.'

Mary bit her lip. 'Such nonsense. I hardly need *him* to do my business.' But wasn't that the whole point? She did need him, right now anyway, to build up the agency.

'Certainly you do not. We females must put up with so much in this life, manage so many things and hide so many emotions. Who better to run a business?'

'And it is not exactly a dream. Mr Campbell and myself.' Though it could be. Wasn't that why she stayed up so very late thinking about him? That was why she was beginning to wonder if this was such a good idea, no matter how it seemed in the moment. She just had to remember it was fake.

'But I am sure it's quite wonderful. It's all over your face! I can always tell when a love is worthy of one of my gowns, and yours assuredly is.'

'So, your gowns are magic?'

Sandrine laughed. 'Something of the sort, yes.'

Mary took a long sip of tea, hiding her embarrassment at being so obvious behind the cup. 'Have you never been tempted to make such a gown for yourself?'

It was as if a grey cloud skidded across Sandrine's elegant face, and Mary felt terrible for bringing up something that obviously caused her friend some sort of bad memory. 'I have never met anyone who could match one of *my* gowns for a wedding day. I shall not marry. I *cannot* marry, I have my shop to think of.'

Mary nodded. Did she not feel the same? A business and a marriage could seldom match, and the agency meant so much to her. 'Well, if you change your mind, the agency would love to be of assistance,' she said, setting down her teacup. 'You would be the great prize of our books! So beautiful and elegant, you would have your pick.'

Sandrine waved this away. 'Nonsense! I am merely passable, it's my gowns that lend elegance.' She ran her fingers over her own dark satin skirt. 'I am just an old spinster and shall remain so now.'

Mary wondered what really could lurk in Sandrine's past, but she knew her friend would never say. Never tell of her old life in France. 'Perhaps you will find someone at Lady Pennington's party,' she suggested. She would so love to think of someone's romance besides her own for Christmas!

'I doubt it. But I shall definitely have the gown ready for Mademoiselle Stewart. I have Mrs Oliver's measurements on file, and they are much of a size, so I can use that to make a start. To make a woman's clothes is to give her armour and be her secret keeper.'

Mary sensed the first secrets Sandrine kept were her own, hidden behind the beautiful facade of the shop, and she would say no more that day. 'Marvellous. And while I'm here, I'll just take a pair of those pink gloves.'

'And put in an order for the Aulde Alliance? I could get a bolt of Campbell tartan. It could make a wedding gown as well as white muslin or blue silk...' Sandrine laughed at Mary's expression and rose to pack the new gloves in fine tissue. 'No, no, I see you will make no such order today. But just in case you need it later...'

Chapter Eight

The Crown Club on Milsom Street was always a masculine haven of silence, far from noisy homes, social obligations with demanding wives and the pressures of business. It was filled with deep, dark velvet upholstered chairs, carved black marble fireplaces and rooms where deep play could take place.

It was also a good hiding place.

Peyton Clark sat slumped in a leather settee near a crackling fire, hoping no one would look for him in such a quiet corner. 'Quiet' was not often a quality associated with him. He lived in chaos and motion, gambling, racing his carriage, betting on horses, finding a willing woman or two. And he certainly did not *enjoy* quiet. It was very boring. Now he found it was forced on him.

He drained his glass of port wine and gestured to a footman for more. He'd had a few glasses before that one and was feeling rather fuzzy-headed, but it wasn't as pleasant as usual. Worries pierced even through wine fumes. And wine was really the only pleasure left to him for the moment. He dared not add to his gambling debts, and Mrs Tolliver's fine establishment of beautiful, obliging women—and a few men—was firmly off-limits. Mrs Tolliver had tossed him out for not paying what he owed there last time and threatened to set her burly watchmen on him if he came back with no coin.

Peyton had hopes that this sad state of affairs wouldn't last much longer. He'd been in utter despair, a black rage, when his stupid old uncle declared he would cut him off.

'Not a single shilling more until you reform your way of life!' Morton Clark had raged as Peyton stood before him, hat in hand, boiling silently with fury that the old man would treat him thus. 'I have tolerated far too many outrages because of what I owe my late brother, your poor father's memory, but no more. This is the last straw!'

So much fuss for one tiny little indiscretion. One little scandal. How was he to know how young the lady had really been? Surely, as Uncle Morton's only remaining family, he was owed some consideration and respect! To throw one's own nephew practically out on the streets was beyond the pale.

At last, Uncle Morton's prosing sputtered off, and he slumped into his chair, staring up at Peyton with burning eyes sunk in his wrinkled face. 'I can give you only one chance.'

And then the sun pierced that crimson anger. A touch of relief. Of course! Peyton was due another chance. 'Oh, Uncle, you won't be sorry! I will reform, I will…' He calculated how fast he could get back to the nearest gaming hell.

'I certainly will not be sorry. Because there are conditions.'

'Conditions?' What did that mean?

'Yes. I will release your allowance, with a substantial increase, as well as purchase a house on King's Crescent…'

'How very generous, Uncle!' That crescent was quite fashionable, the perfect place for a gaming party.

Morton had cut him off with a sharp wave of his walking stick. 'As soon as you marry with my approval. A lady of respectable family and utmost virtuous character. A lady of fortune, a necessity for *you*, I'm sure. One of sturdy morals, who will guide you on a better path.'

Now, he drained his glass again and stared morosely into the fire. Maybe, just maybe, matters were not all *that* dire. He could borrow a bit more, just enough to hold him over, albeit at a criminal rate of interest. And now there was a prospect. One his uncle might even approve of. Adele Stewart.

He remembered when he met her at an assembly, begged for a dance. So young and pretty, with golden-red curls and wide green eyes that stared up at him so admiringly, as if she saw only him. Listened only to him. Exactly what a chap wanted in a wife, someone obedient and sweet. So enticingly innocent.

It was a perfect plan. Except for Adele's monster of a guardian.

Peyton scowled as he thought of Charles Campbell. The man guarded Adele like a dragon, not letting anyone near her. There had to be a way around him.

'Someone sitting here, old chap?' a voice asked, and Peyton glared up to find Percy Overbury standing by the other chair near the fire.

Peyton had enjoyed the quiet for his brooding thoughts, but Overbury was a good enough sort. 'Not at all, do join me,' Peyton said, waving towards the chair. 'Some port?'

'Please. A great deal of it.' Peyton noticed for the first time that Overbury's face looked rather glum under his artfully floppy waves of hair.

'That bad, eh?' he said as he gestured to the footman.

'Dreadful. I was so ecstatically looking forward to the Pennington party, and now—now I am in utter despair about it all. I am done in by true love.'

'True love?' Peyton could not fathom such a thing, though he did understand *fake* romance well enough. It was exhausting to keep it up. 'What happened, then? Some gel throw you over? They all seem to swoon over those books of yours.'

'Worse. I can't even catch her first so she could throw me over! She slips away from me like a—a silk scarf in my hands. Like a summertime breeze. A ray of silver moonlight...'

'Not amenable to poetry, then? No adventure in her? No barque of frailty?'

'She is the most virtuous! The most perfect angel that ever was seen. The most beautiful goddess I have ever beheld. My heart aches to make her mine!'

'Offer a diamond bracelet from Rundell and Bridge and an

account at Mademoiselle Sandrine's shop. That usually does it for me, right quick.'

Overbury looked horrified. 'She is not that kind of female! She is a *lady*. I want to marry her, to possess her fully. But she eludes me.'

'I sympathise with you there, Overbury.' It seemed they both had to fall into the parson's mousetrap, yet the satisfying snap of it evaded them. 'I also cannot secure the hand of the lady I seek.'

Overbury looked astonished. 'You—*you* want to get married, Clark?'

'A sad prospect but a necessary one. My uncle has put his gouty foot down, the old villain. It's marriage or no more allowance.'

'So you are not in love?' Overbury seemed as if he could hardly believe such a thing.

'Oh, I like her well enough. She's a pretty little thing.'

'A pretty little thing? Oh, Clark, you have no poetry in your soul at all! *My* lady is a bright-plumed bird of rarest—'

'Yes, yes,' Peyton cut him off impatiently. 'But it seems that at bottom we both have the same dilemma. Our ladies will not have us. Or rather, her guardian will not let me have her.'

'Mine simply doesn't wish to wed, even as I offer her all the world and my heart.' Overbury looked as if he might break into tears, so Peyton quickly poured him more wine. 'I am going to try my very best to woo her at the Christmas party. It seems an ideal season for romance, don't you think?'

'Perhaps.' The snow was dashed inconvenient for slipping off into dark gardens, but the cold wind could close people in cosily by the fire. But the Pennington party... 'You might be on to something there. Something relaxed about a Christmas house party. I shall be there, too.'

'You?' Overbury asked doubtfully. 'But Lady Pennington does not approve of rakes.'

'No matter about that. I am going with Lord Mountley. They'll be too polite to turn him away. My lady will be there, and I must win her before the New Year.' He had to pay his debts by then, or there could be trouble he would much rather avoid.

'So will mine. My goddess! If I can get close to her...'

'Corner her under the mistletoe?'

'Something like that.'

If Peyton could get Adele under the mistletoe, he'd do more than stealing kisses. If he compromised her, her uncle would have to let them marry. 'So, who is this goddess of yours, Overbury?'

'Miss Mary St Aubin.'

'Hmm. She's pretty, I'll give you that. And seems a merry enough sort. Too marriage-minded, if you ask me. I've heard she makes matches all over the place.'

'Yes, indeed. I only wish she would see her match with *me*. I am becoming quite desperate.'

Peyton sat up straighter, a sudden thought striking him. Mary St Aubin was connected with his Adele! 'I think she knows my lady, too. Adele Stewart.'

Overbury stared at him with wide eyes. 'I say. A bit young, isn't Miss Stewart?'

'She's old enough for her first Season,' Peyton said, disgruntled. 'Plenty old enough to wed. Maybe we could find a way to help each other, you and me.'

Overbury tilted his head, looking dubious but intrigued. Peyton was very familiar with that combination. 'How so?'

'I'm not entirely sure yet, but the two of them are connected, and they will both be at the party. Listen here, Overbury, I'll tell you what I think…'

A Journey to the Western Islands of Scotland; *The Evergreen* by Allan Ramsay; *Highland Topography and its Effects on its People*.

Hmm, Mary thought as she studied the titles on the shelf at Brunton's Bookshop. The clerk had directed her to this dimly lit corner when she asked about volumes on Scotland, but she wasn't sure this was quite what she was looking for, lovely as the poetry was.

She took the Highland study down and looked through some of the engraved illustrations. Rolling hills, ruined castles, deep lochs. In her mind, though, she saw Charles's face as he talked about his castle, the gentle pride of it, and she longed to know more about his home, about what created such depth of feeling in him.

She shook her head and put that book back to take down the poetry. Charles did take up far too much space in her thoughts of late, space she needed for thinking about her business. Instead of balance sheets and finding new clients, she thought of his terrible dancing and wonderful laughter.

Farewell to Lochaber, and farewell, my Jean,
Where heartsome with thee I hae mony day been...

Such beautiful words, she thought. Maybe that was it. Maybe the essence of Charles, the glowing spark she saw when he spoke of his Scotland was just poetry.

The sun in glory glowing, with merry dew bestowing
Sweet fragrance, life, and growing, to flowers and every
tree.

Yes, that was it. The sun in glory glowing, that was him. She flipped to the next page, losing herself in the words, the misty images of rocky valleys and castles overlooking promontories. The shop, the rainy town outside the grimy window, it all quite vanished in silvery heather.

'Lost in a wee *dwam*, are we, lass?' a whisper sounded in her ear, making her jump.

She whirled around, the book raised high to defend herself—only to find herself facing Charles himself, stepped out of her daydreams. A Charles with a delighted, teasing grin on his face.

His ever so handsome face, with its craggy cheekbones and bright green eyes.

'You frightened the wits out of me,' she gasped, and indeed they were still flown far away. Being alone with him in a dim corner would do that.

'So it seems. It must be a fine book to have you so enthralled.' He slid the volume from her hand and studied the cover. 'Ramsay, eh?' He looked up at the row of leather bindings behind her. 'All things Scottish, I see. A new interest?'

'Don't be so egotistical, it's naught to do with you,' she said sternly, and took back the Ramsay. 'I need to be informed about all sorts of cultures for my work, don't I? And...'

One dark brow quirked as he studied her. 'And?'

Oh, how distracting he was! He made every coherent thought fly quite away. 'And—well, yes. Talking to you about your home made me quite curious.' She opened the book and read aloud the words that had just enthralled her.

Overcome by longing for a life, a place she didn't know, for all that was contained in the 'sweet life' of Charles himself, she peeked up at him to find he watched her intently, his eyes very dark.

The book dropped from her grasp as he took her hand and drew her behind the shelf, deeper into the shadows. She leaned into him, breathed deeply of the summer lemon scent of him and curled her fingers into the lapels of his fine wool coat. It always felt so *right* to be with him, even when it was so very wrong.

She couldn't let that perfect moment go. She kissed him, and he met her with such hunger, such eagerness, she knew it did have to be right. He tasted of summer, too, of sunshine and brandy and mint and that wonderful essence that was only him. Their 'no kissing' rule flew right out of her mind. She knew this thing between them had a finishing date, that such moments as this couldn't keep happening, but she couldn't stop what was igniting between them now.

His arms locked around her, and he drew her closer and closer. His mouth hardened on hers, his tongue tracing the curve of her lips before plunging inside to join them even more fully. She wanted, needed, more of that kiss. More of *him*.

He pressed her back against the shelf, his open lips sliding from hers to trace the curve of her jaw, the arch of her neck above the frill of her spencer collar, making her shiver. He lightly nipped at that sensitive little spot just below her ear, and she whimpered.

How could he *do* this to her? She was never herself when she was around him! She never could seem to stop this flood of feelings.

She reached up to twine her fingers in his hair and dragged

his kiss back to her lips. He went most obligingly, eagerly, kissing her with a hot artlessness and need that fired her own.

She pressed even closer to him, wanting to be ever nearer and nearer. Wanting she knew not what. She wanted the poetry that was only him.

And she knew that soon, very soon, she would have to let it go. Not just there, in that bookstore, but in her life entirely. The desire that flared between them when she first kissed him in that garden had only grown stronger, hotter, in the time she'd spent with him since then. It would surely be painful when they parted, when she didn't have him with her any longer, but it was so hard to hold on to caution when they were together. She had only this kind of stolen moment, and she meant to make the most of it all now.

Chapter Nine

The Olivers' carriage turned in at a pair of ornate iron gates touched with gilt at the spiked tips that made them gleam in the winter light. Northland Park was in sight at last.

And soon Mary would see Charles. She slid to the edge of the tufted velvet seat, her toe tapping in her kid half-boot as she tried to see ahead. This fidgety excitement was *not* at the prospect of seeing him, she told herself sternly. Certainly not. It was just having her feet on steady ground again, after the jolting and sticking of the wintertime road. That was all. It had nothing to do with the memory of her kiss with Charles, surely. She had to plant her feet on the ground again, remember her goal, move forward.

Yet she still felt herself trembling with eagerness to see him again.

'I am quite agog to see Northland,' Pen said. She leaned to look out the window beside Mary, Miss Muffins perched on her lap. 'They say it was quite a ruin before! Such a shame, it was rather a showplace, built by a courtier of Queen Anne, I think. I heard the Penningtons have worked wonders.'

'Just as they said the agency worked wonders with the former Miss Evans,' Anthony said, shooting a smile Mary's way.

'She barely said a word when the Evanses first arrived in Bath, now look at her.'

'She didn't need "wonders" worked,' Mary protested. 'She was always beautiful and intelligent. Maybe a bit caught under her mother's thumb. She merely needed to find someone who truly understood her. Valued her, her true self.' Just as everyone should. Just as Mary sometimes longed for, deep in a lonely night. Someone to really look at her, *see* her, as it seemed Charles did whenever her turned his green eyes onto her.

'And surely that was Lord Pennington,' Penelope said. 'They are like two cooing lovebirds in a tree! Perfect for each other.' Anthony took her hand and smiled down at her tenderly, making Mary's heart ache. 'It was so kind of them to open their home. What a lovely Christmas we'll have.'

Mary wondered how lovely it would all be if she had to fight off daydreams of Charles all the time. She'd just have to determine to focus on her work, that was all. Yes. Work.

'Oh, look, there's the house now,' Pen said, and Miss Muffins gave an excited little yip.

Mary peeked out the window again. The drive through towering old oaks was cunningly curved to reveal enticing glimpses of the house and outbuildings, including a round summer house atop a hill and a crumbling brick tower, dappled in light like a painting until the carriage suddenly tumbled out of the woods towards the house itself.

It was quite vast, the centre section of the old Elizabethan manse, with stone walkways, towers, wavy old glass windows, brick chimneys. Covered walkways connected to newer wings on either side, perfect Palladian style in contrast to the rambling old house, with tall, symmetrical windows, pale marble faced in darker brick that echoed the older section. Somehow it all came together perfectly, just like a house Mary would want for herself.

The gravelled drive circled an elaborate Italian fountain, silent now beneath the figure of Diana with her bow raised, past the old house to one of the new wings, two staircases sweeping up to a row of columns and a shaded portico leading to open front doors where rows of liveried footmen waited. She glimpsed gardens beyond, neat beds and mazes sloping down to dark woods. The agency had done well by Miss Evans indeed. She couldn't help but feel a bit proud.

The carriage jolted to a halt at the front of the double stairs, and footmen in green and gold Pennington livery rushed forward to open the doors and let down the steps. Mary climbed down after Pen, holding Miss Muffins under one arm as she studied the dozens of sparkling windows, the Grecian columns, the forest of chimneys, with awe. How happy she was for Lady Pennington. How splendid to have a true home.

The hostess herself rushed out the front doors and down the marble steps to greet them, drawing a fur-edged shawl close against the wind. The skirts of her blue-striped silk gown, surely a Mademoiselle Sandrine creation, swayed around her. 'Oh, you're here at last! We were so afraid the snow would come in again and keep you away. But here you are, and Miss Muffins, too.' She took the delighted pup from Mary and kissed the top of her head as she led the way back to the house. 'Almost everyone is here, except for the Sandfords. We're having tea in the yellow drawing room, you must be famished after your drive.'

The drawing room was a long high-ceilinged space lined with tall windows on one side, looped and draped in pale yellow satin, with paintings on the other wall, gold frames against yellow and white striped silk paper, portraits and still-lifes and grand landscapes. The painted ceiling, inlaid with yellow and cream and pale green, had gods and goddesses and cupids peeking down from fluffy clouds, laughing at human foibles. The faded blue-and-green antique carpet was so thick Mary's boots sank into it, and it was dotted with conversational groupings of yellow brocade chairs and settees. Lord Pennington stood near the huge marble fireplace, talking to guests about his latest scientific experiments. Holly and evergreen boughs around the picture frames and fireplace scented the air with winter and Christmas.

It was all most welcoming, but Mary's heart quite sank when she saw Mr Overbury among the gathering. His expression lit up when he glimpsed her, but luckily he was in conversation with a group near the windows and could not escape. Yet.

'Miss St Aubin, I don't believe you know Mr Clark? An unexpected guest for Christmas, thanks to a cousin of my husband,' Lady Pennington said as they stopped next to a couple on a settee by the window, along with the odious Mr Clark.

Mary's eyes widened at the sound of that name. Adele's unwanted suitor, here, where she could not escape? She pasted on a polite smile; it would never do to give things away by letting him know she saw his game. He took her hand and bowed over it with a wide grin he no doubt thought of as charming and flirtatious. She had to force herself not to snatch her fingers back.

'Miss St Aubin. Delightful to meet you. You're as charming as everyone reports,' he said. Yes. Definitely slippery.

'Mr Clark,' she answered, taking a step back. Miss Muffins growled, and scurried off in search of more congenial company.

They only had to chat for a moment more, before Lady Pennington took Mary's arm and they strolled onward. 'I am afraid there is something about that Mr Clark I cannot find agreeable,' she whispered to Mary. 'But my husband's relations did insist on bringing him, and I didn't want to seem ungracious.'

'I am sure all will be well,' Mary whispered back. But she realised she had to say something to warn her hostess. 'I would just make sure he's not very near Miss Stewart when she arrives.'

Lady Pennington frowned. 'Has he been pressing his attentions on her? Oh! Poor girl. I think I did hear a whisper of some unfortunate young lady in Bristol last year. If I had known...'

'We'll be here to keep an eye on matters,' Mary said, trying not to let her worries show.

'Yes, I shall be vigilant. But I forgot! I did hear you were quite engaged to Miss Stewart's uncle. I was so happy to hear the news! After all the joy you have brought others, you deserve it doublefold yourself.'

'How did you know?' Mary whispered. 'We have made no announcement yet.'

'Such a small neighbourhood, is it not? Everyone loves such happy news. Though I think they love *bad* news even more.' Lady Pennington leaned closer. 'He is ever so handsome, I must say. Almost as much as my darling Pennington! How lucky you are.'

'Yes. Lucky.' Mary once again had to worry if their impulsive plan was such a good idea after all. The 'romance' of it all seemed to be doing the trick for the agency's reputation, but what would happen after? What would she tell her dear friends? And what of herself? She knew she should step back, away from him, guard herself against the moment when they would part. Yet a tiny sliver of her heart, the heart that belonged to the old, romantic Mary, longed to cling onto this connection for just a bit longer, before she resigned herself to industrious spinsterhood.

'So many are bragging that you helped *them* in their fine marriages, that obviously your eye for a happy match is like magic,' Lady Pennington said. 'Just as you did for me. They will be battering down your office doors.'

They stopped at the tea table, its white damask-draped length lined with enticing trays of cucumber and salmon sandwiches, pastel cakes, white-iced Christmas pudding, along with gleaming silver pots and thin china painted with primroses. Lady Pennington handed her a gold-edged cup. 'Will you have time to help them after you are wed?' she said, as she held out a plate of salmon mousse sandwiches. 'I hear that Mr Campbell's estate is in Scotland.'

'We—we haven't yet set a date or made firm plans,' Mary improvised.

'Of course! You want to make sure you perfectly suit, very wise of you.' She smiled as Mademoiselle Sandrine came into the room, glamorous in fur-edged dark blue velvet and matching turban. 'But one thing I'm sure of, Mademoiselle Sandrine will make the gown. All Bath will be so eager to see it.'

'Certainly I will go to her, if it comes to that. Yet, as I said, we have no firm plans yet. We just want to enjoy Christmas in your lovely home. So kind of you to invite us.'

Lady Pennington grimaced. 'I was quite nervous, I must admit. I've never hosted such a large gathering, but I wanted to show what we had done to the estate.' She glanced across the rooms at her parents, Mr and Mrs Evans, looking so proud and so in awe of their daughter's grand drawing room. 'I do hope everyone will find something to enjoy. I have planned games, charades and hide-and-seek, excursions to some local ruins if the weather will hold for us, and a ball for Christmas itself.'

'It all sounds most delightful.'

'I must give you a tour of Northland later. We've been working so hard on it, choosing colours, restoring floors, buying artwork. I wanted to keep the essence of it all, the history, especially in the park and gardens. There's a long gallery in the oldest part of the house, which was Elizabethan, and we can walk there if the snow comes in. And our laboratory, of course! Lord P. is working on his experiments there.'

Mary smiled to see how happy Lady Pennington was, how she glowed talking of her husband and home. And it was true, the agency *had* helped to bring it about. Maybe all would work out after all.

Lady Pennington refilled her teacup. 'I daresay Mr Campbell's home in Scotland is even older than Northland! They say it's a castle. Does it have a moat? Dungeons? So stylish now.'

Mary laughed at her friend's enthusiasm, though she did feel a bit discomfited. She found she didn't know as much about Charles's home as she would like, just the mist and the heather that sounded like such magic, and she wanted to know *everything* about him. His childhood, his favourite food, favourite book! *Everything.*

After chatting for a few moments, Lady Pennington went to greet some newcomers, and Mary wandered to look at a painting hanging near the windows, a beautiful summer scene of children in a garden, laughing and leaping about with their dog. She was lost for a moment in the happiness of the painted scene, and thus did not notice she had left herself vulnerable to Mr Overbury.

'Miss St Aubin,' he said quietly from behind her, making her jump.

She whirled around, and found him lingering close, blocking her exit from the corner. 'Mr Overbury. What a surprise to see you here!'

'It has been much too long since we met.'

Mary made herself smile. 'You did call at the agency only a

fortnight ago, Mr Overbury. I was so sorry we had no new entries on our files that would suit you.'

He leaned even closer, his flowery cologne threatening to engulf her in its cloud. 'You know my very high standards. My very high artistic needs for the lady I can truly love. My sensitive nature could never tolerate anything less than perfection.'

'I am aware,' Mary murmured. When he first arrived at the agency, when she and Ella thought he was a true prospect, they had sent him a few very suitable and beautiful ladies to consider. Then he decided he wanted Mary herself, and that was that. Yet he *was* a well-known poet, connected in Society, and they'd felt they could not toss him out. That his infatuation would fade. What a mistake that had been.

She wished she truly was in possession of a castle with a moat, to keep such suitors at bay. She pictured tossing failed agency applicants into the murky waters and smiled.

Unfortunately, Mr Overbury seemed to think the smile was for him. He stepped even closer, touching her hand. She took another step back but ran into the silk-papered wall. He pressed closer, making her feel a cold rush of panic, the need to flee. That cologne engulfed her, so different from the light crispness of Charles's alluring scent. So different from Charles's *everything*.

'I did so much want to share my new poetry with you,' he said cajolingly. 'There is one verse in particular I hope you will like. That will touch your heart. "When Marian Walks across My Soul."'

'It—it sounds charming, Mr Overbury,' she said, trying so hard to sound polite, to escape without a scene. Polite but discouraging, in a way that would not wound his sensitive feelings and make more trouble for herself. 'About church, is it?'

His eyes widened in a flash of anger. 'No! It is about *love*, worldly love. True, pure, radiant love. For one lady, the only lady. It is most…'

The drawing room door opened, and Charles and Adele came in. Mary felt that cold panic fading away, and she only wanted to run to him. 'Do excuse me, Mr Overbury. I see someone I absolutely must greet,' she said quickly. She slid past him, ignoring his reddened face, the hand he held out to her.

She hurried towards Charles, her feet feeling so light they could surely skim the carpet to carry her to his side. But some of her quick rush of joy faded when she saw Adele notice Clark, saw the flustered blush that spread over the girl's cheeks.

'Miss Stewart,' Mary cried, taking Adele's arm to move her attention away from Clark and subtly draw her across the crowded room. Charles gave her a little nod to show he understood. 'I'm so happy you're here. I know you enjoy Gothic poetry, and there is this painting over here you would most enjoy, it reminds me of such tales. I should love to hear your thoughts on it.'

'Miss St Aubin,' Adele said, glancing over her shoulder in longing. 'Of course. Yet I was just going over...'

Mary inexorably led her around, still chatting about paintings, books, snow, whatever she could think of. Charles shot her a grateful look that made her feel warm all over. They were operating as a team to a good end, a feeling she enjoyed far too much.

'Mademoiselle Sandrine is here, as well,' Mary whispered to Adele. That seemed to catch the girl's full attention. 'I'm sure you would like to converse with her.'

'Oh, yes!' Adele enthused. 'You are so understanding, Miss St Aubin. Charles is kind, and I think he does try, but he is so—so *teuchle*. He doesn't understand how I long for beauty in the world, for emotion and truth, as others—well, as you do.'

Mary gave her a sympathetic smile. She did indeed remember how it was to long for something bigger, wider, more meaningful, to be young and filled with restlessness and desire. And she remembered that Charles, too, had once wanted to write poetry and find a grander world. Surely he could find it in him to connect with Adele now. They both had such good hearts.

'Oh, my dear,' she said, taking Adele's arm. 'I think you must not underestimate him...'

'And how is the servants' hall here at Northland, Daisy?' Mary asked as Daisy helped her prepare for dinner. She studied herself in the dressing table mirror as her hair was curled and pinned, fastened with a ribbon bandeau. Miss Muffins lounged on the large soft bed with its yellow satin counterpane and yellow-and-blue-striped hangings, trying to loll on the precious gown that lay pressed and ready to be donned. It was a lovely, comfortable room, the bright colours bringing a bit of summer into the winter chill, with several cushioned chairs ready to curl up and read in, a fire crackling in the white marble hearth.

'Oh, ever so nice!' Daisy said as she frowned at an errant curl and pinned it firmly in place. 'It's a grand house. You did well for Miss Evans.'

'She did well for herself, standing up to her parents in the beginning.' If only other potential patrons could see what Mary could do for *them*! With or without her own match. 'It is a beautiful house, true. Perfect for Christmas.'

'It's nice to get away from Bath for a time, isn't it, miss? Meet some different people, hear some different conversation...'

Mary thought of the large gathering in the drawing room, of Adele—and Mr Clark. 'Indeed. If we can avoid certain guests and spend more time with the best ones.' Like Charles. She wouldn't mind in the least if the party was *only* him! The two of them talking, walking in the snow—kissing. She turned her head as she studied herself in the mirror, wondering if he would like her hair that way, then scolding herself for even caring. 'Daisy, do you think I need to do something new with my hair? Cut it, maybe? Or grow it longer?'

Daisy's eyes lit up with a challenge. 'Your hair looks lovely as it is, miss, but with this colour and the curl of it, you could do ever so much! Perhaps like...this?' She twisted some up, leaving other curls dangling enticingly against her neck. 'You would be the diamond of the evening!'

'Then let's try it. And it should go well with the new blue gown. Very fashionable.' She wanted to look her best, to gather people interested in the agency and convince them she was *au courant* in all matters. Not for Charles. No, definitely not. Assuredly not.

But what would he really think?

Daisy had just added the final touches to the new coiffure,

making sure it tumbled 'artlessly' like some fashionable milk-maid, when there was a knock at the door. Adele peeked her head in.

'You asked if I could come see you, Miss St Aubin?' she asked shyly. Mary smiled and held out her hand, hoping she could help in some way.

'Oh, yes, Miss Stewart! Do come in, I was just finishing my toilette for the evening.' She stood up and tightened the sash of her dressing gown as she gestured to a chair by the fire. 'I won't take up much of your time before dinner, I just had a small gift for you. A sort of early Christmas.'

Adele's eyes widened. 'A gift for me?'

'Yes. I do hope you'll like it, if not we can find something else to suit, I'm sure.' Mary took out a long white box tied with pale blue ribbons and handed it to Adele. She waited anxiously to see the girl's thoughts.

Adele eagerly pulled off the lid—and gasped. Her hand flew to her mouth as she stared down at the treasures tucked there in tissue. 'Oh, Miss St Aubin! It's—it's…'

'Do you like it? If the colour is wrong…'

Adele clutched the gown to her as if it would be snatched away. 'It is *perfect.*'

Mary smiled in relief. 'Sandrine can make adjustments if it doesn't fit. She says it will be the height of fashion in London with those cap sleeves, but I thought you might want to wear it first for the Christmas ball here at Northland.'

'My very own Mademoiselle Sandrine gown,' Adele whispered. She held it up, and the firelight danced on the small spangles caught in the rosy chiffon. 'But what will Uncle Charles say? He declares I am too young!'

'Leave him to me,' Mary said.

Adele hurried to the mirror and held up the elegantly draped folds of the skirt to her, twirling around. 'Oh, yes, for you are to marry him! I don't see how you can, he's such a stuffy old ogre, but I am very happy you'll be here.'

Charles, a stodgy old ogre? Mary thought of the fire of his kisses, the music of his laughter, and wanted to giggle. He was hardly old. Or stodgy. She wasn't sure about the ogre. 'I hope I can be of some help to you both.'

'You bought me a Mademoiselle Sandrine gown! You are an angel of helpfulness.' She twirled into the chair again as Daisy helped Mary with her own gown, clutching the rose-pink silk and chiffon close. 'I do so miss my mother sometimes. She was so good, so wise. I wish she was here to tell me how to be like her, instead of so confused all the time.'

Mary nodded sadly. She understood that feeling all too well. She'd lost her mother too young, before they had many such moments between them, and she wondered what it would have been like to confide in her, choose gowns together, to whisper and laugh. When her mother was gone, so much light went out of their little family, and she didn't want to hurt that way again. 'I, too, miss my mother. She died when I was just a child. Ella was wonderful, but I know she also yearned for our mother's counsel.'

Adele carefully smoothed the gown, staring down at it. 'Miss St Aubin...'

'Mary, please.'

'Mary. How do you think our mothers would have advised us about—love?'

Mary glanced at Daisy, and they exchanged cautious nods. 'What about love, my dear?'

'How does a person know that they are really in love?'

Mary stared at her for a moment, rather dumbfounded. Surely describing love was rather like trying to explain the colour blue? Impossible. She thought of all the couples she'd met through the agency, what had made her sure they would suit one another.

'Surely it means the way one longs to see the person, counts the seconds until they are there?' Adele said, and touched her heart. 'And the flutterings just here! The longings!'

'It is lovely to first meet someone special and feel like that, yes,' Mary said, squeezing Adele's hand. 'You see someone in a ballroom or across a tea-shop, and they are handsome and charming, and make you feel warm all over. As if you could melt with delight! Yet this feeling lacks what true love needs to grow—vulnerability to another person, showing them our true self and glimpsing theirs in return. Understanding each other. Knowing one's soft heart, the one we usually hide away, is safe with them.'

She thought of Charles, of how when he studied her so closely, she thought he could see everything, that she could say anything to him.

'And those butterflies we can feel?' Adele asked.

Mary laughed. 'They are lovely and very important, of course. One must have passion. Attraction. But also a real, heartfelt friendship. That feeling does not fade but only grows deeper. It takes time, yet you'll want to stay deep in conversation with them, day after day, hear them, look into their eyes. Be together even when there are difficult times. They will help make everything easier. You want to know their dreams and desires, everything about them...'

'And they will desire that, too?' Adele asked doubtfully. Maybe Clark did not wish to converse with her, know her more deeply. Maybe she was realising that now.

'Yes. That is how two people come to be their true selves with each other. To see and accept imperfections...' Mary shook her head, as if she could clear it of her own dreams and hopes, hopes she feared could never really be. 'And if you love things in your own life, art or music or family, you want them to be a part of all that, and they will want that, too. To help and support you. Love does not leave you confused or unhappy. It is like—being on the same cricket team. Making one's life whole.'

Adele giggled. 'I cannot play cricket. But I do like the idea of working together. Very much.'

'As do I,' Mary whispered.

'That's the second gong, miss,' Daisy said, and tied off Mary's sash, smoothing the short sleeves. 'We should finish getting you dressed.'

'Oh, I've kept you too long, Mary.' Adele jumped up, holding her treasured gown close. 'I should go and let you finish.'

'Adele.' Mary reached for her hand, worried, hoping beyond hope she had given her something to think about, warned her subtly away from men like Clark. 'You will think of our conversation? You are so young, and your first Season is about to begin. You have so very many possibilities open to you, you must consider so carefully what *you* really want.'

Adele frowned doubtfully. 'How will I know it's what I want and not what everyone says I must want?'

Ah, yes, there was the rub. 'I have often wrestled with that dilemma myself,' Mary admitted. 'Just—listen to yourself. Make a space of quiet where you can really hear. And remember, you do have time. Don't rush.'

Adele quickly, as if on impulse, kissed Mary's cheek and hurried out.

'There is a sweet girl,' Daisy said as she smoothed the blue organdie skirts of Mary's dinner gown.

'Sweet, yes. And confused, I fear,' Mary murmured in worry. She wondered if this was an inkling of what real mothers felt as they watched their children try to take wing. It was terrifying.

'You'll help her, miss,' Daisy said reassuringly. 'If anyone can help, it's you. Look what you and Miss Ella have done for all your agency folk!'

Mary nodded, but she simply wasn't sure. When it came to her patrons, she could see so clearly what they needed, what they longed for. When it came to herself, things were so much cloudier.

Mary thought she had never seen a more perfect evening before.

Dinner in the elegant Northland dining room had been a delight, white soup and haricot lamb, salmon mousse and cinnamon apples, all amid laughter and talk of all the delightful plans for this party. She'd rather forgotten all her worries, felt like her old, carefree self again.

Now she strolled beside Charles along the windows of Northland's long gallery, the chalky silver moonlight spilling through the old wavy glass of the windows to cast dancing shadows on the dark panelled walls and faded floral carpet runner. Suits of old armour and portraits of people in huge ruffs and wide skirts watched them as they passed, laughing together.

The convivial sounds of dinner went on in the sitting room at the end of the gallery, Adele playing Christmas carols, coffee cups clinking. Best of all, Mary was there with *him*, practically alone at the darker end of the old gallery. They'd been separated at dinner, yet close enough to cast each other glances that seemed to say they understood exactly what the other was thinking about the conversation, about their fellow guests. Now she could feel all the cosiness of winter closing over them like a downy blanket. The cold weather always seemed a time for firesides, quilts, books, cuddling and intimacy. She'd been lonely so long! Maybe all her yearning for Charles was for just this sort of thing, a place to belong, cosy family moments. She feared she was coming to rely on him too much, to long for him. Would she struggle when he was gone? Feel even more alone?

She stopped to stare out the window, wishing she could press her flushed cheek to the chilly glass, to banish the images of cosiness and domesticity. They were much more dangerous than any lust could be, more alluring. But she knew the winter night wouldn't cool her, because he would still be there, right next to her.

'I can see why the Penningtons are so happy here,' she said. 'It's like a fairy-tale house, a dream. Just look at the moonlight on that old tower! And the snow blanketing everything, sparkling under the night sky. It could have been written in a romantic novel and brought to light.'

Charles stepped up next to her, studying the beautiful scene. 'Lord Pennington was telling us at dinner that the tower was built in the 1200s. A maiden of the house was not allowed to marry her true love, and when she heard he was killed in battle, she flung herself from the tower. Only he was not dead but wounded, and came back seeking her. When he found she had perished, he jumped from the highest window to join her. Their souls have walked the gardens ever since.'

'How very sad! I'm glad there's so much happiness here now.' She glanced across the room at Lady Pennington, whose husband stood behind her, his hand on her shoulder, the two of them laughing together. 'Such joy surely banishes old sorrows.'

'Oh, I don't know. They say there's a ghost here.'

'A ghost!' Mary cried with a delicious chill.

Charles laughed, as if he sensed how very much she enjoyed

a spooky tale. 'Probably several, in a place so old. But this one is about lost love.'

'Oh. How can I bear such heartbreaking tales on such a fine evening?'

He smiled as if he knew how much she really loved them. Such romance. 'I would have thought a haunted medieval tower perfect for your poetry-reading heart.'

'For poetry, maybe. But not on a night like this. Christmas just seems made for being cosy, don't you think?'

He looked out the window, a shadow seeming to pass over his eyes, darkening them to moss. 'I don't think my childhood Christmases could have been called cosy. My father was always gone, and the house was very cold in the winter, very silent.'

Mary's heart ached to imagine him so lonely, as she once was. 'Your father was away often, as mine was?'

Charles grimaced. 'In a way. When he was home, he was often in a rage, followed by icy silence. It was often better when he was gone. His estate was his priority, just as your father's parish was his, and that work overcame all else.'

Mary understood such feelings very well. 'And you had no fun at Christmas at all?'

'It wasn't entirely bad. At Christmas, they told ghost stories in the servants' hall, and I would sneak down to listen to them. If I was very good, cook would give me some extra mince pies.'

'Ghost stories?' Mary's heart ached to imagine him as a lonely little boy. She longed to hold him close, make him feel safe as he always did for her. She laid the edge of her hand against his, and he touched her little finger with his, a small, secret link.

He smiled, the wistfulness dissolving. 'A fine old Scots tradition, ghostly tales at Christmas. Didn't you do that?'

'My father was a vicar! He wouldn't have approved. Christmas was all church services, visiting parishioners, serving tea. But when my mother was alive...' Mary looked back out the window, and for a moment she saw not snowy gardens and medieval towers, but the warmth of her mother's firelit sitting room, the sound of the pianoforte playing carols, the sweet cinnamon scents of cakes, and laughter as they tried to play snapdragon. 'She loved Christmas, and when her duties were done there were games and special sweets, gifts and books and music. Ella and I tried to do what we could after she was gone, to remember her, but it wasn't quite the same.'

Charles smiled understandingly, and all the sadness seemed gone like a cloud. She wasn't so alone now, the walls around her heart not quite so high. 'And since you came to Bath?'

'We go to church at the Abbey, of course, and then have a fine dinner and give gifts. But I'm glad to be at Northland now. Just listen to that music! And so many people making merry. Very Christmas-like, and yet nothing like any Christmas I've had before. I enjoy the idea of finding new traditions.'

They walked onward, and when they turned a corner into a silent, dark window nook, he gathered her into his arms. 'What would you choose to do, then, in an all-new, Mary-approved Christmas?'

'Hmm, let me see.' She tapped at her chin, pretending to be deep in thought. 'Make sure everyone has someone to kiss under the mistletoe! That should be on my agency books to instruct everyone.'

He laughed deeply, warmly, making her tingle all down to her toes. 'A new branch of your agency? Christmas instructions?'

'Yes! The Mistletoe Branch. No one should be alone for Christmas.' She twirled around a bit, feeling suddenly lighter, more fun, whimsical thoughts tumbling through her head. 'There must be plum pudding. And charades. And definitely flowers and music!'

Charles took her hand and spun her about until she giggled dizzily. 'That is what you recommend for promoting a Christmas romance?'

'Of course. And dancing! That's the most important of all.'

They listened for a moment to the strains of a waltz drifting from Adele's piano. 'Then I would fail miserably,' Charles said.

'Not with my help. That's what the agency is here for. I did promise you dance lessons.'

'How about now?'

'Right now?' she laughed.

'No time like the present.'

'Very well, then. Take my hand and bow. I know you can do that.'

He took her hand with a flourish, and bowed so low his head nearly brushed the floor, making her laugh. 'I did that well, yes?'

'Very well,' she answered through her giggles. 'Now, step like this—no, to the left. And around. Faster.'

'I can do that, too!' he said, and twirled her around, taking both her hands to send her into a loop. Faster and faster, into and out of beams of moonlight, closer and closer.

Mary threw back her head and laughed giddily as they twirled and spun. How light she felt, how young and free! He held her safe, and she could soar.

They skidded to a halt, both of them breathless. 'See. You are a better dancer already.'

He stared down at her, intent, serious as their giggles faded away. There was that look only he ever gave her, as if he saw everything. Understood everything. 'Only when I'm with you.'

Mary couldn't breathe. 'I—I'm sure everyone would believe us betrothed, then.'

'So we should hold hands more? Sigh and shoot longing glances across the room?'

'Maybe we could—try this?' She held up her hand, palm out, and he pressed his own hand against it. She went up on tiptoe and kissed him. It was soft and tentative at first, just an impulse. But the taste of him, the way his mouth felt on hers—it made her fall down and down into a blurry abyss of sheer need.

His hands closed over her shoulders, and for an instant she feared he might push her away. Then he groaned, a wild sound deep in his throat, and he dragged her close against his body.

His mouth hardened on hers, his tongue tracing the curve of her lips before plunging inside to taste deeply. She only wanted more, more of this kiss, more of *him*.

How could he do this to her? She seemed to lose herself when she was with him, yet she was more truly herself than ever. It was too wild, too uncontrollable, and she loved it.

She twined her fingers in his hair and held him closer. He

went most willingly, kissing her with a heated artlessness and sheer need that fed her own.

A sudden burst of laughter from around the corner startled her, making her jump back from him. He stared back at her, tousled, startled, his eyes very dark.

'I'm sure that was against the rules,' she gasped.

He ran a shaking hand through his hair, leaving the glossy dark strands awry. 'Entirely.'

'We are to be friends.'

'Yes. Friends.'

'And partners in seeing the agency and Adele succeed. That is all.'

'Completely.' He paused. 'Yet, we do seem to break our rules often.'

Mary remembered the bookstore, their sizzling kiss there, and she sighed. 'So we do. It must stop. Immediately.'

'Immediately.'

They stared at each other in the crackling, taut silence. She was altogether doubtful that was a bargain she could keep.

Charles had always been a man of his word, even in his wild youth. A promise was a promise. Now his word was slipping out of his grasp. How could he ever keep his bargain with Mary? How could he ever walk away from her, from their 'betrothal,' and never think of it again?

Friends! Friends with rules, like no kissing. Those rules hadn't lasted long at all.

And how he longed to break them, every one of them, one after another. To catch Mary up in his arms and stride from the room, away from the crowds, to lock her up alone with him until they could work this strange intoxication, this glittering magic that seemed to fly through the air whenever she was near, out of their systems. Surely what he felt for Mary was just desire? Never mind how he loved to laugh with her, talk to her, just look at her, if they could truly be together for just one moment, his feelings would vanish. That had to be it, because he could never bear to make her unhappy in any way, as any wife of his would surely be.

He took a glass of wine from the tray of a passing footman and stood there half hidden in the shadows of a window drapery as he studied the party, feeling so apart from all their merriment.

Mary and Pen stood by the pianoforte, listening to Adele as she played carols. Adele did seem much happier with Mary, more at ease, laughing as they sang a rousing chorus of 'Good King Wenceslas.' Mary turned the page of the music, laughing at something Pen said, breaking up their lyrics. She looked like sunshine in the moment, like happiness personified, and he was captured by it.

He felt that enchantment anytime she was near. She made him feel like himself again, like the weight of the world was slipping off him and he was, or could be, free.

He was still grinning like a foolish schoolboy now as he studied her across the room, as admirers flocked around her. She did have so many suitors, whether she wanted them or not, and none of them seemed to worry whether she could make matches as a 'spinster' or not! They only wanted to be near her, as he did. Seemed to long for her laughter, the warmth of her smile, her attention.

He noticed a young viscount among the circle, a baron who handed her a glass of punch and then lingered. Aye, Mary had declared she was committed only to her business, but anyone could see it didn't have to be that way. She could have any life she chose—any man she really wanted.

So what could she want with him? He had a respectable estate, a fine income, a rebellious niece and more years behind him than he cared to think of.

He glanced at a group of ladies who sat near the vast old fireplace, whispering over their teacups as they studied the gathering at the pianoforte. It struck him that perhaps it was not the gentlemen who stayed away from the agency, who were wary of it, but the ladies. Afraid their matchmaker would take all the attention?

Charles almost laughed aloud. Of course. It all made sense. Mary was ethereally beautiful, with her golden hair and luminous skin, her wide smile. But she also had the kindest heart, the shrewdest, clearest judgement about matches. They were only harming themselves if they wouldn't trust her. He had to fix it all. To help her.

He turned back to watch the pianoforte. Mary had slid onto the bench with Adele, and the two of them played a lively duet, their hands flying together over the keyboard, laughing, their faces alight with fun. Mary glowed with the performance, brighter than the ice-sharp stars beyond the windows, filled with such life. She made him feel alive, too. Made him look forward to things again.

He realised how easily, how very easily, he could fall in love with her, tumble down deep and never be found again. Yet he could not. He knew he did not make a good husband, and he couldn't bear to see any of her glow dimmed.

'Mr Campbell,' a man said, and Charles tore his rapt attention from Mary's laughing face to see Percy Overbury watching him. He scowled at Charles's greeting smile.

Suddenly he remembered what Mary had said about the man's courtship of her. 'Mr Overbury?'

The frown deepened. 'You know who I am?'

'Of course. The poet.'

He ducked his head, as if trying for modesty. 'I see my work does precede me. I do try to circulate my verses only to a few friends, but they will persist in showing them to others.'

'And you know me.'

The man's eyes narrowed. 'Not well, no. The Scots are not regular *habitués* of Bath, are they? I'm surprised you can tear yourself away from the lochs for our theatres, dances and soirées. How strange it must all seem.'

Charles smiled. 'Oh, I am ever surprising, Mr Overbury. A man of many interests.'

'And I think one of them is Miss St Aubin.' The man's chubby white fingers curled into fists.

'It is,' Charles said simply. 'She is a fine lady indeed.'

'She is a goddess! And she deserves far more than some run-down ruin in the Highlands.'

Charles quite agreed about Mary's goddesshood, though his house and park were not really falling down and were not in the Highlands. As for what Mary deserved—Overbury was not wrong there. She deserved everything. All the things Charles couldn't give her, and he thought Overbury certainly could not. She would have plenty of suitors when they parted ways, if she wanted them. She would have her business. He could help give her that. Yet he longed to give her so much more.

'Surely that is all up to her,' he said, trying to sound supremely careless.

Overbury suddenly grabbed his arm, and Charles stared down at him coolly, even as his heart seemed to pause to see if there was to be a fight right in the Northland gallery. 'She belongs with me! I can give her all she needs, all she requires. I adore her! I have ever since I first glimpsed her. We are twin souls.'

Charles arched his brow at the man and slid his arm away. 'As I said, that is up to her. I see no ring of yours on her finger.'

'Nor I yours, though they whisper you are engaged. Surely her true fiancé would have presented her with the largest, greatest jewel.'

'No jewel could ever compete with the light in her eyes,' Charles snapped, and he realised that little flight of his own poetical fancy was very true. Nothing was brighter, more enticing than her eyes as they laughed and danced. *Lud*, but he was as bad as Overbury now! Mary did bring out the romantic fool in him. 'Our friendship is surely none of your business.'

'My business!' The man's face turned an alarming shade of scarlet. 'I *love* her, and I have since long before you arrived. I deserve her. No one can ever understand her as I can. I am warning you—'

'No. I am warning *you*.' He seized Overbury's arm, holding it with seeming lightness as the man's eyes widened with a flash of pain. 'Miss St Aubin wishes to choose her own friends, and they do not include you. You have tried to play the game, and you lost long ago. If I catch you pestering her again, I shall not be accountable for my actions.'

Overbury tore himself away and fell back a step. 'Just like a barbaric Scot! Miss St Aubin will not stand long for such behaviour, I'm sure. Then she will remember who her true friends are. I shall see to that, with the help of others concerned with her happiness.' He smoothed his bright green coat.

'Others?'

'You will find she is not as friendless as you might think, as you try to take advantage of her kindness! There is Mr Clark, and—and others...'

'Clark?' Charles said sharply, suddenly alarmed. What did Adele's unwanted suitor have to do with it? 'Is he your friend, then?'

Overbury seemed to realise he had made some sort of mistake and glanced away. 'He is a man of refinement and feeling, he defends wrong wherever he sees it, just as I do. Those of us with chivalry in our blood will not let you so mistreat ladies, Mr Campbell. You had best stay far away from me! Your threats mean nothing here.' He fled into the crowd.

Charles scowled after him. What did this man and Clark have to do with each other? What did Overbury think he held over Mary? Charles glanced at Adele and Mary at the pianoforte, the two of then laughing together, and a wave of protectiveness washed over him. He would let no one hurt them, ever. They were too precious.

Lady Pennington came up to him with a smile, the plumes on her satin headdress nodding. 'I do hope you are enjoying yourself here, Mr Campbell?'

'Very much. Your home is very beautiful, Lady Pennington, and your cook superlative. How could anyone not enjoy themselves?' Though he did wonder about her taste in other guests, if Overbury and Clark were samples.

'I am so glad you and Miss Stewart could come. I've so enjoyed getting to know her this winter.' She studied Adele at the pianoforte, her head tilted with concentration. 'Her music is sublime. And she does seem to be enjoying herself, now that she is past a bit of shyness! I did worry Northland might be dull for one so young.'

'She always tells me she is not young at all, and I must cease treating her like a child.'

Lady Pennington laughed. 'She sounds like I did with my own parents! You are so good with her, and I will make sure she has a merry Christmas. Mrs Oliver tells me she needs to learn a bit more about Society before she goes to London. And I'll make sure you have a nice Christmas, too.'

Charles thought of dancing with Mary, and knew he'd never had a better Christmas before. 'I just enjoy watching the fun.'

'But you cannot just watch! The Christmas spirit will catch you, Mr Campbell, I promise.' She gave him a sideways, searching glance. 'Miss St Aubin looks beautiful tonight, does she not?'

'She is always beautiful.'

'Indeed she is. And so kind. My husband and I owe everything to her. But tonight she has such...such *radiance* about her. Don't you think?'

He studied Mary again, his very favourite pastime those days, and smiled to see her smile. The golden aura that seemed to shimmer all around her.

And yet there were those blasted rules.

'Very much,' he murmured, and knew he was in deeper trouble than he'd ever been before in his life.

Chapter Ten

'Your home is extraordinary, Pennington,' Charles said as Lord Pennington led him towards the breakfast room after a morning tour of Northland's chambers and corridors, the laboratory where the Penningtons worked side by side. They'd transformed a large cold, old place into a haven of warmth and intimacy, and he wished so much he could do the same. Find just such a home. He'd always longed to create such a feeling in his own castle, his estate, but despite his care for it, it never felt warm. Never felt like the home that hovered just beyond his reach all his life.

Lord Pennington smiled proudly. 'It's almost entirely due to my wife. She has improved my life so much, Campbell, I can't even tell you. My life was quite desolate before I found her! She's transformed it all.'

Charles smiled, even as he felt a pang of jealousy. He'd never wanted to make a home before, never wanted someone to share it all with. Until now.

Pennington pushed open the door to the yellow and white breakfast room, where the long, gleaming table was set with tea and toast, the sideboard groaning with chafing dishes and covered platters, quiet laughter in the air. He saw Mary and Penelope sitting at the far end, whispering together, and his heart ached at their smiles.

All of that warm contentment faded in one icy flash when he glimpsed Adele, sitting at a quiet corner of the table with Mr Clark. Their heads were bent together, their expressions solemn as they whispered. The man touched her hand.

Charles stalked towards them. 'Charles...' he heard Mary say, a warning note in her voice. He ignored her, a haze of anger and—was that fear?—wrapping around him. He strode ahead to get his niece away from that bounder.

Adele looked up, and her eyes widened. 'Uncle Charles!' she choked out, pulling her hand away from Clark.

He took her arm and gave it a little tug. 'Come and sit with me now, Adele.'

She tried to draw away. 'Uncle Charles, really, we were just talking. Surely I am allowed to have friends! To sit where I choose at breakfast.'

'This man is not your friend,' he said. He was aware of the others in the room, the way they watched while trying to pretend not to see, and he couldn't seem to back away. Couldn't just leave her there.

Mr Clark rose to his feet, a smirk on his lips. 'Mr Campbell. If we could just talk, if you could come to know me, I'm sure we would understand each other. This miscommunication could be quickly cleared away. I have nothing but respect for your niece.'

Charles studied him carefully and could see something of his old self in the man's eyes. The sense that he was the only one that mattered, it was of small concern if others got hurt as long as he had what he wanted. Charles hated his old self, the rakish young man Aileen thought he would always be, the one so irresponsible and careless, and he would not let Adele be caught up in the darkness of such a man. He had to try to be worthy of her now, worthy to take care of her. 'Just leave her alone,' he said as cold and steady as he could make himself. 'I shall not say this again.'

Clark stared at him a moment longer, just a beat too long, before he bowed and left the room, not looking behind him.

'Uncle Charles,' Adele whispered. 'How dare you! How can

you ruin my chance of happiness this way?' She, too, ran from the room, and Penelope followed.

Charles was suddenly even more aware of being watched, and he feared he'd ruined what he and Mary hoped to accomplish with their 'betrothal.' He left the breakfast room and made his way towards the library, where he doubted anyone would be at that hour. He had to think clearly, decide how to protect Adele and fix everything. Make it right once more, for the women he cared about so much.

Mary pushed open the library door, Miss Muffins at her heels, and saw Charles standing by the window, staring out at the snowy scene of the garden. The other guests had gathered there to explore the white-dusted pathways, laughing and jostling, tossing snowballs. He looked so lost in stormy thoughts she wondered if she should interrupt.

'How is she?' he asked roughly. He didn't turn around, just seemed to know Mary was the one who stood there. She longed to go to him, take his hand, reassure him, so she did just that. His fingers were warm in hers, and after an instant he squeezed back.

'She will mend.'

'Will she?' he asked doubtfully.

'Of course! She was already smiling when I left her, and Sandrine is looking over fashion plates with her. Adele has a wonderful eye for colour and line, she will be distracted for quite some time.'

Charles glanced down at her, his eyes unreadable. 'What did she say about me?'

Mary smiled up at him. 'That you are a cruel monster, of course, bent on shattering love's young dream.'

He laughed, though it sounded a bit rusty. 'Aye, that's me. I shouldn't have reacted that way. They were only talking, and others were nearby. But when I saw him with her, looking so *small*, I just lost my temper.'

'You were quite right to do so. It's only a small step from a bit of flirtation over the breakfast table to arranging a meeting in—in that summer house over there, maybe.' She gestured to an elegant little folly atop a slope in the garden, its windowless space perfect for liaisons. 'Now Clark can be in no doubt you are watching him. That people know his wiles.'

'And push her closer to him? What was it you said about forbidden love?'

Mary shrugged. 'She is young. I remember what that was like. We need only get her to London this spring, and she will see how paltry Clark looks compared to all other possibilities.'

He tilted his head, watching her closely. 'We?'

She felt the heat of a blush touch her cheeks and turned to the window. 'Well, *you*, I suppose. But I am here to help you now. Was that not our bargain?'

'Ah, yes. The bargain.' The bargain that was meant to help save her business, at least in the short term. Buy her time. For if there was no business in the short term, there could not be in the long term, so the risk of how people would see her match-making skills if her own betrothal ended was worth it.

It had been meant to be all so businesslike. Now all she wanted to do was help him, be beside him, take all those shadows and worries from his beautiful eyes. The risk had turned out to be to her heart. 'Yes, certainly.'

'Adele likes you. I'm glad she can confide in you.'

'I'm glad, too. It isn't easy being between two worlds as she is, not a child but not yet quite a grown-up lady. I'm happy to help if I can.' She made herself laugh. 'And your end of the agreement seems to be working! I've had a few people ask me about the agency, for relatives or friends who wish to find a good match.'

He leaned back, crossing his arms. 'Is that so? Any spectacular matches in mind yet, like the Penningtons?'

'Not quite so grand, but I have hopes. There was a viscount last night during the music, he would like to find a suitable wife who likes riding to hounds as much as he does. And the Penningtons *are* very happy, aren't they?' So happy they positively glowed with it. It made her feel so satisfied and also so, so envious.

'That they are. Lord Pennington showed me his laboratory early this morning and bragged about his wife's intelligence in the sciences. I've never seen a man so in alt about his life.' He shifted on his feet, staring at the crowd outside. 'I admit I was a bit jealous.'

Mary laughed. 'Me too. They are so sickeningly perfect together. They have made such a home here together. A place to belong.'

And she found she wanted that, too. Especially when she was near Charles as she was just then. 'I could—could find you such a thing. Through the agency.'

'Wouldn't that be an odd thing to do for your own fiancé?'

'Once we are…ended. I could help you.' She hated that thought, it made her want to scream and stamp her foot in protest! But that was what a person did for friends, surely. Looked for what was best for them. Even when it hurt.

'Can you, then? Even for such a monster as myself?'

'Well, it would not be easy. I might have to charge quite a sizable fee.'

He laughed again, and she loved to hear it, loved making him laugh. 'Whatever you charge, it isn't enough for such a difficult case as mine.'

Mary sighed. 'I must admit, since Ella and Harry left, I feel rather confused about so many things. They mostly took care of the business side of matters—accounts, ledgers, ordering. I just looked for patrons, thought up matches. Now I must learn it all, and fast.'

'I understand.'

'Do you?' She glanced up at him, at the halo of pale light around him. 'You seem good at everything. Confident. Racing, cricket, riding…' *Kissing.* No, no, there should be no thoughts of kissing at all.

'Before my father died, he'd pretty well cut me off from most things at the estate. His passing was rather quick, and suddenly I was in charge of it all. Staff and tenants, accounts, decisions. I had to grow up in a great hurry, when I realised I could never let them down. I found that my name, my home, really did mean something to me after all.'

'What did you do?'

'Listened, mostly. In many ways, I think a castle is like any other business—like a matchmaking agency. You must put the right people together to get the task accomplished in the best way. Must stay organised. I did it, and you can, as well.'

'You think I could?' she asked.

'Of course! You are one of the most energetic people I've ever known, Mary, one of the smartest and most intuitive. You want to help as many people as possible, I can see that. Just as I do at my estate.'

He did see her, did see what she longed to accomplish. He believed in her. Mary felt like dancing. 'That is true. I want everyone who feels—well, *unique*, different, everyone who is lonely and wants to be seen, to know they can come to me and I will help. I want branches of the agency all over the place! London! Edinburgh! York! All filled with happy couples like the Penningtons that *I* have helped.'

'And you will certainly do so. Employing ladies like yourself everywhere.'

Mary studied his face in the light, all angles and shadows, his jewel-green eyes written with nothing but confidence and admiration. Confidence in *her*.

It was a strange feeling, an intoxicating one. She'd always been the younger sister, the flighty one, the one who had to be looked after. But Charles believed in *her*. Believed she could do more, do what she dreamed of. He treated her as if she were competent and smart. And it made her feel, deep inside, that she really was.

It also made her ache to kiss him. To throw her arms around him and hold him ever so close.

A snowball suddenly smacked into the glass of the window, reminding her they were not entirely alone after all.

'Well, there is still one part of our bargain we haven't completed yet,' she said.

His brow quirked in question. 'And what's that?'

'Dancing! I did promise you lessons. I cannot stake the reputation of my agency on a man who cannot dance.' She held out her hand to him, palm up.

'Right now?'

'When better? We have this vast room, no one is watching,

and Lady Pennington says there will be dancing after dinner tonight. Don't you want to impress all the fine ladies here with your elegance? Sweep them off their slippers?'

'Not treading on their slippers would be a start,' he muttered. But he did take her hand and let her lead him into the centre of the library, under the doubtful stares of the portraits on the walls between the bookcases.

'There's no music,' he said. 'Maybe we should try later...'

Mary held on to him firmly. 'No time like the present. We must seize the chance, before the party ends. It will all go well. You will dazzle the whole gathering!'

'Do you think we will fool everyone into thinking I am the Louis XIV of the Christmas ball, leaping about in a graceful ballet?' he said.

Mary laughed and blew a stray curl from her eyes. 'Well, I suppose we must not get ahead of ourselves. Every journey begins with one step. A chassé step, to be precise. Come, let's try that one.'

As they made their way to a clear space on the carpet, she had to remind herself sternly they were there to dance. To make everyone believe they were betrothed—and then possibly find Charles a true match later, thanks to his dazzling new dance skills. Not to fall deep into the blissful forgetfulness of his kisses again.

'Now,' she said, trying to sound brisk, practical. 'We can do a basic waltz step first. One, *two*, three. Right, left, glide. Right, left, give a little hop here. Like this.'

She demonstrated, and he followed her smoothly enough, landing rather heavily but quite acceptable.

'Very good,' she said with a laugh. 'Are you sure you really don't know how to dance?'

'You've seen me.'

'Indeed. Hmm. Well, let's try to add a few flourishes, then.' She stepped closer, and his warm, clean scent enveloped her, surrounding her, making her dizzy. She swallowed hard and reached for his hand. 'Now, place one hand at my waist, like this.' She laid his right hand close, his touch pressing against her, warm through her gown. She was beginning to think this was a huge mistake. 'And the other can go against my back, lightly, just above my—my...'

A tiny smile touched his lips. 'Your *what*, Mary?'

'Here.' She dared to press his hand into the back of her waist. Suddenly she grew so tense she could barely move, barely breathe, and he stared down at her.

Don't faint, she told herself.

She peeked up at him and found his eyes had darkened in that intense way that always made her forget everything. She could feel the crackle between them as a palpable thing.

'I—now, step,' she whispered. 'I turn thus, we take a forward gliding step. Both with the same foot at the same time, to turn. One, two, and...'

But Charles got ahead of her, stepping forward before she did. His leg tangled in her skirts, and she tilted off balance, falling towards the floor.

'Oh!' she cried, and clutched at his shoulders. He held her close, turning at the last second so he landed on the floor with her on top of him, their bodies pressed closely together. She tumbled off, and started laughing helplessly, laughing until tears ran down her face, and she heard the rumble of his own laughter next to her.

'So, now I'm ready to dazzle them all?' he said breathlessly, helping her to her feet.

Mary gave in to temptation, and reached up to smooth his tousled hair, feeling the silk of it against her fingers, the warmth of him all through her. 'You have the makings of a dancer, I vow it.'

He twirled her in a circle, making her laugh again. 'I shall dazzle them all! My fallings-down will charm all the young ladies, aye?'

Mary was so charmed by his smile, *too* charmed. She just wanted to jump on him, kiss him, muss his hair even more! Forget the dratted bargain.

'It's just the first lesson,' she whispered. 'You surely did not put your estate in order in one day! Have courage, persist.'

'I shall persist!' he shouted, and launched into some sort

of impromptu Scottish leaping dance that made her ache with laughter.

'I am sure that woke up any layabouts here at Northland,' she giggled. Charles seized her hands and spun her in a wild circle, as Miss Muffins stared from her settee. They whirled and whirled until they almost fell down with it all again.

'I think we should find Adele and distract her with carols at the pianoforte,' Mary gasped as they slowed to a halt, and her head kept spinning. 'Show her your reels! She will be astonished.'

'You mean I must sing *and* dance? Ach, lass, you're killing me.'

'So, you cannot sing, either?'

''Tis worse than my dancing.'

'Oh dear.' Mary smoothed the edges of his coat and smiled. 'I think what we need, Mr Campbell, is a Christmas miracle.'

Charles watched Mary as she turned Adele's pages at the pianoforte, smiling at the merry strains of the music, her slipper toe tapping under the fluttering hem of her gown. How beautiful she was, the loveliest thing he'd ever seen. He didn't know how he'd been able to resist her bright pull, like the sun drawing him ever closer into her orbit. He'd almost given up even *trying* to resist it, to step away from her.

He almost laughed at himself and reached for a glass of wine instead of doing what he most longed to—move closer to that glowing circle she created around herself. Lose himself in it. He'd almost begun to think there must be a way to make this permanent, make the betrothal real. Mary was surely worth the risk of marrying again. Days of laughter and nights of passion would make a fine life, surely, for both of them. Even if his heart was guarded, as he sensed Mary's was, they could build a future worth having. The thought made him smile.

But now—now he saw that she deserved more. And her offer to help him find a match after their 'betrothal' ended was just a reminder of that. It made some of that new glow fade, made ice creep in at the edges, just waiting to engulf him again when she was gone.

Did he dare risk his inner heart now? Even if she did not want a real betrothal as he did? Charles had never felt more of a coward—nor braver. He gulped down the wine and resolved to find out once and for all if Mary was worth the risk. If he could begin to give her all she deserved. For she deserved the world.

Chapter Eleven

'How do I look, then, Daisy?' Mary asked, twirling in front of her looking glass in her dinner gown. 'Presentable?'

'Like a Christmas angel, I'd say!' Daisy answered as she clapped her hands in approval. 'All the gentlemen will have eyes only for you.'

'Oh, we can't have that! We're meant to pair up others, make many matches.' But she had to let herself preen just a tiny bit. Her newest Mademoiselle Sandrine gown, spangled silver tulle over paler grey satin, trimmed with silver gilt leaves at the shoulders, draped and swirled just right. Her golden curls were swept up in Daisy's new coiffure, bound with silver ribbon and white silk roses, and seemed to shimmer in the candlelight. She almost wished she had jewels to compare to some of the other ladies—Lady Pennington's new emeralds were scrumptious— but she thought her mother's pearls looked quite well.

Would Charles like it all? That was certainly her main concern—even though it definitely should not be. He was in her thoughts no matter what, he would not be dislodged.

There was a knock at the door, and Mademoiselle Sandrine appeared with her workbox. She cast a professional eye over the silver gown and finally nodded approval. 'Very nice, Mademoiselle Mary. Very nice indeed. You are a credit to my work. Now, let's adjust that hem a titch...'

She knelt down to pin the gossamer hem, tsking over a small tear, pinning and nodding.

'How is Adele faring?' Mary asked, remembering that Adele had gone to look over the new fashion plates with Sandrine that afternoon.

'*Pauvre petite,*' Sandrine murmured as the turned a bit of the silk. 'First love is so very difficult. Especially with someone like Mr Clark.'

'You suspect he is not good for her, as well?' Mary asked.

'Of course not!' Sandrine stood as she lowered her voice to a whisper. 'He owes me for *two* ladies' wardrobes, which he signed the bills for when they were ordered. So expensive! I told him his lady loves would have to go elsewhere from now on. He was quite angry.'

Poor Adele, indeed. Mary shook her head sadly. 'We shall have to keep a close eye on her.'

'Indeed. I made sure her new gown fits perfectly and showed her sketches of a few others I thought she might like for her Season.' She tilted her head in thought. 'If her guardian is one who pays his bills on time...'

Mary laughed. 'I think you need have no fear of that. Charles—that is, Mr Campbell, is most scrupulous. I'm sure he'll want to keep Adele most content now, as well, so I say show all the tempting sketches and swatches you like.'

'I am glad to hear it. I have heard it said he was not quite so responsible in his youth.'

'Where did you hear that from?' Mary whispered. She glanced over at Miss Muffins on the settee, as if she could overhear and spread gossip. The pup just chewed assiduously on her bone.

Sandrine shrugged. 'A modiste hears all sorts of things, *mademoiselle*. Ladies are eager to spill all the scandal broth onto my carpets! They said he once overturned an expensive curricle racing, that he enjoyed cards and ladies and brandy quite excessively. But what man does not in his youth? And he never opened an account for a woman at my shop.'

Mary studied herself in the mirror, studied the shimmering silver tulle that seemed to make her seem taller, more radiant, more elegant. She was glad to hear Sandrine had never worked her magic on a female on Charles's behalf. 'They would certainly have been lucky to have an account with you.' Lucky on all sides, romantic *and* stylish. 'You do the most exquisite work.'

Sandrine packed up her workbox, studying a length of yellow ribbon, a bit of silk thread. 'A gown is like armour, yes? It makes us as we wish we could be; it makes others see us that way, and hides what we do not want seen.'

Mary thought of the shabby muslin frocks of her youth, the way they hid nothing of her circumstances, nothing of her soul. Not like this new silver gown. 'Armour. Yes. I do feel more confident in your gowns than any other, somehow. As if I am perfectly seen *and* invisible at the same time.'

'Our work is very similar, isn't it? We women must always help each other in this world, or we would be utterly lost.' She plucked and straightened the sleeve, arranging a silver leaf so it emphasised the delicacy of a shoulder. 'There! Now you are ready to conquer the world, *mademoiselle*.'

Mary nodded and wished that was true. The world seemed out of control even more than it ever had before.

To Mary's delight, her beautiful armour of silk and sequins would not go to waste, for she was seated next to Charles at dinner. And it did not go unnoticed. He stared at her in silence for a long moment, as if thunderstruck, before he nodded and a slow, lazy smile spread across his lips.

'How elegant you look this evening, Mary,' he whispered warmly close to her ear as the wine was poured and the soup was served.

Mary smiled up at him in return, trying not to giggle. He, also, looked very elegant, his hair dark in the pale amber candlelight, his eyes shadowed. 'Not a dusty old spinster who can't be trusted to make a match?'

'More like Aphrodite, goddess of all romantic matches.'

She laughed in delight. 'Now you certainly exaggerate.'

'Never! I am a blunt old Scotsman. I cannot tell a lie.'

'Mademoiselle Sandrine does make beautiful gowns.'

'It's not the frock, pretty as it is. It is your eyes. Or maybe... your hair.' He surreptitiously touched the end of one curl, his finger brushing her bare neck, and she shivered.

A footman offered a tray of the next course—chicken fricassee in mushroom sauce—and Mary sat back, feeling as if the portraits on the walls watched her. Eyes seemed to burn from somewhere nearby. 'Should we have another dance lesson soon?' she whispered. 'Lady Pennington seems very excited about her Christmas ball.'

His eyes crinkled at the edges with mirth. 'Are you brave enough? Do you have a large supply of slippers with you?'

'You are making great improvements. And there are many ways you can, er, distract a partner from what one's feet are doing. Smile, laugh, compliment...' *Kiss.* Give a lady speaking, searching looks.

He seemed doubtful. 'I can't imagine what I could do to make a lady not notice she's been tripped to the floor.'

'You are learning enough not to fall over! Just move a bit and stare deeply into her eyes. She'll notice nothing else, I promise.' She demonstrated by staring into his eyes, and immediately wished she had not, as she felt quite dizzy and warm. She kicked off her slipper beneath the floor and wiggled her stockinged toes, hoping for some cool air.

'What if there is no one I want to do that with, except you?' he whispered deeply.

And Mary knew she did not wish to dance with anyone else but Charles. She had waltzed and reeled and minuetted with good dancers, excellent dancers, but they'd never made her feel as he did.

She couldn't speak for a long moment, couldn't look away from him. Chatter and laughter went on around them, but neither of them turned from the other. She had no idea what went on near her, no idea anyone else was in the world at all. She stared up into his sharp, handsome face, a face of such masculine power in every carved line, in his strong jaw, his blade of a nose over full, sensual lips, the fierce, dark glow of his mossy green eyes as he stared back at her. His long sun-browned, scarred fingers wrapped tight around the stem of his wineglass.

Yes, a great, masculine beauty of a face, drawn with the tightest of control. She would always be safe with him, or maybe she just imagined she could be. It had been so long since she felt safe, she couldn't even be sure of the feeling any longer. Couldn't shake away the old clinging fear.

She turned away, flustered, fidgety. She needed control, as well. 'What of Adele, then?' she said, trying to keep her tone light, humorous, turn their attention to matters other than that heated sparkle between them. 'She will need more suitable dance partners than Mr Clark.'

They glanced towards Adele, who sat farther along the table between the viscount and a young baronet's heir, most suitable. She seemed deep in conversation with the viscount, surely a good sign. Mr Clark was seated far away and ignored his own neighbours to glare at Adele. Luckily, she didn't even seem to notice between the attentions of her dinner partners and the delectable cheese tarts that had just been served.

'Mademoiselle Sandrine tells me at least two ladies whose bills were meant to be paid by Mr Clark have been left in arrears,' Mary whispered.

'Just as I would expect,' he growled.

Mary watched Adele laugh with the viscount. From all she'd heard, he was a young gentleman with a fine estate, as well as a title and a good reputation as a fair and caring landlord. He did seem to admire Adele very much, surely a good sign for her future prospects.

She turned to study Mr Clark, who was gesturing for yet more wine and still glowered. They only needed to keep Adele away from him long enough for her to see the truth for herself. A tall order, but Mary was determined.

As the fruit trifle was served, she reached her toes out to find her discarded slipper, and accidentally knocked it beyond reach. She searched for the feel of its satin, but it was lost. What would happen when she had to stand and everyone saw her scandalously naked toes?

'Oh, blast,' she gasped.

'What is amiss?' Charles asked.

She leaned closer and whispered, 'I fear I have done something quite dreadful.'

His eyes seemed to sparkle as he looked at her. 'Oh, please do tell.'

'I lost my slipper.'

'Lost your slipper?'

'Under the table. I took it off, and now it's gone.' Somehow, it didn't feel so embarrassing to tell him that. It was as if she could tell him anything, share any silly story with him, and he would not care. He would just join in. It was strange...and delightful.

He laughed, low and rough. 'Never fear, Cinderella. I am here to help.'

For only an instant, he dipped below the edge of the tablecloth, and Mary held her breath as she felt him press close to her leg through her silk skirts. He found her shoe and then took her foot lightly, delicately, onto his palm and slid it into the abandoned slipper. His touch lingered warmly, caressing, along the edge of her stockinged leg, the arch of her foot, and she gasped. Yet it was all over in a flash, and he reappeared next to her to give her a teasing smile.

Mary's shoe was safely replaced when Lady Pennington rose from her seat after the fruit and cheese were finished, her gown of emerald satin rippling in the light. So very different from the girl in garish clothes chosen by her mother who first came to the agency! Mary could only wish for such a thing for Adele. 'Ladies, shall we take our coffee in the drawing room? Don't linger over your port too long, gentlemen; I have a Christmas surprise planned.'

Mary smiled at Charles, feeling such a wrench at leaving him. He seemed to feel the same, trailing his hand over hers under the edge of the damask tablecloth. She pressed his fingers back before she rose to follow Pen and Adele into the drawing room. Lady Pennington poured the coffee as everyone scattered to cosy nests of chairs and settees near the fireside to chat.

'Do sit by me, Mary,' Lady Pennington said, patting the brocade cushions of her settee. 'We have had no time for a quiet cose! I'm dying to know if you have many happy matches in your queue.'

Mary could only hope there would be, very soon, thanks to her scheme with Charles. She told Lady Pennington about a few couples who had come to her recently and her hopes for them.

Lady Pennington gave her a teasing little smile over the painted edge of her coffee cup. 'But surely the happiest match will be your own! Mr Campbell is so handsome, and he has that delicious accent. We're all so envious. When is the wedding?'

Mary felt that terrible heated blush, that curse, flood over her cheeks, and she looked away to the lavishly luxurious room. 'Not as fine a match as your own. And I am not sure about the wedding yet.'

'I'm sure all of Bath will be invited! So many of us owe you so much.'

Luckily, Mary didn't have to stammer over her 'wedding' any longer, as the drawing room doors opened and the gentlemen returned. Lord Pennington came to his wife's side as Mary watched Charles join Adele and Penelope.

'So, what is this surprise, my dear?' Lord Pennington asked, as his fingers entwined cosily with his wife's.

'A game I loved when I was a child at Christmas, though maybe some would think it rather vulgar,' Lady Pennington said with a laugh.

Her husband grinned in delight. 'Even better.'

'What is it?' another guest demanded.

Lady Pennington clapped her hands. 'Hide and go seek! Northland seems just like the sort of home for such games, so many corridors and hidden spaces.'

'Surely it's a child's game?' Miss Tuckworth whispered to her mother.

'No matter! We are all children at heart, *oui*?' Sandrine said.

'Especially at Christmas,' Lady Pennington said.

Adele blushed with joy, peeking across the room at Mr Clark, and Penelope quickly said, 'Dearest Adele can play a tune to help everyone hide! Anthony and I will turn her pages.' Adele's smile faded as she trudged to the pianoforte, and Mary noticed

Mr Clark slip out of the room. She could only hope he was departing for good, but they could not be so fortunate.

'The ladies shall hide first, the gentlemen seek,' Lady Pennington said.

Her husband laughed. 'The way of life, eh?'

'Very well, then, ladies! Adele, are you ready with a song to count?' Lady Pennington asked. 'Get ready, get set—everyone hide!'

Mary was caught up in the stampede of guests running from the drawing room, parted from Charles by the stream of dashing people. She couldn't glimpse him above feathered and ribboned headdresses.

'One, two, three,' Adele called as she played a lively polka. Amid giggles and shrieks, everyone scattered in various directions, up the double staircase, down to the kitchens, into the shadowy corridors, leaving only a cloud of laughter and perfumes behind, the patter of eager footsteps.

Mary wasn't at all sure where she wanted to go without Charles nearby. What if she was 'found' by Mr Overbury instead? The man had been keeping his distance rather oddly in the last couple of days, but could her luck hold? She looked around and headed up the stairs.

'Nineteen, twenty,' Adele called, playing even louder.

Mary suddenly noticed Overbury watching her, his lips set in a most determined fashion. Mary twirled around and ran up the next flight of stairs, lifting her delicate skirts until she reached a hallway on the top floor. Silence closed around her like a winter cloud. It was dim there, lit only by flickering lanterns at each end, revealing rows of closed doors and a dark green carpet runner, the glow of snowflakes drifting past the darkened windows. She heard furtive giggles, the snap of shutting doors. Footsteps clattered, and she hoped Overbury would not dare follow her there.

She ducked behind some heavy tapestry curtains into a window nook and tucked her feet up under her, pressed back to the wall. It was chilly there, the cold from outside seeping into her delicate tulle sleeves, but she didn't care. It seemed quite private and safe.

She closed her eyes and held her breath. The quick patter of her heartbeat slowed in her ears.

And suddenly she was no longer alone. She heard a whisper of movement, felt the breeze of the curtain parting, the heat of someone beside her, banishing the winter.

For an instant, she felt a flash of panic that Overbury had found her, but then she smelled the fresh, springtime warmth of lemony soap, and she knew very well who it was.

Charles.

And her heart pounded in an entirely new way.

She opened her eyes and glimpsed Charles's broad shoulders silhouetted against the lamplight before he dropped the curtain and they were quite alone.

'Are you unwell, Mary?' he whispered, his breath stirring the curls at her temple. She shivered.

'I thought maybe Overbury was following me. I imagined I could be alone here.'

'Shall I go?' He moved as if to leave.

'No!' She grabbed his hand. 'I do feel safe now. With you.'

And she did. She'd never felt so safe in her life. She swayed towards him, drawn to that quiet strength, that delicious warmth he always brought with him. The wonderful way he smelled, the brush of his hand on hers.

His arms closed around her, drew her even closer, as if they were the only people in the whole world. And she felt so wonderfully *un*safe. She felt reckless, wild, excited—joyful.

She threw her arms around his neck and held tight. She pressed her forehead against his shoulder, the fine wool of his evening coat warm on her skin. She closed her eyes and listened to the steady, reassuring music of his heartbeat.

She knew she shouldn't be so close to him in there, knew it was against their own rules of fake courtship. Who knew *what* she would do with such temptation! But she couldn't let go, not yet. It felt all too good. She held him even closer.

She felt the soft press of his kiss on top of her head, and she tilted her face up to his. His eyes, those wondrous emerald eyes, glowed in the darkness. His lips touched her brow, the pulse that beat frantically at her temples, the tip of her cheekbone. Tiny drops of flame on her skin, trailing dizzying desire with every touch. Flames that burned all the way to her heart.

Mary stretched up on tiptoe and pressed her lips to his, giving in to that insistent desire. It was a small, questing kiss at first, but the soft heat of his lips made that flame roar out of control. He moaned, the sound ragged against her lips, and he dragged her so close there was nothing between them at all. How perfectly they fit together! As if made to be just so.

Her lips parted at his touch, and his tongue slid lightly over hers. He tasted of wine and strawberries, and that darkness that was only him. He seemed to question, to seek, and as if finding whatever he sought, he delved deeper.

She curled her fingertips in his rough silk hair, trying to hold him with her forever. He gave no sign of running away. The kiss plunged even deeper, and she fell down into hot, blurry *need*. Mary felt she was on fire, and she swayed as if she would tumble to the floor her legs were so weak.

Charles pressed her against the wall, and she felt his lips trail from hers in a ribbon of fire over the arc of her throat, the edge of her collarbone along the edge of her gown, nipping and teasing with the tip of his tongue to soothe the little sting.

'Oh, Mary, *m'usghair...*' he whispered roughly, his brogue heavy. She blinked open her eyes and saw that he rested his forehead against the wall beside her. His own eyes were closed, his brow furrowed as if he were in pain. His shoulders shuddered as he drew in a ragged breath. He seemed to struggle with the raw, hot longing between them, just as she did.

She reached up and touched his cheek, feeling the stubble over his satin-smooth skin. He turned his head and kissed her palm.

'Oh, Charles. I think, that is, I—'

Suddenly, the real world seemed to crash and clang into their secret little haven. Footsteps and muffled laughter echoed from the corridor, and she remembered the party, the games.

And this little game, this masquerade of a betrothal, didn't seem like a game at all any more. It felt like a heartbreak about to happen.

She knew she couldn't stay there wrapped up in him a moment longer, or she would never want to let him go at all. She softly, gently kissed his cheek. It felt rough and delicate all at the same time, just like he was. She slid away, but his hand seized hers as she passed, strong and hot.

'Just one more moment, Mary,' he muttered. 'Please.'

She was deeply tempted. She leaned against his shoulder, resting her cheek on him. His whole body was rigid, perfectly still, except for his hand on hers. His iron control was still there, but she could feel it cracking almost like she heard it, a whip-lash in the night.

'You know Shakespeare?' he asked.

Mary was quite surprised by the change in topic. 'Shake-speare? Of course. I am a poetical sort of female, you know.'

'This party seems to have run mad. We need Puck's reverse remedy to set it right again.'

'Are you saying it's a love potion?' She laughed. 'My grand-mother, when I was a very little girl, used to tell tales of spirits hiding in the Christmas wreaths, and that was why we put out holly. To keep them at bay. I can imagine them now.'

A smile wrinkled his brow, despite their situation. 'Spirits caught in the holly boughs?'

'Yes. It could very well be Puck or Oberon, or Queen Mab. Everything feels quite topsy-turvy lately.'

It certainly did feel like something had been set free inside of Mary, something wild she'd spent her whole life fighting against in order to be safe. To be responsible. She had to find a way to catch it back again, to put it back into the jinni bottle before her life, her heart, shattered. She couldn't afford to fall in love with Charles Campbell. She needed the agency; he needed a proper wife and to help his niece. That was that.

'But if I remember correctly, Puck's schemes only create more chaos! It's Christmas, yes? We only need a little time, for reflection and planning, and all will be well. We cannot lose control.'

He turned his head to look at her, his hair tumbling over his brow, shadowing his eyes. 'My sweet Mary, I'm sure we need more than this one Christmas to set things right. My mistakes are—'

There were more voices outside, lighter, closer, more raucous, as if the Penningtons' cellar had been dipped into deeply. Mary trembled and edged away from Charles. Her whole being urged her to *stay, stay, stay!*

She smoothed her hair and dress, and tried to paste on a careless smile. It was truly as if the mad Christmas spirit had taken over her world—security, control, was flying apart. She remembered too much when she was younger: the fun, the longing for adventure, the passion. All the things she'd thought packed carefully away in order to take care of herself, build her independence. Now, with Charles, they were soaring free out of Pandora's box! And she loved it. She loved feeling like her old self again, even if just for a moment.

She didn't want to leave, but she knew she had to, for both their sakes. She kissed his cheek one more time and slid her hand out of his. She tiptoed out of their little alcove and blinked at the sudden flare of light after the shadows, the rush of people dashing past.

On the top step of the staircase, she glimpsed Adele—standing with Mr Clark. Adele did not look guilty or defiant now; she looked horribly shocked and chilled, her arms wrapped around herself, as if Clark had tried something with her.

Oh, how terrible Mary was for being such a bad chaperone, she scolded herself as she hurried forward, no time to summon Charles. 'Adele!' she called, sharper than she intended.

Adele jumped, a startled expression on her face, followed by a bad sign—stubbornness.

'Did you become lost? This house is quite a maze.'

'I—yes, lost. I am so glad to see you, Miss St Aubin!' she said, and as Mary drew closer, she saw that Adele was shaking. Not so stubborn after all. What had Mr Clark been saying to her?

He smiled innocently, smoothly, and Adele would not look at him.

Mary slipped her arm around the girl's trembling shoulders and noticed a rip in her embroidered sleeve, a red mark on her shoulder. She sucked in a deep breath, trying to contain her fury until she could get Adele away. If she was caught looking like that, Mr Clark would not be the one blamed but Adele herself. 'Come along, it is late. Let's see if I can find something warm to drink, and we can have a chat.' She glanced back at Clark, who looked rather infuriatingly smug as Adele trembled against Mary's shoulder.

'He—he kissed me,' Adele whispered as Mary led her into her own bedchamber and wrapped her up in a soft blanket. 'I thought it would be wonderful, but...'

'It was not?' Mary asked gently. She rang the bell to summon Daisy to bring some tea and sat down next to Adele.

Adele just shook her head. 'I don't want to talk about it, I pushed him away and he reached for me just as you appeared.' Her eyes widened. 'Uncle Charles! He will be so angry.'

'Oh, my dear,' Mary whispered. 'He would be angry, yes, but not with you. And he need never know. We can keep it between ourselves if you feel the need. Come, tell me about it, and I know we'll find a way to help you...'

Chapter Twelve

'Oh, the holly she bears a blossom as white as the lily flower...'

Mary laughed as the wind caught at her pelisse and made her cheeks sting with the cold. Was it really the best day to look for fresh greenery to deck Northland's halls? But it *was* pretty outside, she had to admit as the cart lurched along the path that wound through the park and out the gates, led along by their singing.

The pale gold sunlight, peeking through dove-grey clouds, shimmered on the dusting of snow, and everyone laughed and sang louder as they jostled amid picnic baskets, warm blankets, tools for cutting the greenery.

Best of all, she sat beside Charles on the narrow bench. His hand brushed hers, lingered, and she remembered the overwhelming bliss of him kissing her behind the curtain.

'Oh, the holly she bears a berry as red as any blood!'

The cart suddenly jolted around a corner, and Mary tumbled against his shoulder. He caught her, his arm coming close around her. She laughed and clutched at the edge of his coat as if she would fall. She wished she *could* fall, right into his arms.

Mary studied the scene around them, finding it more and more like a party under an enchantment. Even Adele laughed today, enjoying herself with Mr Clark nowhere in view. The trees grew thicker, the shadows more dappled, the little dome of the elegant summer house peeking above the branches. The notes of the song echoed as if floating along down a long corridor.

'How lovely it all is,' she said, and pointed out the summer house to Charles. 'Couldn't you just go inside there and stay forever?'

'Not much like town life, is it?' he said wistfully, and she wondered if he missed Scotland so much. 'Do you long for streets and shops here?'

Mary considered this. She'd always been rather a town sort of person, liking people and activity, but this peace was addictive. 'Not really, no. Yet I always thought I was a town mouse! After my childhood in a country vicarage, I yearned for parties and fun. But this is too enchanting. Like a fairy story, I almost expect to see gnomes around this corner. I could get used to this beauty. Are you missing Scotland and your castle?'

He quirked a smile down at her. 'I can't miss anything at all when you're here.'

And just like that, Mary couldn't breathe.

Before she could find words to answer, or even remember what words were in her jumbled, confused, lustful thoughts, the cart lurched to a halt in a clearing surrounded by circles of trees. Like a fairy ring for her story, where elves would dance. She stared around her, dazzled.

'Now,' Lord Pennington announced as he hopped down from the drivers' seat and helped his wife to alight, the two of them smiling into each other's eyes as if no one else existed and they saw only each other. 'I command you all, as lord of this demesne...'

Everyone laughed and teased him, and Lady Pennington gave her husband a playful shove.

He laughed, too. 'I do command you all to go out and find as much greenery as possible to deck the halls of Northland for our ball. The winner shall have the first glass from the wassail bowl! And I assure you, our cook mixes her wassail very strong indeed.'

A great cheer went up, loud and raucous as if they'd already been dipping into the wassail, and everyone scattered into the woods like a flock of brightly plumed birds in their pelisses and cloaks and greatcoats. Adele wandered off with Penelope and Anthony, who kept her close, and Mary noticed Mr Overbury starting towards her in a most determined fashion. But before he could get far, Charles held out his hand to help Mary down from the cart and held on to it, making Overbury back away scowling and kicking at the snow.

Mary's flat boot sole slid on the rung of the cart, and Charles quickly caught her around the waist before she could fall, her stomach clenched in sudden panic. She held on to him, breathless at the sparkling jolt of pure, clear, bright pleasure his touch gave her, wiping away any fear. It made her tingle all the way to her toes.

He slowly, oh, so slowly, slid her to her feet. He felt so warm, so strong, so safe. She wished with all her strength she would never, ever have to let him go again. Never lose that heady blend of protection and excitement he always brought. She wanted him to twirl her free in the winter light, spin her in a dance—kiss her. To let the fizzing Christmas spirit take over.

But she did have to stand on her own two feet. As she always did. 'Th-thank you, Mr Cam—Charles,' she whispered as she stepped back from him and felt the cold wind on her skin again. She glanced around and saw no one paid attention to them. They had scattered on their own errands, their own flirtations. 'So clumsy of me.'

He watched her carefully, intently. 'Not at all. I fear it is *I* who must beg *your* assistance.'

'My assistance?' She wondered dazedly what he could need. If he might *need* their kisses, as she feared she now did. She remembered thinking she should enjoy these moments together, these bright, fleeting days, and she knew she could do just that.

'I see a fine patch of holly over there just begging to be a mantelpiece decoration, but I don't have quite the adept nature I once had, and it's rather high. I think teamwork is needed.'

Mary laughed, distracted and charmed all at once, as she always was with him. 'I'm sure between us, we can defeat the holly and bear it home in triumph.'

Charles offered his arm, and she smiled up at him as she slipped her gloved hand through the curl of his elbow, feeling him press close to her. They followed the others between the thick stands of trees, hearing laughter bounce off the bare branches and twine into the sky. Mary found it easy to chatter with him, to talk about light matters such as favourite Christmas carols, Christmas traditions in Scotland, as if they had known each other forever. A cold wind swept through the trees high above them, swaying the branches, making the voices a mere blur. It felt like they were all alone, together.

'So, what are Christmases like in your castle, then?' she asked. She paused to clip a clump of low-hanging mistletoe, pearly with white berries, perfect for enticing someone into Christmas kisses.

'There's the ghillies' ball. I always looked forward to that as child, it was the only time there were people and noise and music in the place! I must organise it myself next year, with reels and lots of food and drink.'

Mary looked around at the silent trees, the pale, quiet sky, and imagined dancers in tartans twirling and spinning. 'This must seem rather dull after such a thing! Just a plain English country Christmas.'

'Oh, Mary,' he said, slanting her a sad little smile. 'An English country Christmas is one of the finest things I could ever imagine. Especially right now.'

Mary looked away, feeling shy, flattered—hopeful? Yet, what was there to be hopeful about? After this perfect Christmas, they would go their own ways. 'Shall we conquer that holly, then? I see some with particularly luscious red berries twined just up there.'

She took his hand in hers, revelling in the feel of his warm palm through their gloves, and led him to the holly bush, dark green against the snow. She held up the branches as he sawed them off to fill their baskets. They would surely bring back more than anyone else, and the wassail would be theirs! She could hear the voices of everyone else on the wind, far away, and she was just there wrapped in his warmth.

'It does remind me of some Christmases when I was a girl,'

she said. 'Ella, Papa, and I would find decorations for the vicarage and the church. It all smelled so delicious, of evergreen, and we would sing as we searched. And in the evenings, my father would read us the nativity story, and sometimes we could even get him to talk of our mother, of when they first met. Christmas was her favourite time of year.'

'It sounds wonderful,' he said wistfully. 'Like a family.'

'What did you do at Christmas, then? Besides the ghillies' ball, and the cook's mince pies and ghost stories.'

'That is just about it. When my mother was alive, she was usually in London, and I seldom saw my father. He did not enjoy Christmas, or anything that might dare to try to be fun.'

'Oh,' Mary whispered, her heart aching for the lonely boy he'd been. He smiled as he spoke, as if it were all of no consequence, a normal sort of life, but she knew there was sadness behind the words. She pictured a little boy wandering the stony halls of a castle, longing to hear carol music. 'And what about later?'

'When I was married, you mean? Oh, Aileen loved any chance for a party, but she usually found them much more easily in Edinburgh!' he said, and snipped off another branch of holly. 'In truth, I knew very soon after we wed that we were not compatible. But had to figure out a way ahead. *I* had to figure out a way.'

'And did you?'

'For a time. She liked the idea of being mistress of a castle, more than she liked the reality, and who can blame her. It's not easy. But she seemed to enjoy it for a while, and I was happy to have someone to share the work, as I thought. Then she found someone far more to her liking and stayed in England more and more until she did not come back.'

Mary gasped. 'She eloped?'

'You could say that. She declared I could never understand her, never give her the excitement she wanted. She imagined when we married that I would be someone else entirely, would be my young, reckless self forever, when I could not be. And she could not be other than she was, too. So she lived with her lover and died not long after, from a lung disease they said. So you see why I have been rather reluctant when friends urge me to marry again. How could I do such a thing to another woman? I am no fine husband.'

'Indeed, I can see why you would hesitate. But you are so very wrong about being no good husband material,' Mary murmured. She longed to take his hand, to hold him, to heal his past, even as she knew she couldn't. All she could do was try to give him a bit of help. 'You are a good guardian to Adele, you worry about her, watch over her. Her unhappiness is not your fault, she is just young and unsure. Just as I once was.'

'You, Mary?' he murmured, his eyes filled with understanding and concern as he watched her. 'Unsure?'

'Yes, certainly. The world is new to her, it all looks strange and frightening. I had Ella to help me, and I think that's why I love the agency so much. It's a way to give back to Ella for all she sacrificed for me and a way for me to find meaning in myself. Adele will find such a thing, too, with you to back her up.'

'And is the agency all you really want?'

Mary stared up into his eyes, and something hit her like a boulder to truth. No, it was not *all* she wanted; she had other longings, other dreams that she'd buried for a long time. She'd thought she'd never have to see them again, until Charles. 'No,' she whispered. 'I want...want...' She paused, tilting her head as she considered, as she let the enormity of this moment between them wash over her. 'I fear I may be about to do something rather naughty. That's what I want.'

He smiled lazily and leaned closer. 'I am all attention.'

'See that beautiful cluster of mistletoe up there? Every house must have plenty of mistletoe for Christmas. I'll climb up and fetch it.'

'Climb it?' he said doubtfully, tilting back his head to take in the tree that soared up into the winter sky. 'Mary, I don't think—'

Before he could stop her, Mary ran to the tree and found the perfect foothold in the bark. She remembered her childhood, running with Ella and Fred at Moulton Magna, playing in the woods, and it was wonderful to feel that free again, even if only for a moment. She reached up to grab at a thick branch. 'Ella and I used to climb trees all the time when we were children and no one was watching. I'm sure I remember how to do this.'

He frowned and rushed towards her, his arms outstretched to her. 'Mary, it looks dangerous.'

'Says the man who used to race his curricle! And not so dangerous as going back to Northland with not much greenery to show for it. We want that wassail, don't we?' She kept pulling herself upward, her shoulders aching with the long-forgotten strain, yet it felt marvellous. Strong and free, even when her hat tumbled from her head and spiralled to the ground.

She felt a strong, warm touch on her leg, heated through her stocking, holding her steady while helping her upward. Charles, ready to catch her if she needed it. To hold her safe even as he grinned up at her with shared mischief.

She reached up and snapped off the alluring cluster of mistletoe. As she climbed back down, the toe of her boot caught in her hem, and she tumbled backward again in a flash of clumsiness. But, as he always did, Charles was there to catch her. He held her high in his powerful arms for a moment, above the rest of the world, just the two of them. Breathless, she held on to his shoulders, safer than she'd ever been before.

'Thank you,' she whispered. 'How clumsy I have become lately! You've saved me once again.'

'I have to find some way to make myself useful, aye?' he said, and gave her a playful little bounce that made her laugh. 'Rescuing fair damsels seems as good a job as any.'

'You are very good at it, indeed,' she said as he slowly, slowly slid her to her feet. He didn't seem to want to let go yet, either, and they stood there holding on to each other. 'And just look at our lovely mistletoe! Not a single berry lost. Surely it was worth the danger.'

They smiled widely at each other, letting the fun sweep them into the wind, the moment of lightness.

'There you are,' Lady Pennington called. Mary reluctantly stepped away from Charles and turned to see their hostess marching towards them through the trees, Adele behind her. 'We're setting up for luncheon near the old summer house, a fine reward for all our hard work. Oh, look at all that beautiful mistletoe you've found, marvellous! Adele here has been helping me look for evergreen boughs, but we found nothing so beautiful as that. And what we did find was all on her.'

Adele held up a branch and smiled shyly, and Mary was glad to see she'd stayed away from Mr Clark, that she seemed to be stepping forward from what happened.

'More than a few romantics will find their way beneath it, I'm sure,' Lady Pennington laughed. 'This is our destination.'

They had made their way to the round pale stone summer house atop the hill, its rotunda roof a beacon in the grey sky, its high small windows glittering. A white tent lay at the foot of the hill looking up towards its beauty, luncheon waiting beneath it.

'Talk about a fine place for a princess,' Mary said. 'It is beautiful.' She remembered the story Charles told of a maiden and her knight who perished for love at the old medieval tower, and she wondered if the doomed pair of spirits ever came here for a little rest.

'I'm quite sure I can never return to prosaic old Bath after all this loveliness,' Adele said wistfully. Mary took her arm and gave it a reassuring squeeze.

She found them spots near the end of one snowy linen-draped table, near Charles, Sandrine, Pen and Anthony. They were laughing, merry, trading tales of Christmases in their youths, and soon even Adele was giggling, and happily whispering with Sandrine about fashion. Charles squeezed Mary's hand under the edge of the cloth, and she was sure she'd never had quite such a golden afternoon in her life.

After luncheon was over, the guests lingered around the table in a late meal lassitude, sipping the last of the wine, nibbling the fruit and pastries. Adele rose from the table and strolled outside the tent, away from the sweet-scented braziers, and was hit by the cold wind tugging at her fur-edged pelisse and making her eyes water. She thought about running back inside again. But she couldn't bear to hear her future marital state laughed about again. She knew she only had a few moments before her protective guardian and Mary came after her.

She gathered the folds of her coat closer around her and

plunged into the circle of trees, taking comfort in their silent dignity, in the scudding grey clouds sliding overhead. None of them cared about her matches, about what she wanted and didn't want, didn't care about her confusion. She just needed to be alone to *think*. She was tired of being so blasted confused!

She was careful not to wander too far; the sun was fading, and she had no desire to be lost in cold night woods, nor to make her friends upset again. She paused beside one of the carts and sat down on the narrow seat, close enough to hear the chatter from the tent, far enough away she wouldn't be immediately seen.

Especially by Peyton Clark.

She drew up her knees beneath her chin, as she had when she was a child. She'd so hoped for romance when they returned to Bath! Charles's castle was filled with romance, of course, but of a quite different sort than what she sought. Cold stones that whispered of old battles, of ghostly wanderings, could not compare to the thrill of a dance with that special someone. She was sure she'd find poetry in a town.

As soon as she saw Peyton Clark at an assembly, his golden curls, his tall figure, the heated way he watched her, she was elated to find her heart's desire so quickly. And then they'd danced, and her heart soared. It had to be love!

But Uncle Charles did not approve. All true meant-to-be-together couples faced prejudice and misunderstandings that drove them apart, surely. It only gave them a chance for secret notes, hurried meetings in Sydney Gardens and behind pillars at the Pump Room. It felt so wonderful to feel *she* could decide something, for once! She could love who she chose, create her own future.

Now she was not so sure at all. When he had found her on the stairs, tried to kiss her—those flutterings she'd felt before when she imagined such a thing turned into panic. Could such a thing be part of true love? She thought of what Miss St Aubin said, that love was listening and understanding. Dear Miss St Aubin, Mary! The only one who seemed to understand how Adele felt, who didn't shriek and demand and say they knew better. Who listened. Uncle Charles was so lucky to have wooed such a lady.

But then, if Mary was engaged to Adele's uncle, was she not like all the rest? Sure they knew her heart better than Adele did herself?

'Adele! My bright flower, my angel, where are you?' Peyton called now on the wind, and Adele feared she hadn't hid so well, after all. She tucked her feet tighter under her.

But he peered over the side of the cart, smiling broadly. 'I have been looking everywhere for you. They are getting ready to go back to the house, and I needed to speak to you alone. To explain.'

She remembered what happened in the confusion of the hide-and-seek game, the way he kissed her, his open mouth devouring hers, frightening her. But now he smiled as if nothing happened at all. She was very confused, frightened.

'I just needed a breath of fresh air,' she said. 'All that claret...'

He gave her an indulgent smile. 'Fuzzy-muzzy-headed? My silly little mouse! I shall hold you steady.'

He laid his hand on her arm, and it didn't feel at all the way it once did. It felt icy, and she wanted to be by herself, to think quietly. 'I am quite well. I can make my own way back.'

'But I am in alt that we can be alone at last. This is all I could ever desire, to be near you.'

'My uncle says—'

'Your uncle! What does he know about true love, such an old stick in the mud? You and I are made for each other. You shall never find anyone more perfect together, no matter how many Seasons you have. It's why I couldn't help myself last night, I was overwhelmed by my love for you.'

'What are you saying?' she whispered.

He frowned, and it was as if his sunny smile had never been there in only an instant. 'I am saying, Adele, that I cannot wait for you to be my wife. To make you mine entirely. Come away with me to Gretna Green.'

Adele was shocked. She'd wanted romance, yes, but—was this too much? 'Gretna Green?'

'You are Scots, are you not? It will be like marrying at home for you.'

But Adele did not want to go home. She wanted to see more

of the world, meet more people. And then she wanted to marry in a real kirk, not some grubby blacksmith's shop. 'I—I just don't know. This is very sudden. I cannot think…'

'No thinking, my love, just feeling. It's time for us to begin our lives together.' He stared deeply into her eyes, confusing her. 'Don't you love me, Adele, as I do you?'

She had thought she did. So very much. Then he grabbed her on the staircase during hide-and-seek, kissed her when she did not want it. 'I must think about it.'

A dark cloud seemed to slide over his golden features as he frowned at her. Something cold touched her deep inside, some fear. 'I thought I was sure of you, Adele, sure of our true love. That you were wise beyond your years, special.'

And she had been so flattered he called her wise, told her she was special, different from other ladies her age. 'Of course. I must just—'

He pushed himself to his feet in a whirl of anger, and she shrank back in sudden apprehension. 'We have until the ball. Arrangements are made.'

He departed, leaving her alone with all her doubts and fears, and she bent her head to her knees and cried with the loneliness of it all.

Chapter Thirteen

⟨ornamental flourish⟩

Mary thought she'd never known a more idyllic Christmas moment than this one. The guests were gathered around a giant carved fireplace that crackled with warmth against the cold wind howling at the windows, wrapping them in safety and cosiness. Goblets of spiced wine and platters of cinnamon biscuits and hothouse fruit passed around as Adele played carols at the pianoforte and everyone laughed together.

It felt just as a home should, Mary mused wistfully as she studied the scene. The Penningtons held hands, and Charles watched them, his gaze faraway…wistful, even. Did he think of his lost wife now? Mary felt such a sharp pang to consider it.

As Adele's song ended, she rose from the pianoforte and asked if anyone else would like to play. Mr Clark applauded her loudly from his seat at the back of the room, but she ignored him. Miss Tuckworth took her place, and she came to sit beside Mary and Charles, smoothing her pale blue muslin skirts around her.

'Uncle Charles,' she said, and he broke away from his thoughts to smile at her. 'Didn't you say when you were young, people would tell ghost stories for Christmas?'

He laughed. 'Aye, we did. I had many a nanny who could tell hair-raising stories, they kept me quite awake on Twelfth Night.'

'It's an old tradition,' Anthony said. 'To bring in the New Year and sweep the old out.'

'Well, I think we should try it now,' Adele said. 'That howling wind makes it seem just the thing. Shall you start, Uncle?'

Charles smiled and launched into a tale of a haunted castle harbouring a terrible beast in its dungeons, whose shrieks and cries brought curses onto the family living above him. He told of ghostly pipers wandering the hillsides as mournful music echoed in the distance. Sandrine added a story of a chateau in the French countryside, abandoned when its family perished under the guillotine, but now their pale shades drifted through the chambers, wailing. By the time Lord Pennington related the stories of Northland's own ghosts, grey ladies and fiery-eyed monks, everyone was quite on the edge of their chairs with tension.

In the last tale, a wailing white lady who warned of the death of someone near her, Mr Clark crept behind Lady Tuckworth's chair and shouted, 'Boo!' making everyone shriek. That was quite the end of the tales, and Lady Pennington quickly called for wine. But an unease still lingered in the air.

Mary felt very silly indeed, for she couldn't sleep at all. Every clang or clatter, every whistle of the wind beyond her bedroom draperies made her jump and shriek. She wrapped her arms around Miss Muffins under the bedclothes and held on tight.

As if the pup could keep spirits away. She shook as if just as afraid as Mary.

'Fool,' Mary whispered. She never should have listened to ghost stories! They'd made her have such horrors when she was a child, imaging faces at windows, footsteps on empty stairs, and it seemed nothing had changed.

When a branch skittered across the window pane, sounding like a skeletal touch, she'd had enough. She gave a little scream and leaped out of bed, grabbing up her dressing gown as she ran across the room. Miss Muffins was right at her heels.

She wasn't sure where she would go. The rest of the house seemed silent, shadowy. All the doors were closed, and surely spirits walked free at that hour. As a child, Mary would run to

Ella's room, but Ella wasn't there. So she turned to her other source of comfort, books.

She found a lantern on a table at the top of the stairs, a beacon for unwary wanderers, and tiptoed down. She passed niches where sculptures seemed positively phantom-like, curtains that trembled as if someone touched them. At last, she found herself safe in the library.

A fire still burned in the grate, light dancing on the rows of books that waited for her. She gave a sigh of relief and made her way towards its welcome, towards a stack of leather-bound volumes on the gilt table.

Only to find she was not alone in her sanctuary.

She shrieked as she came around a large brown velvet armchair and glimpsed an arm clad in dark blue brocade, a scarred, strong, sun-browned hand holding a glass of brandy.

Yet it was not a ghostly visitor. A head peered over the back of the chair, and Mary laughed in relief to see it was Charles, his hair tousled, his eyes wide as if she had startled him just as he did her.

She felt so very safe in only one instant—and then not safe at all, for her emotions roiled and turned at being alone with him.

'I—I'm so sorry, I didn't know anyone was here,' she said. 'I couldn't sleep.'

'Neither could I.' He gestured to the chair beside his, smiling ruefully. 'The Northland spirits seemed rather restless.'

'I always was a beastly coward about ghosts,' Mary admitted. She sat down as Miss Muffins found a cushion near the hearth, and Mary was suddenly wrapped in cosiness with Charles. 'I hope you aren't reading *The Devil Monk*.' She nodded at the book in his hand.

He laughed, warm and rich. 'Not at all. John Donne. I often find comfort in his verses.'

'I love it, too. Would you read some to me?'

'Of course.' He put his glass down and reached for her hand as he lifted the book closer. His touch was steadying, warm, but it made her tremble all the same.

Mary remembered his words about his first marriage, how

he'd had hope at first. Had he read poetry to her? Longed for her, as Mary longed for him right now?

'Is this how you spent evenings when you were married?' she dared to ask shyly.

He frowned down at the book. 'Never. Aileen did not care much for books. She enjoyed excitement, romance, danger.'

Danger, like running off with someone else when she could have had Charles, and was the luckiest woman in the world to have him. 'Then she was very silly. Books have quite enough excitement for me. And danger will find us whether we look for it or not, so why create more of it?' She squeezed his hand. 'I wish life could always be just like this.'

'As do I. Such nights are made for seeking warmth and safety, a fine fire, a good book, a dog. A...' He studied her, unreadable in the firelight.

'A friend?' she whispered.

'A twin spirit, if we are lucky.'

'Such things are rare indeed,' she said. 'Like jewels.'

'Yes. More precious than rubies. They should be cared for, cherished.'

Mary had no words, nothing she could say about her own longings and dreams. She could only stare into his eyes, those beautiful eyes, and wonder if he could possibly feel the same. The whole world was narrowed to that one room, that one fireside, the two of them, and she yearned with every inch of her being to succumb to it all, possess it forever.

And yet—yet there was still such fear, always lingering in the background of her mind, her heart. The fear of losing what she had, losing the work she'd come to rely on, losing the wondrous love she'd just found.

He seemed to sense her unease. 'Mary,' he said gently, and reached for her hand again. He eased back the lace ruffle of her sleeve, revealing the pulse that beat there, strong and fast with desire. He bent his head and pressed a soft, lingering kiss to her lifeblood.

She could not turn away from him, leaned towards him as if caught in his orbit. She reached up with her free hand and swept a tousled lock of hair from his brow, letting her touch drift over him. And at last he dipped his head and kissed her, a kiss full of all the longing and need she could find no words for, couldn't even understand. Her arms wound around his neck, holding him with her, leaning into his strength. He was all she should have fought against, this surrender to emotion, yet instead he felt like her only haven. She just couldn't stay away from him.

Their lips slid away from each other, from the desperation of that kiss. He leaned his forehead to hers, and they stood together there in sizzling silence, wrapped up in longing. Mary never wanted to let go again.

Chapter Fourteen

Mary sighed and sank down lower on the library settee the next morning as she tried to concentrate on the book she held, the morning light from the windows bright on the words. She'd thought she could hide there, press away thoughts of Charles and the temptations of his kiss, his touch. But probably the library, where they kissed, wasn't the best place for such forgetting. She looked at the chairs and remembered him reading Donne to her. Looked at the carpet and remembered their kiss.

She could hear laughter outside the room as everyone rushed about decorating. It seemed unlikely they would find her there, yet she wondered if being alone was really a mistake. Alone with her thoughts and daydreams and yearnings. She'd seen such obsessions and emotions from people at the agency before, but had never thought she would be their victim.

She snapped the book shut. When she was with Charles, it all felt so perfect. Fun and full of light. When he was gone, when she closed her eyes at night and was alone, she was beset with doubts and fears.

There was a quiet knock at the door. Happy for some distraction, she put aside the book and called, 'Come in!'

It was the butler. He held a folded note on a silver tray in one hand and a fur-lined cloak with the other. 'I beg your pardon for the interruption, Miss St Aubin, but I have an urgent message for you.'

'For me?' Mary said, alarmed. Was it her sister or one of the twins? She jumped up from the settee and reached for the note, quickly tearing it open. It was quite short, a dark, swift, spiky scrawl, and it seemed no one was ill or injured. Quite the opposite.

Meet me outside in ten minutes. A Christmas surprise. Charles.

Mary blinked, her heart racing as she read the message a second time. From Charles! He wanted to meet her!

The butler gave a discreet little cough and offered the cloak. 'I was told you would need these, Miss St Aubin, as it looks like snow outside. And these.' He picked up gloves and a pair of sturdy boots. An outdoor surprise, then. Her mind whirled with imaginings, hopes, fears.

'Thank you.' In a confused, excited, hopeful haze, she quickly put on the warm clothes and hurried out of the library, avoiding the merriment in the drawing room to slip out the front doors.

Charles was indeed waiting there for her, holding the reins of his curricle at the foot of the stone stairs. She thought of their day snowbound at that inn, the heated intimacy of it all.

'Come out with me, Mary,' he called. 'It's a beautiful day!'

Mary laughed and drew her hood closer. 'If you enjoy freezing your nose off,' she said. She dashed down the steps towards him, and he caught her to lift her high onto the seat. He tucked a fur-lined robe around her and slid a hot brick under her now booted feet. 'It's a perfectly warm day. See?'

And so it was—with him. She couldn't remember ever being quite so warm, so sparkling with sunlight, before. He climbed up beside her and flicked the reins, setting them off on this unknown adventure.

'I do like surprises,' she said, leaning against him.

'Then you will especially like this one. Lady Pennington helped me set it up.'

Lady Pennington. Of course. She'd forgotten everyone thought them betrothed, and with so much romance wrapped around Christmas, they would want to help their engagement along. It made her feel terrible for deceiving them—and filled with fun laughter at the little secret.

The carriage flew along a narrow path just off the main drive. Frost sparkled on the bare tree branches like diamonds, and it was so quiet there, so magical, not another being in sight. She wound her arm through his and rested her head on his shoulder, wishing their mysterious journey might go on forever.

But it could not, of course. He guided the horse down a circular drive and drew up in front of the little summer house where they'd had luncheon. Up close, the tiny building looked even more as though it belonged in a fairy tale, with its columns and high windows, the winter ivy twining up its stone walls. A grey plume of smoke curled up from the chimney, a sign of real life.

'Does someone live here, then?' she asked, looking for faces at the windows.

'Yes. We do. At least for this afternoon.' Charles leaped down from the carriage and came around to help her. But instead of putting her down on the frosty ground, he swept her high in his arms, making her laugh, making her feel as light as a feather against his strength. He carried her through the little fence surrounding the summer house, through a tiny sleeping garden to the vine-covered front door, as if she were one of the agency's brides. Mary decided to forget all her doubts and fears today, to just linger in this perfect moment.

She giggled and held on tight to his neck as he swung her through the door and down a narrow little corridor, through a low portal and into a pocket-sized sitting room. She gasped in delight when she saw what waited there.

A bright fire burned in a little stone-fronted grate in the octagonal room, surely used for tea parties and liaisons in warmer months. Spread before its warmth was a picnic arranged on a silken quilt. Bread, cheese, Christmas cake with icing like white lace, hothouse strawberries and bottles of wine, with dried flower petals scattered over the polished parquet floor to cast the faint scent of summer in the air.

It was beautiful, like a romantic gesture she would recommend to agency patrons. Not like something she would imagine for herself.

'Oh, Charles,' she whispered. 'Is this the surprise?'

'Do you like it? I wasn't sure...' He glanced around doubtfully, and she kissed his cheek.

'I *love* it. It's the most perfect thing ever.'

'Such a delicious meal,' Mary sighed as she fell back onto the cloud-like softness of the quilt. She was so warm and content, the heat from the fire dancing over her, the wine drifting lazily through her veins making her feel she could float. How long had it been since all felt so very *right*?

Never. She'd never felt like that before, as if she was just exactly where she was meant to be. All due to Charles.

She rolled to her side and propped her head on her arm to study him. She'd never seen him look so very handsome, his hair tousled, cravat loosened to reveal the strong lines of his throat, smiling and content. In one hand he held a half-full goblet of wine while his other lazily stroked the folds of her skirt where it draped over his leg, binding them together.

'I do like your kind of surprise,' she murmured. She reached out and softly traced her fingertips over the sculpted, lean angles of his face. His cut-glass cheekbones, the rough dark bristles over his square jaw, his closed eyes, the satiny sweep of his dark brows. He lay there, very, very still, like a jungle panther about to pounce, eyes shut as he let her explore. She glimpsed the pink scar she'd seen at the inn and traced a healing touch over it.

Then she swept a gentle caress over his lips, and he suddenly snapped, catching the tip of her finger lightly between his teeth. She laughed in surprise, fading to a longing sigh as his tongue swept over her skin and he nibbled at her fingertip. A flash of fireworks went through her, crackling, sizzling. She pressed her palm to his cheek and wished they could be here like this forever, just the two of them.

He put down his glass and wound his arm around her waist, bringing her down next to him on the blanket. His palms planted to either side of her as he held himself over her on his powerfully muscled arms, bared by his rolled-up shirtsleeves. His green eyes were darkened, hooded and intense as he stared down at her, as if he could see into her very soul.

'Mary,' he said, universes in her name. 'Let me make all time like this for you. Let this engagement be real, I beg you.' He looked as surprised as she felt, but then he smiled and plunged on. 'Maybe I can't give you all you need, but let me try. We have such fun together!'

Mary was shocked. She stared up at him, frozen, tempted. Oh, so tempted. 'W-why?'

'Why? We like each other. We understand one another. We want the same things, I think.'

Like. Mary turned her head away. He said everything, except love. And she longed only for him to love her. 'Oh, Charles. It's not enough. I'm afraid.'

He turned her back to look at him, stark—was it fear on his face? 'Afraid of me? I would not hurt you for the world.'

'No, not of you! Of me. Of how I feel with you. So—so wild and free. As I once was. I couldn't bear losing myself, losing *you.* If you turned away from me, I could never...' She broke off, unable to explain even to herself. If he did not love her, only liked her, laughed with her, the future would be bleak for her. Would she become as unhappy as his first wife had been, as he had been in his marriage? Would she make him unhappy? She couldn't bear that.

She nearly blurted out that she needed him to love her as she did him, but she bit her lip to hold those most powerful words back. She let go of him and rolled over to cover her face with her hands. It was such a shocking but not surprising realisation. She *loved* him. More than she had ever imagined she could love anyone.

She'd seen such things at the agency, seen it with her sister and Fred, with the Penningtons and the Olivers. Love that transcended all else. When it was for other people, she could see it, control it. With herself, she felt like she was spinning away wildly and couldn't catch it. Couldn't get back her heart.

'Oh, Mary.' She felt his hands, those powerful scarred hands caress her shoulders. He drew her closer against his chest, his arms tight around her. She spun around to bury her face in his shoulder, and inhaled deeply of his lemon scent. Her only refuge and the only thing that could really hurt her.

He pressed a lingering kiss to the top of her head. 'I would never hurt you, my *cuisle*. Please believe me.'

'You would not, on purpose.'

He held her face between his palms as if she were the most delicate piece of porcelain, his thumbs caressing her cheekbones. She peeked up at him, everything blurry and bright through the sheen of her unshed tears, and she saw his tender wonder-filled smile.

His lips met hers, softly at first, gentle, questing.

'This is against the rules,' she whispered. She couldn't marry him if he did not love her; but she could take this moment and store it into her memories.

'Hang the rules,' he growled. 'We never paid mind to them, anyway.'

Very true. She closed her eyes and he pressed deeper, the tip of his tongue tracing the curve of her lower lip until she moaned with delight. His tongue slipped inside, twining over hers, tasting her deeply as if she was the sweetest wine. She felt his fingers in her loosened hair, tilting her head so he could kiss her even more deeply. More intimately.

How wondrous he tasted, of wine and strawberries, and that dark, swirling essence of himself that she always craved so much. She wrapped her arms around his shoulders and pressed herself even closer to him.

He groaned against her lips, and carried her down deep into the blankets. His kiss turned harder, wilder, and something inside of her answered his need with a burning passion of her own, a desire she'd fought against for too long.

She pushed his coat off, tossed aside his loosened cravat, and reached for the hem of his shirt to drag it up so she could at last touch him. He shifted, letting her fingertips explore the warm silk of his skin, running a caress over him as she felt his muscles grow tense. How she longed to feel all of him, see him, know him.

'Mary,' he whispered, his voice so hot and rough. His lips

slid from hers to kiss her cheek, the pulse beating at her temple, the edge of her ear. His teeth nipped lightly at her earlobe, brushed over a tiny, sensitive spot just below, his breath warm in her ear. He traced a ribbon of tiny kisses along her arched neck, the curve of her shoulder above her gown and, shockingly, the upper swell of her breast, making her whimper.

'Charles,' she sighed.

As if the sound of his name unleashed something inside of him, he tugged down her gown, her chemise, until she lay bare before him, and she did not even care. She felt wanton and free and delicious! She felt beautiful under his avid stare, his hungry touch. She'd never wanted anything more than this.

'Please,' she whispered. He nodded, and his head bent as his mouth closed hard over her bared nipple, his tongue swirling around its tip, his teeth lightly stinging then his kiss soothing again. She gasped and twisted her fingers in his hair to hold him against her. She followed her instincts and wrapped her legs around his hips as her skirts frothed to one side, pressing to the curve of his backside in tight woollen breeches, feeling the hard strength of him.

Her eyes closed tightly as she felt his mouth on her bare skin, felt his hand slide down over her side, feathering lightly along her body, closer and closer to that most aching part of her, then teasingly away.

'Please,' she whispered. 'Touch me. I need to know...'

He moaned and at last gave her what she craved. His fingers traced over that delicate spot between her legs, then one fingertip staggeringly, wonderfully, slid deep inside of her, and she knew that everything she had imagined, everything she had desired, was a hundred times better. It was perfect.

'Do you like that?' he said tightly, his lips against her neck.

'Yes. Oh, yes,' she sobbed as he thrust his touch deeper. Her legs fell away from him so she could plant her feet to the floor on either side of his lean hips to hold herself to the earth, sure she would soar away into the stars.

'Charles, please,' she moaned. He moved faster and faster, until she cried out, bursting into sparks of hot, wild joy.

Slowly, slowly, she drifted back to earth, still shivering, her skin tingling, until she found herself not among the stars, but beside the fire, with him. She held on to him tightly. She didn't want to let him go yet, didn't want to let the cold world outside encroach on this dream. It frightened her to realise how she forgot everything else here in his arms.

She felt him bury his face in her shoulder and press his lips to her damp, trembling skin. His arm looped close over her waist, holding her against him, as if he didn't want to let her go, either.

She sighed and glanced at the high windows. It was still light outside but turning pinkish-grey at the edges, the day waning. She gently stroked the damp strands of his tousled hair, felt the softness of his breath on her skin. She closed her eyes and wanted to cling to him and flee all at the same time. What had she done?

'We should go back,' she murmured.

His arms tightened. 'Stay. Just for a little while longer, please, Mary.'

Just a little while longer.

She wanted to stay forever just like that, wrapped in his arms. But she knew so much waited beyond those doors. If he did not love her, she could never stay. And she knew this moment was all they really had. 'I can't marry you, Charles. You know I cannot, not if it would make you unhappy later. We can continue until Adele is safe, of course, but—'

He sat up straight to stare into her eyes, his own narrowed, dark. 'But after what just happened...'

Mary reached up to gently touch his cheek, to let herself feel the ache of that moment, that longing and sadness and resolve. 'It wouldn't work, you know that. We would come to hate being together, resent our time, our responsibilities. This moment is perfect! Let it be just that. Please, Charles. I couldn't bear anything else.'

He stared at her as if he would argue, but then she saw the knowledge come into his eyes, the realisation that she would not budge. Could not move, for the sake of their hearts. He nodded and lay down beside her again. Mary wrapped her arms around him and held on for every ounce of her heart for as long as she could.

Chapter Fifteen

'This is intolerable!' Peyton Clark shouted. He paced the clearing in the woods, kicking at the drifts of snow, hitting a low-hanging branch. He'd never known fury like that before, never been denied what should be his in such a brutal way.

Overbury watched from the edge of the circle, his face red, his hands clutching at the edge of his cloak. He glanced behind him uncertainly, a scared rabbit who Clark realised would never have been a reliable ally. 'I am sure matters cannot be so very dire,' he bleated.

'Not so dire!' Clark clenched his fists as he longed to grab the man by that ridiculous fur collar and shake him until his teeth rattled. But he knew Overbury was not the enemy here. It was Adele and her uncle. They were the ones who had to pay. 'I shall soon be cut off without a shilling, thanks to my uncle and Charles Campbell. How dare they put me, *me*, in such danger! All because of that rabbity girl. That fickle minx.'

Overbury's eyes widened. 'I thought you loved her! As I love Miss St Aubin.'

'Love?' Clark laughed incredulously. 'How could I love someone like that? Simpering and spoiled. But I liked her well enough, when I thought her a true lady, and she seemed happy with what I offered.' And, most important, happy to offer her dowry. That was what he was due; that was what he needed so desperately. 'Do you not feel you are owed Miss St Aubin's affections, for all you have done for her?'

Overbury's mouth dropped open. The man really was quite like a trout. 'Not—not *owed*, I suppose. Just owed the chance to show her how very devoted I am, how much I love her, how I would strive to make her happy. If she would just see that!'

Clark shook his finger at the man. 'Exactly. We know what is best. And yet they stand in our way at every turn. They must be taught a lesson.'

He sat down on a fallen log, his thoughts racing, time running out around him. It felt like his world was melting into nothingness. 'I fear time is short for us, Overbury. We must act quickly.'

'Act?' Overbury squeaked. 'Have we not been...?'

'Indeed we have not. We have behaved like simpletons, waiting for them to see what they must do. We have tried to show them what should be, what could be, and they refuse at every turn.' He tapped the toe of his boot against the snow. 'It is nearly Christmas. This party will soon be over; we must be bold.'

'Bold,' Overbury echoed.

'Once we bring the issue forward, make it a reality they cannot deny, they will have no choice. They will see it is all for the best.'

Overbury fell back a step. 'What—what exactly do you mean by that?'

Clark leaped up again, pacing, the excitement of a plan washing over him. That was the problem! He had not stood up for himself when he should have, had not been strong. That would change. 'Do you truly love Miss St Aubin, man?'

'Of course I do!'

'Then you must *show* her that. Catch her attention. Overpower her, as women long for men to do.' A plan finally started to take shape in his mind, one he was sure must work. 'First, we shall lure Adele out of the Christmas ball into the garden, and then...'

Everything was quite ready for the Christmas ball.

Mary stood by the window of her bedchamber, watching

the snow falling thicker outside as the day had promised earlier, closing them all inside like a winter painting. Daisy fluttered around behind her, putting the final touches to Mary's ball gown.

Mary tried to push down her sadness at what should be such a happy time, tried to smile and pretend. She'd been pacing her room all day, wondering if she had been too hasty to reject Charles's proposal that they marry for real. Surely she could have, *should* have, trusted in the connection they had built. She could help him move forward, as he had with her. She had to talk to him, to see if it was even possible!

Was she really, really, really ready to take a step into a new life? When Charles held her in his arms, vowed never to hurt her, she knew she could. Now, alone, she was afraid of the unknown.

'You should smile, Miss Mary!' Daisy cried as she held up Mary's new gown. 'It's Christmas. And just look at Mademoiselle Sandrine's new creation.'

Sandrine had indeed surpassed herself, Mary had to admit. As Daisy helped her into the gown and started to fasten up all the tiny pearl buttons along the back, she saw it was the most beautiful thing she'd seen, a creation of darkening shades of blue, satin and organdie, held up with silken bunches of lilies of the valley and edged with old lace. She felt like the fairy queen Charles called her. A fairy queen who could be brave and risk her heart.

As Daisy added the last-minute touch of a wreath of white silk roses and loops of pearls to Mary's upswept blond curls, she peeked out the window to find carriages arriving ahead of the snow, filled with ball guests to supplement the house party and fill the ballroom. Their occupants stepped down onto the green carpet that lined the gravel drive, wrapped in their furs and velvets, laughing with excitement.

There was no time to hesitate. She slipped on her mother's pearl earrings, borrowed from Ella for Christmas, and drew on her gloves.

'Are you ready, Miss Mary?' Daisy asked, and Miss Muffins gave a little bark from her cushions. Mary drew in a deep, steadying breath.

'Yes. I am ready.' And she knew she was. Ready for anything at all.

Even if what she really longed for was to hide under the bed. She, who'd always loved parties! But only if Charles would hide there with her. Instead, he waited for her in the ballroom.

Daisy handed her a lace fan, straightened her short pearl-edged train, and Mary held her head up high as she marched out of the chamber into the night.

The dining room was empty as she paused to examine it; everyone was still in the foyer or reception room. A buffet supper for midnight was being set up there, while she could hear the musicians tuning up in the ballroom. It all quite sparkled and dazzled as a Christmas party should, the rooms festooned with large wreaths and swags of greenery, gathered on their outings. Crimson hothouse roses, palm fronds twining in gilt vases, tables lined with round bunches of more roses, carnations, holly, all beautiful.

The warm air smelled of greenery and the spices of the Christmas punch, smoke from thousands of wax candles, the Yule logs in every fireplace.

Mary found Lady Pennington waiting on the staircase to greet her guests, empress-like in a golden silk gown. But there was no sign of Pen or Anthony, or of Adele, and luckily no Overbury.

And no Charles. What if he didn't appear that night? What if the summer house was a dream, and all her excitement and fear were for nothing?

At last, she glimpsed Charles strolling down the stairs, still smoothing his hair, straightening his cravat. He looked splendid, like her Scots warrior, powerful and tall, his hair gleaming, his smile warm and inviting even across the room.

His face lit up when she waved to him, brighter than the Yule log. 'Forgive my tardiness,' he said as he hurried to her side, taking her hand for a lingering kiss. 'I had an important gift to fetch.'

He handed her a small, ribbon-bound package. Eagerly, she

opened the little box to find a brooch, an amethyst set in a silver thistle. It was delicate, elegant, beautiful. 'Charles,' she whispered.

'It was my grandmother's, from the Highlands where she was born. It was said she wore it at the ball where she met my grandfather, and it's blessed. That is her family crest etched on the back.'

'Oh, Charles,' Mary breathed. 'It is so pretty.' And so precious, so personal. What could it mean?

'If it is too plain...' he began doubtfully.

'It's the loveliest thing ever. But you should not give it away! It's too precious.' She held it out as if to return it, and he pressed it into her hands.

'It belongs with you,' he said simply. 'No matter what.'

She couldn't say anything else, for the ballroom doors opened, and a kaleidoscope of silks, satins, diamonds, pearls, feathers all flowed inside, set off by the stark black and dark blue of the gentlemen. The orchestra struck up the first dance.

'Shall we?' she said.

He grinned at her. 'Do you dare?'

'We can only try!'

She held tightly to his hand as they took their places on the dance floor, keeping her smile firmly in place even as she started to worry about what might happen next. If they might find themselves flat on their backsides in front of the whole party.

The music grew louder, a most lively tune. She squeezed his hand, and they stepped off—right, left, right, left, hop. Turn, spin. To her joy, the whirling movement went off perfectly, and they landed lightly together. They looked at each other, a thrill of accomplishment sparkling between them.

After that, the dance sped forward like magic. They spun and turned, clasped arms in allemande, twirled. It was a grand dance, perfect in every way, and she hated to see it ever end. She wanted the ball, Christmas, everything to stay just as it was so she would never have to part with him.

Yet it did end, of course, and they made one last slow turn together.

He bowed to her, and she dropped into a curtsy. She stared up at him, and they seemed to be the only two people in all the world. All the other guests, the grand sparkle of the room, faded away, and she was sure this was where she was meant to be.

Flustered, scared, exhilarated, she stepped back. 'I—excuse me, just for a moment.'

He nodded, and she felt him watch her as she hurried away towards the ladies' withdrawing room. She needed to take a deep breath, think for a moment in the quiet chamber.

Yet once there, she found her fears seemed to fade quietly away and left only the shine of the dance. She couldn't help but smile at herself in the mirror. She suddenly longed to giggle and twirl around and around! She saw his smile in her memory, the glow of his eyes, and wondered if they really could find a way to be together. Surely it was possible? Anything was possible at Christmas.

She patted her hair into place, and the candlelight caught on her new silver brooch. He had given her his grandmother's jewel. Surely that meant something? Surely that meant he wanted her, that he could love her. All their scheming, their falsehoods, had somehow come true.

She wanted to be by his side again. She hurried out of the room and along the corridor. She could hear music in the distance, beckoning her onward, and she noticed a half-open door to the terrace that ran along the back of the house, looking to the gardens and the woods. Snow was falling, lacy, silvery, delicately against the glow of lights from the lanterns strung along the terrace. She went outside to take it all in for a moment, let the magic of Christmas wrap around her.

A flash of movement at the edge of the garden, just at the corner of the light thrown around by the lanterns, caught her attention. A pink streak, something pale and quick.

To her shock, she saw it was Adele. And Mr Clark held her by the arm, dragging her towards the darkness of the trees. Mary couldn't hear very much from that distance, but she saw Adele's mouth open in panic. This seemed no romantic elopement, but a kidnapping.

Her heart pounding, Mary opened her own mouth to scream

and found that no sound came out except a terrified squeak. No one was nearby, the ballroom noisy with music and laughter, and she saw Clark and Adele were farther away at every second. Another figure emerged from the woods, and she knew there was no time to lose.

She ran down the steps of the terrace into the garden, her slippers sliding on the frosty ground, panic racing through her veins.

'Let her go!' she shouted.

Clark and Adele spun around. Adele managed to wiggle free, but only for an instant before he caught her again, making her cry out. His handsome face was twisted with fury and frustration.

'Mary,' Adele sobbed, and to Mary's horror, she saw a dark bruise on the girl's cheek. 'No, no, go back! I'm not worth it!'

'This has nothing to do with you. You have interfered enough!' Clark snarled. 'She has agreed to be my wife. If you don't want anyone hurt…'

Someone suddenly grabbed Mary's arm from behind, and she screamed in panic. She whirled around and lashed out, trying to hit them—and saw it was Overbury. He looked as shocked as she felt, his face pale in the moonlight, but she had no sympathy for him.

'You are a part of this villainy?' she hissed at him. 'I should have known.'

'It isn't what it looks like,' he begged her, but his grasp didn't loosen on her arm. She knew she'd have bruises there soon. 'I swear it! I only wanted you to notice me, and he said—'

'Enough blabbery. We have to be gone,' Mr Clark said. 'Bring her or not. I don't care.'

He swung Adele up into his arms roughly, making her scream. Mary started to run after them, and Overbury reeled her back towards him, stronger than he looked. Mary had only an instant, and she loosened her new brooch with her free hand and let it drop to the ground so Charles would find it and know she'd been there.

Overbury moved to pick her up, and she fought with all her might, kicking and shrieking, desperate to get free. In mid-swing, a sharp pain flashed through her head, and she fell to her knees, dizzy and in agony. A warm wetness spread at the back of her neck, and she tumbled down and down, hearing Adele scream, a dog bark, all from a great distance.

Then she saw only blackness.

Chapter Sixteen

Charles was sure he'd never felt so nervous before, so filled with doubts and yet certainty, as he paced the floor waiting for Mary to return. Surely it would all come right now. He could dance! She wore his grandmother's brooch. He could persuade her this should be real, permanent. That he loved her. Truly loved her.

'Charles!' he heard Penelope call. He smiled and turned to her, only to freeze at the expression on her face. Her eyes were wide with panic, her cheeks pale. Penelope never looked like that; she was always calm and collected and serene. She held Miss Muffins under her arm, and even the dog seemed frozen silent. A footman trailed behind them, looking terribly confused.

Charles forgot the party, forgot everything. The world seemed to have stopped. Some sort of old battlefield instincts were roused within him, and he hurried to her. 'Pen? Is someone hurt, ill?'

She shook her head and gasped in a breath. 'No, no! But this footman—he saw something most strange, most alarming.' She waved the man forward, and he seemed nervous.

'What is it?' Charles demanded.

'I—I did see something odd, sir. From the music room window as I was collecting glasses. A lady was in the garden, arguing with two gentlemen just where the lanterns were strung in the trees, so I could see her pink dress. I thought that was strange, as it was starting to snow even harder out there.' He took a gulp of air. 'She pushed one of them and started to run away, but the other man grabbed her arm. I think—I think it was Miss Stewart, sir.'

'Adele,' Charles whispered, appalled, terrified, furious.

'It must be Mr Clark,' Penelope cried. 'I should have watched her better, I should have followed her every moment. And now surely he's taken her. This is my fault.'

Charles felt chilled to his very core. He knew he had to hold onto that coldness, had to use it to help him think straight and find her. 'What happened then?' he asked the footman.

'I started to run outside, and I saw another lady appear. She—I think she wore a blue gown, but I can't be sure. There was a fight, and she fell down. By the time I got there, they had gone. There was this on the ground at the edge of the trees.' He held out a silver thistle brooch. The very one Charles had just given Mary. It must have been wrenched from her.

He took it, turning it over on his palm as fear and anger washed over him. 'It must be Mary.'

'I was in the dining room, and Miss Muffins came bursting in, running to me,' Penelope said, cradling the shaking dog. 'She must have known something terrible happened.'

Charles patted the dog's head. If something happened to Mary, Miss Muffins would never abandon her. 'Which way did they go?' he asked the footman.

The man shook his head. 'It was too dark by then. But there must be some footprints in that fresh snow.'

'Gather as many men as you can find and follow me on the search. Fetch lanterns, blankets. Have a doctor waiting. Pen, find our hostess and tell her what is happening, try not to let anyone else know yet. Ask Anthony to come with me. We don't need a panic to frighten Clark.'

He hurried out the front doors into the snowy garden, knowing he had to stay calm. Stay frozen. He had to think only of finding them. They could not be hurt, they could not. He would find them soon. Mary needed him now.

He wouldn't let her down, as he had too many people in his life. And he could never bear to lose her.

Mary felt like she was sinking down into the dark waves of some warm ocean, falling deeper and deeper, more and more tired. She somehow knew she had to fight against it, pull herself up to the cold surface, but she only wanted to sleep.

Yet there was something she had to battle against, something most important she had to remember. If only she could think, think...

Then it came to her, a great flash of light. She'd gone after Adele, and they'd been kidnapped. She remembered screams, panic, a pain in her head, then darkness.

She could smell the faded remains of a fire, damp wool, could feel something under her cheek that was warm. She heard a ragged sob close by, felt arms holding her.

She sucked in a deep breath, nearly choking, and forced her eyes to open, that warm water rushing away from her. Pain shot through her head, sharp and frigid, and she thought she would be sick. She ground her teeth against it and took quick stock of her surroundings.

She saw a domed ceiling high overhead, and realised she was in the summer house. It was completely transformed from her beautiful afternoon there with Charles. The firelight and blankets were gone, leaving only freezing stone walls and flagstone floors.

It was Adele who held her close. Her strawberry-blond hair hung loose and tangled, the sleeve of her gown torn and a bruise on her cheek. Mary reached out for her, terrified she was hurt. Terrified she had not been able to protect her.

'Oh, Mary, thank heavens you're awake,' she sobbed. 'I was so, so afraid.'

Mary carefully touched the back of her head, and found a bandage wrapped there, a bit of organza from Adele's gown. 'What happened?' she whispered. She wrapped her own arms around the girl, and they held on to each other against the cold and fear.

'They locked us in here and ran off when they heard someone

and were afraid of being found.' Adele sniffed. 'They said they'd be back for us. Cowards. Probably they're in the next county by now. Everyone was absolutely right about what a scoundrel Peyton is. Too scared to face what they've done.'

'Let's hope they stay gone, then, until we can figure out how to get out of here,' Mary said, trying her hardest to think straight, make a plan.

'I was so stupid,' Adele cried. 'How could I be fooled by someone like that? He would have ruined me. He hurt you!'

'You were not stupid,' Mary said. 'You were deceived. How could it be otherwise? How could you have known?' She glanced around at the dark walls. 'There is no way out?'

'I couldn't find one,' Adele said. 'The windows are too high and small, and the door is firmly locked.'

Mary sat up slowly, her head swimming, and tried to remember something, anything, that could help. She searched the seemingly empty room until she found a bread knife left from her picnic there with Charles, dropped near the empty fireplace. It wasn't much, but it was something. She knelt down by the door and tried to pry it open, Adele hurrying to help her.

After what seemed like an eternity of futile digging at the stone, her hand throbbing, her head on fire, they saw the flash of light in the windows.

Adele grabbed her arm and whispered, 'Could it be...?'

'Mary! Adele! Are you there?' she heard Charles shout. Warm, wonderful relief washed over her, and she knew she'd never heard anything so sweet. For an instant, she wondered if she was still in a faint and this was a dream. But then his voice came again, louder, stronger, along with a pounding at the door. 'Mary! If you're there, please answer me.'

'I'm here! We're here!' She and Adele rushed to bang on the door together. 'Overbury and Clark have fled and locked us in here.'

'Are you hurt?'

Mary glanced at Adele, at her loose hair and bruised cheek, and wrapped her arm around her. 'I was hit over the head, and something is wrong with my shoulder. Adele has a bruise on her poor cheek, but other than that we are fine.'

'We'll have you both safely to Northland and with a doctor in only a trice, my love. Now stand back.'

Mary grasped Adele's hand and they hurried across the octagonal room as the blasts of the door being beaten down echoed around them. People came flooding in, footmen, Lord Pennington. But all Mary could see was Charles. He embraced Adele, held her close to make sure she was uninjured, before she broke away and ran to Pen, who stood tensely at the edge of the rescue party.

Mary almost burst into floods of tears as Charles gently gathered her into his arms and wrapped her in his heat. She clung to him and knew that she was truly no longer alone. That she was safe and always would be with him. She closed her eyes and held on to him, her rock in a storm. It was like the moments after they kissed and caressed here in this very place, all the worry and strife of life gone perfectly still and quiet.

'Let me help you stand, my love,' he said, his brogue strong with worry. 'I have you safe now.'

'I know you do. Always.' She took a deep breath and gathered every ounce of any courage she might possess. 'I love you, Charles.'

He stared at her, his eyes glowing. 'As I love you. You must know that. So very much. I never thought I could feel like this, not until I found you.' He pressed a gentle kiss to her brow. 'I won't ever let you leave me again, if you really do love me. I won't let anything hurt you ever again.' He lifted her high in his arms, carrying her out of the cold room into the snowy night, the stars blessedly sparkling above them.

'Beautiful,' she whispered, holding on to him, staring up into their beckoning freedom high above her. Above them.

'It may not be the most auspicious moment,' he said as he carried her towards the waiting cart, where Miss Muffins barked anxiously from the seat. 'But, I beg you, say you will be my wife. Say we will never be apart. I can do anything if you're with me.'

And she knew she could do anything with *him*. He was truly the very best man she'd ever known, the bravest, the kindest, the strongest. The most handsome for certain. He would never hold back her dreams in life, no matter what they were; he would only add to them, make them even more glorious.

'Yes, Charles Campbell,' she said. 'I will marry you.'

He smiled down at her, the brightest light breaking through all the dark fear of the night. It was the most glorious moment she'd ever imagined.

As he placed her gently onto the seat beside Miss Muffins, who huddled close, Mary heard Penelope call to them. She peeked over the edge of the cart to see her friend rushing towards them, her pale cloak a beacon in the shadows. 'Oh, Mary, you're safe! They just found Clark fallen from his horse on the icy road, but Overbury is nowhere to be found yet. Such brutes!' She turned away to find Adele, still crying.

'It seems we are both found now,' Charles whispered to her. 'And it seems I owe Clark some thanks.'

'Thanks!' Mary cried.

'If not for almost losing you, almost losing what we had just found, I wouldn't have been able to say—I love you. Truly and with my whole heart. No fears should have stood in my way. You are the most perfect thing I have ever known, and I will never let you forget that again. Never let you doubt my feelings.'

Mary was sure her heart would burst with joy. This was all she could have dreamed of, all she could have wanted! 'If only our rescuers had waited a moment more for us to kiss,' she whispered back.

He laughed merrily. 'Well, we shall have all the time for all the kisses for the rest of our lives.'

Mary held her breath as she tiptoed away from the impromptu party that echoed with music and laughter in the grand gallery. The party meant for her and Charles, to celebrate his rescue of her, to celebrate their betrothal.

'Better late than never!' everyone had said with a laugh.

Little did they know her *real* betrothal hadn't begun until now.

She hurried down a narrow back staircase, trying not to laugh with giddy glee, with the feeling of delightful naughtiness that always came upon her when she was near Charles.

She went farther and farther down a shadowed corridor, empty except for a few lanterns and wine barrels, her heart pounding. She almost ran around a corner, and shrieked when a voice suddenly called, 'Well, Miss St Aubin, there you are! Running away from our appointment?'

'Ack!' Mary sounded, though she certainly should have expected it. Wasn't the voice the one she was seeking? The one she ran towards? Yet she had been so wrapped up in hurrying to their rendezvous that she was startled, and she gasped as she lost her balance and almost slid down on the flagstone floor. 'Blast it, Charles!'

He caught her in his arms, holding her close to his heat in the gloom. Her heart pounded even harder. 'I'm sorry, my love, I thought you heard me here. Are you all right? I didn't mean to frighten you, not after all you have been through.'

'I am well, except my dignity,' she laughed. She clung to him, their bodies pressed so close not even a breath could come between them. Not now that they were safe together at last. 'What a terrible maiden of olden days I would make, falling down as I rush to meet my white knight. You might change your mind about our betrothal.'

'After I almost lost you because of my foolishness, because of my fear of love? Never,' he answered roughly.

'And my blindness,' she whispered. She feared she might start crying to think of it, to think of how close they came to living their lives apart. 'I can't believe we almost let this slip between our fingers!'

'We never will again.' He stepped back to hand her a cloak, and bowed low as he offered it to her. 'Will you accompany me, my lady, on the night of our betrothal celebration? We have time all to ourselves, Adele will make sure no one looks for us for a while.'

Mary studied his glossy hair in the flickering light, the long fingers of the hand he offered to her, and she nodded. She feared she could barely manage to speak. 'Of course. I would follow you anywhere.'

He swirled the cloak around her shoulders, enclosing her in its warmth and took her hand in his. As she held on to him, she felt the strong safety of him envelop her until all the ghosts of the past vanished and *they* were all that was in the world. As he drew her closer to him, his other arm slipping around her shoulders, she felt that excitement expand and grow within her, tingling and irresistible, like life itself. Life with him.

She didn't want him to let go, ever. She didn't want to lose this glittering spell that wove around her when she was with him.

She smiled up at Charles and let him draw her down the corridor and out a side door into the night. The air was cold and icy sharp, catching at her upswept curls, and she laughed as they ran down a pathway through the moonlit garden. Behind them, the house was lit from every window, and she feared someone might see them, call out to stop them slipping away from their own party. But there was only the whine of the wind, their muffled laughter.

'Where are we going?' she asked, whispering even though no one could hear her.

'Can't you guess?' he said, leading her down another pathway, and suddenly she knew.

'The summer house!' she gasped. It rose up before them, shadowed against the stairs, a tiny flicker of amber light at its small window, its half-open door.

'Our place,' he said tenderly. 'I wanted it to be cleansed of any bad moments, any fear, and leave only happy memories here. I enlisted your maid to help me set it up, and crept down here after our first dance to make sure it was perfect for you.'

He suddenly swept her off her feet, making her laugh. She clung to his neck as he carried her through the door into their own little haven.

Just like it had been before when they were together there, a fire crackled in the grate, welcoming and warming. Spread before it was a nest of fluffy blankets and satin cushions, bottles of wine, plates of delicate pastries like wedding cakes. Mary's heart felt it would burst as she studied it all, studied what he had made to show her how special he thought she was. How special *they* were together.

'Magical,' she whispered. He slid her to her feet, and she

smiled up at him. She wound her arms tightly about his neck so he could not fly away from her, so she could not lose this dream. His hair, so soft, like silk, curled against her bare fingers, and his body felt so solid and warm and delicious against hers. She yearned to stay right there, in his arms, all night—forever! To kiss him, *feel* him, and forget about kidnappings and agencies and Seasons and everything else.

'How very beautiful you are, Charles,' she whispered.

His emerald eyes widened in surprise, but before he could say anything, she went up on tiptoe to kiss him as she longed to do. She pressed one swift, bold caress to his lips, then another and another, teasing him until he moaned and pulled her even closer. He deepened the kiss, his tongue seeking hers, and she was utterly lost in him. Lost in her need to be just this close to him, always, to taste him, smell his summery scent, draw all he was into her soul until he was hers.

He was right. They had nearly missed out on this, but now their whole lives were before them.

He groaned against her, and their kiss slid into a humid hunger, filled with all the yearnings of their time together, their drive to be close and know this was real. This was forever.

Mary didn't question herself, didn't question her emotions for the first time in so long.

She shrugged off her cloak and reached for his coat, catching his arm in her frenzy to be ever closer to him, making them both laugh. It was always thus when they were together: fire and fun, all mixed up so perfectly. The coat fell away, and she unwound his cravat, tangling the muslin, making them laugh even more until they clung to each other.

She pressed her face to the curve of his neck, bare to her now, and inhaled the salty, heady scent of him. This was what she had always sought.

'Mary,' he whispered, 'you are the other half of me.'

'And you of me.' She knew what she had to do. She had to let go of the past, of her emotional fears. She had to be bold. They were reborn there in that summer house, together.

She kissed him again, shaking with the force of her need, and he shuddered against her. She knew he felt as she did. This was their real betrothal, their real pledge. He lifted her to her feet, and she felt him carry her backwards, down into that nest of blankets, like falling into a heavenly cloud.

She opened her eyes and gazed up at him, the firelight a corona around the tousled waves of his dark hair, and was sure they were in a magical fairy circle, sparkling ribbons binding them together.

'Mary...' he began, his voice hoarse. 'We shouldn't—I didn't bring you here just to take advantage of you.'

'Shh.' She pressed her fingers to his lips, feeling their softness under her touch. She was finished with words, with worry and with thoughts. 'Just look at me.'

'I could do that forever.'

'Then know how much I want this with you. Forever and ever.'

He rose up over her to shed his shirt, revealing those old scars to her once again, never taking his gaze from her before he dove back to her, to a rain of kisses, caresses. Mary pressed up into him, kissing his cheek, his neck, as she felt his hands slide the bodice of her gown away from her shoulders, the touch of cold air and firelight and, *oh*, his lips on her bare skin.

Any words were beyond her now, lost in their kiss, open mouths, not to be denied any longer. She slid her palms over his back, feeling the damp silk of his skin, the heat of him. When she peeked up, she saw he was exquisite, more handsome than any classical sculpture for he was *alive*, glowing, vibrant with breath and desire and strength.

He caught her in his arms again, their heartbeats melding, nothing at all careful about this kiss. It was too urgent, too filled with need that couldn't be denied any longer. She felt free at last, and there was only this one moment with the man she loved.

She closed her eyes tightly, revelling in his caress, the press of his mouth on the bare curve of her breast as her bodice fell down. Her legs parted as she felt his weight lower between them, her skirts swept away. She knew what would happen; she had read things, and she had a married sister who was always honest with her. But the images mere pictures in books and whispered words conjured never hinted at how it all *felt*. Of that heady, dizzy sensation of falling and falling, lost in another person.

'I—I don't want to hurt you,' he gasped.

She smiled against his shoulder as she felt the press of the tip of his manhood against her. Her entire body ached for that final union with him, that moment when they were together entirely. 'You never could.'

She spread her legs wider, invitingly, and he slid inside her. It did hurt, how could it not? A sharp, burning pain, but it was nothing compared to the way it felt when he filled her, came to her at last. She arched her back against the pain, wrapping her arms and legs around him so tightly he could never escape her.

'You see? It doesn't hurt now,' she whispered. 'I feel completely perfect.'

He laughed tightly. 'Not half as perfect as I do right now. My beautiful, wonderful Mary.'

Slowly, ever so slowly, he moved again within her, drawing back, lunging forward, just a little deeper, a little more intimate every time. Mary squeezed her eyes closed, feeling that ache ebb away until there was only the pleasure. A tingling delight that grew and expanded, spreading through her arms and legs, her fingertips, out the top of her head like the flames from the fireplace. Pleasure unlike any she had ever known or even imagined. No wonder so many people came seeking matches at the agency! This type of love and passion was the most perfect thing in the world.

Mary cried out at the wonder of it all, at the bursts of light behind her closed eyes, blue and white and red like fireworks. The heat and pressure were too much, too much! How could she ever survive it without being burned up and consumed? But what a wondrous way to go.

Above her, around her, she felt Charles tense, his back arch. 'Mary!' he shouted out. And she exploded, consumed by those lights. She clung to him, and he to her, falling down into the flames.

After long moments—hours or days?—she slowly opened her eyes, sure she must have tumbled down into some bonfire or volcano. That she would find herself in a different world entirely. But it was the same room in the summer house, cleansed of fear, filled only with love. The stars outside, the fireplace, the blankets—transformed.

Beside her, collapsed on the pillows, his arms tight around her waist, was Charles. Her Scottish *laird*, her love. His eyes were tightly closed, his limbs sprawled out in exhaustion.

She smiled, feeling herself slowly float down to earth again. She felt the blankets beneath her, the heat of the fire on her skin, the soreness of her limbs. It didn't matter, though. Nothing mattered, in this moment out of time. They would have to return to the party soon, pretend they had been engaged for many weeks, but they would know the truth of what had just happened. That here, in this summer house, they became their true selves together.

She snuggled closer to him, half drowsing, feeling as if she could float up and up into the stars. His arm was heavy over her waist, and she curled herself tighter into the haven of his body, feeling his breath on her bare shoulder, the strength of his muscles as she traced her fingertips over his forearm.

'Oh, Mary,' he whispered into her hair. 'I think I shall have to spend the rest of my life trying to discover everything about you. But I know one thing.'

She smiled. 'And what is that, my love?'

'That you are the most magnificent lass I have ever seen.'

She laughed and rolled over to face him. The moonlight and the orange flames outlined his beautiful face, casting sharp angles, mysterious shadows over his eyes, darkened now. She reached up and traced his features carefully, all those commonplace things like eyebrows, a nose, cheekbones, that made him up into what he was. The perfection of Charles. 'And you are unlike anyone else I have ever known or even imagined.'

He laid back in their nest, his arms stretched under his head as Mary sat up to gaze down at him, study him. 'Me, Mary? I am the simplest creature, easy to read as a book.'

She laughed. 'A book in Scots, maybe. I need translations.'

He caught her around the waist and drew her close again. 'You understood me well enough tonight.'

'Don't tease!' she giggled. 'But I suppose we have time to learn those mysteries now, don't we?'

'Oh, yes,' he whispered, just before he kissed her again. 'Every single little mystery is ours to discover now.'

Epilogue

'There now, Miss Mary,' Daisy said with a satisfied air as she straightened a wreath of white and pink silk roses on Mary's upswept golden curls. 'I think we've done a fine job here.'

Ella and Adele clapped in agreement, and Miss Muffins let out a long bark.

'Oh, Daisy. You have indeed!' Mary answered in glee, giving a joyful little twirl in front of the mirror. Her Mademoiselle Sandrine gown was a dream, palest blue silk with a froth of a white lace train. It looked like a summer's day, like a gown to hold dreams of warmth and sun and happy-ever-after. The future seemed bright, full of everything she could have longed for: a social season with the agency in Bath and the rest of the year spent in Scotland, with managers put in place to run the business in her absence. Work and family! Adele had even voiced ambitions to take over matchmaking herself one day, which filled Mary with such happiness, knowing she could pass on all she'd learned.

But today was only for wedding dreams.

Sandrine knelt to adjust a frill on the train. 'Just one more inch here—there, perfect. My finest creation.'

Miss Muffins barked again, and spun about until the bow around her neck came untied.

Mary spun in the glass again, taking in her mother's pearl necklace, the short lace veil attached to the wreath, the little silver thistle brooch attached to her bodice. It had been long weeks since she and Adele escaped their kidnappers, days of bad memories and bad dreams, but also days of wondrous healing. Wedding plans, a honeymoon trip to Scotland, Adele's new excitement for her Season as a chance to move forward, they had a great deal to anticipate.

Adele handed her a bouquet of hothouse roses, pink and white bound with looping ribbons. 'Are you ready... Aunt?' she whispered shyly, and Mary hugged her close.

'Much more than ready,' she answered, and they proceeded out of the chamber and down the stairs, Daisy holding the train high as they crossed the courtyard to the waiting Abbey amid streamers and confetti and beaming guests.

But Mary could only see the man who waited for her at the church door, her very own Christmas husband. The best match she had ever made.

He smiled wide, filled with joy, the shadows of the past forgotten. He hurried to her, as if he was unable to wait a moment longer, and took her gloved hand in his, raising it to his lips for a tender kiss. They were both exactly where they belonged, at long last, as the blessings of Christmas showered down on them.

* * * * *

HISTORICAL

Your romantic escape to the past.

Available Next Month

The Trouble With The Daring Governess Annie Burrows
The Earl's Marriage Dilemma Sarah Mallory

....

One Waltz With The Viscount Laura Martin
When Cinderella Met The Duke Sophia Williams

4 brand new stories each month

HISTORICAL

Your romantic escape to the past.

MILLS & BOON

Keep reading for an excerpt of
What Happen's Ay Christmas...
by Yvonne Linsdsay.
Find it in the
Christmas Blockbuster 2024 anthology,
out now!

CHAPTER ONE

"MOM, I'M SORRY. I won't be able to make it tonight. I have too much work on my plate."

Kristin eyed the Christmas decorations that festooned her office, with a baleful eye. She wasn't lying, exactly. She did have a ton of work to get through, but she wasn't in the mood for yet another happy family gathering where everyone except her was paired up with a significant other. Normally, it didn't bother her, but lately she'd been more unsettled than usual.

"Kristin, I won't take no for an answer. I'm done with your excuses. Tonight is important to me and I expect you to be here at seven sharp."

Kristin's mom, Nancy, abruptly ended the call, leaving her daughter staring at the phone on her office desk with a mixture of frustration and curiosity. Kristin rolled her chair from her desk, pushed her hands through her long hair and massaged her scalp with her fingertips. It didn't ease the perpetual headache she'd had for the past several months.

Her identical twin brothers, Keaton and Logan, had been putting pressure on her to cut her workload, citing their father's massive fatal stroke almost a year ago as a fine example of why you shouldn't burn the candle at both ends. She was doing the work of two people at the moment since she hadn't yet been able to bring herself to replace the man she'd trusted as her right hand here at work, and as her lover in the bedroom.

And all along Isaac had been a spy working for their biggest rival, Warren Everard. While everyone involved in the corporate espionage was now facing charges, it still galled her, even all these months later, that she'd never suspected—not even for a moment—that he was capable of such subterfuge. And it made her doubly wary of replacing him—in the office, or at home. Business was hard enough right now, without worrying about having to second-guess everyone around you. It had been the easier option to simply assimilate Isaac's workload into her own. After all, it wasn't as if she had any reason to rush home.

Isaac's betrayal was doubly cruel because she hadn't shared with her family how intimate she and Isaac had become. They'd kept their relationship under wraps. Not a single person in the office had ever suspected that they were more than boss and employee. She'd technically been in a position of power over him. Forming a relationship would have been frowned upon, so when he'd suggested they initially keep things quiet, she'd been in full agreement. But all along his plan had been to abuse her trust, which was, in her book, far more damaging. And she'd borne the pain of that betrayal and her broken heart alone.

Kristin rose from her seat and turned to face the darkening sky outside her office window. The Richmond Tower commanded exceptional views of the Seattle cityscape, but she rarely took the time to appreciate it. Christmas was only a little over three weeks away but her gaze remained oblivious to the glittering outlook spread before her like a pirate's jewel casket.

Instead, her thoughts turned inward. So much had changed in the past year. Courtesy of the double life her father had successfully lived, right up until the moment he'd dropped dead in his office, she'd gained not just one brother—Logan had been kidnapped as a child and was now reunited with the family—but two half brothers, and a half sister to boot.

And while it had been a joy to watch her full brothers both find love with amazing women whom she respected and adored, seeing her brothers' happiness only made Isaac's duplicity all the more painful.

Was it too much to expect to be able to build a relationship founded on mutual attraction, affection and trust? Kristin shook her head. Apparently, for her, it was. And now she had to present a cheerful face at another family dinner. Ah, well, she thought as she returned to her computer and backed up her work, at least she could depend on a better meal than the microwave instant dinner option in her apartment's freezer. She chuckled ruefully. She sounded like a total loser.

Kristin checked that the backup was complete, grabbed her bag and coat and locked her office door behind her. She fingered her car keys, wondering if she should drive to her mom's place in Bellevue. No, she decided. She'd order a driver and leave her car in its secure parking space below the building. The way she was feeling right now, she might indulge in a glass or two of wine tonight.

Half an hour later, Kristin let herself into the large two-story mansion that had been her parents' home for as long as she could remember and shrugged off her coat. She loved coming here. There was a sense of stability about the place that she desperately craved now. The clipped sound of heels on the parquet floor alerted her to the arrival of the family housekeeper, Martha.

"Ah, Kristin. It's good to see you. Your mom and the others are in the main salon having drinks before dinner. Here, let me take your coat."

"The main salon? I thought this was a casual thing," Kristin commented as she passed her coat to the older woman.

Martha had been in her parents' employ since Kristin had

been a baby and, since Kristin's father's death last year, had become more of a companion to her mom.

"Mrs. Richmond asked that I send you through when you arrived," the housekeeper continued smoothly without actually answering Kristin's question.

A sense of unease filled her. Her mom only used the main sitting room for formal occasions. What was going on? Realizing it would be useless to press Martha, who was already walking away to hang up her coat, Kristin made her way across the foyer to the double wooden doors that led to the rest of her family. A murmur of voices came through the door and she hesitated—reluctant, for some reason, to join them. A burst of laughter from inside the room motivated her to reach for the handle and join her family.

She scanned the room as she entered, noting the beautifully decorated Christmas tree her mom had erected immediately after Thanksgiving, and relaxed as she identified her brothers and their partners, her mom and Hector Ramirez. Hector was the family's attorney and had been an absolute rock of support for her mom since Douglas Richmond's sudden death. So much so, the two of them had vacationed together in Palm Springs a few months ago.

As Kristin entered the room, her mom rose from Hector's side and crossed toward her daughter to welcome her.

"I made it," Kristin said with a smile as her mom enveloped her in a loving embrace.

"Thank you, my darling girl. It's always so good to see you."

"You know, if you came back to the office we'd see each other every day."

Nancy had worked side by side with her husband until his death nearly a year ago and had been heavily involved in the family's charitable foundation. But now she rarely entered the building where he'd died and had established a base here at home to manage the Richmond Foundation remotely.

"What can I get you to drink?" Nancy asked, ignoring Kristin's not-so-subtle comment.

"My usual white wine would be great, thanks."

Kristin turned to say hi to her brothers and their partners. Logan and Honor had married in the summer and, last week at Thanksgiving, announced they were expecting a baby. While Honor wasn't showing yet, there was a glow about her that inspired a prick of envy in Kristin's heart. And the way Logan looked at Honor these days? Well, his love for her and their child was tangible. More than anything Kristin ached to have that level of commitment with someone else.

Keaton and Tami were equally tightly knit. They'd originally started as an office romance at Richmond Developments, but Tami now worked as a project manager and liaison between the Richmond Foundation and other charities on special ventures. Tami rose from her seat and hugged Kristin in greeting.

"I was hoping you would make it," Tami said with a welcoming smile. "We hardly get to see you outside of work these days."

"Do you know what this is all about?" Kristin whispered to her.

"Not a clue. It doesn't quite feel like Nancy's regular family dinner vibe, does it?"

"True," Kristin conceded. She couldn't quite shake the apprehension that niggled at the back of her mind.

Her mom returned with Kristin's glass of wine and then turned and faced the room. Some silent communication must have passed between her and Hector, because he rose and stood next to her, one arm casually draped around Nancy's waist.

"If I could have all your attention, please," Nancy started, sounding a little nervous.

That niggle in the back of Kristin's mind grew stronger.

"Hector and I have an announcement to make. As you know, we've been friends for many years and he's been an incredible support to me since Douglas passed away. In fact, he's become so important to me that I can't see my future without him…

and I'm very proud to tell you that he has consented to be my husband."

There was a sudden murmur in the room and Kristin felt her stomach twist in a knot.

"You asked Hector to marry you?" she blurted.

"He was too much of a gentleman to do it so soon after your father's death. But if Douglas's passing taught me anything, it was to grab hold of what's important and keep it close to you. I didn't want to waste any more time following other people's expectations or beating around the bush." Nancy turned and faced Hector and beamed at him, her love for him radiating from her. "I love him and that's why I asked him to marry me. He said yes and I couldn't be happier."

The others rose from their seats, offering their congratulations and hugging Nancy and shaking Hector's hand, but Kristin stood on the periphery. Nancy extricated herself from the rest of the family and came over to Kristin.

"Kristin? Aren't you happy for us?" she asked, a worried frown pulling at her brows.

"Isn't it a bit soon, Mom? Dad hasn't even been dead a year. I mean, I have nothing against Hector and I know how much he's come to mean to you, but don't you think you're rushing things?"

Nancy laughed and patted Kristin's arm. "Oh, my darling. We're both nearing sixty. We want to spend the rest of our lives together, properly, as husband and wife. It's important to us both and I trust Hector. He would never let me down the way your father did. Seriously, Kristin, you wouldn't stand in the way of our happiness, would you?"

Kristin hesitated. Of course she wanted her mom to be happy.

Hector joined them. "Everything okay, ladies?" he asked.

"Everything is fine," Nancy assured him and gave Kristin a look that brooked no argument. "Isn't it, Kristin?"

"Yes, absolutely," Kristin said, forcing a smile to her face. She still couldn't put a finger on why she felt uncomfortable.

Sour grapes because everyone around her was paired up and living their happily-ever-afters and she wasn't? She raised her glass. "Congratulations to you both. May you be exceptionally happy together."

"Thank you, Kristin," Hector said, his eyes glistening with moisture. "It means a great deal to us to hear you say that. We understand how close you were to your father and how much you miss him. He was my best friend but I can't deny that I've loved Nancy for many years and I feel privileged to be able to plan the rest of our lives as one."

His words struck Kristin to her core. There was no doubt Hector's feelings for Nancy were genuine.

"And what about your work for us, Hector? Will you remain our family attorney?" she asked.

"I'm glad you asked." He smiled. "It leads us to our second announcement for this evening. I've decided to take early retirement—I sold my practice to a longtime friend and colleague. To facilitate a smooth takeover, I will remain on in an advisory capacity for the next six months."

"A longtime friend? Who?" Kristin pressed. "Have we met him before?"

"I don't believe so," Hector replied.

"Then how can we be sure he'll be a good fit for us? How can we trust him?"

She spoke the words without thinking. Hector was saved from answering by the echoing tones of the front doorbell.

"Well, it sounds as if he's arrived to join us, so you can find out the answers to those questions yourself," Hector said with a confident smile.

Kristin helped herself to a generous swig of her wine. While the fine vintage was like a kiss of velvet on her tongue, it burned all the way to her stomach, reminding her she hadn't eaten much today. She didn't like the sound of any of this. What if the new person wasn't good enough? Their family had been through hell and back these past several months, first with Logan popping out of the woodwork thirty-four years after his abduction as a baby, then her dad dying, then the discovery that he had a another family and business mirroring theirs on the other side of the country. After that there'd been the corporate espionage, of which Isaac had been an integral part.

How could they be expected to trust a stranger?

"Darling, don't worry so much. Hector's friend has an exceptional reputation," her mom murmured in her ear.

"He'd better have," Kristin muttered before taking another sip of her wine.

She turned to face the sitting room doors as they swung open. Martha announced the new arrival.

"Mr. Jones has arrived," she said before ushering him through.

Logan and Keaton had moved forward and obstructed her immediate line of sight to the newcomer.

"Good evening, everyone. I hope I'm not late?"

The man's voice was deep and resonant and there was something disturbingly familiar about it. The niggle in Kristin's mind morphed into a full-blown sense of misgiving.

"No, not at all," Hector hastened to assure him. "Everyone, please welcome my good friend Jackson Jones."

And there he stood. All six feet three inches of him clad in bespoke Armani and, according to her accelerated heart rate, looking even more fiercely attractive than she remembered. His dark blue eyes focused on her with laser precision. His nostrils flared ever so slightly on a sharply indrawn breath.

Jackson Jones.

The first man she'd ever loved.

The first man she'd ever slept with.

The man who'd walked out on her without a single word or a backward glance.

The man she'd sworn to hate for eternity.